HAWKE

TED BELL

POCKET BOOKS
New York London Toronto Sydney

This book is a work of fiction. Names, characters, places and incidents are products of the author's imagination or are used fictitiously. Any resemblance to actual events or locales or persons living or dead is entirely coincidental.

 POCKET BOOKS, a division of Simon & Schuster, Inc.
1230 Avenue of the Americas, New York, NY 10020

Copyright © 2003 by Theodore Bell

All rights reserved, including the right to reproduce
this book or portions thereof in any form whatsoever.
For information address Atria Books, 1230 Avenue
of the Americas, New York, NY 10020

ISBN-13: 978-0-7434-6669-1
ISBN-10:   0-7434-6669-1
ISBN-13: 978-1-4165-1630-9 (Pbk)
ISBN-13:   1-4165-1630-1 (Pbk)

First Pocket Books trade paperback printing July 2005

10 9 8 7 6 5 4 3 2 1

POCKET BOOKS and colophon are registered
trademarks of Simon & Schuster, Inc.

Manufactured in the United States of America

For information regarding special discounts for bulk purchases,
please contact Simon & Schuster Special Sales at 1-800-456-6798
or business@simonandschuster.com.

HAWKE

PROLOGUE

· · · · — · · ·

The boy, barely seven years old, was dreaming what was to be the last completely happy dream of his life.

He was sound asleep in the top bunk of his tiny berth as images of his dog, Scoundrel, bounded across his mind. They had taken a small picnic down to the edge of the sea, just below the big house where his grandfather lived. Scoundrel was plunging again and again into the waves, retrieving the red rubber ball. But now some terrible black storm appeared to be howling in from the sea, and there was a voice calling him to come home quickly.

And then someone was grabbing his shoulder, whispering in his ear. *Alex! Alex! Alex!*

Yes, someone was shaking him, telling him to wake up, wake up now, even though he knew it was still nighttime, could hear the waves lapping against the hull of the sailboat, could see the blue moonlight streaming through the porthole onto his bedcovers, could hear the faint whistle of wind in the rigging of the tall mast that towered above the decks.

"Wake up, Alex, wake up!" said the voice.

He rolled over and opened his sleepy eyes. In the dim light of the tiny cabin he could see his father standing at his bedside, wearing an old gray T-shirt that said "Royal Navy." His father's jet-black parrot, Sniper, was perched on his shoulder. The bird was unusually quiet.

His dad had a terrible look on his face, almost scared, the boy thought, which was silly because his father wasn't afraid of anything. He was the best, bravest man of all.

"Time to rise and shine?" the boy asked.

"Yes, it is, I'm afraid, little fellow," his father said in a hurried, gentle whisper. "You have to get up quickly now and come with Daddy. Here, I'll help you down."

His father reached up with one hand to pull back his covers and help him onto the little ladder leading down from his berth. At the last moment, the boy clutched the blanket he'd had almost since birth and gripped it to his chest as he descended the ladder. Then his father picked him up in one arm and carried him out of the cabin and into the dark companionway. They turned left, and ran through the darkness toward the front of the boat, the bow it was called, his father still whispering in his ear as they ran.

"It's going to be all right, we just have to hide you for a while and you have to be very, very quiet. Not a single noise till Daddy comes to get you, understand? Not a peep, okay?"

"Yes, Father," the boy said, although he could feel himself growing scared now. They'd reached the end of the long corridor and his father put him down. "What's wrong?" the boy asked.

"I don't know, but I'm going up on deck to find out," his father said, taking him by the hand. The boy, still trying to rub the sleep from his eyes with the corner of his blanket, followed his father into the small compartment all the way in the bow.

This bow compartment was too small to be of much

use for anything really. So it was just piled high with coiled ropes and boxes of canned food and other supplies. There was a wooden box filled with dark bottles of "hootch," which is what his father called the stuff he drank up on deck every night before dinner. Behind all the boxes, on the forward wall, was a door. Alex had once stacked boxes under the door and tried to pry it open, thinking it would make an excellent hiding spot. He didn't know what was in there, but the door was always locked.

His father used a key now to open the little door.

"This is where we keep the extra anchor and mooring lines, Alex," his father whispered. "And a few things we don't want stolen, like Mummy's good silverware from home. But there are other things in here, things I don't want anyone to ever find. I'll show you one right now."

The locker itself was a very small V-shaped space, too small to be even called a room. From it came a smell of oily, muddy chain and ropes. The big anchor was in use, of course, holding them to the sandy bottom of a little cove.

They were in the Exumas, a chain of islands stretching south of the Bahamas, and had been mooring in a different cove every afternoon. This one was the prettiest of all. His father had shown it to him on the chart. The anchorage he was searching for was called the Luna Sea, which his dad had thought quite a clever name.

Alex pointed out that the island itself had a funny shape. "It looks like the mean old wolf," he'd said. "The one that ate up the three little piggies."

"Well, then, we'll call it Big Bad Wolf Island," his father had said.

It was a small bay of deep blue water, rimmed by a crescent of white sand. At one end of the beach was a stand of palm trees, bending and rustling in the wind. There were brilliantly colored fish swimming all around the boat. Alex, standing on the bow, dove into the water as soon as they'd anchored. His father had been teaching him the names of all the fish. He was looking for his newest favorite, the black and yellow striped ones called Sergeant-Majors.

He and his father had had a splendid evening of it until it got dark, diving off the bow, then swimming around to the ladder hanging from the stern. Mother had been waiting on deck at sunset with a big fluffy towel and, hugging him while drying him off, she'd asked him to name all the fish he'd seen.

So many beautifully colored fish in the clear water, he'd told her, it was hard to remember all their names. Triggerfish. Clownfish. Angelfish. That was the one. Did they come down from heaven? he wondered. But you could reach out and touch the Angels and they would nibble your fingers. Ticklish bites. It seemed long ago.

The boy bent forward and peered into the anchor locker, so dark in the nighttime.

"I'm not scared, Dad," the boy said in a small voice. "Maybe I look scared, but it's only because I'm a little sleepy." He was looking up at his father with a serious expression on his face.

"Is everything okay? Is Mother okay?" he asked.

"She's fine, fine," his father whispered. "She's hiding as well, you see, back in the stern. And keeping just as quiet as a church mouse, too. Isn't that fun?"

"I guess so, Daddy."

"Yes. Do you have a pocket on your pajama top? Yes, you do, don't you? Splendid!"

His father reached up inside the locker and ran his hands along its ceiling, feeling for something. Then he had it and turned to his son.

"I want you to put this into your pocket and save it for Daddy, all right?"

His father handed him a small blue envelope with something folded up inside.

"What is it?" Alex asked.

"Why, it's an ancient pirate treasure map, of course! So, take good care of it. Now, I want you to climb inside this little room and then I'm going to close the door and then you'll lock it, like a game. When I come back, I'll knock three times and that will mean it's time for you to come out. Hurry now, upsy-daisy, in you go."

"Yes, Father, it's going to be fun, isn't it?"

"Right you are. Here's the key. I'm going to stick it into the lock on your side of the door. I want you to lock the door from the inside. And, don't open it for anybody but Daddy, all right? Now, three knocks, remember?"

The boy crawled up inside and pulled his tattered blanket in after him, tugging it up around his chin. The chains were rough and hurt his skin through his thin pajamas. They were his favorite ones, covered with cowboys and Indians and six-shooters. He wore them every night of his life, never allowing anybody to even wash them. They would certainly get dirty now. It was hot in this place and it didn't smell very good either.

They'd been sailing for almost two weeks now, and the child had explored every inch of the vessel, learning the names of everything. His father's new boat, a beautiful yawl he'd christened *Seahawke*, was on her maiden voyage to the Bahamas and Exumas. She was almost as large as his grandfather's ancient schooner in England, the one he kept moored at Greybeard Island: a wonderful boat called the *Rambler*.

"All shipshape in there, my laddie boy?" his father whispered through the opened door. "Still wearing the St. George's medal Mummy gave you for your birthday?"

"Aye, aye, Captain," the boy said, reaching inside his pajama top and lifting it up on its thin gold chain for his father to see. "Anchor locker officer of the day, awaiting further orders, sir!" He raised his hand to his forehead in a little salute.

His father smiled and leaned inside to kiss his son on the cheek. "I love you, Alex. Don't you worry, Daddy will be back soon. Don't forget, three knocks."

"Three knocks," the boy replied, nodding his head. "Aye, aye, sir."

As his father started to close the door, the boy saw that he had taken something else out of the locker. It was in his hand. His gun. The one from the war days that he always kept in his bedside drawer at home in England. The gun was dangerous and he was not allowed to touch it, even though he knew where it was and had peeked at it countless times.

"What's wrong, Dad? Please tell me," the boy said, trying desperately to be brave and not to cry. The gun scared him more than anything did.

"Sniper heard funny noises up on deck, that's all. He woke me up. I'm going to go up on deck and see." His father had trained Sniper in the old pirates' ways. The black parrot would screech or squawk in alarm whenever anyone approached or if he heard any unusual noises.

His dad smiled then and held up the gun. "Look. I'm taking my service revolver, too. Whoever it is, they'll be dead sorry they picked out this particular boat and this particular naval officer, I'll tell you that."

"But who, whoever would come on our boat in the middle of the night?" the boy asked.

"I'm not sure," the man said with a little smile. And then, just before his father closed the door, the boy heard his father say, "Maybe it's pirates, Alex."

Little Alex Hawke's eyes went wide.

"Pirates," he repeated to himself in the darkness. He dreamed, it seemed, of pirates almost every night.

"Pirates," he whispered in the darkness, turning the key in the lock. He put the key in his pajama pocket with the map. He had a great love, and a great fear, for pirates in his little heart. They were certainly bad, murdering thieves, weren't they? But, still, their adventures were thrilling to hear about late at night with the wind howling about the eaves of the great house overlooking the sea.

Sitting by a crackling fire on rainy nights, listening to his grandfather tell of buccaneers and their bloodthirsty deeds, was one of his life's great joys. Grandfather seemed to know every horrific pirate story by heart. And every single one of them, he told Alex, was absolutely true.

There was one story Alex cherished above all others.

The bloody tale of the life and horrible death of little Alex Hawke's famous ancestor, the notorious cutthroat Blackhawke himself.

Alex heard a sharp metallic noise beyond his door.

★ ★ ★

There were three small ventilation slits in the locker door, and Alex pressed his eye to one of the openings. He could see his father checking his gun, cocking it, and then starting up the steel ladder that led to a big hatch at the top. The hatch opened up on the deck, right up on the bow of the sailboat, the boy knew. When his father reached the hatch, all Alex could see were two bare feet on the middle rung. He could hear his father unscrewing the two latches and pushing the hatch cover ever so slowly open. Moonlight poured down into the compartment, and cool night air, and he knew the hatch was now open.

His father's feet quickly disappeared up the ladder and then it was quiet for a few moments. Alex took a deep breath and sat back on his blanket. It was still very stuffy and hot in the locker, and he hoped this game wouldn't last too long. He groped for one of the life preservers he knew was stored here and placed it close to the door where he could sit on it and see through the vents.

No pirates about. Nothing. Just the empty storage compartment outside his door, and, beyond it, the empty companionway.

Still, a thought pushed its way into Alex's mind.

A bad thing is coming.

He sat back on his makeshift cushion, telling himself it would all be all right. He started to count his blessings, which were many, the way his mother had taught him to do each night at bedtime.

He had a wonderful, happy family.

His mother was beautiful and kind. Famous, too.

His father and grandfather were both retired military

men, and later British intelligence officers. His grandfather, upon retiring from the Royal Navy, had ended his long career as one of England's greatest spies during the Second World War.

His father, whose name he'd inherited, was a commander in the Royal Navy, a great hero. But what he did mostly, Alex thought, was roam the world looking for bad guys. Of course, he didn't have a big battleship like other captains, but he was a pilot, after all. He was now more of a policeman, really. Tracking down pirates, most likely, Alex thought, for, surely, there were still plenty of them lurking about.

Besides, he had a real pirate treasure map right in his pocket, didn't he?

Suddenly, there was a sound above—a muffled shout, in some foreign language. Spanish, he thought, like his nanny back in England spoke to him, and he heard his father cry out something in Spanish, too.

The boy put his ear to the door, his heart thudding in his chest. He heard more shouts and more arguing in Spanish and then a loud thump on the deck just above his head. Then footsteps running this way toward the bow and much more shouting just above the hatch.

Alex put his eye to the slot. Nothing. Suddenly, his father came tumbling down through the hatch, landing with a shuddering thud on the cabin floor not four feet from his hiding place. There was bright blood streaming from a wound on his father's forehead!

A scream was rising up in the boy's throat, when he saw two feet descending the ladder. Two bare feet and legs coming down the rungs, and then a long black ponytail. The man had something on his shoulder, too, a drawing of a bug? A tattooed spider, he now saw, black with a red spot on its belly.

Spiders were bad. Alex had been terrified of them ever since he'd awoken one night to find one crawling across his face. On his cheek. By his mouth. Had he not awoken, it would have crawled inside—

The man with the spider on his shoulder dropped to the floor and looked around, breathing hard. He had long, dark eyelashes, just like a girl.

"I am looking for a map, *señor,*" the man-girl said. "This map, this treasure you search for, belongs to my family! Every five-year-old in Cuba knows the story of the English pirate Blackhawke stealing the great treasure of de Herreras!"

The man then kicked his father in the stomach, hard enough to make him cry out and try to get to his feet.

"I don't know what the bloody hell you're talking about, old chap," Alex's father said, breathing hard.

"I will tell you," the man said, and kicked his father so hard Alex heard something crack inside his dad's chest.

"The ancient treasure, stolen by the pirate Blackhawke, *señor,* it belonged to my famous ancestor, Admiral Andrés Manso de Herreras. I claim my ancestor's gold in the name of my family, *señor!*"

The intruder stepped over him and turned so that he was now facing Alex. He was a slender, brownish man, who wore only a filthy pair of shorts and one gold earring. He was staring calmly down at Alex's father. He had some kind of small machine gun, too, pointed at his father's head. His father no longer had his gun. Alex forced himself to be still, though he felt his heart would explode.

"Dónde está el mapa, Señor Hawke?" the pretty man said. *"Cuántos están en el barco?"*

He was about to kick Alex's father again, but, suddenly, Sniper swooped down through the open hatch, screeching, with his claws out. The bird flew right at the man's face, slashing his cheek and drawing bright red blood.

The man cried out and tried to bat Sniper away, but the bird kept up his attack. Alex's father, rolling over, grabbed the intruder's small brown foot and yanked him off balance. He went down hard. Alex heard the whoosh of air coming out of him; and then his father was upon him, going for the hand with the gun. They both grunted, rolling over twice before they slammed against the doorframe. His father pinned the man there, and slammed the hand with the gun hard on the floor.

"Either drop the gun, or I break your wrist, choose one, *chica,*" his old man said. It seemed his father wasn't hurt nearly as badly as the boy had feared! One eye to the slit, Alex held his breath, praying as he never had before.

please let him be okay please let him be okay
please let him be—

The gun went off then, not one shot but hundreds, it seemed, a deafening staccato filling the tiny compartment, splinters of wood and glass flying everywhere. And so much smoke Alex couldn't even see who had the gun now, but then his father was backing toward him, pointing the gun down at the long-haired man who was slowly getting to his feet. He was holding his bare shoulder, and blood was streaming through his fingers, splashing on the floor. He hissed something at Alex's father in Spanish, but stayed where he was.

His father, his old gray T-shirt soaked with blood, had his back pressed against Alex's hiding place. Alex could hear him breathing heavily, strongly. Alex's heart heaved in his chest, sheer joy filling him inside, as his father, his great hero, spoke.

"There is no goddamn map, *señor*," his father said, holding out his forearm so Sniper could perch there. "How many times did I tell you up on deck? No map, no treasure, no nothing. Just me, alone on this old boat, trying like hell to have a little fun. Then you showed up. Now you get the hell off my boat, *comprende?* Or I'll spatter your brains on that wall right here and now."

"*Señor*, I beg you," the man said, in good English now. "It's all a big mistake. Listen. Was not your yacht last week down in Staniel Cay? My brother, Carlitos, he say a descendant of Blackhawke the famous pirate is down here in the Exumas, looking for the famous lost treasure of de Herreras and—"

"I got it. So you decided to smoke a little ganja and row out to a total stranger's boat in the middle of the night, carrying a bloody machine gun, and hoping to find some nonexistent map, right?"

"Oh, no, *señor*, I only—"

"Shut up, please!" Alex heard his father say, pulling back on the slide that cocked the machine gun. "You're losing a lot of blood, old chap. You need to get yourself to a doctor. Put both hands on your head and turn around, got that? Right now!"

His father moved away from the door and Alex could see the compartment again. Pressing his eye to the slit once more, he felt something warm and sticky on his face. His father's blood. He watched the ponytailed man moving toward the door with his hands on his head. Suddenly, he stopped, and turned to Alex's father with a horrible grin on his face.

Sniper let out a blood-curdling screech and fluttered his big black wings wildly.

"Oh, God, Kitty," he heard his father say in words that sounded broken and full of pain.

In the doorway, two more men stood on either side of Alex's mother. One man, tall, whose bald head was glistening with sweat, held his mother roughly by one arm. Her long blond hair was matted and wild, her pale blue eyes red, brimming with unshed tears. She was clutching the remains of her torn nightgown with her other arm, terror plain on her beautiful face. The other man was fat and had a big gold cross hanging from his neck. He had a long flat knife at Alex's mother's throat, right under her chin.

Sniper squawked and flared his wings angrily.

"Sniper, no!" Alex heard his father say, and the bird calmed itself and remained perched on his arm.

In the fat man's other hand, he clutched a handful of sparkling jewels. Diamond necklaces and bracelets and the pretty thing his mother had worn in her hair the night before. A tiara. The boy had told her it made her look like a fairy queen.

"Ah, *la señora,* eh, the beauteous Lady Hawke, no?" the pony-tailed pirate said, smiling now. He bowed from the waist. "Allow me to introduce myself. I am called *Araña,* the spider, but my name it is simply Manso. And these are my two brothers, Juanito and Carlos. It was *mi hermano,* Carlitos, who served you, dear lady, all that rum at the Staniel Cay Yacht Club."

"*Sí,* I am Carlitos," the fat young Cuban said to Alex's mother. "Remember me *now*, dear lady? We celebrated the New Year's Eve together!"

"My brother, he is the bartender there, see?" Manso said. "He hears many things. And my brother, he tells me all about your great beauty. And how you dance up on the bar. And, of course, your husband's search for the lost treasure of Blackhawke. A treasure, *señora,* that the English pirate stole from my ancestor, Andrés Manso de Herreras, the greatest Spanish privateer of them all! It is a story passed down through my family for endless generations."

The man stepped closer to Alex's mother and stroked her cheek. "So, please, *Señora* Hawke, would you be so kind as to come in and join our little fiesta?"

A small sob escaped his mother's trembling lips. Alex saw her angry blue eyes and pale cheeks in the moonlight that was still streaming down through the opened hatch. His eyes pressed against the narrow slit, he could see that his mother was fighting desperately to hold back her tears.

She reached out to her husband. "I'm so very sorry, Alexander. So very, very sorry."

Now the boy had tears of his own, burning his eyes. He wanted to shrink back from this, away from the door. Crawl down under the chains. Disappear back into his dreams. A little red ball, riding the crest of a breaking wave.

But he couldn't look away. He knew his father was locked in a desperate struggle to save his mother's life and his own. He had to be there for his father, even if he could not help him.

The fat Cuban called Carlitos said something in Spanish that caused his mother to wrench her head around and spit in the man's face.

Then the tattooed pirate called *Araña* gripped the fat Cuban's hand, the one holding the machete to his mother's throat.

"No, Carlitos," *Araña* said. "Not until she shows us the map. He won't do it. But I can make her do it, that I can promise."

But the fat man, anger and spittle on his face, disobeyed and drew his blade slowly across his mother's taut skin, leaving a thin red line that instantly became a torrent of blood.

"Carlitos! You stupid fool!" the ponytailed man screamed.

Alex shrank back from the vents, clawing his way across the chains, as far as he could go into the sharp V-shaped space of the bow. He squeezed his eyes shut and stuffed the blanket into his mouth to stifle the deep sobs welling up from his throat.

There was a murderous cry from his father and fast upon that furious shrieking from Sniper and screaming voices in Spanish and English; then his father's terrible wails made him clamp both hands to his ears to shut it out, shut it all out.

The last thing he heard was something slamming hard against the little locker door, hard enough to splinter it inward.

Bahamian fishermen found *Seahawke* adrift nearly thirty miles off Nassau four days later. She was dismasted, her anchor ripped from the bow by a fierce tropical storm that had roared northward up the Exuma Sound just the day before. Finding the yacht abandoned, the owner of the fishing boat and two crew boarded her. Starting at the stern, Captain Burgess McKay and his two paid men worked their way forward, shocked at the amount of destruction that had been wreaked inside the beautiful yacht. Nothing aboard had escaped someone's fury. Nothing and no one could have escaped such blind ferocity.

At some point they noticed a faint hum coming from somewhere toward the bow of the boat. They moved slowly along the companionway, gaping at the ruinous destruction of compartments to both sides. They searched the whole of the dead and drifting yacht. Someone had taken an ax to all the pretty mahogany woodwork, all the furniture, all the beautiful fixtures. The vessel was ruined, destroyed. Bad.

In the main stateroom they found an open safe, empty. A robbery at sea, piracy, was not all that uncommon in these waters. And the yacht flew a large British Union Jack flag at her stern. That made her a likely target for the growing number of island people, all descended from slaves, who were coming to despise their former British masters.

There was still a strange hum emanating from the forward compartment. They all mistook it for a noisy generator. But when they arrived they saw that it was nothing but a lone fly batting itself again and again against the door, as if trying to get in. One crewman swatted the fly away, but it was only momentarily distracted from its efforts. They tried the knob. The door swung inward.

The first thing they saw was a blood-caked machete.

Then, the bodies. The two crewmen were suddenly staggering backwards into the captain.

He prodded them forward into the compartment, but, unable to stomach the buzzing flies, the stench, and the spattered walls, they quickly scrambled up the ladder and instantly heaved their breakfasts into the sea. The captain tore off his shirt, covered his mouth and nose, and remained below. Taking a deep breath, he entered the compartment.

Two nude and mutilated bodies. One, a woman, had had her throat slashed. There were other wounds, but the captain quickly averted his eyes. The other victim was worse. It was a man, and he was pinned to the forward bulkhead wall by two stiletto daggers driven through his hands. The captain stared at the corpse in disbelief. The man had clearly been crucified. He had also been disemboweled.

There was something else on the cabin floor. A large black bird, its feathers matted with blood. The captain saw faint movement of one wing and lifted the bird in his hands. It was badly hurt but still breathing. It squawked weakly as he cradled it in his arms.

Staggering backwards through the door of the small compartment, he made the sign of the cross.

"Mother of God," he said softly to himself.

He fell back into the corridor and collapsed against the wall. He found himself struggling for breath. It was oven-hot in the little cabin, and he turned away, headed for the stern to fill his lungs and gather himself for what he knew he must do. He had only taken two steps aft when he stopped, listening carefully.

There was another sound coming from the compartment, different from the sickening buzz of the countless black flies. It was the sound of short, sucking breaths. Human. Somehow, there was a living being in that room.

McKay filled his lungs with air and stepped once more through the door to the horror inside. It seemed impossible, but the sound of breathing seemed to be coming from the man impaled on the wall.

He went up to the hanging corpse. There was no possibility that this man was alive. Still, he could hear it. Fast, shallow breathing.

It was coming from behind the body.

Captain McKay gritted his teeth and placed the injured parrot carefully on the floor behind him. He reached up and pulled both stilettos from the palms of the dead man. He had to step back as the body fell toward him and collapsed at his feet.

On the bloody wall where the man had died was a small door. It had three small vents. There was a gaping crack down the middle, as if the man had been hurled against it with great force. The sounds were coming from behind that door. He turned the knob. Locked from the inside.

Looking around desperately, he spied the blood-caked machete propped up against the back wall. He grabbed it and quickly pried the small door open with the blade's edge. He bent and peered inside, his eyes adjusting rapidly to the darkness. The breathing was replaced by a low, keening whimper.

There was a figure, a small child, curled into the V-shaped sides of the bow. Not moving, but breathing. Small, shallow breaths. The captain climbed up inside the locker and gathered the child to his chest. It was a young boy, plainly delirious, and he was whispering something rapidly and repeatedly. Captain McKay put his ear to the boy's lips.

three knocks three knocks three knocks three knocks

Lifting him out, the captain was amazed the boy was still alive. It must have been days since he'd eaten, and the child was obviously dehydrated. In an instant, the captain realized that this child must surely have witnessed the murder of his parents through the three ventilation slits.

He covered the boy's eyes with his free hand, shielding him from the sight of the two bodies, and stepped out into the companionway.

In his mind the captain could see it now. How it might have been. The crucified man had hidden the boy in the locker. And died shielding the little door, and behind it, his son.

The captain went quickly to the stern of the yacht and gently handed the boy up to a crewman aboard the fishing vessel. Then he quickly returned for the wounded bird, gathered it up, and closed the main hatch on the horror below. Once the boy was safely aboard their vessel, they left the mutilated yacht untouched. Rigging a line to her bow, they took her in tow, and Captain McKay in the pilothouse got on the radio to the Nassau Constabulary.

The poor fishermen were shocked at what the child must have witnessed and endured. He was barely alive. They prayed for him all the way back to Nassau Harbor. The captain relinquished his berth and the three men tended the boy round the clock. The black parrot, who recovered quickly, never left the boy's side. The only thing the child could keep down was some weak tea. He didn't speak at all, other than to whisper a strange phrase over and over during his few brief spells of consciousness.

three knocks three knocks three knocks three knocks

The fishing boat, *Misty II*, towed the big yacht all the way into the main dock at Nassau Harbor, where a waiting police ambulance took little Alex Hawke, along with his parents' bodies, to the Royal St. George's Hospital. His grandfather was contacted in England, and immediately began making arrangements with the naval secretary to bring them all home.

He then flew to Nassau and spent every day at Alex's bedside, holding his hand, telling him stories about his dog Scoundrel's latest adventures at home on Greybeard Island.

It would be several weeks before Alex was well enough to travel. During that period, the Nassau police investigating the crime visited the hospital, hoping to learn something, anything, about what had happened aboard the *Seahawke*. They quickly realized the boy, mercifully, had no memory whatsoever of the terrible events.

One nice policeman continued to come every afternoon. He was a kind man with a big smile, and he never asked any questions. Every day he'd appear in the doorway, and he always brought some new toy along. A small bird he'd whittled or something from the straw market.

When Alex was about to be discharged from the hospital, the navy secretary at the admiralty in London sent two senior staff officers to the Bahamas to accompany the elderly Admiral Hawke and his grandson home.

The big Royal Navy plane flew from Nassau to Heathrow, refueling at Bermuda and Madeira. Alex sat with his grandfather, sleeping or holding his hand most of the way. His parents were somewhere in the back of the plane, he knew. Something bad had happened to them, he knew. Something terrible. He couldn't remember.

They finally landed in England. A thick fog blanketed everything. They took his parents, who were in narrow metal boxes covered with flags, and put them into the back of a long black car.

The next day, more black cars took them all to a naval cemetery. It rained hard. It was very cold. Sailors fired rifles into the air. As his mother and father finally disappeared into the ground, he saw his grandfather salute. He did, too.

He couldn't cry anymore, so he didn't. He wanted to go home with his grandfather.

Home was on the smallest of four small islands in the English Channel, just off the coast of France. The Channel Islands, they were called. Alex's island was named after the dense fogs that often swirled around its peaks and valleys.

Greybeard Island.

The pirate dreams finally stopped when little Alexander Hawke was about nine.

So the nights were better, and, as Alex grew, the days were never long enough. The sun always stopped before he was ready for it to disappear. He rose each morning at first light and ran down the twisting steps to the sea.

Scoundrel was always right on his heels. He loved diving from the rocks into the cold water of the channel with his dog leaping in right behind him. Later, he would sit for long hours on the craggy hillside, looking out to sea, listening to the crispy sound of late-afternoon breezes in the canopy of trees above his head.

There were long weeks at sea with his grandfather aboard the *Rambler*. They often sailed the schooner north, off the coast of England, sometimes as far as Portsmouth before turning for home. The boy learned to hand, reef, and steer by the stars. He learned to keep one eye aloft, looking for the telltale luff of lost wind in the mainsail.

On endless sunlit days, when Alex had the helm, he would sail the boat through vast floating fields of red krill, cheering the leaping dolphins and whales as they feasted there. Minkies and Humpies, the whales were called, and he came to recognize and love them.

He was learning something new every day. His grandfather taught him the names of the stars and shells, birds and fish. How to tie a bosun's knot. How to knot a bow tie. How to gut a fish. How to write a poem. How to cook fresh clams and mussels in seawater. How to sew a sail. How to spell Mississippi.

He even tried to learn the art of falconry, using his pet parrot, Sniper. Sniper was not interested in becoming a falcon, however, and little Alex soon gave this up. He'd learned the bird's genealogy from his grandfather.

The bird and its descendants had been in the family for generations. Sniper's ancestor had belonged to Alex Hawke's ancestor, the famous pirate Blackhawke, who always kept the bird perched on his shoulder. Pirates,

Alex learned, had for centuries taught the wily birds to warn them of unseen attackers. Each generation of Hawke parrots had been taught these old pirate ways and Sniper was no exception.

Alex Hawke said his prayers every night, kneeling beside his bed and always blessing his grandfather and also his mother and father in heaven. Then he climbed up into the big four-poster bed. Through the open window beyond his bed, he could see the stars shining over the black surface of the English Channel. And hear the waves crashing against the rocks far below his grandfather's house.

He would let his sleepy eyes drift, floating over the familiar toy boats and soldiers and pictures arranged about his room.

Over his bed hung a large painting of Nelson's flagship, *Victory*, her towering masts flying acres of billowing white sail. Bright pennants fluttering from the mastheads. Next to his grandfather, of course, Admiral Lord Nelson was Alex Hawke's great boyhood hero. It was Nelson who was struck down at the moment of his greatest triumph, when the British soundly thrashed the French fleet at Trafalgar.

Hanging from a nail beneath that painting was a very old brass spyglass that had belonged to one of his ancestors who'd sailed under Nelson. A Captain Alexander Hawke himself. Alex spent long hours sitting in his open bedroom window with that battered telescope, tracking birds and ships, imagining his famous namesake doing the very same thing.

When he was twelve, he acquired his first sailing boat. A little dory his grandfather had found, moldering away in a nearby boat yard. He kept the name, even though he had no idea what it meant. He just liked the sound of it. *Gin Fizz*.

As he grew bigger, the island grew smaller. He dreamed of flying, he dreamed of sailing away. He dreamed of joining the Navy one day as his father had done at his very age.

As it happened, his grandfather had attended Dartmouth, and Alex was admitted there as well. He loved books, and his grades were very good. He developed a great longing to go to sea, and his grandfather made a few discreet introductions for him at the very top echelons of the Royal Navy.

He was accepted into the naval officer air corps. Soon after he won his wings, he was flying Harrier jets off aircraft carriers. Then he moved on to fighter jets. He was decorated for valor many times. He was simply good at war.

When peacetime flying no longer thrilled him, Alex joined the special forces branch of the military known as the SBS, the British equivalent of the U.S. Navy SEALs. He gradually became an expert in the art of blowing things up and killing people silently with a knife or one's bare hands. These were all skills he knew he would need.

Because Alex was dreaming of pirates again. He had pirate blood in him, after all. And, as the old expression has it, it takes one to know one.

1

The Englishman looked at his unsmiling reflection in the smoky mirror behind the bar and drained the last of his pint. He'd lost count of how many he'd downed since entering the tattered old pub. It was called The Grapes, and it was one of the more respectable establishments in a rather bawdy little quarter of Mayfair known as Shepherd's Market.

Pink and rose lights were glowing softly in many of the small windows of the narrow buildings that lined the winding lanes. Hand-lettered names could be found beside the illuminated buttons inside each of the darkened doorways. Fanny. Cecily. Vera and Bea. Their pale faces could often be seen at the window for just a moment before the shade was drawn.

He had drifted aimlessly through the narrow streets of Mayfair, having decided to walk home from dinner at the German ambassador's residence. He'd left rather early when, after he'd downed yet another flute of champagne, it occurred to him that every single thing he'd said all evening had bored him to tears.

He'd meant to go straight home, but the miserable weather so perfectly matched the texture and color of his current state of mind that he'd decided to embrace it, dismissing his driver for the evening and electing to hoof it to Belgrave Square.

Damp. Cold. Foggy. Lowering clouds threatening rain or snow or both. Miserable. Perfect.

There was an electric fire in the coal grate of the smoky pub, and now, brooding upon his perch at the end of the bar, he looked at the thin gold Patek on his wrist. Bloody hell. It was considerably further past his bedtime than he'd imagined. Not that it mattered much. He could sleep in next morning. Had nothing on until lunch at his club at one. He tried to recall whom he was lunching with and was damned if he could.

The days had become an endless blur and, except for the constant dull ache in his heart, he would have sworn that he'd died some time ago and no one had bothered to inform him of his own passing.

The pub had thinned out quite a bit, only one or two chaps remaining at the bar and a few young foreign backpackers necking in the curves of the dark banquettes. At least there were fewer patrons to stare at him and the ones remaining had finally left him bloody well alone.

He was aware, of course, that he stood out.

He was, after all, wearing white tie and tails, and his feet were shod with black patent leather pumps. His long black opera cloak, sealskin topper, and gold-headed cane lay atop the bar. He knew he must cut quite an amusing figure at The Grapes, but he was long past caring. He signaled the barman for a check and ordered what would definitely be his last pint before heading home. Sticking twenty quid under the ashtray, he returned to his stormy thoughts.

Part of it was sheer boredom, of course, what the cursed French called *ennui*. He was rotting away so rapidly that it would hardly surprise him if he awoke one morning to find mildew growing on his—

"Got a match, guv?" someone suddenly said at his side. He turned to regard the newcomer and saw that there were three of them. Leather jackets, shaved heads, black jeans shoved into heavy black boots. All staring at him, sneers on their pallid faces. They looked, what was the word, itchy.

He hadn't even seen them come in.

"Matter of fact I do," he said, and fished his old gold Dunhill out of his waistcoat pocket. He flicked it open and lit the cigarette dangling from the lips of the grinning skinhead who was staring at him with glittering eyes.

Whatever drugs he was taking had definitely kicked in.

"Ta," the youth said. He'd had blond hair once, but the stubby new growth was some sort of acid green.

"Pleasure," he replied and, pocketing his lighter, returned to his pint.

"Me mates and I," the lout continued, "we was wonderin' about you."

"Really? I'm not at all interesting, I assure you."

"Yeah? Well, what we was wonderin', me mates and me, was whether or not you were a, you know, a poofter."

"A *poofter?*" he asked, putting down his pint and turning his cold blue eyes toward the sallow face and wide grin full of bad teeth.

"Yeah. A fooking flamer," the man said, though something in the older man's eyes made him take a step backwards.

Two well-manicured hands shot out and pinched the skinhead's ringed earlobes cruelly.

"Poofter?" the elegant man said, smiling, twisting his

fingers. "You don't mean the sort of chap who wears earrings and dyes his hair, do you?"

This drew a laugh from the two sullen mates and brought an angry flush of color into the cheeks of the green-haired fellow.

"Nice meeting you lads," the Englishman said, releasing the chap's bright red ears. He stood, picked up his cloak, and shouldered into it. Then he donned his top hat, picked up the ebony cane, and turned to go.

"Wot's at?" the green-haired boy said, blocking his way.

"Wot's wot?" the gentleman replied in a perfect mimicry of the fellow's accent.

"Wot you said. Wot you called me—"

"Get out of my way," he said. "Now."

"Make me, guv. C'mon. Give 'er a go."

"Pleasure," he said, and he brought the flat hard edge of his hand down on the fellow's right shoulder with such blinding speed that the youth felt the sharp stab of pain before he even saw the hand coming.

"Christ!" he screamed in pain, staggering backwards, his shoulder blade sagging at an odd angle. "You broke me bloody—me bloody—"

"Clavicle," the Englishman said as the fellow stumbled backwards over a barstool and collapsed to the floor.

He then stepped over the chap on his way out the door. "Good evening," he said, tipping his hat as he strolled out the open door and onto the empty street. No one about. It was a good deal later than he'd imagined.

He walked to the next corner and paused beside a lamppost to draw out his gunmetal cigar case. He lit his cigar, listening carefully for their approach. It didn't take long. He let them get within six feet, then whirled about to face the three thugs. The green-haired one was holding his broken collarbone, his face contorted with rage.

"Ah, my new friends," the Englishman said, a pleasant smile on his face. "I've been expecting you. Now. Who wants to go first? You? You? Perhaps all of you at once?"

He waited for one of them to move and when it happened he attacked. His senses were surging back to him, and, like an animal, he rejoiced in the feeling.

He broke two noses first, then lashed out at the third chap, his right foot the blur of a scalded piston. He connected, first hearing the snap of the fibula and then the deeper crack of the tibia, the inner and larger of the two bones of the lower leg. Sadly, it was enough to take all the fight out of them, and so he turned away and headed for home. It had started to rain, a raw, cold rain, and he removed his hat and turned his face up into it, enjoying the sting of the icy drops. He reached the house in Belgrave Square, and Pelham swung the door open for him, taking his hat and cane.

"Good heavens!" the old fellow exclaimed when the man removed his cloak to reveal his blood-spattered shirt-front. "What happened, m'lord?"

"Bloody nose, I'm afraid," he replied, mounting the broad stairs. "Two of them, in fact."

Ten minutes later, he was in his bed, yearning for sleep and the American woman he seemed to have fallen deeply in love with, Victoria Sweet.

★ ★ ★

A few hours on, the Englishman was staring at the ringing bedside telephone and the clock with equal disbelief.
"Bloody hell," he said to himself. He picked up the
phone.

"Yes?" he said, with no intention of being polite.
Christ, it was barely a quarter to five in the morning.

"Hi," said the throaty female voice at the other end,
altogether too cheery for the ungodly hour.

"Good God," he said, yawning. He'd been in a deep
sleep. Having quite a pleasant dream as he remembered.
Vicky was undoing her—he'd lost it.

"No, not Him. But close. It's the brand-new secretary.
First day on the job!"

"Do you have even the faintest idea what time it is
over here?"

"You sound put out."

"May I be frank?"

"Oh, don't be mad. I've had the most amazing day. I'm
not calling to flirt, either. It's strictly business."

The Englishman, fully awake now, propped himself
up against the many large pillows at the head of his bed.
A hard rain, now mixed with sleet, was thrashing against
his tall bedroom windows. The fire, which had been casting shadows on the vaulted ceiling when he'd at last
fallen asleep, was now reduced to a few glowing coals,
and a damp chill pervaded the lofty chamber.

He pulled the blanket up under his chin, cradling the
phone against his cheek. Another soggy January day in
London was about to dawn. He was sluggish. He was
bored. His limbs, his mind, his very cells, had gone soft
and flaccid.

The little scuffle in the street had been a pleasant distraction, but nothing more. The Englishman was in fact a restless warrior who, for far too long now, had been "between assignments," as the euphemism has it.

Which is why the single word *business* had crackled like lightning around his languishing synapses and stirred his lazy blood.

"You mentioned something about business," he said.

"Are you disappointed? Tell the truth. You were hoping it was phone sex. I could hear it in your voice."

"Your voice does sound rather—never mind. Smoky. I thought you'd stopped smoking."

"I'm trying to quit. I'm going hot turkey."

"Excuse me?"

"It's the opposite of cold turkey. You fire up your first one the second you wake up and then smoke as many as you possibly can before you go to sleep at night."

"Sounds brilliant. Well. You said business. Tell me."

"First, you have to know something. This is not my idea. Your pal the president asked for you specifically. I'm telling you that just in case you've got too much on your plate already."

"All right."

"It's not me who's asking. It's him."

"Doesn't matter to me who it is. My plate, dear girl, is as clean as your proverbial American whistle."

"You have no idea how glad they'll be to hear that over at *Casa Blanca*."

"All right. I'm no longer annoyed. I'm awake. Razor sharp. Tell me."

"Your MI6 picked this up, tossed the ball to us. CIA has checked it out and it's serious. Confirmed through the captured Al Qaeda commander, Abu Subeida."

"The Gatekeeper."

"Yes. Ever heard of something called Project Boomerang?"

"Hmm. I do seem to remember that. Some kind of wildly experimental submarine program. The Soviets were building a prototype at the Komsomolsk yard. Tail end of the Cold War. Never got it operational as I recall. Is that it?"

"Exactly. The Russians called it the Borzoi. They'd gotten their hands on a lot of our stealth technology. And they'd also developed some of their own. Plus a three-foot-thick coating of sonar- and radar-absorptive material, advanced fuel-cell technology, and a virtually silent propulsion system. The sub carries forty of their SS-N-20 SLBMs. Long-range Sturgeon ballistic missiles."

"*Carries?* As in present tense?"

"Yes."

"Christ."

"The thing is huge. Shaped like a boomerang, hence the name. Two airfoil-shaped hulls join at the bow to form a V shape, twenty missile silos on each hull. Virtually invisible to detection. When she's running submerged at speed, a single conning tower at the bow is retracted entirely within the hull."

"An underwater flying wing."

"Yes. An invisible underwater flying wing. At least three times faster than anything either of us has got."

"Bloody hell. They actually got one up and running?"

"They built two."

"Yes?"

"We can only account for one."

"What do our new best friends have to say about that?"

"Moscow says it was stolen."

"Security never being their strong point."

"Exactly. They say they have no idea where it is. The theory both at Defense and here at State is that one sub has probably been sold. The president would like you to find out who sold it. And more importantly, who bought it. And when."

"Consider it done," the Englishman said, springing from his bed and grabbing his robe from the back of a chair.

"We could have phone sex now if you'd like," the woman said.

"I wouldn't even dream of taking advantage of you at a moment like this, darling."

"I'll take that as a no. Go back to sleep. Good night, baby."

"Good night."

"I love you, Alex," the woman said.

But the Englishman's heart was in another place entirely, and he had no reply to that.

"Good night," he repeated softly, and replaced the receiver. He had told her that their relationship was over. And that he was very much in love with another woman. No matter what he said, or how frequently, however, it didn't seem to take.

He stood up, stretched, and pushed the bell that would alert Pelham down in the kitchen that he'd be having an early breakfast. Then he dropped to the floor by his bed, did his customary thirty push-ups and fifty sit-ups, followed by the rest of his exercise program. Muscles aflame, he then headed for the shower.

Under the scalding water, Alexander Hawke was surprised to find himself singing at the top of his lungs.

An old Beatles tune.

"Here Comes the Sun."

2

The sun was still brutal as the slender white launch arrived at Staniel Cay. It was precisely three o'clock in the afternoon.

At the helm, a man wearing a crisp white uniform reversed the twin Hamilton whisperjet thrusters, boiling the water at the stern. The long slim vessel slowed instantly, gliding to a stop alongside the dock. The tide was out, but a long ladder hung nearly down to the launch's portside gunwales.

The launch was all gleaming brass and highly varnished mahogany. There was such spit-and-polish perfection about her that she seemed too pristine for this remote backwater of the Exumas; it was as if some alien, other-worldly craft had landed.

Two crewmen, dressed identically in starched white shirts and shorts, climbed quickly up the ladder onto the dock and secured the bow, stern, and spring lines. One crewman posted himself by the ladder to aid disembarking passengers. The other, who was also discreetly but heavily armed, cast a keen eye over the deserted docks. Satisfied nothing was amiss, he caught the helmsman's eye and made a slashing motion across his throat.

The helmsman killed the twin engines and, minus their throaty rumble, the sleepy harbor fell silent once more. The only sound, save the cries of the whirling gulls and terns, was the crack of the large English Union Jack, snapping in a smart breeze on its staff at the rear of the launch.

There were only two passengers aboard, both Englishmen. Standing in the stern of the launch, they were chatting amiably, shielding their eyes against the glare of the Caribbean sun. The taller and younger of the two was a man in his late thirties named Alexander Hawke. He stood something over six feet, but was so lean that he seemed taller. He had thick black hair, piercing blue eyes, a long thin nose, and a prominent square chin that gave him an air of resolution and determination.

It had been scarcely more than a month since Hawke had received the early-morning phone call from Washington. Now, on a blistering afternoon in February, the Englishman scanned the tiny marina with an expression of intense curiosity. He then turned to his companion, Ambrose Congreve, smiling.

"This is where they shot the film *Thunderball*," Hawke said, a somewhat bemused look in his eyes. "Did you know that, Ambrose?"

"What's that?"

"Sorry. I'd forgotten. You'd never set foot inside a cinema unless it was a John Wayne picture. *Thunderball* was a James Bond film. Sean Connery. My favorite, actually."

Hawke's companion was a shortish, rounded man in

his late fifties. He had a pair of deceptively sentimental blue eyes set in a baby's face, a face partially obscured behind a colossal moustache. He heaved a deep sigh and mopped his brow with one of his trademark monogrammed linen handkerchiefs.

"I prefer John Wayne to James Bond simply because the Duke did less talking and more shooting," Congreve sniffed.

"Yes, but Bond—"

"Excuse me, Alex. But, do you really think we ought to be standing out here in the blazing sun discussing ancient heroes of the cinema? Your two agents are sure to be waiting for you on shore."

"Giving you a little local color, that's all, Constable," Hawke said, smiling.

"Well, I don't need any local color. What I need is liquid refreshment. Let's just get this over with, shall we?"

"You *are* a bit cranky, aren't you? You need a nap is what you need."

"Oh, rubbish! What I *need*," Congreve said, "is an enormous fruity rum concoction or vast quantities of very cold beer."

"You can't drink, Constable, you're on duty."

"I would hardly call meeting with a pair of real estate agents duty."

"Did I say real estate agents? Ah. I may have misspoken."

Ambrose just shook his head and said, "You never misspeak, Alex."

Ambrose Congreve, Hawke's oldest and closest friend, had, to his parents' chagrin, begun his career in law enforcement as a bobby on the streets of London. He'd studied Greek and Latin at Cambridge and had thoroughly distinguished himself in modern languages as well. But his true love was reading the tales of his two heroes. The dashing detective, Lord Peter Wimsey. And, of course, that Homeric figure, the incandescent Holmes.

He didn't want to teach Greek. He wanted a life of derring-do. He didn't want chalk on his fingers; he wanted to be a copper.

Early on in his new career, he'd shown a preternatural aptitude for investigation. His almost eerie ability to link seemingly trivial details helped him solve one famous case after another. He'd eventually risen to chief of New Scotland Yard's Criminal Investigation Department. Unofficially retired from the CID now, he still maintained close ties with the Special Branch at the Yard. Still, he detested the nickname "Constable," which is why Hawke enjoyed using it so frequently.

"My sole reason for accompanying you on this afternoon's excursion," Inspector Congreve said, "is that I envision a chilled adult beverage awaiting me in some disreputable saloon. I might even order the one thing your great hero did manage to get right—a properly shaken martini."

"If you had any sense, Ambrose, you'd stop drinking so much and stop smoking that damnable pipe. Wasn't a six-shooter got the Duke carted up Boot Hill, you know. It was a herd of unfiltered Camels."

Congreve heaved an audible sigh and removed the old tweed cap from his head. He ran his fingers through his sparse thatch of chestnut brown hair.

Bloody hell, he thought, here was one mystery solved anyway. The precise latitude and longitudinal location where the phrase "Mad dogs and Englishmen go out in the midday sun" had originated. He'd been absolutely

barmy to go along with Hawke's scheme. It was hot as
Hades in these godforsaken islands. The obvious notion
of removing his woolen bow tie or mismatched tweed
jacket and waistcoat never occurred to Congreve.

Notoriously indifferent to his own wardrobe,
Ambrose seldom noticed whether his suit trousers and
jackets matched and his socks were frequently opposing
colors. Wearing clothes appropriate for the season or the
weather would simply never occur to him. Ian Baker-
Soames, his tailor at Anderson & Sheppard, Savile Row,
London, had long ago resigned himself to Congreve's
sartorial eccentricities.

Rara avis, the tailors whispered whenever Ambrose
Congreve strode through the hallowed portals of A&S. If
he had acquired the reputation of a rare bird, he was
blissfully unaware of that distinction.

Hawke was still willfully ignoring his mutterings and
pleas, going on and on with his geology lecture.

"That little atoll over there," Hawke said, continuing
despite his audience's cool reaction. "It's called
Thunderball because of a small blowhole at the top.
Bloody thing bellows like thundering gods when the sea
blows in hard out of the west."

"Most exciting, I'm sure," Congreve said with a yawn.

"Isn't it?"

"Quite."

"Hullo, Tommy!" Hawke said suddenly, calling up to
the young blond crewman standing guard on the dock.
"You might take a quick stroll down the dock and see if
our new friends have arrived. Won't be hard to spot. Bad
suits, bad haircuts, and bad neckties. Anything odd catches
your eye, give me a quick call on the walkie-talkie."

"Aye, sir!" Tommy Quick said, and took off down the docks at a run.

"You see, Ambrose," Hawke said, continuing his dissertation, "Thunderball is completely hollow inside. The sea surges inside, forces the air out the top. Boom! Hear it for miles around, apparently."

"A true geologic wonder. You'll forgive me if I don't hurl my cap into the air and prance about on the tips of my toes?"

"Yes," Hawke said, too caught up in his enthusiasm to acknowledge the sarcasm. "I swam inside the thing early this morning. Certain aspects of its geology should make it an ideal spot for negotiating with a pair of arms dealers. You've got your bathing trunks with you, I assume? We're going to take these bloody Russians on a little undersea adventure."

"*Arms dealers? Russians?* You plainly led me to believe we were meeting some real estate agents."

"Did I say that? Last-minute change of plans, I'm afraid," Hawke said, scrambling up the ladder. "It's cloak-and-dagger time again, old boy. Come along, Ambrose, the Russians are coming!"

Congreve was busy contemplating the shadowy movements of an especially large shark. He leaned over the rail and watched the fish patrolling the clear waters directly beneath the stern of the launch. Going for a *swim*? Is that what Hawke had said? Congreve considered all forms of athletic endeavor save golf to be sheer barbarism. He heaved what could only be called a wistful sigh. His idea of heaven was puttering and putting around his beloved Sunningdale links just outside London. There, at least, the fiercest creatures one was likely to encounter were surly caddies with apocalyptic hangovers or the odd dyspeptic chipmunk.

He had a standing foursome at Sunningdale, every Saturday morning, rain or shine. Been teeing it up for nearly a quarter of a century. To Ambrose's great chagrin, he was the only member of his foursome never to have achieved a hole in one. It had become a lifelong obsession. He was hellbent on doing it one day, and—

"That's a nurse shark, Ambrose," Hawke shouted from above, interrupting his reverie. "Stop staring at him, you'll scare the poor bastard to death."

Congreve looked up and saw Hawke standing next to Quick at the top of the ladder. Hawke said, "Come along, will you? According to Tommy, we've still got a few minutes to stroll the docks before the Russkies arrive."

Congreve grunted something and started wheezing his way up the ladder. He joined Hawke on the dock, pausing to catch his breath.

It was a pretty little cove, really. Four houses perched on stilts just beyond the docks, each one painted a more brilliant pastel shade than its neighbor. Brightly colored fishing boats bobbed on their moorings in waters too many shades of blue to count. Rather fetching, to be honest.

One rainy afternoon in January, about a month earlier, there'd been a long liquid lunch at White's, Hawke's club in London. It was there Hawke had first broached the notion of this little Caribbean cruise. Congreve was ambivalent at first.

"I don't know. How long a voyage do you envision?" he asked. "As Holmes put it so well, 'My prolonged absence tends to generate too much unhealthy excitement amongst the criminal classes.' "

But Hawke wouldn't take no for an answer and finally got Congreve to agree. After all, it meant an escape from the cold drizzle of midwinter London. Not to mention his tiny Special Branch office in Westminster. A few weeks of "sun, sightseeing, and a bit of shopping" was how the jaunt had been ladled up, and Congreve signed on.

Shopping?

Congreve had hardly been able to imagine what Hawke would want to buy in these godforsaken Bahamian backwaters. An island or two, perhaps? Of course, that was long before he'd learned Hawke was meeting not with real estate agents, but with arms dealers. Congreve looked at Hawke, who'd suddenly stopped dead in his tracks and gone stone silent.

"I've been in this harbor before, you know, Ambrose," Hawke said, his eyes going somewhere else, getting very hard for a moment. "A long time ago. I was just a boy, of course. Barely seven years old. I really can't remember much else, though."

"Is that why you chose these particular islands for the meeting?"

"I don't know," Hawke said. "It's odd. It was this mission that brought me here. Obviously. Still, I do feel drawn to the place. I've been having these peculiar dreams about these islands that—" He paused and looked away, unwilling or unable to continue.

"At any rate," he finally said, "I've brought along a map. Had it since childhood. A map of a treasure that might be buried somewhere in this neck of the Caribbean. But, to be perfectly honest, I'm not sure it's the map that's making me feel—feel like I'm on the verge of something here, Ambrose."

"Yes?"

"I have no idea what it is," Hawke said, looking at his friend with helpless eyes. "I just know somehow the map may be a part of the thing."

"*Shrouded in mystery* is the term, I believe," Congreve said, looking closely at his friend.

"Hmm. Yes," Alex replied, staring at some imaginary point on the horizon. "Shrouded."

Then he shrugged off whatever feelings he was having and said, "Anyway, it's as good a place to meet these dodgy bastards as any other, I suppose."

Constable Congreve put his hand on his friend's shoulder and squeezed. He had been expecting this moment. Dreading it, actually.

Like many people, Ambrose knew the awful story of the murder of Hawke's parents. Not from Hawke, certainly, who, in all these years, had never acknowledged the murders to a soul. Hawke had, Ambrose was sure, completely erased the tragedy from his conscious mind. At the very least, the horrific memories were submerged so deeply in his subconscious, Ambrose wondered if they'd ever resurface.

But in a large leather satchel Ambrose carried everywhere were certain CID files. Files whose existence was known only to Constable Congreve. A cold case for decades, the Hawke murders remained an unsolved double homicide that, without Congreve's determination and commitment, would be moldering away somewhere in the Yard. In the dimly lit cemetery where they kept all the dead files buried.

Of course he'd never dared to raise the subject with Hawke. For his friend's sake, such gruesome memories were clearly better left unstirred. But the murders, Congreve knew, had occurred somewhere in these islands. Quite possibly in these very waters, in fact. He couldn't help but wonder if something, a particular sight or a sound, might trigger Hawke's memory.

Now, Hawke's odd expression as he gazed out over the harbor set Ambrose to wondering. What if all Hawke's deeply submerged memories started to surface sooner rather than later? Pop up, exploding to the surface like some ancient underwater buoys whose unseen tethers have finally rotted and suddenly snapped? And if that happened, where would it all lead?

For a moment, it looked as if Alex might say something more; but then his eyes flickered and blinked and it was all gone, flown from his face in an instant. Hawke smiled at his friend.

"I'll tell you one thing true, Ambrose Congreve."

"Yes?"

"Everything in this world happens in the blink of an eye. Never forget that. *Everything*."

3

Gomez, bruised and bleeding, emerged from the gloom of the ancient and crumbling hospital with just two things on his mind. Sex. And murder. Not necessarily in that order, either.

At least the rain had stopped. The broad tiled steps of the Hospital Calixto García were steaming under the wicked sun. Christ. The light made him squint as he walked down the slippery wet steps to the palmy court-yard, which was full of old soldiers in wheelchairs who had just rolled outside the former military hospital for a little air. It wasn't all that great out here, but it sure beat the hell out of *inside*.

He saw the neon glow of the tiny bar where he'd had breakfast across the Avenida de la Universidad. He could really use a couple of cold ones about now. Like, about twelve should do it.

"I'm not having a good day," he said to some old broad who was staring at his bloody mouth as he went through the wrought-iron gates. "Okay with you?"

He walked out into the sweltering street beyond, cup-ping his hand to the side of his mouth. Hurt like hell.

Taxi? Not when you need one. Lots of Flying Pigeon Chinese bicycles, but very few cars. He'd heard gasoline rations were down to three liters a month. Most of the cars he saw had red tags. Government cars. Hard times in the old hometown, baby. After five minutes he started to walk in the direction of the *Malecón* that ringed the bay. At least he could get his bearings there. Figure out where the hell he was going.

After the stink of sick people, now he had the stink of the streets up his nose. It was like somebody whipped up a big batch of what, sugar cane juice, motor oil, and rot-ten mangos. Popped that pudding in the oven at five hun-dred. Yum, that does smell good.

Oh, and sprinkle with sweat. Lots of sweat. Had these people never heard of Ban Roll-on? And stir in some of the stinky perfume the little *jineteras* wore who followed him everywhere, that'd be good, too.

Hookers, they were everywhere, and cops, too, cracking down on the hookers. It was like cracking down on roaches. They were in the woodwork.

There were two kinds of cops, he'd found out the hard way. The "tourist cops" who were okay, merely a pain in the ass. But the other ones, the ones with the berets, the national police, they were definitely not okay. You even look at them funny they whack you with a baton or haul your ass to jail.

But even they couldn't stop the *jineteras*. Talk about a kid in a candy store. He'd landed in hooker heaven. There were crowds of them outside his hotel, morning, noon, and night. There had been a bunch waiting when he came out of the little family-owned *paladar* where he'd had lunch the day before.

Christ. He couldn't shake 'em. It was like, despite his *guayabera* and his chinos, he had "American Sailor" tattooed on his goddamn forehead. He wondered if this was how movie stars felt. Or Elvis. Not that he especially minded being chased by hookers everywhere he went. That was the only good part of this whole two-day pass. The bad part, the really bad part, had been the last two hours at his dying mother's bedside listening to her scream.

She had cancer of the gut. Bad. Now, you would think that the quote unquote best hospital in Havana would have some kind of painkillers for her. Let her die with some kind of goddamn peace and dignity. He had certainly been wiring her doctor enough money under the table to take special care of her.

Pain management, they called it, every time he called the hospital to check on her. All they could do at this stage, one doctor had said to him. Pain management, *señor.*

Yeah, well, that doctor had zoomed right to the top of Gomez's personal shit list. A true chartbuster.

What had he given her for the pain today? Or yesterday? Or the whole last month as far as he could tell? *Nada.* Zippo. Not even one teensy little baby aspirin. No, the United States government had taken care of that department with their stupid embargo on food and medicine. Still, they had to do something for her.

Finally, he'd pitched a complete shitfit with the doctors and nurses. They told him it wasn't their fault. Blamed it all on America. He'd nearly beat that doctor's brains out before they all pulled him off the guy. Some gorilla orderly had whacked his head on the floor and split his lip. The coppery taste of blood was still in his mouth and he bent over and spit his bloody saliva in the gutter.

Jesus H. Christ, was that a tooth going down the drain? He felt around inside his mouth with his tongue. Yes indeedy, one tooth missing. Okay, now he was getting major league pissed off.

That's why he was now on his way over to the Swiss embassy. Kick some serious butt. Open a big can of whupass on somebody. The head nurse said they had an American desk there. A desk? She said she meant there were some American officials there, even though it was the Swiss embassy.

Make sense? No, but what the hell. Nothing in Cuba made sense anymore. Anyway, he was going to go over there to find one of those little bureaucratic dipshits and rip his goddamn head off.

Murder. That was the ultimate pain management.

That was the plan. First, kick some ass. Next, go *get* some ass. He bought a tourist map and some condoms from a street vendor. He paid one dollar American (nobody took pesos, only greenbacks) and located the embassy on the map. Only eight blocks. He'd hotfoot it over there and pound a few more heads.

Problem was, he found out when he finally got there, the damn embassy was closed. He banged on the door for ten minutes before he realized it was Sunday. Weren't embassies supposed to be open seven days a week? Like 7-Eleven? What if he had an emergency? Which, by the way, he did. He needed some medicine. He was an American citizen. Hell, he was military. U.S. friggin' Navy.

Not that the Navy could give a rat's ass, either. He'd spent the last three nights in the Guantánamo brig for breaking into the base dispensary at three in the morning. He'd copped some morphine and Dilaudid and was just easing out the jimmied back door when the MPs nailed him. The fact that he was stealing medicine for his dying mother didn't even register.

Tell it to somebody who gives a shit, the MP who busted him had said.

He was sitting on the embassy steps drinking one of his little airplane Stolis and trying to figure out his next move when the weird chick appeared. Blond hair, cut short. Green eyes and big red lips and tits out to here. Christmas in July. Tank top and some kind of black spandex thing that stopped way above her knees. Yellow high heels. That clinched it.

He'd definitely died and gone to prostitute paradise.

The girl stopped and looked at him, lounging there on the steps of the Swiss embassy, Mr. Casual. Weird, but she looked familiar. She had these slanty Chinese eyes, but she didn't look all that Chinese. Her skin was the color of one of those three-dollar mocha lattes at Starbucks.

Couldn't tell if she was a working girl or not, more he looked at her. She had this gold collar thing around her neck that looked real. Had a little gold ring hanging down at the front. Hooker jewelry? Hell, they were all working girls, weren't they? One way or another when you got right down to it, everybody and everything was for sale around here.

Amazingly enough, she climbed up the steps and banged on the door. He let her rap it a few times, then said, "It's closed. Sunday."

"What?" she said in English. All attitude this chick.

"You want a mink coat?"

She flipped him the finger and said something that didn't sound too encouraging.

"How about we start with a big pitcher of sangria over at the Floridita?"

She stopped again, thought about it, turned around. She was checking him out. He yawned and stretched his legs out, cool as a Popsicle.

"*Americano,* huh?"

"Home of the brave, baby."

"Yeah, right, Ernesto Junior here wants to buy me sangria at El Floridita, Papa's favorite saloon. You're just another Hemingway sucker, *chico.*"

"A who sucker?"

"Never mind. What happened to your lip?"

"You should see the other guy," he said, liking how fast it came out.

"Yeah, that doctor. You broke his jaw. You're the one who caused all that trouble at the hospital, right?"

He looked at her.

"You were there? I thought I'd seen you before."

"My sister is head nurse there. She's the one who told you about the embassy."

"So you—like, what, followed me over here?"

"Don't flatter yourself, *chico*. I had some business at the embassy, too—something to deliver for my brother." She pulled a manila envelope out of her shoulder bag.

"Stick it under the door," Gomez said.

"No."

"Why not?"

"It's full of money."

"Oh," he said, thinking, definitely not a working girl delivering cash to an embassy.

"So, *adios*," she said, sticking the envelope back in her bag. He wondered how much money was in there. He could grab it and run. The *Malecón* was only a block away. He could melt into the crowds. Could she catch him wearing those bright yellow fuck-me shoes? I don't think so.

"Hey, wait a minute, baby! Where you going?"

"Back to work."

"You work on Sunday? Christ."

"My brother has a club. I work there."

"Yeah, what do you do?"

"Whatever it takes."

"Hey, that sounds good. Can I come?"

"It's very exclusive. Members only."

"I could join."

She laughed so hard it pissed him off.

"You think I can't afford it?"

"I know you can't afford it. It's the most expensive club in Havana. On the other hand—"

"What?"

"My brother might like you."

"Why's that?"

"He likes guys who like to beat the shit out of other guys. They're always useful."

Five seconds after she put two fingers in her mouth and blew the loudest whistle he'd ever heard, the biggest, blackest Chrysler Imperial on earth pulled up in front of the embassy. The driver, some muscleman in a black T-shirt, reached over and swung the door open for her. She hopped in the front, leaned over, and gave the guy a big kiss.

Gomez didn't see her sliding over for him up front so he climbed in the back. The car was mint, like just off the showroom floor. Even had that smell.

"What year is this?" Gomez asked as the guy took off down the narrow street.

"Fifty-nine," the guy said, and turned around and smiled at him. Big gold tooth up front. *"Está bueno, no?"*

"This is my cousin Santos," the chick said, squeezing the back of the guy's neck. "Sorry, I don't know your name."

"Gomez."

"I'm Ling-Ling," she said.

"Ling-Ling," Gomez said, liking the sound of it. "You know how Chinese people name their kids?" he asked. "They throw all their silverware up in the air and name the kids after the sound it makes when it hits the floor. Ling-Ling, huh? Sounds like a salad fork."

Nobody said another word until they pulled up in front of a big wooden gate set in a high pink wall. Gomez had been following their route on his map. They'd driven all along the *Malccón* with the Castillo del Morro on his far right, looking like an ocean liner entering the stormy harbor. Big rollers came in from the Atlantic, crashing over the seawall at Punta Brava, the spray misting the Chrysler's windshield.

Now they were in the shady El Vedado section where all the big old houses were. Most of them built sometime before 1959 B.C. Before Castro.

Gomez and the chick climbed out.

"Hasta mañana," her cousin said, slapping his meaty brown hand on the door a couple of times. Guy must have been wearing ten gold bracelets. Gomez watched the Imperial slide off into a tunnel of green branches hanging dark and heavy, brushing the top of the car as it slid away.

"Well, this is it," Ling-Ling said, pushing a button in the wall and waving up at one of the video cameras.

"What's the club called?" Gomez asked as the heavy doors started to swing inward.

"The Mao-Mao Club."

They stepped through the gates, and Gomez said, "This isn't a club, it's a jungle."

"It's beautiful, isn't it? We have every kind of bird and animal. Even jaguars and leopards."

"No kidding," Gomez said, trying not to sound scared. He seemed to remember somebody getting eaten by a leopard in a movie.

After five minutes of ducking under trees and climbing over banyan roots that had buckled the old walkway, they came to another gate. This time, the gate swung open automatically into a courtyard and there was a little Chinese guy standing there in red silk pajamas. He had a silver tray in his hand with some kind of drink in a tall silver cup.

"Every new guest receives one," Ling-Ling said. "It's called Poison. Try it."

"I love poison," Gomez said, and took a sip. It was the best thing he'd ever tasted in his life.

"You make this stuff?" he asked the Chinaman. The little fellow giggled and scurried away. Probably doesn't speak a word of English, Gomez thought, hardly surprised.

"This way," Ling-Ling said. "My brother is probably at the bar in the casino."

They walked around a pool about half the size of a football field that had a huge splashing fountain in the middle of it. The fountain had some guy with a giant pitchfork riding in some kind of Roman chariot pulled by a bunch of dolphins and whales. Guy had his arm around this mermaid. Biggest damn mermaid tits you ever saw. Solid gold? Had to be.

Gomez heard a shriek and saw a girl climb out of the pool, naked, and watched her get chased by this old fat guy into one of the cabanas that lined both sides of the pool. The girl was wearing the same kind of gold collar around her neck as Ling-Ling.

He noticed that a lot of the cabanas were occupied and most of them had the thick striped curtains closed. He also saw more beautiful girls wearing gold collars at the far end of the pool. He took another swig of his drink and tried not to stare too hard.

At the far end of a wide grassy strip lined with a double row of tall palms stood a big pink building with white shutters that had to be four stories high. Could have been a hotel at one time. Or some dictator's house.

"I like this club," Gomez said, following Ling-Ling into the cool shade of the main house.

She stopped and looked at him. "There is one rule," she said. "There are many famous people here. If you recognize someone, you don't look at them or speak to them. Okay?"

"Got it," Gomez said, searching the faces at the roulette tables for someone he recognized. He saw one cat looked a lot like Bruce Willis, but he wasn't a hundred percent sure because of the dark glasses.

They found her brother sitting at the far end of the long mahogany bar, talking quietly to some guy with a long black ponytail. "*Ciao,* Manso," her brother said to him, and the ponytailed guy immediately stood up and turned away.

"Rodrigo," Ling-Ling said. "This is *Señor* Gomez. He is someone I thought you would like to meet."

Rodrigo stood and stuck out his hand to Gomez. Manso, the ponytailed guy he'd been talking to, wandered off through the casino. Probably famous, because he was careful not to show his face. Swishy walk, Gomez thought, watching the guy. Gay bar? No way. Too much stuff running around bare-ass naked.

"*Buenas tardes,*" the man said. "A cordial welcome to Club Mao-Mao." Smooth as silk, man.

Still, Gomez almost lost it.

The man's eyes were completely colorless.

There was the normal white part. And then, in the middle, where the color usually is, they were totally transparent. Like the guy had a pair of clear marbles in his eye sockets.

"Do I frighten you, *señor?* Sorry. I sometimes have that effect on strangers."

"No. I just—"

The guy was a piece of work all right. Tall and thin and movie-star handsome. Dressed in a white linen suit with a pale blue silk shirt. Thin gold chain around his neck. Had the same mocha latte skin as his sister. Same peroxide blond hair, too. But those eyes were out of some horror movie.

"What do you do, *Señor* Gomez?" Rodrigo asked. "If I may ask?"

"United States Navy. I'm a sailor. Stationed over at Guantánamo."

"So, what brings you to our ancient capital?"

"A two-day pass. My mother, she's, uh, in the hospital. She's dying. Stomach cancer."

"You are *cubano,* no?"

"Yes. My mother stayed here when my father took me from Mariel Harbor to Miami in eighty-one. He died last year at Dade County. Prostrate cancer."

"Prostate."

"What?"

"I believe the word is *prostate, señor.* In any case, I'm sorry to hear of his passing. Won't you have another drink?" He signaled the bartender and another silver cup arrived.

"Thank you," Gomez said. "These are great." He was

already feeling the first one, but what the hell. Stuff was frigging delicious.

"You had an unfortunate experience at the hospital, I understand," Rodrigo said.

"Yeah, this goddamn American embargo. My mother is in such pain that—wait a minute, how'd you know about the hospital?"

"My sister. We talk on the phone all the time. You are opposed to the American policy?"

"You could say that."

"The *americanos* try to punish Cuba but they only hurt women and children. Do you like to gamble, *Señor* Gomez? Blackjack? Baccarat? Chemin de fer?"

"Twenty-one," Gomez said. "Is that the same as Blackjack?"

"*Exactamente,*" Rodrigo said. He opened a white marble box that was sitting on the bar. It was full of chips, one hundred–, five hundred–, one thousand–dollar chips. He counted out ten one thousand–dollar chips and stacked them in front of Gomez.

"Compliments of the house," he said, flashing a big white smile. "Ling-Ling, would you introduce *Señor* Gomez to our head croupier? Make sure he's well taken care of at the tables, darling."

"Of course," Ling-Ling said. "Won't you come with me, *Señor* Gomez?"

"Love it," Gomez said. "And, could I, uh, get one more of these poison things?"

Gomez followed Ling-Ling's sashaying little spandex butt out toward the casino floor, thinking, have I absolutely died and gone to heaven here or what?

"Jack!" he said, passing a guy in a very sharp sharkskin

suit who was rolling the bones. Guy had to be Nicholson. He recognized the haircut and shades from *People* magazine. "My man, what's up?"

"Jesus Christ," Ling-Ling hissed at him. "Didn't you hear what I fucking told you?"

"Yeah, right. Sorry."

Chick was pissed. All right, we can deal with that. How many times in his life is a guy going to rub elbows with Jack Goddamn Nicholson? A little slack here, Ling-Ling, please.

"Autograph out of the question, I guess," he said, following her through the maze of tables.

"You got a pen?" the chick says, giving him a look over the shoulder. "I'll autograph your dick if there's enough space to write on."

"Hey, ease up. I said I was sorry."

"Here's your table, sailor boy. This is Francisco. He will take care of you. Okay? *Bonne chance. Ciao.* Whatever."

The chick started to walk away. He grabbed her arm.

"Hey. Question. What's with your brother's eyes?" Gomez asked her. "You don't mind me asking."

She turned and stared at him.

"My brother was imprisoned for twelve years," Ling-Ling said. "He was kept in a small room with no light. None. No natural. No artificial. The lack of light just leaches all the color out."

"Man. So, how did he get out? Seems to be doing okay now, I mean."

"He said that if they'd let him out for just one day he would do anything. Literally anything they asked. They gave him something to do that was extremely—unpleasant. He was permanently released the following day. Now my brother and I are together again."

He didn't know where he was when he came to, but he was pretty damn sure that it wasn't Hugh Hefner's bedroom at the Playboy Mansion.

He was sitting in a hard wooden chair in a room with no other furniture. Nothing on the floors or the walls. Not even windows. His hands were duct-taped to the arms of the chair, his ankles bound to the chair's legs. He didn't know how long he had sat there with his head pounding before he heard a door open behind him.

"Ah, *Señor* Gomez," he heard a familiar voice say. It was, what was his name, Rodrigo. "Did you have a nice siesta? You've slept for almost twenty-four hours."

"What's the—what's the deal here? I thought you, uh, that you—" His tongue felt way too big for his mouth.

"The deal is this, *Señor* Gomez. You owe the Mao-Mao Club one hundred thousand dollars."

The guy pulled out a piece of paper and held it in front of Gomez's face. He tried to focus but everything was out of whack.

"There is the ten thousand I extended you as a courtesy. When you exhausted that, you indebted yourself to the house for another hundred thousand. At the bottom is your signature. I am forgiving you the ten, because it was a gift."

"What's the, uh, what do you—"

"You have exactly one week to repay. You must understand that I am not one who forgives his debtors as they forgive him."

"I can't . . . I don't . . . how will I get the money?"

"That is hardly my concern, *señor*. Now, turn your left palm upwards."

The man pulled a pair of nasty-looking silver scissors from his pocket and snipped the blades a couple of times.

"Hey, wait! What are you—"

"Two associates of mine will contact you in a few days. Tell you where to bring the money. I'm going to mark you now so that they will recognize you. Turn your left palm upwards, please."

"I can't . . . please . . . the tape is too tight."

"Here, let me help you."

Rodrigo slashed the tape that bound Gomez's wrist, flipped his hand over, and crushed his left wrist to the arm of the chair.

"Hey, you can't—"

Rodrigo looked into Gomez's face with his two colorless eyes as he slashed the sailor's palm with the scissors blade. Gomez saw all the bright red blood spattering this guy Rodrigo's white linen suit, and the lights went out again.

For a while, Gomez thought the angry red letters carved into his hand were *WW*. After a couple of days, he realized maybe he was looking at the letters upside down.

Maybe it was *MM* instead of *WW*.

Mickey Mouse? Marilyn Monroe?

The Mao-Mao Club?

Yeah.

Maybe it meant he was a member.

4

•••——•••

The Staniel Cay Yacht Club baked beneath a torpid afternoon sun. The old haunt had been built in the late forties, sometime just after the war and prior to the time in the fifties when, in Hawke's view anyway, a vast majority of the world's architects had gone completely off the rails.

The pink-hued British Colonial–style clubhouse had the faded façade and the boozy, sunburnt charm of a timeworn playboy. Little of the former glamour remained but, underneath it all, Hawke saw as he strode toward it down the long dock, good bones.

Still, to call it a yacht club was stretching things a bit.

Yachts? Certainly a few serious sport-fishing boats showed up from time to time, especially when the marlin were running. Most of the time, however, there were just small fishing gigs and dories bobbing in the clear blue waters around the docks.

It was a club only in that its membership shared a common partiality to lethal rum beverages, ice-cold Kalik beer, and fishing lies of an order of magnitude seldom found outside these parts of the Caribbean. The "president" of the club was whoever was sober enough to remain standing when the bar closed.

The faded club rules, mimeographed and tacked above the bar, stated that it was absolutely forbidden to sleep on the horseshoe bar. Still, in the very early morning, it was not uncommon to find a few members dozing peacefully atop it.

Suffice it to say, one didn't stroll through these aged

portals expecting limbo nights, cocktails with tiny umbrellas, or the quaint melody of "Yellowbird" wafting through the palms. Perhaps the club had seen better days. Perhaps, worse.

The music on the club's PA system consisted of either reggae in the evenings, or, as now, scratchy recordings of early American bluesmen such as Son House or Blind Lemon Jefferson.

Amen Lillywhite, the club's chief bartender, was all smiles when Hawke and Congreve walked in. He was an ancient blackbird of a man, tall and bare-chested with golden hoop earrings. His enormous white grin and a necklace of shark's teeth had been a primary attraction at the club since the night it opened.

"Welcome, welcome, gentlemen!" he boomed. "What can I get for you two young fellows?"

"Two ice-cold beers would be lovely," Congreve said.

News both good and bad traveled fast in Staniel Cay. Amen, presiding at his horseshoe bar, was at the very epicenter of information flow on the small island. News of the launch moored at the end of the dock reached his ears seconds after its arrival. His excitement grew when he learned the name *Blackhawke* was scribed in gold leaf on the launch's transom. The famous yacht had arrived almost a week earlier, mooring in the deeper water offshore. This was the first time her launch had ventured into Staniel Cay.

It was dark and cool inside the bar where Hawke and Congreve stood waiting for the Russians. The two agents had finally arrived, but remained out on the docks, having a frightful row. Meanwhile, the two Englishmen, each sipping from a cold bottle of Kalik, were gazing up at a wall covered with faded snapshots, a kaleidoscopic jumble of sunny days and rum-soaked nights.

There was an eclectic mix of locals, charter skippers, international boat bums, rich American or British yachtsmen, and even a surprising number of movie stars. Everyone posing with his or her arms around Amen. Amen's appearance changed with the passing decades, but he was the only constant.

"I'd say there are only three ways of getting one's picture up on this wall, Constable," Hawke said. "No doubt you have arrived at a similar conclusion, you being the famous bloodhound, after all?"

"Better hound than hare," Congreve replied, rubbing his chin and perusing the photographs. "I would say that there are actually four."

"Yes?"

"You've got to be rich, famous, or an alcoholic," Ambrose declared.

"And the fourth?" Hawke asked, delighted.

"All of the above, of course."

"Precisely," Hawke said, looking at his friend with an admiring smile. "Ambrose Congreve, Scotland Yard's own Demon of Deduction," Hawke added.

Alex then looked out toward the docks, frowning. The Russians were still there, shouting. Arguing about just how much money they might gouge out of the rich Englishman, Hawke imagined. Bloody hell, he hated waiting.

"What the devil is keeping those two? And what are they going on about anyway?" Hawke asked. "Are we having this bloody meeting or are we not?"

"I've been eavesdropping. They're fighting over a

woman. Grigory came back to their boat last night and found Nikolai having a go at someone Grigory fancied. Not being very nice to her either, apparently. Someone named Gloria. A local girl from what I can make out."

"Your Russian seems sound enough."

"Flawless."

"Here's the thing. Go tell those bastards I'm walking out of here in fifteen seconds."

"Right-ho," Congreve said, and pushed through the screen doors and out into the sun.

Hawke looked around the ancient saloon. Every arched wall was festooned with fishing nets, buoys, giant mounted marlin and sailfish, conch shells, shark jaws, and endless strings of Christmas lights. Somehow, he thought to himself, it all worked.

Two or three "members" were seated at the bar, wholly absorbed in some kind of dice game, paying scant attention to Hawke or anyone else. The tables were all empty. Lunch crowd gone, cocktail crowd not yet arrived. Good.

The two crewmen from Hawke's launch had scouted the yacht club yesterday and proclaimed it ideal. Now, both armed, they had stationed themselves none too discreetly on either side of the club's front door.

The younger of the two, ex–U.S. Army sharpshooter Tommy Quick, was happily tossing fried bacon rinds into the waters surrounding the docks. In the gin-clear water, Tom could see literally dozens of large nurse and bull and sand sharks cruising over the white sandy bottom, instantly rising to snap up his treats as quickly as they hit the surface.

Hawke had met Sergeant Thomas Quick at the U.S.

Army's Sniper School at Fort Hood. Hawke had audited a course there one summer and successfully recruited the Army's #1 sniper. Quick could easily see that working for Alex Hawke would be a far more exciting and lucrative career than anything the U.S. Army offered.

The world knew Hawke as one of the world's most powerful businessmen and head of a massive conglomeration of diversified industries. A very select group of people knew that he frequently did highly secret freelance work for the governments of the United States and Great Britain.

Since joining Hawke, Inc., Quick had bought gold mines in South Africa, been in a room deep in the Kremlin while Hawke chatted with the Russian defense minister, and spent a long night helping Hawke attach limpet mines to the hulls of ships full of illegal weapons sitting in the bay off Bahrain. On the first anniversary of his employment, Quick had given Hawke a gift that the man still wore, an Army Sniper School T-shirt that read:

You Can Run But You'll Only Die Tired!

The older crewman, Ross Sutherland, who was actually on permanent loan to Hawke from the Yard's Special Branch, kept one eye on the two bickering Russians and one hand inside his shirt, lightly gripping the nine-millimeter Glock he always wore strapped under his arm. These Russians didn't look like much, but, in his years spent protecting Hawke, he'd learned the hard way never to go by appearances.

Sutherland was a man who'd think nothing of laying down his life for Alex Hawke. One night, in a makeshift prison some thirty miles south of Baghdad, Hawke had almost died saving Sutherland's life. Somehow, Hawke managed to get the two of them safely out of the Iraqi hellhole where they'd been held for over two weeks after a SAM-7 brought their Tomcat fighter down. Ross had no memory of the escape. He'd literally been beaten senseless by the Iraqi guards.

Both men had been brutally mistreated, especially Sutherland. If they had not escaped that night, Hawke knew it was doubtful Ross could survive another day's "interrogation." As it happened, Hawke had killed two guards with his bare hands and they'd fled south across the desert, using the stars for navigation.

Ross had barely survived their endless trek across the scorching sands. For days and nights on end, Hawke had carried Sutherland on his back before an American tank command finally stumbled upon them. By this point, they were wandering in circles, staggering blindly up and down the endless sea of dunes.

The Russians continued their tiresome squabbling and Ross knew Hawke must have been getting impatient. Idly, he fingered the Glock beneath his shirt. Not that Sutherland was expecting trouble. The night before, he'd reread the Russians' dossiers. They were both former Black Sea Fleet officers. Both had originally served at the sub base at Vladivostok. They'd been classmates at the academy and were surviving the end of the Cold War by peddling what remained of the Soviet navy.

Ross allowed himself a smile at the sight of Congreve barging into the middle of the heated argument, barking at them in Russian. After a moment of stunned silence, the two nodded their heads. Ross opened the screen door and the two men meekly followed his colleague from Scotland Yard back inside.

"Well, isn't this cozy?" Hawke asked when they'd all been seated. "Refreshments? Vodka, I'd imagine. Get everyone in a festive mood." He signaled to a waitress lingering in the doorway to the kitchen.

"I think perhaps beer might be a better choice," Congreve said, giving Alex a meaningful kick to the shin under the table. Hawke understood immediately that the Russians' vodka quota for the day had already been met and nodded his head.

Ambrose was yammering away with the Russkies, so Hawke leaned back in his chair and took their measure.

These two legionnaires of the former evil empire were bleary-eyed and a sickly gray beneath their suntanned exteriors. The heavy one had salt-and-pepper hair, cut short in the old Soviet military style. Steel-rimmed glasses completed the look. Long, greasy dark hair, tied loosely at the back, a pair of shiny black marbles for eyes, and a rather uncooperative black beard on the other chap. He bore, Hawke observed, an uncanny resemblance to the notorious Russian "Mad Monk," Rasputin.

Unlike the woolen suits Hawke had pictured them wearing, they were casually dressed in bathing suits, sandals, and sport shirts depicting multicolored billfish leaping gaily about.

Looking at them, Hawke felt a twinge of pity. At one time, these two cold warriors had surely been formidable men, accustomed to a sense of purpose, power, and command. Now they had a dissolute air about them, stemming no doubt from too much sun, too much rum, too little self-respect. It was more than a little humbling, Hawke imagined, to be peddling the arsenal of your once vaingloriously evil empire.

"Well," Hawke said, suddenly restless. "I'm Alexander Hawke. My esteemed colleague, Mr. Ambrose Congreve, whom you've met, will be handling the translations. Ambrose, you have the floor."

As Congreve translated this bit, the waitress approached Hawke. Her flashing eyes and body language indicated that she was not in the best of moods. Surprising, since he'd heard so much about the sunny disposition of the people in these islands. This singular exception to that rule presented herself at the table.

"Hello," Hawke said, though his smile went unreturned. "Four Kaliks should do it, thanks." *Blackhawke*'s crew drank nothing but the local Bahamian beer, and that was good enough for Alex. The girl nodded grimly and headed for the bar. Her walk did lovely things to the back of her shift.

Congreve coughed discreetly to get Hawke's attention.

"May I present Mr. Nikolai Golgolkin and Mr. Grigory Bolkonski," Congreve said to Hawke. "Golgolkin, the Russian bear with the steel glasses, seems to be the one in charge. The chap on the left, who is a dead ringer for Rasputin, is a former submarine designer and weapons expert from the Severodvinsk shipyard on the Kola Peninsula. Both are very pleased to meet the famous Hawke."

The little "mad monk" didn't seem all that pleased. He turned his black eyes on Congreve, anger suffusing his face. He'd clearly heard the Rasputin reference and was not amused.

"Lovely," Hawke said, smiling.

"They apologize for their rudeness in keeping you waiting and beg forgiveness. It seems they are uncomfortable having this discussion in such a public place, but they have brought a gift. Vodka."

"They certainly have a gift for drinking the stuff, judging by appearances," Hawke said.

Golgolkin produced a small, rectangular red velvet box, which he placed in front of Hawke. Hawke opened it and smiled. It was Moskoya Private Label. Quite rare. Bloody marvelous stuff after a few hours in the freezer.

"Very kind," Hawke said, looking from one Russian to the other. "A most generous gift. Let's get to it. According to our mutual Syrian friend in Abu Kamal, they will have a portfolio of their wares with them, correct?"

Congreve began translating and soon they were all chattering again in what was, to Hawke's ear, still a most unlovely language.

The waitress arrived with a tray and placed a sweating bottle of Kalik in front of each man. Her angry eyes avoided those of the two Russians and her volcanic mood sent tremors to her fingers as she served them. Such a pretty girl, Hawke thought. Pity she was so unhappy.

As she handed Hawke his beer, he couldn't help but notice the rough red abrasions around each of her wrists. A quick glance down at her bare feet and ankles revealed that they, too, were red and raw. This poor girl had recently been abused, and badly.

"What is your name?" Hawke whispered to the girl, taking her gently by the hand.

"Gloria," she replied, her eyes downcast.

"Gloria," he repeated, remembering it as the name of the woman Congreve had heard the Russians arguing over. "Yes, I might have guessed that."

5

It was hard for Hawke to conceal his unbridled loathing for the two Russians. To think, just moments before, he'd actually been feeling sorry for these two sodden degenerates. Make that godless Commie sodden degenerates. In Alex's world there was right. And there was wrong. And there were no shades of gray.

The kind of work Alex Hawke did, covert assignments for both the British and American governments, often meant dealing with cretins like these two. But Hawke was a man who loved his life's calling deeply and passionately. He relished each and every assignment. Now, after the long, restless hiatus that had been January, he looked forward to this one with keen anticipation.

He stared at the two men sitting across from him. According to everything he'd learned from Cap Adams, the CIA station agent in Kuwait City, they were a pair of heartless pirates, perverse enough to make their fortunes selling weapons of mass destruction to the world's terrorists. He'd gathered sufficient information from enough sources to suggest that these two just might be the ones to lead him to the disappearing Borzoi submarine. After that, he planned to put these two parasites out of business. Permanently.

Congreve said something briefly in Russian, and Golgolkin pulled a faded red leather folder from his satchel, pushing it toward Hawke. Embossed in gold on the cover was the old Soviet symbol itself, the hammer and sickle.

"Suggestion," Hawke said, tapping the symbol with his finger. "You boys ought to find yourselves a new logo. When somebody's sickle has been hammered as badly as yours has been, it's time to move on."

As Congreve translated this bit to the puzzled Russians, Hawke perused a stack of glossy eight-by-ten photos until a certain item caught his eye. It was a huge jet-powered hovercraft, capable of carrying at least sixty or seventy soldiers. Or, Hawke thought, passengers. He separated the photo from the stack and placed it on the table.

Hawke owned a handsome castle in Scotland. It was on a lovely rugged island in the Hebrides and he'd gotten his chum Faldo to build one of the most gorgeous links golf courses in all of Britain on it. Hawke was a terrible golfer, but his love of the game remained undiminished.

He didn't get to use the Scotland property as much as he'd intended and was now thinking of converting it into a small hotel. This hovercraft would make a splendid way of transporting guests to and fro. The fact that it was ex-Soviet would only add to the cachet.

"How fast?" he asked.

Rasputin muttered something and Congreve translated, "On a calm day, flat, no wind, in excess of sixty knots."

Hawke said nothing and continued to look through the pile of photos. It was an amazing assortment of weapons and military craft. Scud missiles and missile launchers, helicopter gunships, high-speed attack boats; indeed, just about everything except what Hawke was really interested in. He returned the photos to the folder, slid the red leather case across the table, and stood up.

"Well," Hawke said, "you've piqued my interest. I'd like you to join me aboard the launch. We'll continue this discussion at a more private location."

The Russians were instantly all smiles, positively giddy at the sudden prospect of a major sale, and happy to go someplace less public. Getting to their feet, they extended their hands as if to seal some bargain already agreed to. Hawke ignored them and turned to Congreve.

"Ambrose, be so kind as to escort these two characters out to the launch. I'll linger here a moment and take care of our tab."

"So, this is what you meant by 'shopping,' eh?" Congreve leaned to whisper in Hawke's ear. "You might have mentioned it sooner, and I could have had this pair of cads thoroughly checked out."

"No need to bother you with it. I had Sutherland do it, before we left London. I told you, Ambrose, this is a holiday. Relax, get some sun, have a bit of fun. You've been quite morose since your Maggie died."

Congreve looked away, sadness overtaking him.

"Mags was a fine old hound. I had a dog once," Hawke said. "Scoundrel. I loved that dog so much, it frightened me to watch him grow old, knowing that he would die one day."

"It's so awful when they do," Congreve replied. "But

they do die. And then you are alone." The older man turned away, squared up his shoulders, and hustled the two arms dealers out through the screen doors and into the afternoon sun.

I've always been alone, Hawke thought, looking after him. Always.

Hawke shook off the feeling and walked over to the bar. He took one of the many empty stools, smiled at the bartender, and said, "Lovely day for it, isn't it?"

"The Lord has indeed blessed us once more, sir," the bartender said with his big white smile. He stuck out his hand. "My name, sir, is Amen Lillywhite. Please call me Amen. We are honored to have you here at the club, Commander Blackhawke."

Hawke nodded and took the man's scrawny mahogany hand and shook it. "Rum, please, Amen. Neat. Gosling's Black Seal 151 if you've got the stuff."

"Not much call for it, but I do, sir!" he said. "Let me find it."

Commander? Hawke was amazed. Commander *had* been his rank when, after a successful career, he'd retired from the Navy. Hardly anyone used it anymore.

And *Blackhawke*? Who knew how that had gotten started? No one, save perhaps Congreve, knew that Alex was indeed a direct descendant of the famous pirate. Perhaps it was a creation of the idiotic society reporters in London who relentlessly followed his every move and romantic misadventure. "Blackhawke's Latest Bird Flies the Coop" was typical of the tabloid coverage he'd endured.

And there were more than a few captains of industry around the world who, having been broadsided by a

Hawke hostile takeover, considered him somewhat piratical. In any event, the swashbuckling sobriquet had stuck, and it amused Hawke no end. He and Congreve alone knew that there was a very *real* Blackhawke perched atop the uppermost branches of the Hawke family tree.

"An honor to serve you," Lillywhite said, placing a healthy tumbler of rum on the bar before him.

"I only drink on two occasions. When I'm alone or with somebody, Amen," Hawke said, taking a sip of the dark liquid. "Will you join me in a glass?"

Amen smiled and shook his head.

"Haven't had a drop since my first day here, near to fifty years now. Good Lord surrounds me with temptation, sees what I do. I sometimes imagine myself at the pearly gates. And maybe the Lord might say, 'You've had a long trip, Amen. Would you like a drink?' "

Alex laughed and said, "I was wondering. Those pictures over there on that wall. How far do they go back?"

" 'Bout fifty years or so, sir," Amen said. "To the club's most early days, I think, right after the war. I started working here, let me see, in forty-nine." Hawke nodded silently, gazing at the wall. Strange, but he found himself studying the jumble of old photographs with solemn intensity. Almost as if he expected to find an old friend or relative amongst the countless strangers.

He caught Gloria's eye. She had been standing at the window, watching Congreve and the two Russians stroll down the dock. She walked over, keeping her eyes on the floor, and handed him the handwritten chit. Hawke didn't even look at it. He took her hand and pressed a folded hundred-pound note into it. He caught her gaze and held it.

"I don't know what happened to you last night. But I'm the one who invited those two men to your island and so I feel responsible. I promise you this. They will never, ever bother you again."

She looked up at him with gleaming eyes. "You'll keep them away?"

"Actually, I plan to *put* them away," Hawke said with a smile. "Now, you take care of yourself. Cut some fresh aloe and rub it into those abrasions."

"I will," she said, not looking up into his eyes.

Hawke paused once more before the wall of photographs on his way to the door. Spying a tiny Polaroid amidst the jumble, he found himself unthinkingly reaching up and plucking it from the wall. Without even looking at it, he stuck it in the breast pocket of his shirt, then walked out into the heat of the tropical sun.

At the end of the dock, the launch's powerful twin engines rumbled in the somnolent afternoon. Congreve had raised the hydraulic engine hatch cover and was busy showing off the twin supercharged Rolls-Royce power plants to the Russians. Rasputin had climbed down into the engine room for a closer look.

"Giving away the latest of Her Majesty's technology for free, eh, Constable?" Hawke said, looking down from the dock. Congreve guiltily pushed a button, and the big hatch cover started to close with a hydraulic hiss. The sight of the Russian scrambling out in the nick of time delighted Hawke.

"Everything shipshape?" Hawke asked Tommy Quick after he'd climbed down the ladder and stepped aboard.

"Aye, Skipper," Quick said. "I've got snorkels, fins, and masks for everybody. Tide's full in now, so the entrance to the grotto is submerged. About six feet below the sur-face. A few sharks milling about in the vicinity, but I shouldn't worry about them, sir."

"I shouldn't worry about them either, Tommy, if, like you, I were remaining aboard the launch," Hawke replied.

"Sorry, sir, I only meant—"

"Relax, Tom," Hawke said, smiling. "Just a bad joke. Why is everyone so bloody touchy lately? Even that aged party Congreve. Somebody pour a wee dram of rum down his gullet for this epic voyage, please? And let's shove off, shall we? It's getting late."

Hawke turned to the Russians now seated in the stern. "You chaps ever done any snorkeling? Great fun. You're going to love it. Everybody all buckled in?"

Hawke relieved his helmsman and leaned on the twin-chromed throttles. In a second, the launch was up on a plane and screaming out of the Staniel Cay Marina, bound straight for Thunderball Island.

"Look back there, Ambrose," Hawke shouted, point-ing at the two fellows huddled behind them in the stern. "Not the hardy outdoors type, are they? No wonder they lost the stomach for the bloody Cold War."

Congreve looked back at them. And, indeed, they'd both gone pale as ghosts.

"White Russians, I'd say, by the looks of them," Congreve said, and Hawke couldn't help laughing.

6
● ● ● ━ ━ ━ ● ● ●

Petty Officer Third Class Rafael Eduardo Gomez,
United States Navy, Guantánamo, had the shakes so
badly he had to duck into a bar. He ordered a double
brandy, beer back, and downed the jigger of brandy
in two gulps. Which was perfectly okay except that it
wasn't even eight o'clock in the morning yet and he
had the most important meeting of his life in fifteen
minutes.

But the brandy calmed his nerves all right. Yes, sir, it
did! He swallowed the ice-cold beer in one long, Adam's
apple–bobbing gulp and slammed the empty mug down
on the bar. Yes! Breakfast of champions.

It was the last day of his family emergency leave from
Gitmo. He'd wangled this second leave by using his
mother's death in Havana. Said he had to go to Miami to
tie up some important family business. At the last
minute, he decided it'd be a good idea to take his family.
Make a little holiday out of the thing. Quality time, his
wife, Rita, called it. Time to get Rita off his ass for a couple of days, anyway.

It had been raining in Miami for forty-eight straight
hours. So, since it was sunny today, he was supposed to
be taking Rita and their two daughters to South Beach
this morning. He'd promised, she'd reminded him.

"Something has come up," he told Rita in the kitchen
of his Aunt Nina's apartment in Little Havana.

"Like what?" Rita said.

"Like something," he replied. "A business deal. I can't

talk about it. It's an idea my cousin Pablito has. We could make a lot of money, baby."

"Your cousin, he just got out of jail last week! He misses prison so much already? You know, honey, maybe your cousin, he's not into crime for the money! Maybe he likes—"

"What you saying? You saying my beloved cousin, he is a—"

That's when he'd lost it. Slapped her hard enough to hurt. So much for quality time. She was still yelling at him when he slammed the kitchen door behind him and made a beeline over to Calle Ocho. It was the main street of Miami's Cuban barrio. The two men he was meeting had told him to be at the San Cristóbal Café at eight sharp.

He walked in at one minute before, feeling good now, feeling the *glow*, baby. There was one old guy sitting at the counter sipping a café con leche and watching the waitress's short skirt hike up as she bent over to fill an ice bucket; otherwise, the bodega was empty. So he was here first, which was good.

Basic military training. Do a little recon. Get the lay of the land. He was tempted to take a seat at the counter and recon the waitress bending over the ice machine. Incredible booty on this bitch and—no. This breakfast is strictly business, he had to remind himself. He took a seat at a table by the window where he could keep an eye on the door. He wanted to check out these two dudes before they checked him out.

He pulled out the folded *Miami Herald* he'd been told to bring and set it on the table open to the sports section, just like the guy had said. Frigging Dolphins. What were they, fourth in the division? Ever since Marino had retired—a large black shadow fell across his paper.

"*Señor* Gomez?" a big tall guy in a white *guayabera* said. Christ, he hadn't even seen them walk in. So much for his recon and surveillance plan.

"That's my name," he said, trying to pull off a cocky grin but not too sure he had it working just right. Maybe the double brandy hadn't been such a good idea. His teeth felt funny.

"Are you a Dolphin fan, *señor?*" asked the second guy, who was shorter than the first guy but way *wider.* This one was carrying a suitcase, a beat-up old gray Samsonite. Amazingly enough, it looked exactly like his own suitcase. *Exactly.* The guy put it on the floor very carefully and looked at Gomez, waiting for an answer.

Both of them badass, he could gather that much pretty quickly. Gooey hair. Big black sunglasses, heavy gold chains, Rolex watches with diamonds, all that *Scarface* shit.

"I used to be," he said, trying to get it exactly right. "But now I root for the Yankees."

The two Cuban badasses smiled and sat down across from him, and he knew he'd nailed the goddamn secret password thing. *Nailed* it. When you're good, you're good, that's all there is to it.

"Your left hand. Show me," Wideload said.

Gomez turned his palm up and showed him the two initials carved into his hand. Guy didn't say anything, just nodded to the other guy.

"What does that stand for, anyway?" Gomez asked. "The *MM?* Is that Mao-Mao? Or is it, like, *WW?*"

They both looked at him like he was crazy.

"Why don't you shut the fuck up and let us ask the questions, okay?" Wideload said. "We ask the questions. You answer the questions. Got that?"

"Okay, okay. Sorry. I was just wondering, you know, what it stood for. You guys have names, by any chance? Just curious."

"Guy simply don't understand English," Wideload said, shaking his head.

"No. He speaks English okay. But he got the attention span of a fuckin' *moquito*," the tall guy said.

"Hey, wait a goddamn second," Gomez said. "I don't—"

"Shut up and listen. Okay?"

"Okay. Hey, I'm all ears."

"That's good. You want to do business? Shut your mouth for five seconds. It was us who spoke to you on the phone. I'm Julio. He's Iglesias," Tallboy said.

"Man," Gomez said, slapping the table, "you guys are good. Code names and everything!"

"You believe this guy?" the tall one said.

"It's not code, okay? Our names really are Julio and Iglesias," the white *guayabera* said.

"Fine," Gomez said, bobbing his head up and down. "Cool. Julio. Iglesias. Whatever. I'm down with that."

"Give me a look at your newspaper," Wideload said. Major Cuban accents here. Two heavy-duty hombres just off the boat from *La Habana*. A blind man could see that.

"All yours," Gomez said, and slid the paper over to the guy.

The guy opened to the page where Gomez had stashed all the ID they'd asked for. His Navy papers,

Florida driver's license, Social Security. While one guy checked his ID, the other guy called the waitress over and ordered them all café con leches. Not that he'd do it, this was a business meeting, but a cold one at this point would really hit the spot.

She bent over to hand them all menus and gave everybody a perfect photo op of her lacy push-up Wonder Bra. Gomez almost came out of his seat. Perfect goddamn wonder breasts! Christ Jesus, he thought, how come this place was so empty? Forget the food, this waitress's knockers alone ought to be packing them in. He was watching her rumba her ass on back to the kitchen when Wideload brought him back to reality.

"We were both saddened to hear of your mother's passing," the Cuban guy said, picking something out of his teeth with a gold toothpick.

"Yeah? How'd you know about that?" Gomez said. "Rodrigo tell you?"

"You're smart, you never say that name again, *señor.* You're not smart . . . well . . ."

Gomez just nodded, looking from one to the other, making sure they knew that he got the picture.

"Rodrigo?" he said, grinning. "Who the hell is Rodrigo?"

"You just said it again, asshole," Wideload said. "Twice."

"Hey, I was just—"

"How about you shut the fuck up while we finish looking at your papers, okay?"

It was just after he got back to the base after the little episode at the Mao-Mao Club that he'd gotten the phone call from these two guys. Before he left Havana, he'd gone back to the hospital and said his goodbyes to his mother. She was still wailing in pain when he'd walked out the door. He'd immediately split for Gitmo.

His mother died an hour after he left the hospital, Rita told him when he walked in the door.

Headed home to Gitmo he'd been sad and pissed about his hand, which stung like crazy, but what he really was, goddammit, was scared shitless about coming up with a hundred large. On the other hand, what could they do? Way he had it figured, if he never left the base, how could they get to him? Fact was, it didn't take long.

They'd called his house at the base. Late the same night he got home from Havana. He'd been sitting in the kitchen drinking Budweiser tallboys. Crying some, thinking about his mom. The kids were asleep and his wife was upstairs watching some stupid movie. Two Cuban guys on the phone. They wanted to know did he have the money and when he'd be coming to Miami next to visit his Aunt Nina.

Some truly unbelievable shit, man.

They'd known her name, where she lived, everything. They said they'd heard a lot of good things about him and they wanted to hook up with him somewhere. Soon. Before his deadline ran out.

He told them right up front he didn't have the money. Didn't see any way of getting it in a week. Could he, maybe, get an extension? He had friends in Miami. He'd done a little dealing before he joined the Navy. Maybe he could work something out with some of his old pals. Seeing Rodrigo's colorless eyes as he said it. Getting that really sick feeling in his stomach.

Like he really had a chance to score a hundred large in three days. Make that three lifetimes.

Then, a miracle. The more they talked the more he began to understand that they weren't going to whack him for a chickenshit hundred G's, after all! No, they had some kind of weird-assed business proposition for him! A deal that would not only erase the unfortunate debt he had gotten into in Havana, but a deal that would make him rich!

They said they wanted to meet up in Miami. They were sure he would find they had a proposition that would interest him greatly.

"Yeah, how greatly?" he'd asked the guy on the phone. He'd heard of these phone scams before. These guys sounded legit, but he wasn't stupid.

"Is one million dollars greatly enough?" the guy said.

"One million dollars?" he said, almost choking on the figure. "Yeah, I'd say that was greatly."

So he agreed to meet them and wangled the family emergency leave. Took his family to Miami. He'd listen to what they had to say. Hopefully, it wasn't some con to get him off the base so they could waste him. He was a pretty good judge of character, though, and these guys sounded okay to him.

So, here he was, Johnny-on-the-spot at the San Cristóbal on Calle Ocho just like they told him. A million bucks? For that kind of money, he'd meet anybody. Friggin' Adolf and friggin' Hitler, man. Friggin' Frank and friggin' Sinatra, much less Julio and Iglesias here.

Who wants to be a millionaire? Petty Officer Third Class Rafael Gomez, that's who.

He was starting to think that the chance meeting with Ling-Ling was the beginning of a major shift in his luck. Luck that, frankly, hadn't been all that hot lately. Hadn't been that great since high school, if you wanted the truth.

Gomez noticed they still hadn't bothered to properly introduce themselves. Because they knew *his* real name, it bothered him a little. Probably the way these kinds of things went down, though. Less he knew the better, he figured, when and if the fit hit the shan. But, still—

"So let me skip the chase and cut directly to the outcome," Gomez said, liking the way that had come out. "What exactly does a guy have to do around here to make a million bucks? What's the plan, guys? And, since we're going to maybe be in business together, let's cut the crap. You guys have any, like, real names?"

"I am Julio," Tallboy said. "Like we told you, amigo."

"I am Iglesias," Wideload said.

Gomez looked at them for a second, shaking his head. What were you going to do?

"Right, Julio and Iglesias. Okay, fine, and I'm Elvis and Presley. Split personality, get it? So, if it ain't too much trouble, how about bringing me up to speed on what, exactly, is the big plan? You guys were kinda vague on the phone, know what I mean? Julio?"

"*Necesario, señor.* Is very simple plan, *Señor* Elvis," Julio said with a smile. He had a gold tooth right up front that was catching the morning sun bouncing off the windows big time. Made it hard to concentrate on what the guy was saying. The tooth and the fact that there might be a million bucks in that suitcase.

"Simple is good," Gomez said, feeling his heart pumping. He'd started shaking again, only from the inside out now. He was going to have to, what, whack somebody? Would he do that for a million smacks? Maybe.

He'd killed a guy once. Accident. Fed him to the

gators late one night in the big ditch along Alligator Alley. Way the hell out the Tamiami Trail in the deep 'glades. Nobody ever knew nothing.

No biggie, he thought, remembering.

"Man, it's hot in here. Anybody for a brewski?" They both shook their heads. "No? Man, I could go for one. Breakfast of champions, man, the King of Beers."

Thing about these guys, no sense of humor whatsoever.

"All you have to do, *Señor* Presley, is take this fine piece of luggage home to Guantánamo with you tomorrow." The guy picked up the suitcase and placed it on the table.

"That's it?"

"That's it."

"You guys aren't going to believe this," Gomez said, "but that suitcase looks exactly like *my* suitcase. Exactly."

"Maybe that's because it *is* your suitcase, *señor,*" Julio said.

"What? No way, man. My suitcase is under my bed at my aunt's place."

"Really? When was the last time you checked?"

Gomez looked at all the old stickers and shit on the Samsonite. Old United bag tags from when he was flying back and forth from Cecil Field, N.A.S. JAX all the time. Sonofabitch. It *was* his suitcase.

"What's inside my suitcase, you don't mind me asking?"

"It's difficult to describe, *señor,*" Iglesias said. "You've heard of a Roach Motel?"

"Yeah. The bugs check in but they don't check out."

"Well, inside that suitcase is a kind of reverse Roach Motel," Julio said.

"*Sí,* he's right," Iglesias chimed in. "In this motel, the

bugs they are already checked in, but they *can't wait* to check out. Check out and kick some gringo ass."

"But here's the good part, *señor,*" Julio added. "The bugs? Decoys. The real killer is some kind of bitchin' new nerve toxin, man. It's a deadly combo, one-two punch, I'm serious."

"The hell you guys talking about?" Gomez said. He was getting shaky again. He could *really* use a cold one right now. But, and it was a big *but,* all right, he knew he had to keep his cool if he was ever going to see one million smackers up close and personal.

"It's a new kind of bug bomb, Elvis," Iglesias said. "The very latest in modern biological technology. Cause some very serious fuckage, man."

Julio and Iglesias both looked at him. Hard.

"Bug bomb," Gomez said. "What the fuck's a bug bomb?"

7

Hawke perched on the gunwale in his mask and flippers, waiting impatiently for Congreve and the Russians. All were struggling to get their gear on properly.

"You've got your mask on upside down, Ambrose," he said. "That's why the snorkel's mouthpiece is above your head instead of below it. Quite useless, the way you're wearing it. Don't forget to spit in it, before you put it on."

"*Spit* in it? Bloody hell," Congreve muttered, and reversed the thing.

"You only need the mask and snorkel until we're through the underwater entrance. Once we surface inside Thunderball, there's plenty of air. Tell your little friends to hurry it up, please. The tide waits for no man, Constable."

"You know, of course, that those are sharks in the water," Ambrose said.

"Hmm, yes," Hawke said. "The vast majority of sharks around here generally prefer plankton to people, old boy. The poison coral is what you need to watch out for. Here, put these gloves on."

"And what about the vast minority of sharks?" Ambrose asked, but Hawke had neatly executed a frog-man's backflip into the water and he was gone.

He kicked down a few feet below the surface, looking for the entrance. It was right where he remembered it would be. Only now, some very large sharks guarded it. Luckily, they were mostly of the nurse variety, timid and easily frightened by man.

Ignoring them, Hawke swam straight for the opening.

One particularly resolute shark stood his ground as Hawke approached. There was no getting around him. He was hovering directly in front of the entrance and wasn't planning to budge. Hawke hovered a foot or so away, eye-to-eye with the blackest pair of eyes he'd ever seen. Hawke patted him on the snout, and the fish bolted like a scalded cat.

Hawke smiled. Ambrose and the Russkies were probably going to encounter this very same fellow. Ambrose, he hoped, would recognize him as strictly a sushi devotee.

Kicking forward, he carefully avoided the jagged coral surrounding the entrance. Some of the coral, he knew, was poisonous. Problem was, he had no idea *which* coral. Glad of his diving gloves, he had to grab the jagged out-croppings to pull himself through fairly tight quarters. In a moment, he was inside the grotto and bobbing up to the surface, floating in the pure beam of sunlight from the blowhole some fifteen feet above his head.

It was staggeringly beautiful inside, he saw, pulling off his dive mask. Far more stunning than in the early-morn-ing light he'd seen earlier. A natural cathedral of coral and stone; sunlight shimmering on the sculptured walls and turning the water inside a most amazing shade of clear green. Hawke replaced his mask and ducked his head back underwater. There were dozens of fish of every size and description, including a school of yellow and black striped creatures packed so tightly they seemed a single, darting mass.

Sergeant-Majors.

That's what the striped fish were called. The name had just popped into his head. He flashed on himself as a child, reaching out to touch the fish. Odd. How the hell would he know that name? Must have been a documen-tary he'd seen on that BBC nature program.

Diving down to the rocky floor, exploring a forest of stalagmites, he came upon a massive dark shape lurking in the shadows. Swimming closer, he was just about to reach out to rouse the creature, when the thing darted upward toward his outstretched hand, opening its jaws. All Hawke saw as he yanked his hand back were the spiky fangs filling the wide mouth and he spun around, kicking hard for the surface of the grotto. A moray eel. Powerful jaws, razor-sharp teeth. Reflexes almost as good as his own. But, thank God, not quite.

Thinking about introducing Ambrose to this truly scary character, Hawke was surprised to see the man himself when he reached the surface.

"Smashing, isn't it, Constable?" Hawke said, lifting the mask from his face. "Welcome to Thunderball!"

Congreve mumbled something in reply, but he still had his snorkel mouthpiece in place. Hawke reached over and popped it out of his friend's mouth. "I'm sorry, what were you saying?"

"I was saying that I will get you for this," Ambrose Congreve spouted, spewing seawater and coughing.

"A little dicey getting in, I'll admit, but those sharks are harmless. Besides, look around you, Ambrose! Rather surreal, wouldn't you say?" The resounding echo of Hawke's voice added to the magical quality of the grotto.

Congreve ignored him, looking around for the damnable Russians who'd been swimming right behind him. Terrified they might have panicked and, worse yet, that Hawke might ask him to go get them, he was thrilled to see first one, then the other, pop to the surface. Coughing and sputtering, they removed their masks and didn't bother to try to conceal the terror that was plain on their faces.

The bearded bear shouted one word over and over to Congreve and made a jerking gesture with his hand.

"What does that word mean, Ambrose?"

"Sharks, sharks, sharks," Congreve translated. "They are extremely unhappy about your choice of venue, absolutely petrified of sharks, and would like to leave immediately. I must say I have a lot of sympathy for their position."

"Sorry. It's here or nowhere."

Congreve translated and, after a rancorous exchange, the Russians seemed to resign themselves to their fate. The four swimmers formed up into a circle, paddling to stay in place.

"I'll be brief," Hawke said. "I am interested in making a purchase. Extremely interested."

The translation brought smiles back to the faces of the Russians. They spoke rapidly to Congreve.

"They will be happy to oblige you," Congreve said. "The hovercrafts are reasonably priced. Only sold in lots of three. Two million pounds each. Guaranteed delivery in eight weeks."

"No, no. No bloody hovercraft," Hawke said.

Congreve gave him a puzzled look. "What then?"

"Tell them I want to buy a 'boomer.' A Soviet Akula-class submarine."

A nuclear submarine? But Congreve didn't even blink. He'd been with Hawke too long. He told the Russians what Hawke had said. Both men bobbed their heads excitedly.

"I assume that's a yes," Hawke said. "How much and how long until I get it?"

The exchange was brief. Congreve said, "They have an Akula. Excellent condition. One of the last to be built. Fifty million dollars, half up front, the other half payable upon delivery. Six months to get the vessel seaworthy and assemble a trained crew and shoreside maintenance team."

Hawke eyed the Russians evenly. "How old?" he asked.

Congreve asked and said, "One of the last Soviet subs produced. The Akula Typhoon. Built in 1995."

"No, no," Hawke said. "No Typhoon. I want the very last series they built. The Akula II. Code name *Borzoi*."

Congreve told them and it generated a lot of head-shaking protestation by the Russians. Ambrose finally said, "They don't know anything about a Borzoi."

"My information says they're lying. Tell them I want a Borzoi. I'm prepared to pay a considerable sum of money. And I want to speak directly to the last person to purchase one. For this kind of money, the emptor better damn well caveat."

Upon hearing this wrinkle, the bobbing heads of the Russians conferred with each other. Rasputin clearly wanted to proceed; the other one did not. He'd been expecting this to be the hard part. It was why he'd chosen this location to negotiate.

"You'll notice," Hawke said, "that the tide has been rising. Very shortly we will be banging our heads on those nasty-looking coral stalactites up there. Some are poisonous. After that, we run out of air. Also, notice how rapidly the sun's angle through the blowhole is changing. It will be almost completely dark inside soon. Even now there's not enough light to swim out without getting yourself chopped up by the poisonous coral. Unless, like me, you have one of these dive lights."

Hawke switched on the high-powered light mounted above his dive mask and directed it toward the Russians, who grimaced in the glare and turned away.

"The experimental Akula II," Hawke said. "Borzoi. Twin-hulled sub shaped like a boomerang. Carries forty warheads. Tell them that's the only boat I'm interested in."

Congreve translated after a brief parley and said, "They say they don't know anything about a second-generation Akula. They say the Akula I was the last sub produced before the collapse of the Soviet Navy."

"Fine," Hawke said. He switched off the light and plunged them all into shadowy darkness. "We'll all just bob around in here until their memory improves or they drown. Whichever comes first."

Thirty seconds later there was a sharp cry of pain. The surging tide had smashed one of the Russians up against the jagged stalactites that formed the grotto's ceiling. Hawke switched on the light and aimed it at the Russians. The skinny little one had a bloody gash over his right eye.

"I want a Borzoi, comrade," Hawke said, swimming up to him and getting right in his facemask. "Nothing else. Is that clear? Borzoi."

The Russian sputtered something, shaking his head and peering into Hawke's mask.

"What's he say?" Hawke asked Congreve.

"He says yes."

"Pithy," Hawke said, smiling behind his mask.

"He says, yes, it's possible he may be able to locate a Borzoi for you. The price will be very high, however."

"Good," Hawke said, smiling at Congreve. "I thought they'd rise to the occasion. Tell them we'll talk money over dinner aboard *Blackhawke*. The launch will pick them up at the dock. Seven sharp. Dinner at eight."

Hawke dove and kicked down, his powerful beam catching the brilliant fish and multicolored coral and lighting the way out of Thunderball. He wasn't surprised to find his little flock paddling right behind him.

8

Colonel Manso de Herreras sat on the unshaded platform next to the empty chair of his closest friend, the
Maximum Leader. Fidel Castro. The Cuban *caudillo.*

Manso was sweating profusely. His uniform was
drenched. Perspiration burned his eyes. It wasn't the heat
that was bothering him, though. It was the chain of
events he planned to unleash when and if this never-
ending ceremony was concluded. The last Communist
leader in the Western Hemisphere had already been
speaking for well over an hour.

The platform where Manso sat baking beside the
empty chair was on the white marble terrace of the old
Habana Yacht Club. They were in one of the old neighborhoods, only a few blocks from the leader's primary
residence. Still, there were six big black Mercedes parked
in the circular drive. The leader never rode in the same
car twice. Never slept in the same house two nights in a
row.

Manso had been sitting in the sun on the flimsy folding chair for almost two hours now. He'd turned a deaf
ear to the ceremony and passed the time gazing out over
the drowsy harbor. There were a few fishing trawlers
crisscrossing the mirrorlike sea. He'd followed their pas-
sages idly, trying to tune out the papery voice at the
lectern.

It was a dedication ceremony of some kind, God
knows what. It was easily the third one he'd attended this
week. He no longer bothered to find out who or what

they were honoring at these events. They were constantly honoring or dedicating something or other lately, he'd noticed. It hardly seemed to matter what it was.

They would dedicate a tractor if they could find one that was running, he thought, scanning the crowd for any pretty *señoritas*. He had come to believe that *el jefe* either enjoyed being handed wilted carnations by endless processions of schoolgirls or was convinced such festivities took the people's minds off some of their more immediate problems.

Like eating.

An American joke had circulated recently amongst the higher echelons of the Cuban military and State Security. The joke had it that Castro had gotten everything right in Cuba but three little things. Breakfast. Lunch. And dinner.

Since their beloved comrades in Moscow had abandoned them in the early nineties, his country's economy had crashed and burned. Cuba now had one of the lowest per capita incomes in the Caribbean, ranking right up there with that other economic powerhouse, Haiti. He was sure that *el jefe* wasn't mentioning *that* little economic tidbit in his remarks.

The Soviets had poured a hundred billion dollars into the island of Cuba. Where had it all *gone*, Manso and his band of disgruntled confederates wondered.

A short list: the army, its uniforms, and missiles. The now-outdated electric power system. A nuclear power plant intended to wean Cuba off foreign oil and left two-thirds completed. A twenty-six-square-mile intelligence-gathering complex outside of Lourdes that Fidel was now trying to peddle to the Chinese. And countless enormous, hideously ugly residential buildings now falling down around their ears because of the amazingly shoddy construction.

And of course, there was the highway system. Ah, yes. Since shortages of fuel, oil, and machinery parts had paralyzed transportation, the endless miles of highways were utterly useless. Sugar production, the economy's mainstay, had been cut in half. New tourism efforts were helping some, but not nearly enough. Unless drastic measures were taken, Cuba, already running on fumes, would soon be running on empty.

Manso shifted in his chair. The metal seat had begun to roast his backside to a crisp. The hot seat reminded him of yet another misery, the shortage of paper. No books, no magazines, no *toilet paper*. Thank God for the limitless supply of Marxist economic textbooks that the Cuban populace had finally, after forty years, put to good use.

They also found the Communist paper, *Granma,* very useful. Published only every other day, it consisted of eight pages full of pap about *la lucha,* the "struggle," and how the people must endure these sacrifices for the greater glory. Manso had read an article that very morning stating that not eating was *good* for you! Privately, Manso had taken to calling *Granma* the Toilet Paper.

But there was no shortage of speeches and dedications like this one, Manso thought, mopping his brow. The production of speeches, dedications, and pontifications, always high, had recently gone through the roof.

The *comandante,* at the podium well over an hour or so already, was warming to his theme. As if it weren't warm enough already, Manso thought, reaching for a cup of iced lemonade beneath his chair. The ice had melted but the tangy juice helped a little.

Out on the lawn, Manso's olive-green helicopter was waiting. In approximately one half hour, God willing, he and the *comandante* were scheduled to depart for Manso's retreat on the southeast coast for the weekend. The two of them would be flying out alone, with Manso at the controls of the aging Kamov 26 helicopter gunship.

Before Fidel had made him head of State Security, Manso had been the highest-ranking colonel in the Air Force. He had a distinguished flying record and many decorations. He was also the only pilot in Cuba to whom the *comandante* would entrust his life.

The flying time to his personal estate, Manso estimated, was just less than two hours. The weather was perfect, but it still promised to be an exciting flight.

Manso's estate occupied a good deal of the five thousand acres of an island just off the town of Manzanillo. Manso, whose boyhood nickname had been *Araña,* the spider, had called the place *Finca Telaraña,* the Spider's Web. Originally, it had been just a *casita* on the balmy shores of the Golfo de Guacanayabo. A little retreat, where he and the great leader could escape the pressures of *La Habana* and have a little fun.

Over the years, Manso had gotten very good at finding ever newer and more interesting ways of keeping *el comandante* amused. There was, of course, no shortage of girls willing to do anything for money or *el jefe.*

The most recent event Manso had staged at *Finca Telaraña* was a tree-climbing contest. About ten local beauty queens had participated. They had stripped and raced for the trees. The winner got an expensive jeweled watch, while the losers had to shave their heads, eat a few live insects, and perform an elaborate dance number while everyone else enjoyed an exquisite buffet.

Manso supplied the female pipeline and he kept it full. This talent had helped his career in the Air Force enormously. Not to mention the size of his personal fortune. Manso had also done many favors for his leader. Favors Castro would entrust to no one else.

"He has become an inconvenience, Manso" was all that needed to be said. The man, or his entire family, would disappear. Always with a knife, never a gun. Guns, Manso had discovered very early in life, were no fun at all. He had grown up in the cane fields of Oriente province. He had learned that a razor-sharp machete made him the equal of bigger, stronger, and even wiser men.

When he was still a boy, he had formed a small band known as the *Macheteros*. The machete wielders. Once, barely twelve, he and his two brothers had kidnapped a staff member of the Soviet consulate. The Russian bastard had insulted his mother in the street. They'd placed him in a cotton sack and taken him at midnight out into the cane fields. Swigging rum up in the cab of the stolen pickup, the three brothers laughed at the man bouncing around in the back of the truck's bed as they careened through the tall cane.

His two brothers held the man's arms. Manso suddenly stepped forward and whipped off the sack covering the man's head. When the man saw a glint of moonlight on Manso's upraised blade, he started begging. He was still pleading when Manso casually lopped off his head, spraying the three boys with blood. It was Manso's first taste of blood and he found that he liked it.

He'd had the head delivered in a piñata to the Soviet embassy. This spectacular crime, and the ensuing manhunt for Manso and his two brothers, had caused them to flee their homeland. They headed straight for their uncle's village in the mountains of Colombia. Their mother, a Colombian, had a brother who was a coca farmer in a thriving little hamlet called Medellín.

In the long chain of lucky events that would mark his life, the murder of the Russian brought Manso to the attention of Fidel Castro himself. Normally, this would have resulted in his capture, torture, and execution. The Soviets wanted Manso's head, that was certain. They'd even sent investigators and detectives all the way from Moscow in search of the murderous de Herreras brothers.

By the time the Russian investigators reached Cuba, Manso and his young brothers were in Colombia, at the forefront of a burgeoning new industry. They were using high-powered speedboats, committing acts of sea piracy, and running cocaine for a Colombian madman called *el doctor*.

9

· · · — · ·

El doctor, it didn't take Manso long to discover, was not a doctor at all.

He was a murderous psychopath. A squat little man who'd gotten his start stealing headstones from the local cemeteries, sandblasting them, and then reselling them. *El doctor* was the honorary sobriquet given to the young drug kingpin Pablo Escobar in honor of the first man he murdered, a man who happened to be a doctor.

Murder was not an unusual way to earn a nickname in Colombia. But this particular murder would mark the beginning of a reign of terror that would end only when Pablo himself was murdered at age forty, in 1989. At the time of his death, the former tombstone salesman, Pablo Escobar, was the richest, most powerful criminal in the world.

Manso had found his role model.

Shortly after fleeing Cuba and arriving at their uncle's farm in the tiny mountain village of Medellín, the three de Herreras brothers began learning the thriving new coca business literally from the ground up. They planted and tended the shrubs, native to the Andes, with the pretty yellow flowers. Among other alkaloids, the leaves of *Erythroxylum coca* yielded a miracle powder called cocaine.

They worked in their uncle's fields at first, and then graduated to the corrugated tin labs where the miracle money dust was refined and processed.

It wasn't long until the brothers' ingenuity, intelligence, and ruthlessness brought them to the attention of *el doctor* himself. Six weeks after arriving, they had officially been taken under the wing of Pablo Escobar and his Medellín cartel. Pablo was the vicious but wily thug whose murderous assassinations of judges, journalists, and presidential candidates would one day almost topple the Colombian government. Eventually, he blew an Avianca jetliner out of the sky and rocketed to the top of the world's most-wanted list.

Pablo Escobar was the first billionaire Manso had ever

met. He was also a legend to his people. The Colombian Robin Hood took millions in drug money from the stupid *norteamericanos* and used a small portion of it to build villages and soccer fields for the poor *campesinos* of Medellín. To the terrorized and oppressed poor people of Colombia, Manso saw, Escobar was a national *hero*.

Neither a revolutionary nor an idealist, Pablo was merely an outlaw. But in a country where the laws are hated, a charismatic and benevolent desperado can find himself a figure of adulation. Even worship.

Manso kept a keen eye on every move Pablo made. He was mesmerized, like all the rest, by Escobar's penchant for casually extreme violence. He watched the ruthless Escobar with endless fascination as he went about the daily business of creating and embellishing his own mythic stature.

Manso immediately understood what worlds were opened once a man decided to make his own laws, his own rules. The young Cuban *machetero* in the thrall of *el doctor* now had a philosophy to live by. It was simple. You accepted either Manso's *plata* or Manso's *plomo*. You took his silver. Or you took his lead. It made not the least bit of difference to him which one you chose.

Under Pablo's tutelage, the three de Herreras brothers became ever more lethal and sophisticated assassins. Before you killed a man, for instance, you first made him scream and beg. Or, even better, before you killed him, you first killed those he loved most.

Before you raped, you assembled an audience. Fathers and mothers, sisters and brothers were forced to watch. It was work his two brothers took to with enthusiasm. Manso had far grander ideas.

A very bright and keen observer of things, he saw that the *norteamericanos'* seemingly insatiable demand for the Colombian product was rapidly overcoming supply. He sensed that this was only the beginning. The American appetite for coca powder was proving to be enormous. Many billions would be made in the next five or ten years.

The demand was there. How to supply it became increasingly problematic. Pablo even built a fleet of remote-controlled submarines, each capable of carrying two thousand kilos of cocaine from the shores of Colombia to the waters off Puerto Rico. It wasn't enough. Manso had an idea.

It was obvious to him that Pablo would need ever increasing numbers of pilots to ferry the huge loads of his product north. So, he'd learn how to fly. But Pablo's *pilotos* were a close-knit group and shunned the young Cuban hothead. He begged the pilots for flying lessons. But, another pilot meant less money for them, so they resisted.

He finally persuaded one of the younger pilots to teach him to fly by abducting the man's sister. The man took his case to Pablo, who applauded Manso's audacity. The next day, Manso was airborne.

He soloed after only six hours of instruction.

Pilots were in fact paid a lot more than the mere *sicarios*, or paid assassins, that Pablo employed in ever increasing numbers. It was the happiest time of Manso's life. He was a swaggering *piloto* in gleaming aviator sunglasses, playing the *narcos* version of aerial cat and mouse with the government troops on his weekly runs to Managua in his C-123 transport plane.

With his newfound wealth, he purchased an American Cigarette speedboat. When the weather was too bad for flying, Manso and his brothers took to the sea to make their deliveries. Once the product had been delivered, they went in search of isolated tourist yachts, robbing and murdering at will.

The de Herreras brothers had become the deadliest pirates in the Caribbean. But it was not to last.

After an ill-considered midnight run north to Cuba to see their mother, a bloody shoot-out with Cuban gunboats off the Isle of Pines finally ended in their capture. The three brothers were taken to Havana. They were whisked from the airfield directly to the *Palacio de la Revolución* and brought before *el comandante*.

Castro stood up behind his massive desk and stared at them, his hand on the sidearm that always hung from his belt.

"Ah," Castro said. "The three little boys who murdered the Russian diplomat? *Sí?*"

"*Sí, Comandante,*" Manso said, smiling. "It was a great pleasure. The man was a pig. He insulted my mother in the street."

"So, you cut his head off and sent it to the Soviet embassy in a piñata," Castro said, walking around the desk.

Manso stiffened. Waiting in the anteroom outside the Maximum Leader's office, under the guns of the elite guards, he'd concluded that they were all to be shot where they stood. "We will die like men," he had told his brothers. Now, it was simply a matter of waiting for the bullets to come. He'd seen men die badly. He didn't intend to disgrace himself.

"*Sí, Comandante*. I used my machete. It was a clean cut! I am a *Machetero!* So are my brothers. We are proud sons of Oriente!"

Castro walked up to Manso and stared hard into his eyes. Then his face broke into a grin and he embraced the startled boy in his two strong arms.

Manso was too shocked to speak.

"This man you killed. His name was Dimitri Gokov. We suspected the Russian of being a double agent, spying for the *americanos*. This very morning, another Soviet agent confirmed under torture that Gokov was part of a U.S. group plotting an overthrow of our revolutionary government."

"*Comandante*, I don't—"

"You are a brave boy. And you have an absolutely amazing sense of timing! Had we caught you yesterday, you would have been shot!" Castro said, and laughed. In Castro's mind, Manso's piñata had sent a brilliant, if unwitting, message to both the politburo in Moscow and his enemies in Washington. He embraced Carlos and Juanito and handed all three brothers small black boxes. The three brothers looked at each other, grinning. Inside each box was a shiny golden star attached to a red silk ribbon.

In time, he further rewarded Manso with a commission in the Air Force. He gave Juanito and Carlos commissions, too, in the Army and Navy. All three had shown surprising initiative and risen swiftly to the highest ranks.

Carlitos was now one of the highest-ranking officers in the Navy. Both he and Juanito, *comandante* of the Western Army, had also secretly returned to the lucrative *narco* trade they knew so well. Manso's only fear was that

Carlitos's insatiable love of the product was increasing his already frightening instability.

Carlitos was valuable, but he would have to be watched. Pitting brother against brother, Manso gave that responsibility to Juanito.

Castro's reprieve had been the beginning of a long, profitable relationship for all of them. Those closest to the leader always reaped the largest rewards. As Fidel himself had once remarked, "I bathe myself, but I also splash others." There were rumors of hundreds of millions in Castro's Swiss bank accounts. Manso grew adept at siphoning off his share and more.

In time, all three brothers grew immensely rich from many sources. It was far easier to export your product to America from Cuba than it was from Colombia. Juanito, through his vast drug-running operations in the Exumas, got the product into Cuba. Manso and Carlos got it out of Cuba and into the United States. There were rumors, of course, about *narco* traffic at the very highest levels of the Cuban military. But Manso's private security force made sure it was all kept very quiet.

Even the leader, if he knew of the de Herreras brothers' sideline businesses, never mentioned it. *El jefe* was famously antidrug, and had even been trying to negotiate some kind of crackdown with the U.S. for years.

Manso and his leader had grown ever closer over the years. The leader, who was never able to sleep at night, would roam the streets of the old city with Manso, pouring out his frustrations and fears. Time passed, and the two men became, not brothers, because their age difference was too wide, but something akin to father and son.

Fidel had been born in 1926 at Las Manacas, near Biran, in northeastern Cuba. Manso had been born twenty-five years later in Mayari, the nearest neighboring town to Biran. They shared a common loathing for the gringo imperialists who had exploited the natural resources and the peasants of their beloved Oriente. This had been one of the earliest bonds between the aging leader and the promising young Manso.

He looked at his leader now, red-faced and shaking his fists in the anger he seemed to summon so easily. Manso took a sip from the cup of the warm lemonade and tried to relax. He was going to need every ounce of his courage and strength of mind to do what he had to do.

It had been six whole months since he'd been to *Telaraña*. It had become too dangerous for him to be seen there. His brother Juanito had been flying down from Havana once a week, supervising most of the construction. His other brother, Carlos, had been put in charge of planning and organization. He was also in charge of Manso's personal security force. Castro had an imperial guard said to number ten thousand. Manso's guard, though not nearly that size, had grown exponentially in recent months.

Manso didn't like to admit it, but his brother Carlos, who'd risen to the highest echelons of the Navy, was by far the smartest of the three and certainly the most politically astute. He was also the most unpredictable. A life-long addiction to the poppy and the coca leaf had made him dangerously unstable.

But it was somewhere inside the scrambled brains of

Carlos that the little seed of rebellion had begun to grow. Manso, with his limitless financial resources, had provided Carlos's tiny seed with all the water and sunshine it needed to thrive.

Then there was his brother Juanito, a great general of the Army. There were in fact three distinct armies in Cuba. The army of the East, the Central army, and the army of the West. On pain of execution, the leaders of the three armies were not allowed to communicate with one another. This Manso and Carlos had used to their great advantage.

Juanito, in complete secrecy, had used his position as commander of the Western forces to turn Carlos's little seed into the vast secret complex of bricks, mortar, missiles, and men called *Telaraña*. Manso had originally modeled *Telaraña* after Escobar's own grandiose estate in the mountains of Medellín, Hacienda los Napoles.

Telaraña had become far more than the jungle pleasure palace, which, to a casual observer, it still appeared to be. An influx of many millions had turned *Telaraña* into a powerful military fortress that would soon be the birthplace of a new Cuba.

Manso looked at his chunky gold Rolex. Three-fifteen. The speech seemed to be winding up to a climax. Good. With any luck, they could be airborne in twenty minutes or so. If God was truly on his side, and how could He not be, the birth of a new Cuba was less than three hours away.

10

·· · — — · ··

She lay about a half mile outside the channel markers for Staniel Cay and when she was lit up at night, as she was now, she was magnificent. The name, illuminated in huge gold type on her towering stern, said it all.

BLACKHAWKE.

Hawke's yacht, completed in great secrecy just two years earlier at the Huisman yard in Holland, caused a unique stir wherever she went in the world. And the world, it delighted Hawke to know, had no idea just how singular a vessel this truly was.

At just over two hundred forty feet in overall length, she was a mammoth silhouette against the evening sky. Tonight, since there were to be guests, her gleaming black hull and towering white topsides were illuminated with halogen lighting from stem to stern. Her crew, who, with the exception of the galley staff and the launch crew, wore simple summer uniforms of black linen, had been given the night off.

Congreve, who loved messing about in kitchens, had sent Slushy, the executive chef, ashore. He'd elected to do the cooking tonight himself. Local lobsters, fresh corn, and salad. In deference to the Russians, he was serving caviar and iced vodka before dinner.

Twilight had congealed into starlit darkness.

The two old friends sat conversing comfortably under the umbrella of stars, as their guests weren't due for another half hour or so. They were all the way aft on the top deck. Quick, now disguised as a steward, was serving drinks and hors d'oeuvres.

Hawke had let his parrot, Sniper, out of his cage, and the big black bird was now perched in his favorite location on Hawke's right shoulder. The bird had been a gift from his grandfather on Alex's eighth birthday. Hawke had no idea how old Sniper was. Parrots, he'd learned, lived to be ninety to one hundred years old.

It was Hawke's habit at cocktail time to feed the bird whatever hors d'oeuvres were being served. Sniper seemed to like everything except pigs-in-blankets. But he had an enormous fondness for Russian caviar. At the moment, he was making do with the cheese.

Congreve was busy trying to get his pipe lit again. They were sitting some fifty feet above the water and it was breezy out on deck.

"Another Dark & Stormy, Ambrose?" Hawke asked, feeding Sniper his fifth gob of warm Brie cheese. Dark & Stormy was his friend's favorite cocktail, a heady mix of dark rum and ginger beer.

"No thank you, Alex. I anticipate a lengthy evening."

"God, I hope not. I don't want those two cretins aboard this ship one second longer than absolutely necessary."

"Sketchy, aren't they?"

"You have no idea."

"Pity about that poor waitress."

"You noticed," Hawke said.

"Please," Congreve replied with a withering stare.

"I forgot. You notice everything."

"I don't want to be an old Nosey Parker. But, I have to ask, what in the bloody hell are you going to do with a nuclear submarine?"

"You actually thought I was serious? That's quite good."

"You're not?"

"Hardly."

"I see. And your reasoning for subjecting me to life-threatening encounters with poisonous rocks and man-eating marine life?"

"Simple. Call from Washington. A Soviet Borzoi-class boomer disappeared six months ago from its pen pal at Vladivostok. It took me a while, back-channel, but I was eventually able to determine who might have stolen the damn thing. From there, it was fairly easy to identify who was peddling it. You remember Cap Adams. Middle East CIA station chap in Kuwait City? He finally put me on to the two human ferrets we went snorkeling with today. Pretty sure they sold it. The Americans are desperate to know who bought it. It's my job to find out."

"Borzoi? Never heard the name."

"Not surprising. Last gasp of the Soviet Navy. A highly experimental sub. Only two were built. They used pilfered American stealth technology and some of their own to create the world's first stealth submarine. Radical delta-wing design. Retractable conning tower. She carries forty warheads and, for all intents and purposes, the bloody thing's invisible."

"Good God," Congreve said, leaning forward. "Anyone in possession of such a weapon could stick up the whole world."

"I'm afraid you're right. Global, reach-for-the-sky type hardware. She's monstrous. Lethal. Undetectable. The pan-Arabic terrorist organization that first tried to buy the sub gave it the code name Operation Invincible

Sword. My CIA friend Cap Adams spent a few tough weeks in Kuwait, making sure something went wrong with that plan, thank God."

"So the Russians had to find another buyer. Who on earth other than the Arabs or the Chinese has got that kind of money?"

"Good question. Cap finally put me on to our two dinner guests. His information indicates they've located a new buyer. She has been purchased. Being delivered now. Our job is to find out who the proud new owner is. We need to ensure that the delivery does not happen. The U.S. Navy has deciphered certain radio codes that might enable us to intercept it at sea."

"Who, exactly, is 'we'?"

" 'We,' in this case, is Washington, the U.S. Atlantic Fleet, and me. They're footing the bill for our little Caribbean cruise, actually. Jolly generous, I'd say."

"Who in Washington? Anybody I know?"

"High."

"Your friend POTUS?"

"Yes. And the brand-new American secretary of state."

"Your old friend Conch."

"Indeed. She called me in early January just as I was about to shoot myself out of sheer boredom."

"Ah. I thought you had successfully extinguished that long-flickering flame."

"Her motives are hardly romantic, Constable. She has hired me to find out who bought that damn submarine and why. Most importantly, where the hell she's located. They like to keep track of these things, you know."

"Hmm. One suspects Madame Secretary's motives are

always romantic where you're concerned. Speaking of suspects, who's on the list of potential buyers?"

"Oh, the usual madmen and megalomaniacs, naturally. All the rogue states. North Korea. Iran. Some kind of pan-Islamic movement. The one who scares me most is Muammar Useef, the erstwhile Saudi playboy."

"Long-range ballistic missiles bearing germs. That's how Muammar would go. And he's got the money and the motive."

"And the track record, of course. Not to mention the opportunity. No question. That's why the Yanks are taking this one so seriously," Hawke said.

"Funny," Congreve said. "The world seemed a much safer place when all we had to deal with was a bunch of drunken Russians stumbling around the Kremlin knocking over the samovars."

"Yes. Praying they didn't all wake up with hangovers and bang their bloody bums up against the wrong button," Hawke said. He paused a moment, looking at his friend thoughtfully before he spoke.

"Actually, there's another matter I'm pursuing down here, Ambrose. I mentioned it to you on the docks this afternoon. At the risk of being dramatic, I'm going to show you something I've never shown another living being. Or even a dead being for that matter."

"Nothing *too* personal, one would only hope."

"Please, Ambrose. This is quite serious."

"*Hawke!*"

Sniper had squawked a warning, and Hawke knew Quick must be approaching the banquette where they were sitting. It was one of the oldest pirate tricks in the books, but it still worked. Over the years, Hawke had been working on Sniper's vocabulary, and the bird had a surprising range of expressions.

Tommy Quick was carrying a small metal box with an electronic keypad embedded in the top. He placed it gently on the table in front of them.

"Put Sniper back in his cage, will you, Tom?" Hawke said, waving his hand before his nose. "I don't think this Brie agrees with him. Upset stomach." Quick held out his forearm, and the bird immediately flew from its owner's shoulder to the steward's outstretched arm.

Ambrose leaned forward to touch the silver box, and Hawke grabbed his hand in mid-air. "Don't touch the box, Ambrose. It's alarmed and will respond to my fingerprints only. Sorry."

"A lovely box."

"Isn't it? Polished titanium," Hawke said, punching in his code. The lid of the box snapped open with a hiss, then started rising slowly. Peering over the edge, Congreve saw a small scrap of blue paper, now yellowed with age. There was some kind of crude drawing and quite a bit of scribbling below the picture. Hawke punched another key, and the interior of the box was illuminated. Then a thick piece of glass lowered from the raised lid to cover the opening. It was, Congreve saw, optical glass designed to magnify the contents.

"It's the map, Ambrose. The one I spoke of. Early eighteenth century. My grandfather gave it to me."

"A map of what, exactly?"

"Oh, buried treasure, and all that sort of thing. My grandfather loved to tell stories of cutthroat buccaneers and bloodthirsty swashbucklers and buried booty. This map you see here belonged to one of my more infamous ancestors."

"They were all infamous, as far as I can tell. Right down to the present day."

"Every family has a few black sheep, I suppose. Only in my family, it was a black *hawk*."

"Blackhawke, the pirate. Yes. Your great ancestral role model. I've always been curious about that bloody chapter in the Hawke family history. So, tell me the story for God's sake. The barbarous Russians won't be here for another half hour!"

"Well, if you're really interested."

"Hawke, you really do try my patience at times."

"All right, all right. I'll tell you the tale."

11
• • • — • •

"The pirate stared at the skulking black rat," Alex Hawke began, and he was off.

"Last meal, Rat!" the ragged old man shouted hoarsely at the creature. "Here's the totality of me bleeding generosity at last, down your bleeding gullet, I'm afraid." The pirate eyed a lively morsel of weevil-infested bread and lobbed it at the oily-looking creature. The rat had backed into its favorite dank corner of the prison cell, all eyes and haunches. Man and rodent had grown quite companionable these last few months, and the proffered tidbit was quickly consumed.

The rat's black eyes glittered as it turned away from its benefactor with nary a trace of gratitude for past favors.

There then came a sound from the pirate's throat that could have passed for a sigh, had it not been so mournful, and he collapsed back upon his pitiful rack. Wrapping a threadbare blanket around his shoulders, he lifted his gaze. One patch of sky was visible in the moldy wall opposite, and he could see the light was fading. With it went the pirate's chances for a long and happy life.

Unlike his friend Rat, the ailing buccaneer would not be enjoying the hospitality of Newgate Prison when the sun rose next morning. The prisoner coughed and smiled grimly in spite of himself. Six months prior to his arrest and this miserable circumstance, he'd been out on the open seas of the Caribbee, his ship bursting to the gunwales with captured booty he'd relieved from a Spaniard, on a hard reach, flying up the Gulf Stream, finally to home and family after long years afloat.

They'd be coming for him shortly, he knew, for what would be his last journey. King's men, horses, and soldiers. Coming to load him into a cart, him and a few of his miserable shipmates, and haul them all away, down Holborn Street, through the laughing, taunting crowds. This trip was known poetically as "heading west." But every lost soul rolling out Newgate's gilded archway for the last time knew he was eastbound. East, for the muddy banks of the Thames and Executioner's Dock. Where waited a length of stout rope and the hangman.

"It's old Blackhawke himself that's cornered now, ain't it, Rat?" he said, watching the animal scurry to the corner opposite. The man dipped his quill once more into the inkwell and returned to his unfinished letter. He coughed and shivered in the chill, damp air.

His recent trip across the icy North Atlantic, chained

like a dog in the brig, and subsequent few months in this notorious pesthole of a prison had left the famous pirate captain much diminished. Once the mere sight of his flagship masthead appearing on the horizon had struck fear into every man afloat. Now Blackhawke was a figure of mockery and derision, wrongly consigned to the hangman's noose by high-placed friends now turned lower than dogs, treacherous enemies who had betrayed him to save their own hides.

Blackhawke straightened and turned once more to his letter. Such thoughts of doom weren't befitting a man of his stature and fame. And, besides, there was still the chance of the king's pardon, wasn't there? He dipped his quill, put it to the blue paper, and made a few scratches, trying to sketch in the outline of the island's coastline. He wasn't much used to drawing maps and figures, and it taxed him sorely.

"Now, where was that bloody rock?" he said to Rat, scratching his raggedy beard. "I remember a spiky rock standing just above the cave, looked like a ship under sail it did, but where? Here, I think," he said, and drew it on the map.

He'd been trying to finish the letter to his wife all week, but his mind was clouded with fear, anger, and rum. The rum was courtesy of the Newgate Prison parson, who'd been smuggling it into his cell in ever more copious quantities as his days dwindled.

"See? All smugglers in some ways, ain't we, Parson?" he'd said between sips of rum to the clergyman that very morning. Both knew it was possibly the pirate's last drink. "Piracy! There's a laugh! Who *ain't* a pirate? It's the way of the world they're hanging me for! And me not even guilty! Why, I had me that letter of marque from his majesty and two French passes for all them East India ships I took, didn't I?"

He and the parson both knew that wasn't exactly true. The famous pirate captain had been sentenced to death for the murder of a Mr. Cookson, a former bosun on his ship. The captain, strolling his quarterdeck, had overheard an unflattering remark from the bosun and banged the man smartly on the head with a wooden bucket. Unfortunately, the poor fellow expired two days later.

At his trial for both murder and piracy, Blackhawke had claimed it was manslaughter, a crime of passion. Suppression of mutiny, he'd argued in the dock. But the jury had decided otherwise. In words that tolled like solemn bells in the gloom of the Old Bailey, each prisoner learned his fate that evening.

> *"You shall be taken from the Place where you are, and be carried to the Place from whence you came, and from thence to the Place of Execution, and there be severally hang'd by your necks until you be dead.*
> *"And may the Lord have mercy on your souls."*

The pirate scratched some more on the scraps of blue paper that Parson had given him. His fever had parched his memory. He was having trouble remembering the outline of the rocky coast on the nor'west side of the island. This was information vitally important to his purposes. It was his last chance to provide sustenance for his soon to be grieving widow and children. As he drew, he tried to call up the night he'd buried the last of his illgotten treasure.

On a chilled, moonless night, he and two mates had left the moored English Third-Rater and rowed the skiff toward the island's rocky coast. Though Blackhawke had paid careful attention as the shoreline hove into view, the exact geography of the place had long receded now from his mind's eye.

Well, he'd just do the best he could and hope his dear wife would find the location. Surely she'd recognize the twisting river that he roughed in there on that jagged coast jutting into the sea? And the coconut trees here, and the big rock above the cave? His drawings looked something like cocoa trees, didn't they?

He put a bold black X where he thought the treasure should be. Yes. That was it. Just about that far west of the river.

The captain and two shipmates had done their digging inside the cave right there, two leagues west of the mouth of the river. Boca de Chavon, the Spaniards called it, whatever that meant. And exactly one hundred paces from that big rock jutting into the sea, the one that nearly chewed the bottom out of that skiff all right.

Three men had rowed ashore. There was a hidden cave, the mouth of which was completely underwater all the time save dead low tide. At the very back of that cave was where they did their digging, hacking deep through coral and wet sand.

But after the bags of gold were safely concealed in a deep hole in the deepest part of the cave, only one man had returned to the sloop that night. Blackhawke himself. The two mates remained behind to "guard" the treasure, although they were in a most unhealthy condition. As they held their lanterns, leaning over, peering down into that black hole full of gold, both had their skulls stove in by a mighty swipe of Blackhawke's spade.

Under the crude illustration, Blackhawke wrote to his wife in his crabbed hand:

Gold! Aye, there's gold in that cave on the Dog's Island, dearest wife, verily some hundred odd bags of it that we lifted from the good ship Santa Clara, being the barge of the Spanish corsair Andrés Manso de Herreras, which we took as a prize off the Isle of Dogs.

This Manso de Herreras, he was the most blood-thirsty of cutthroats and we lost many a man in a pitched battle on his decks once we'd boarded the Santa Clara. He almost got the better of your beloved husband, advancing on me from behind, but my faithful parrot Bones sung out in time and I sent the cur to his maker and his gold to my hold from whence I stashed it in the cave. I pray you, care for old Bones, since the wily old bird will live a long life and 'twas mine he saved.

But also in that cave you'll find two unfortunate souls who I had to dispatch so as to keep my secrets. Prepare yourself for them skeletons before you lift your spade, my Darling. And do your digging as I do mine, on nights when the moon has fled the sky or the clouds abet your endeavours.

A caution, dear Wife! There's grave danger for a body wanting to go ashore on that rocky coast. Cave Canem! Its teeth are sharp enough to bite you into bits. Many have died trying. But, once past those cruel teeth, I war-

*rant that my poor family's salvation lies beneath my
mark on the old Dog himself.*

  *At least I go to my maker knowing I've provided for
you and our dear children. I've got some fancy this letter
will prove my farewell, although the king may spare me
yet. I only hope my good name will not be forever sullied
by this treacherous betrayal—*

There was a sharp rap at his cell door, and Blackhawke
looked up. Surely they'd not come for him so early as
this? Blackhawke hurriedly reached beneath his threadbare bedcovers and withdrew a battered brass spyglass.
He removed the eyepiece and set it aside. Taking up his
quill, he scrawled under the map and letter "With undy-
ing affection, your husband Richard" at the bottom of his
letter.

He then rolled up this document and inserted it into
the body of the spyglass. As good a hidey-hole as any and
his only one at that!

Another rap at his door and he called out, "Away with
you, whoever you may be! Captain Blackhawke is not
presently receiving!"

He was screwing the eyepiece back into place when
the heavy cell door swung open. It was only Parson, carrying another jug of prison grog.

"Good Parson!" Blackhawke said. "Have you happy
word from my beloved monarch?" Blackhawke was at the
window, the spyglass to his eye, peering through the bars
at the dark and lowering clouds. Good, he thought, the
letter was not visible inside the shaft of the glass. He'd get
the thing to his wife somehow, with the parson's help.

The parson came forward and handed the jug of grog

to Blackhawke, who immediately took a deep swig. "Come, what news? I beg you."

"The king's men are in the courtyard," Parson said. "The carts are being harnessed as we speak. Only one of your crew was pardoned. A Mr. Mainwaring, who finally produced convincing evidence of his innocence, Captain."

The old pirate collapsed back upon his cot and uttered one word, "Lost."

12

"Splendid yarn!" Congreve exclaimed just as the heavily armed steward came to stand beside Hawke. "For God's sakes, man, don't stop now!"

"Sorry for the interruption, sir," Tom Quick said. "But the stern watch just rang up to say the launch has left the dock and your guests are on their way."

"Thank you, Tommy."

Ambrose slapped his knee in delight. "Astounding. Really quite remarkable!"

"What do you mean?" Hawke asked.

"Well, I mean to say it gave me goose pimples. The 'skulls stove in with spades.' All that blood and thunder sort of thing."

Hawke smiled at his friend. He had to admit he had gotten rather caught up in the telling of the tale.

"So what happened next, old chap?" Ambrose asked. "You've certainly captured my imagination!"

"Well, I'll continue it later, if you insist. I'm not much

of a storyteller, but I must have made Grandfather tell it a hundred times. I've been anxious to tell you the story, and show you the map, ever since we got down here to the tropics. Get your old brain working on the thing. I've been chewing at that map all my life and made a little progress, of course, but I've only gotten so far."

"It's fascinating. Once I've examined the document more closely, I'll compare it to some of the older maps in the ship's library. First thing tomorrow and—heavens—look at the time! I'd better get hopping. I've got a few very nervous crustaceans awaiting me in the kitchen and I think it's time to get them into a nice hot bath." Congreve got to his feet.

"It's called a galley, Constable. How many times must I remind you? On a boat, the kitchen is the galley."

"In my view, a kitchen by any other name is still a kitchen."

"I give up," Hawke said, raising his glass. "Show those lobsters no mercy."

"Yes, once the lobsters have been murdered in cold blood, I'll rejoin you and your new comrades in arms," Congreve said. He wandered off, cocktail in hand, pipe between clenched teeth.

Hawke noticed Quick coming up the steps with a bottle of Chateau Montrachet on ice.

"Love a splash of that, Tom," he said.

"Pleasure," Tom said, and poured him a glass.

"These two men coming for dinner," Hawke said. "Russians, as you know. Arms dealers, in fact. Highly untrustworthy. Has Sutherland alerted the crew and staff remaining on board tonight?"

"Yes, sir."

"I don't expect trouble. A fairly pathetic duo. But keep your eyes open all the same, Tom. You look a proper steward, but you're armed to the teeth, I suppose?"

Quick opened his loose-fitted starched white jacket to reveal twin holsters strapped across his chest, a pair of nine-millimeter automatics in each one. There was a bandolier of extra magazines around his waist.

"Ah, good. I wonder. Do you find yourself missing good old Fort Hood much, Sergeant Quick?"

"Every minute of every day, sir," Tom said, smiling.

"Good lad. I'm grateful to have you aboard."

"Shall I escort the guests up here when they arrive?"

"Yes, and do me a small favor, would you?" Hawke asked, keying the code that would close the metal box. "Would you return this box to the library? I believe you know where it's kept? And, also, there is a rather large black Halliburton travel case in the same locker."

"Yes, sir. I know the one."

"Please bring the case up to wherever Congreve has us dining this evening. And stow it out of sight."

"Yes, sir. You'll be in the small dining room, just off the library," Quick said, and turned to go. He paused. "Sorry, the wine steward asked if you'd chosen a dinner wine."

"Do we have any more of this sixty-four Montrachet left?"

"I'll speak to the steward, sir."

"Good. I hate to waste good wine on bad company, but perhaps it will loosen their tongues."

"I've got the audio recording system set up in the dining room, sir."

"Fine. Keep a close watch while these two redbirds are

aboard, Tommy. I don't want them going anywhere on
the ship unaccompanied. Even if they need to use the
head, someone stands outside."

"Aye, aye, sir."

Hawke rose and strolled over to the ship's stern rail.
He gazed out over the polished black ocean and breathed
deeply. On the horizon, humped silhouettes of islands,
bone-white in the moonlight, looked, in a trick of light,
like a slouching white bear, sleeping. About half a mile
out, he could see the launch approaching. Her bow was
up on a plane, throwing white water to either side, red
and green running lights winking. A long trail of frothy
wake streamed behind her in the moonlight.

Christ, it was beautiful. Was that why, since he'd arrived
in these islands, he'd noticed this strange feeling, like a tug
on his soul? He could have invited Victoria down here to
share all this with him. Bad idea, he'd finally decided. The
trip was, after all, strictly business. Sticky business, probably. Make that definitely. Maybe even risky business.

Vicky. The mental picture of her standing right here at
the rail was so strong he felt he could almost reach out
and stroke her lovely hair. It had been a long few weeks
since she'd waved good-bye to him on a rainy afternoon
outside his home in Belgrave Square.

Something caught his eye and he looked up just in
time to see a flaming star's brief arc across the deep blue
bowl of the heavens.

So lovely here. A dusting of stars and a fat moon
played hide-and-seek now among a few tattered clouds.
The hearty salt tang in his nostrils smelled of seaweed
and iodine. Something about the place was definitely tugging at his heart. Caribbean moons and stars were not

the sort of thing a boy of seven or so would remember, of course. He had little memory of being here at all. Still, here he had been, and now his work had brought him back.

Gazing out, Hawke was astounded to find his eyes tearing up. What on earth? He was hardly the type to get all leaky about a pretty view or even a beautiful woman, was he? He shook his head, trying to clear it. Something about this place that—

He had turned and started to go below when it hit him. A kind of chill ran through him, then a shudder so severe it rattled his bones. He staggered, reached out, and gripped the rail with both hands. He'd gone all light-headed and short of breath. Seeing his knuckles go white on the rail, he realized he was literally holding on for dear life. Had he actually blacked out?

He managed a few deep, slow breaths and it seemed to calm him a little. Still, his heart was jackhammering in his chest. Was this what a heart attack felt like? A stroke? Good Lord, it couldn't be! He was only thirty-seven years old. He exercised like a fiend, smoked only the occasional cigar, drank only the odd cocktail or two. He was fond of his wine, true, but that was good for you, wasn't it? he asked himself, weaving his way over to the banquette where he collapsed.

If this was some severe illness announcing itself, the timing couldn't be worse. He clasped his hand to the back of his neck, squeezing hard, feeling the spike of panic abate just a bit.

He'd been thinking, while shaving just this very morning, that he'd never felt better in his life. In a world besieged by dirty little wars and full of evil, dangerous people, he was doing his duty. Work he felt was vitally important. At the same time, he'd managed to rebuild his family fortune and fund causes and charities he believed in.

And, at last, he'd met a beautiful woman he couldn't get off his mind, Dr. Victoria Sweet. Doc, he'd taken to calling her. She wasn't practicing much medicine anymore. She'd been a pediatrician, specializing in children's neurological disorders. Then she'd published a children's book called Whirl-o-Drome that had become an enormous success on both sides of the ocean. Hawke had adored the story. And so had the public. There was talk of Hollywood.

He leaned his head back on the cushion and looked up into the night sky. He remembered the rainy night Vicky had read the thing aloud. It was soon after they'd met. And he remembered telling her that such wonderful stories would probably do more, for far greater numbers of children, than her medical practice might ever accomplish. Especially Whirl-o-Drome.

It was a tale of a child's enduring love. A young boy, whose father's Spitfire has been shot down in flames during the Battle of Britain, is sent to live in a seaside village with his aunt. Every night, he goes down to an old amusement park by the sea and rides the Whirl-o-Drome, an ancient merry-go-round with toy airplanes secured at the ends of long poles. The little planes spin round and round, and climb or dive when the children use the airplane's control stick.

One night, just before closing and after many, many rides, the boy's little silver plane comes to life. The lights inside the cockpit suddenly illuminate. Needles are spinning on the dials. Tiny red lights are winking out on the wing tips. Suddenly, the boy hears static and a faint voice. It's coming from the headphones of an old leather flying helmet that has somehow appeared between his feet. He places the helmet on his head and pulls the goggles down over his eyes. Suddenly, a button he's never seen before begins to glow bright red at the center of the console. The voice in the headphones tells him to push the red button in front of him. He does, and the little airplane disengages from the arm of the ride, and the boy soars out over the sea.

"Climb, climb!" says the strangely familiar voice in his earphones, and the boy pulls back on the stick, soaring higher and higher. Finally, he bursts through a canyon of clouds into clear starlit air. He sees an old Spitfire doing barrel rolls in the moonlight. He races to catch up with the plane and sees the number on its wing.

Number Seven. His father's number.

"Timmy? Is that you?" the voice in his earphones says. The voice sounds an awful lot like—

"Y-yes?"

"See that big bright moon on the horizon? You stay right off my starboard wing and follow me all the way there. There's something I want you to see!"

"Are you really—Number Seven? Because Number Seven was my father's plane and—"

"It's me, Timmy," the voice said. "It's your father. You can find me up here most nights, if you'll just believe in your little plane."

It was a lovely tale.

"Skipper?" Tommy Quick said. "Sorry to bother you. But the guests have arrived."

"Ah, yes. The guests. Thank you, Tom. I'll be along in a few minutes."

He realized his heart was still racing. He willed the image of Vicky to appear out there before him. He let her smiling eyes finally cause the triphammer of his heart to slow gradually to a near normal pace. What on earth was the matter with him? He wouldn't admit it, even to himself, but this wasn't the first time he'd suffered one of these little, what did they call them, seizures. They'd begun shortly after *Blackhawke* had arrived in the Caribbean. Ironic. People came here to relax.

After a little while, he felt somewhat like his old self once again. He sprang from the banquette and headed for his stateroom to shower and dress for dinner. He looked at his watch on his way down the aft stairway. He had maybe ten minutes to collect himself before it was time to go down and suffer his insufferable guests.

13

· · · — · ·

The huge twin rotor blades of the olive-green Kamov-26 helicopter started spinning rapidly as Manso spooled up the revs of the jet turbine engine. He looked over at his lone passenger, Fidel Castro.

"All buckled in, *Comandante?*" he asked over the intercom. Both of them were wearing headphones with speakers. It was the only way you could communicate because of the turbine engine's whine.

"*Sí, Manso. Vámonos!*" Castro said.

Manso flipped a switch that killed any transmission in the leader's headphones.

"Havana Control, this is Alpha Bravo Hotel One," Manso said. "Do you copy?"

"Copy loud and clear, Alpha Bravo, you're clear for takeoff. Over." Manso recognized the silky voice of Rodrigo del Rio, owner of the Club Mao-Mao and, more importantly, Castro's former deputy head of State Security. Now he'd been bought and paid for by Manso. His loyalty to Manso was unquestioned. Only this morning, the air traffic controller typically in the tower at this time of day had been stabbed to death in his bed by del Rio. Rodrigo had used his weapon of choice, a gleaming pair of silver scissors that had earned him the nickname Scissorhands.

"Roger that, tower," Manso said.

He took a deep breath and said the three code words that would change Cuba forever. Upon hearing the code, Rodrigo, in concert with Manso's brothers Juan, General of the Army of the West, and Carlos, Commander in Chief of the Navy, would unleash their forces. They would initiate the first military takeover of Cuba in forty-some years.

"Mango is airborne."

"We copy that, Alpha Bravo," Rodrigo said. "Mango in the air. Over."

Safety checks complete, rotors engaged, the Kamov-26 rose vertically some forty feet into the air. Manso tilted the nose over to initiate forward velocity and roared across the bay. The old yacht club fell away quickly, but Manso liked to fly low, almost brushing the tops of the sailboat masts in the marina.

The skippers on the fishing trawlers all knew *el jefe's* chopper on sight, and he saw many of them lift their caps and wave as Manso executed a sharp looping turn to the southeast and headed back across the Malecón that ran along the bay, climbing up over Morro Castle and the crumbling city of Havana.

"The speech, it was excellent, *Comandante,*" Manso said, once they were out over the countryside.

Castro turned and gave him a look. Manso knew as the words were coming out that it had been a foolish remark. They'd known each other too long for such trivialities. Castro had an innate genius when it came to selling himself. It had allowed him to dazzle millions of people around the world. This speech was simply more anti-American self-promotion, done brilliantly, nothing new.

Beads of sweat had popped out on Manso's brow and threatened to run down into his eyes. He realized he was too nervous for small talk. Tense. It would be wise to just shut up and fly.

"*Gracias,*" Castro said, the word dripping sarcasm, and turned to gaze out the window at his failed utopia, falling away beneath him as the chopper gained altitude. God knows what he's thinking, Manso thought, surreptitiously eyeing his leader. Look at him. He has confronted and defeated ten American presidents. He has made himself a martyr through sheer defiance, spitting in the face of Uncle Sam. With the Cold War ended, he has used America's outdated trade embargo to further burnish his shining star. A cunning actor, strutting across the stage of the world, occasionally luring popes, potentates, terrorists, and presidents to the little island, adding a little glamour to his cast.

This earnest, brave-hearted, little off-off-Broadway production, Castro's Cuba, had been running for over forty years. The star of the show was still shining bright, his name still up in lights all over the world.

The secret? Manso had learned it well from Escobar. Every great hero needs an implacable enemy. *El jefe* had the perfect enemy. The one country the world loves to hate. America. Manso had watched, first Pablo and then Fidel. He'd learned every sleight of political hand and every brilliant move, and was now ready to implement his former masters' concepts for himself.

Castro, at seventy-five, obviously had no idea what the immediate future held for him, or Manso would be dead. Were there even a trace of suspicion, the leader would never be up in this helicopter alone with him. So, why the tightness in Manso's chest, the sweat stinging his eyes?

It had been a tense six months. Days and nights of endless planning and tense debate. Even this simple moment, timing a flight from the Havana Yacht Club to *Telaraña*, had been a subject of elaborate study and conjecture.

In the beginning, the problems they had faced had seemed insurmountable. Manso's rebellious confederates needed constant reassurance. Manso, however, had been steadfast in his belief that such an operation could succeed, and even have a kind of simplicity.

They had not been easy to convince, of course. But gradually, Manso had been able to boost their confidence: The unthinkable could be thought, and the undoable could be done. He had been unwavering, and in the end, he had prevailed.

He told them in detail about the perfect simplicity of

Batista's coup back in 1952. Like their own, the '52 rebellion had originated with a few young military officers, mostly *campesinos* and middle class. They had become completely disenchanted with the corruption of President Prio's regime and recruited Batista, a former president himself, to lead the coup that would bring down Prio.

It had gone off precisely as planned. Perfectly.

Batista had arrived in the capital at 2:43 A.M. one Wednesday morning. It was *Carnaval,* and the merrymakers were still reveling in the streets. Batista was wearing brightly colored slacks and a sports jacket. The guards at Camp Colombia, where nearly two-thirds of Cuba's armed forces were housed, didn't even notice him. He literally did a samba through the security gates with his boisterous comrades singing and laughing.

The higher-ranking officers at the camp were all sound asleep. Many had been drinking heavily and simply passed out on the floors of the barracks. At Batista's signal, they were all arrested and driven to *Kuquine,* Batista's palacial country estate outside the capital. Not a single officer had offered any resistance.

Simultaneously, rebel officers were taking over the telephone company and the radio and television stations. By sunrise that morning, the entire operation had been completed.

President Prio returned to the capital and tried to rally his supporters. But without the army or access to the radio and television, his old civilian government was paralyzed. Prio was forced to acknowledge the inevitable.

The only thing Manso always left out of the story was *el presidente* Prio's addiction to morphine. When the man wasn't sleeping, he was sleepwalking. Batista knew this, of course, and used it to his great advantage. Castro, of course, was another story. He hardly ever slept and was constantly surrounded by secret police and vigilant body-guards.

The plotters had decided to give their operation the code name Mango after a popular song that ridiculed Fidel in his omnipresent green fatigues. Their joke was that you can't have "mangos" without "mansos."

Secrecy surrounding Operation Mango had been keeping Manso awake lately. The possibilities of a leak increased with every passing day. He'd lain sleepless many nights during these last months of intense plan-ning, wondering who might betray him, even acciden-tally.

He had constantly reminded his band of rebels, "When you are sitting on a secret this big, be careful. Because everybody notices that there is something under you."

And right now, he felt surely the man next to him *must* see the enormity beneath him. He drew his sleeve across his brow, wiping the sweat from his eyes, hoping Castro wouldn't notice.

"Did you ever read the book *The Last Tycoon* by F. Scott Fitzgerald, Manso?" the voice of the *comandante* crackled suddenly in his earphones. *El jefe* had been gaz-ing out the side window of the cockpit and Manso thought he had dozed off.

"No, *Comandante*," Manso said, intensely relieved that Castro's mind was on his books at the moment.

"Too bad," Castro said. "There is a wonderful parable in the book. The hero, who is a young Hollywood film producer, is on a cross-country airplane trip. He is interested in learning to fly, so he goes up into the cockpit. The questions he asks, the pilots think he could learn solo flying in ten minutes, he had such a mentality."

"*Sí, Comandante,*" Manso said, a hot spasm of nerves suddenly sizzling at the edges of his brain. Where was *this* going?

"The plane is flying over a large mountain. Just like the one up ahead of us. Do you see the one I mean?"

"*Sí, sí, Comandante,*" Manso said. "It's no problem. Our altitude—"

"Listen to the story, Manso. This mountain is important in the story. The producer tells the pilot and copilot to suppose they were railroad men. And they wanted to build a railroad through the mountains below."

"*Sí, sí.* But the mountain is in the way, no?"

"*Claro que sí,*" Castro said in agreement, looking down through the lexan nose of the cockpit at the green mountain now fast disappearing between his feet.

"They have surveyor's maps. Showing three or four possibilities, no one better than the others. So, he asks them what they would do, since they have no basis for a decision. The pilot says he would clear the forest on the left side of the mountain and put his railroad there. The copilot says no, it would be simpler to go around to the right where the river has already cleared the trees. I paraphrase, of course, but this is the point. No one is sure."

"It's an excellent parable, *Comandante.*"

"It's not *finished,* Manso," Castro said sharply. He looked at his pilot. "Is something wrong? You are pale. You sweat."

"No, no, *Comandante,* I feel fine. A little too much

chorizo at lunch, I think. Please. Continue with the story."

"If you're ill, it's dangerous. We should land."

"Is nothing, I promise. Please tell me the end." And, after regarding his pilot carefully for several seconds, Castro did.

"This producer, Monroe Stahr, he was a boy genius. He said to the pilots that since you can't test the best way, you just do it. Pick a way, any way, use powder and nitro-glycerine and simply blast your way right through. He said that, then he left the cockpit."

"Ah," Manso said.

"You do not understand the parable, my old friend, neither did the two pilots in the story. They thought it was valuable advice, but they didn't know how to use it. It is the difference between us, Manso. I learned long ago that the best way out is always *through*. Never *around*."

Madre de Dios, Manso thought. Does he know? Suspect? What is the point of this story if he does not?

Manso elected to make no reply, and they flew for another hour in silence. It was the longest hour of Manso's life.

When they were some fifteen minutes away from landing at *Telaraña,* Manso finally broke the silence.

"*Comandante,*" he said, "do you remember a certain Petty Officer Third Class Rafael Gomez? The American sailor Rodrigo recruited in Havana some time ago?"

"Of course I remember him. I read the reports. Rodrigo believes he could prove to be one of our most productive moles inside Guantánamo Naval Station. Is there a problem? Is he compromised?"

Manso took a deep breath and stepped off the wide

platform that had been his support, his life, for almost as long as he could remember.

"More of an opportunity, *Comandante.*"

"Tell me."

"This Gomez, he is . . . more than a mole. I have ordered Rodrigo to make arrangements for Gomez to smuggle a weapon inside the U.S. base. A biological weapon. A bomb containing a completely new strain of weapons-grade bacteria developed by the Iraqis. The bacteria are only a diversion. In addition to the bacteria, the bomb contains an indescribably powerful nerve toxin. With a delivery system also created by the Iraqis unlike anything seen before. Expands to cover any predesignated area, kills, and then expires."

Castro looked stricken. His face suffused with blood as the enormity of what he'd just heard sank in. He turned in his seat and glared at his trusted friend and comrade.

"You? *You* ordered such a thing without my consent?"

"*Sí, Comandante.* I ordered it. The Cuban people have suffered the indignity of the Americans on their sovereign soil for over forty years. And you allowed them to do it! I intend to rectify this insult!"

"And Rodrigo? Don't tell me the deputy chief of Secret Police has complicity in this? Rodrigo has aided you in this madness?"

"I have his support, yes."

"Have you both gone insane?"

"*Comandante,* it is you who has allowed the American presence on our island! You should have forced them out decades ago!"

"Your ignorance of political realities would be laughable if it were not so pathetic."

"There is a new political reality, *Jefe*."

"Yes. You and your fellow traitors would rain fire down upon our heads, just like the Al Qaeda brought to Afghanistan!"

"No, *Comandante*. It is a brilliant plan. We will give the gringos forty-eight hours to evacuate. If they do not—well, once exploded, this bomb will kill every man, woman, and child inside the American compound within hours. Then, it simply expires."

"My God, Manso," Castro said, collapsing back against his seat. "What drives you to this?"

"Vengeance, my *comandante*. I watched Escobar. I watched you. I spent my life watching two magnificent performances. I was inspired, but I was patient. I saw how brilliantly you picked your enemies. How you would toy with them and bring the spotlight upon yourself. But this humiliation at the hand of the fucking *yanquis* must end. It's my time, now. I feel this."

"You *feel* it? Your time? To do what? You're a madman! You have no credible support around you. No political infrastructure. You can't even control your two brothers! Carlitos is totally unstable. A borderline psychotic. The state will spin out of control!"

"I will deal with my brothers when the storm subsides. I have assembled a cadre of young and trustworthy advisers. As for now, I am ready to wreak havoc and seek vengeance. I am ready to fulfill my destiny."

"It is not vengeance you seek, Manso," Castro said with a bitter laugh. "It is only the limelight."

"Be careful what you say, *Jefe*."

"You are beyond transparent. You think you are unique? You have a destiny? You are nothing but a pathetic cliché! You merely want the world to see your face on CNN! Once a man has all the money and power in the world, the only thing left for him to seek is fame."

"I learned from the master, *Comandante.*"

"And once you blow up your little bomb, Manso, what then? What's to stop the Americans from obliterating our country in the space of an hour?"

"They won't lift a finger, *Comandante.*"

"You will not succeed, Manso."

"I think I will. Have you ever heard of the submarine the Russians call Borzoi, *Comandante?*"

14

Hawke carefully folded his linen napkin and pushed himself back from the table. An hour ago, he'd been knocking on death's door. Now, he felt bloody marvelous. His speedy recovery from the strange malady had been nothing short of miraculous. Whatever had gotten into him up on deck was gone.

"My compliments to the chef, Ambrose," Hawke said. "What was in that sauce?"

"A simple blend of butter, lime juice, and a lot of Appleton rum. The one-fifty-one proof."

"That explains it. Feeling tipsy and I've only had one glass of wine."

He wasn't tipsy at all, but the Russians were. At first, they'd been quiet, a little awed by their surroundings perhaps. But now, having imbibed large quantities of vodka and some of the flashiest wines in the ship's cellars, they'd acquired a rosy glow and gone quite chatty.

The dinner, from Hawke's point of view, had gone off well. There'd been no talk of business, and Ambrose had carried on the bulk of the conversation completely in Russian, with only the odd "I say" or "Hear, Hear!" necessary on Hawke's part. As the steward cleared the table, Congreve refilled the Russians' glasses with vintage Sandeman port, saying something or other which they found amusing.

Hawke sat back and savored his surroundings, nursing his own small port wine. He loved this room and everything in it. The Minton china and porcelain currently gracing the table had been in the Hawke family for generations. White, with gold trim, each piece of china featured the same magnificent black hawk on a circular field of gold. The same symbol was on Hawke's flag, the massive ship's burgee, painted in gold leaf on *Blackhawke*'s twin smokestacks, and it adorned the crew's uniforms. The symbol was even emblazoned on the cufflinks Hawke was wearing at this very moment.

But this room. He'd taken great pains with the room itself, making every effort to reproduce a small study at his grandfather's home on Greybeard Island. This cabin was filled with artifacts from that very room. The paneled walls were of black walnut, hung with the tattered battle flags of regiments of yore.

In an illuminated corner display case were rows upon rows of lead soldiers, a collection Hawke had started as a boy. On occasion, even now, he would re-create famous battles on the dining room table, challenging Ambrose's own formidable generalship.

There was, too, the magnificent sword collection that had been in the Hawke family for centuries. The swords were mounted everywhere, the most valuable of them locked up inside illuminated glass cases.

Hawke's eye fell on one sword in particular. His favorite. It was an ornamental rapier with the most exquisite provenance. One of his ancestors had taken it from the body of Marshal Ney, the bravest of Napoleon's generals. The sword had been in Ney's hand when he led the last French charge at Waterloo.

His grandfather had taught him the art of fencing with it. Later, at Oxford, he'd mastered the sport and been thrice champion. He still practiced it fiendishly.

He rose from his chair and removed the sword from its pride of place above the small fireplace. Amusing himself, he made a few parries and thrusts.

"Brian," Hawke whispered to the tall, sandy-haired steward hovering by the door, "that black case that Tom Quick stowed in the pantry? Would you mind?"

"Certainly, sir," Brian said, with a smart salute, and pushed through the swinging door that led to the pantry.

Brian Drummond was only one of the many "stewards" aboard whom Hawke had recruited from various branches of the British military. Royal Navy, SAS, and the Special Boat Squadron, where Brian had served, an elite unit on a par with the Navy SEALs. The stewards on board *Blackhawke* were, in fact, a small, highly trained fighting force under the joint command of Brian Drummond and Tom Quick.

Hawke, in a jolly mood not to be knocking on heaven's door, after all, raised the gleaming sword and pointed it directly at the bearded Russian called Golgolkin.

"Do you fence at all, comrade?" Hawke said to him, and Congreve, highly amused, translated.

"*Nyet,*" said Golgolkin, and that was good enough for Hawke.

"Pity, it's my favorite sport," Hawke said, and, drawing his dinner jacket aside, he slid the rapier through his cummerbund so that he was now wearing it on his hip. "Rather rakish, don't you think, Ambrose?" Hawke had donned black tie and evening clothes, a tradition he kept whenever company came to supper.

"Everyone should wear one," Congreve replied with a sly grin. "You never know when you might want to make a point."

Standing at the stern just as the launch arrived, Congreve and Hawke had come up with a novel way of extracting the desired information should their guests prove less than forthcoming. Congreve could see that Hawke now felt it was time to put their plan in motion.

"Ambrose, please tell our guests that we're about to serve dessert. Something I whipped up especially for them," Hawke said.

The Russians, whose cheeks were flushed with vodka and wine, smiled broadly as Congreve spoke. They had never expected to be invited aboard the famous *Blackhawke*. And, now, to be served a dish created by the famous owner himself? Well, they'd be dining out on this tale back in Moscow for years to come, that much was certain.

Hawke pushed a button mounted under the dining table. In the pantry, Brian saw the flashing light above the door and entered the room, carrying the small Halliburton metal case. As Hawke had instructed, he placed it on the dining table in front of the two Russians and stepped back.

"Gentlemen," Hawke said, walking around the table toward the Russians, "we have a special treat for dessert this evening. I think you're going to enjoy it."

As Congreve translated, Hawke reached across the table and released the two latches. The case lid cracked open.

"Tonight, we're serving"—he opened the case with a flourish—"money."

The Russians' eyes went wide, startled at the sight of the neatly wrapped and arranged stacks of U.S. currency that filled the case.

"Not at all fattening," Hawke said. "Only twenty million calories, after all."

The Russians were speechless. They kept looking at each other, the money, and then each other again. This Hawke was unlike anyone else they'd dealt with. Neither was quite sure how to respond to a man so cavalier with his cash.

Hawke closed the case, locked it, and handed it back to Brian.

"Ambrose," Hawke said, "our guests are invited to continue discussing this transaction up on deck. Perhaps a brief tour of the yacht while we talk."

While the translation was in progress, Brian walked to the bookcase beside the small hearth and reached up to a large leather-bound volume, *Life of Nelson,* and pulled it halfway out. There was a faint whir somewhere, and the bookcase slid back and to one side, revealing a small elevator.

"This goes directly to the bridge, gentlemen," Hawke

said. "We'll begin our tour there." He stood back and let the astonished Russians and Ambrose enter, then stepped inside and hit the button for the bridge deck. The elevator started up.

The door slid open to reveal the bridge, a massive room, inky black save for the vast array of multicolored display screens that filled an instrument panel stretching some thirty feet across. Above the screens, large black windows ran from one side of the room to the other. The windows were tinted, but you could see the starry skies beyond.

A single captain's chair was mounted before the center of the panel.

A large screen just to the right of the chair seemed to show a live view from space. Through the moving cloud layers, you could see a scattering of small winking lights below in the darkness.

Hawke, seeing the guests eyeing the screen, said, "A live satellite view of our precise location. Were I to zoom in, we could see the lights of *Blackhawke* itself."

Congreve translated this to noises of amazement from the Russians. Hawke hated showing off, but with these two he had no qualms.

"Captain Robbie Taylor is normally in charge of this ship. I gave the captain the night off," Hawke said, escorting the Russians into the room. "So the ship is essentially running itself. There are twenty-two mainframe computers monitoring every system aboard and talking to each other twenty-four hours a day."

"Frightfully boring conversation, I should imagine," Ambrose whispered to Hawke, and then translated what Hawke had said to the Russians.

There was a sudden low screech in the darkness, and then a dark shape was darting toward the larger of the two Russians. The man cried out, more in fear than in pain, and Hawke quickly shouted, "Sniper! Release!"

The Russian—it was Golgolkin—was cursing loudly, and Congreve touched a wall panel that brought up a soft, diffused lighting from the domed ceiling.

Hawke's beloved parrot had Golgolkin's right wrist clamped in his sharp beak.

"Sniper!" Hawke shouted. "I said 'Release'!"

When the bird still did not obey, Hawke said mildly, "Ambrose, Sniper has taken a strong dislike to this fellow. Ask our guest if he is carrying a weapon of some sort, won't you?"

The Russian replied to Congreve's question, and Ambrose said, "Pistol. Right pocket of his jacket."

"Take it," Hawke said, and Congreve pulled a small automatic pistol from the man's pocket. He handed the weapon to Hawke. The parrot immediately released the Russian's wrist and removed himself to perch on Hawke's outstretched forearm.

"Mr. Golgolkin, I'm disappointed. I didn't subject either of you to the ship's metal detector out of common courtesy. And now I find that you come to my dinner table with a gun in your pocket. What were you planning to do with it?"

Ambrose questioned Golgolkin, who was grimacing, rubbing his wrist, and replied, "He says he always carries it. He has many enemies. He offers his deepest apologies."

"These enemies," Hawke said, stroking his parrot's head, "trouble me. Are they the unhappy result of any recent transactions?"

Congreve asked, and said, "He says they are political enemies, not business enemies."

"Mildly reassuring, I suppose," Hawke said. "His gun will be returned to him at the launch. In the meantime, we'll continue our little tour."

After the translation, Congreve said, "He apologizes once more and hopes this unfortunate mistake on his part won't have a negative effect on this transaction."

Hawke waved the notion away.

"Come, gentlemen, I'd like to show you the view of the islands from the bow of the ship. It's magnificent."

Hawke touched a panel on the wall, and a giant gull-wing section of the starboard-side bulkhead opened upward out into the night sky, silently above the deck. He stepped through and waited for the others to follow.

"This way, please," Hawke said, striding briskly forward along the teak decks. The others had to hurry to keep up.

"They should know," Hawke said over his shoulder, "that they are free to take five million dollars cash with them tonight when they leave the ship. In return, I want a written commitment for three things. A delivery date six months hence. The right to see the actual submarine prior to commissioning. And acknowledgment that the boat will be finished precisely to my personal specifications. Still with me, Ambrose?"

"Of course."

"Splendid," Hawke continued. "In addition, as I said earlier, I want to speak directly with their most recent purchaser. Assuming he's a satisfied customer, and they fulfill the other obligations, they will receive my commitment for the balance. To be determined, of course."

The foursome had reached the bow of the ship. There was a narrow bow pulpit extending some ten feet out over the water. The pulpit itself was some forty feet above the ocean's moonlit surface.

"They agree to all conditions," a slightly winded Congreve said, "save one. They cannot divulge the names of any prior purchasers. It is, apparently, a no-no in their trade."

"Ah, well, progress of a sort," Hawke said, extending his hand toward the pulpit. "In order to enjoy the full splendor of the view, they need to walk out on the pulpit to get out over the water. No need to fear, it's quite sturdy."

Congreve told them, and the two Russians, followed by Hawke and Congreve, walked out onto the narrow pulpit. Hawke removed a remote control device hanging from the pulpit's stainless steel rail. He pushed a button, and the entire pulpit started extending silently forward from the bow of the ship.

"Don't be alarmed, gentlemen," Hawke said. "We use this as a gangplank for docking in the Mediterranean. When it's fully extended, you'll be able to look back and see the entire superstructure of the yacht. Quite a sight."

The Russians said something and Congreve translated, "They say the great height makes them nervous."

"To hell with height," Hawke said. "Tell them to look at all the bloody sharks circling down below. And ask them if they'd like me to take a picture of them together. A souvenir of the evening. I brought a little camera."

Congreve told them and both Russians were clutching each other in a boozy embrace and breaking into silly grins.

"What a fabulous photo op," Hawke said, backing up and putting the small camera to his eye. "Splendid, but I'm a little too close. I've got to back up a few feet—hold that smile—yes, this is going to be brilliant. Hold it one more second—" Hawke and Congreve stepped off the pulpit and back onto the bow and the camera flashed.

And then he did something that struck terror into both the Russians' hearts. He pushed another button on the remote that caused the steel guard railings running along either side of the pulpit to withdraw into the hull. The two arms dealers shouted and clung to each other for dear life, staring down at the sea far below.

They were essentially standing at the end of a narrow diving board forty feet above shark-infested waters. They screamed something in Russian, but Hawke ignored them.

Instead, he drew his sword and walked toward them.

"How much for this Borzoi?" he asked.

"They say one hundred fifty million."

"Done," Hawke said. "And the owner of the other Borzoi? I want that name."

The Russians said a few words.

"Impossible for them to reveal it," Congreve said.

"Operation Invincible Sword," Hawke said. "Remember that little fiasco in Bahrain, Comrade Golgolkin?" He flicked his sword tip across the fat man's belly and said, "Welcome to the sequel."

Congreve had to smile. Alex Hawke was nothing if not a shrewd negotiator.

15

•••——•••

Gomez looked at his watch. He was already half an hour late for the birthday party.

This was unfortunate because the party was in honor of Lucinda Nettles's fourth birthday. Little Cindy was the only child of Admiral and Mrs. Joseph Nettles. And Joe Nettles was the commanding officer at the United States Naval Air Station, Guantánamo Bay, Cuba. In other words, Joe was Gomez's boss. *El nacho grande* here on Gitmo, as they called the joint.

Normally, of course, lowlife swabbies like Gomez didn't get invited to the CO's pad for parties, hang out, have a cold one, shoot the shit with the old man himself. But Gomez's two girls, Amber and Tiffany, were in the same class as Cindy Nettles. And that was the only reason Joe's wife, Ginny, had even invited them to this damn party, he knew that much for sure. Also, Gomez's wife, Rita, had gotten pretty palsy-walsy with Mrs. Nettles lately. Went to some friggin' card game there every week.

Fightin' Joe ran a tight ship. The invitation with all the little balloons said three o'clock sharp. It had been right there on the refrigerator door all week. Three o'clock it said, and now it was three-forty. And Fightin' Joe didn't like it when you were late.

Joe went to Annapolis, but, face it, he was still a damned redneck. Hell, he used go up on those watch-towers sometimes, the ones looking out over no-man's-land, the minefield around the base perimeter. His friend Sparky Collins was a guard up there. Sparky told him Joe would climb up and say to the guys on guard, bored shit-less, "Hey, watch this, boys!"

Joe, knowing the Cubans—the Frontier Guards, they called themselves—were up in their own towers, had their scopes trained on him, goes up there, turns his back on 'em and drops trou! *Moons them,* for chrissakes. The friggin' CO of the whole friggin' outfit! The Marines all went apeshit and everybody started calling him the Moon-man.

And then one day he has this fancy-ass barbeque for some big shots from the State Department and he's laughing, telling them all about mooning the Cubans, and this wise guy from the Cuban Desk says, "But, Admiral, you obviously don't understand Cuban culture. In Cuba, they don't see your action as an insult. They see it as an *invitation!*"

Whoa.

Everybody within hearing range was smart enough not to laugh right out loud except Gomez, who doubled over with tears in his eyes.

Gomez had never been invited back to the CO's house, which caused his wife Rita to pitch a shitfit every time the Nettleses had a party and they didn't make the cut. That's why she was so hopped up about this damn birthday party. Maybe they'd gone from the shitlist to the A list.

Rita and their two daughters had gone straight to the party from school. The party was going to be out around the pool in the CO's backyard. Man. He could see it all now. All those screaming kids running around with ice cream and Oreos all over their faces. He hoped they'd be serving something besides Kool-Aid for the grown-ups.

Maybe he'd stick a couple of his little airplane Stolis in his pockets for insurance.

Gomer, as his buddies on the base called him, had called his wife and explained that he might be a little late getting to the party. He was stopping by the house to fin ish wrapping a special present for little Cindy. That's what he was doing now, at the workbench out in his small garage.

He placed a large box on the bench, opened it, and pulled out a teddy bear. One big teddy bear. The biggest, fluffiest one he could find at the base exchange. Thing had to be at least three feet tall. The tag around its neck said it was a Steiff, imported from Germany or some-where. Expensive, but, hell, he could afford it. He was a goddamn millionaire!

The bear was snow white. And nice and plump, with a big fat belly too, which served his purposes. The idea for the birthday present had come to him over a few too many beers one recent afternoon in the PX. One minute he'd been mulling the whole thing over. The next minute he had it. It was just the way his brain worked. It was an ability that had brought him a long way from the barrios of Miami.

A long way from the *gusanos* of Little Havana, *señor.*

Los Gusanos. That's what Fidel called his people. The Worms. Like his father and all his aunts and uncles. The ones who'd abandoned their homeland and tried to make a better life in America. The *worms.* He couldn't decide who was worse, the *fidelistas* or the *americanos.* They were all shit, weren't they? The Cuban *people* deserved better, he knew that much.

Castro? America? He could give a shit. That's why he'd

agreed to go along with the Million-Dollar Plan, right?
No shit, Sherlock.

A toy. He'd been sitting there at the bar, and whammo!
The idea had just popped into his brain. Poof! But not
just a toy. A toy inside the home of Guantánamo's commanding officer. A toy in the room of the CO's little girl.
It was perfect. He had actually started giggling when he
thought of it, and his buddies at the bar had looked at
him funny.

Damn, he was good, though. You had to admit.

He stopped giggling and started gulping. He'd noticed
he was drinking a lot of beer lately. Beer and tranks and,
at night, cold potato juice, Vitamin V, right out of the
freezer. Then a couple more beers before bedtime. It
seemed to help. Bam, he was out like a light. Gonzo. Up
at six and he never missed a day of work, did he? Hell, he
still pumped iron at the gym. He was doing just fine.

But Rita didn't think so, obviously. She was ragging his
ass day and night. Still bugging him about the goddamn
initials on his left hand. A tattoo, he'd told her. It just
looked a little weird 'cause it had gotten infected. Then of
course she has to know whose initials. Whose? *Whose?*
Some little whore in Havana he'd gotten drunk with?
Some AIDS-infected *puta?*

At that exact moment, a moment when most guys he
knew would have lost it, what's new, he'd nailed it. Just
looked her right in the eye and hung it out there.

"MM. 'My Mother,' " he said.

"Oh."

"The one who *died?* Remember her?"

That shut her ass up. But she still never let up about
the hootch. Afraid a little booze now and then was ruin-

ing his Navy career. As if it wasn't ruined enough already. You didn't exactly get promoted for spending a lot of consecutive nights in the brig.

What she *didn't* know was that it didn't goddamn matter! *They were rich!* That would shut her up on a permanent basis. He'd made them so goddamn rich they could thumb their noses at anybody in the whole stinkpot Navy.

Who wants to be a millionaire?

Rafael Goddamn Gomez, that's who, and by God, he was one.

He even had this number he could call in Switzerland. He called it every day and gave the guy at the bank his secret account number. They'd give him the current balance in his secret numbered account. Money was growing like weeds over there. Hell, the interest *alone* was more than his shitty Navy salary.

Did he feel guilty taking all that money? Well, that was a good question. Did Uncle Sam feel guilty about the agony of his sainted mother in that hospital in Havana because of the goddamn U.S. embargo on medicines? That was *another* good question. How many innocent people had to die in pain before the idiots in Washington lifted that friggin' blockade?

Guilty? Him?

"I don't think so," Gomer said aloud, looking out the greasy garage window at some little kids on their bikes. American kids with lots of Armour hot dogs and Diet Coke and individually wrapped American cheese in the fridge and eardrops in the medicine cabinet if their little ears got little friggin' earaches. Hell, they even had a McDonald's here.

Happy Meals! While everybody else in Cuba was

going to bed hungry, these little rugrats were wolfing Happy Meals!

Guilty? Not in *this* friggin' lifetime.

Gomer took out his pocketknife and flipped open the big blade. He held the teddy bear down on the worktable with one hand and slit it open along the seam under its arm with the other. White stuffing popped out and flew all over the bench. Christ. He looked at his watch again. Four-fifteen. How long did birthday parties generally last anyway?

It would look weird if he didn't get over there pretty soon. The phone in the kitchen had been ringing off the hook and he was pretty sure it was Rita, wondering what the hell was keeping him. He was doing the best he could, wasn't he? Providing for his family? There was a cold Budweiser sitting on the table that he didn't remember bringing out to the garage. Weird. He took a gulp and felt better already. Beer was a goddamn miracle food and nobody ever gave it any credit.

Gomer walked over to his car and pulled the keys out of the ignition. It was an old car, a goddamn embarrassing heap to tell the truth. Well, his days of tooling around in crap like this would be over before you knew it. He had a stack of Corvette magazines under his bed to prove it.

He unlocked the trunk and opened it.

That's where he'd hidden the package that Julio and Iglesias had given him in Miami. The one they'd wrapped up in his own friggin' T-shirts and jockeys and put inside his own friggin' suitcase! Which they'd given back to him in the coffee shop the day he'd agreed to go along with the Big Plan.

The package was in there, right under the spare tire.

Since he was the only one who drove the damn car, he figured it'd be pretty safe under there. And there it was, too, right where he stowed it soon as he'd returned from stateside. Man. When you got it going right, you got it going right.

It took him a few minutes to get the package open. First there was all this goddamn Cuban newspaper wrapped in twine. And then all this goddamn bubbly stuff wrapped around the box. And you get that off, then it was goddamn shrink-wrapped inside! Christ. They certainly weren't making it easy for him. He probably should have done this earlier in the day. Before he'd gone to work.

So he was a little late. Shoot him.

He was curious to see the thing itself. He ripped at the bubble stuff, just throwing it on the floor, trying to get to the box inside. Then he had it. The box was made of some kind of heavy black plastic. High-impact stuff. It had latches on all four sides. He flipped them open, easy.

It was like Christmas. What was in the box?

Oh. A thermos bottle.

That's what it looked like. A silver thermos with some kind of foam packing all around it. And two other little gizmos packed in the foam right next to it. Everything wrapped in newspaper with some kind of damn Arabic writing on it.

He lifted the thermos out very carefully because he knew what it contained of course. *El Motel de los Cucarachas,* baby. He set it down on the workbench next to his beer. Careful. Don't want to knock either of these two babies over! Then he pried the first gizmo out and placed it next to the thermos thing.

The gizmo was round, and threaded inside. And, man,

it was heavy. He could see that the threads inside matched the threads outside the bottom of the thermos bottle. He had a vague recollection of the Cubans showing him a drawing, telling him to screw the little gizmo on the—the—what the hell had they called it, the *canister*.

That's it. It was a canister, not a thermos bottle. He picked up the gizmo and screwed it to the bottom of the canister. The thing made a little electronic noise that surprised him, but it sounded like a happy noise. Like he'd done it right. Surprise, surprise.

Piece of cake. Birthday cake, he thought, and laughed out loud. You weren't supposed to laugh at your own jokes, but still.

He turned the whole thing upside down and looked for the switch they'd told him about. They were very nervous that he'd forget the switch, he remembered that. But he hadn't forgotten to remember, had he? Even though he'd had a little buzz on all day.

The switch was under a little clear red plastic cover that you had to slide back. So far, so good. He slid the cover back and flipped the switch. He took a swig of beer. Then he held the thermos up and looked at the gizmo end. There was a digital readout window with red letters that had now appeared.

He liked the look of the word he saw blinking there. It was just the kind of word that got a whup-ass alpha male like himself hyper-jazzed. In bright red letters it said:

ARMED

How awesome is that? Armed and *extremely* dangerous. He knew you weren't supposed to laugh at your own jokes, but you had to chuckle at that one. Okay, now, by the book. Step one: Drink more beer. Step two: Put the thermos inside Mr. Bear, sew up his fat little tummy, and then wrap him all up in the pink paper and the big red ribbon. Put him very *carefully* into the car.

He's shaking now, from the inside out. His whole body is thrumming like the frigging G-string on Axl Rose's Fender Stratocaster.

Okay, the second little gizmo. What had they called it? A soda pop name. 7UP? No, RC. That was it. Leave the second gizmo, a little metal box with an antenna on it, right where it was, inside the black plastic box. He wouldn't be needing that little item, not until he got The Call. Till then the box could go right back in the trunk under the spare.

Time to amscray on over to the Moonman's birthday bash.

Easy as peas.

When you've totally and completely got your shit together and know exactly what you're doing, that is.

16

• • • ▬ • • •

"Nothing stirs the human blood quite like the sight of large dorsal fins knifing through the water," Hawke said, pointing his sword down toward the sharks circling below. "Wouldn't you agree, gentlemen?"

Grigory and Nikolai looked ready to vomit.

"Can anyone identify the various species?" Hawke

asked. "There are over three hundred and fifty, you know. Look. There's a big bull for you. I saw a few tigers and even a white-tip earlier. Nasty fellows. Carnivores. Strictly the man-eating meat-and-potatoes type."

The big Russian had started to edge his way gingerly back toward Hawke, who pointed his rapier directly at the man's midriff. The man stopped short.

"Here's my point, Nikolai," Hawke said, pressing the sword's sharp tip against the man's stomach. "You want my hundred fifty million dollars. I want your nuclear sub. But I insist you give me the name of your last customer. All clear?"

Suddenly, Brian Drummond appeared at Hawke's side carrying a large stainless steel pail. It was filled with two gallons of pulverized fish entrails, guts, gristle, and blood. What fishermen call chum.

"Ah," Hawke said, "look, Nikolai. Here's our steward Brian, who's brought along his chum. Throw it overboard, please, Brian. Bit ripe for my taste."

"Aye, aye, Skipper." Brian walked to the forwardmost part of the rail and flung the putrid contents of the pail overboard.

Seconds later the water below the extended pulpit was a churning pinkish froth as the sharks went into a feeding frenzy. The Russians looked down in horror.

"Speak up, boys," Hawke said. "I'm running out of patience, and you are running out of time." The two men started gibbering.

"They say revealing names is not only unprofessional; it's suicide," Congreve said. "To reveal any of their contacts' identities would mean certain death for both of them."

"Ask them what, at this point, they think *not* revealing those identities means."

The petrified Golgolkin started talking very rapidly. Rasputin was cringing behind him, speechless with terror.

Congreve listened to all this and turned to Hawke.

"Here we go, Alex. He received a DHL parcel containing five million dollars cash and a telephone number," Congreve translated. "When he called it, the party did not identify himself, but gave another number to call. After countless calls like this, he finally spoke to someone who claimed to be negotiating for a third party. This party wished to buy a Borzoi-class Soviet submarine. He was willing to pay the going price. He insisted on remaining anonymous."

"Very good," Hawke said. "Progress. What was the country code of the last number he called?"

Congreve asked, and said to Hawke, "There were so many numbers, so many different voices, he says he can't remember. They were all cell phone numbers in various countries."

"Did he receive the deposit?" Hawke asked.

"He says yes."

"*How* did he receive it?"

"He says it was a wire transfer. Into his numbered account in Switzerland."

"Excellent. And now, please, where was the money transferred from?"

"He says he can't remember. He begs you to spare his life."

"Pity. It's always sad when memory fails us at just the wrong moment," Hawke said. Sword extended, he walked out over the water toward the cowering Russians.

"Do you know our English expression 'to walk the plank,' Comrade Golgolkin?" Hawke asked.

"He says no," Ambrose said.

"Really? It's an old Hawke family tradition, invented a few hundred years ago by one of my more rambunctious ancestors, I believe."

He flicked the sword's point across the man's belly.

"Ai-eee!" the Russian cried.

"Sorry, old chap, but this is how it works. You can talk. Or you can walk. Should you choose neither of the above, I can happily run you both through."

The sword penetrated the man's shirtfront, and a bright red flower of blood began to bloom on his belly. The Russian looked down at the blade in his stomach, horrified.

"Last chance, Golgolkin," Hawke said. "Where was the money wired from?"

Rasputin was screaming something, undoubtedly encouraging his colleague to cough up the information. The fat Russian squeezed his eyes shut and uttered something between his clenched teeth.

Hawke turned to Congreve. "I'm sorry, Ambrose. What did he say?"

"The money was wired from a private account. A bank account. In Miami, he thinks." Congreve said.

"And the name of the bank?"

Congreve translated. A huge sob escaped from the big Russian. "He's praying," Congreve said.

"His prayers will go unanswered. I want that bloody bank's name! Now!" He twisted the sword blade.

"Sunstate Bank," the Russian blurted out in English.

"Now for the hundred-and-fifty-million-dollar question," Hawke said. "Who bought the bloody Borzoi? Who? Give me that name on the account in Miami or you're a dead man!"

"*Telaraña,*" the Russian finally cried. "*Telaraña!*"

"That's better," Hawke said. "Such a relief when the truth comes out at last."

Withdrawing his sword but keeping the tip poised at the man's belly, Hawke said, "Bloody good show! Now, tell this fat bastard two things. If he's lying, there's nowhere in the world he can run. I'll find him and slice him to bloody pieces with this very sword."

Hearing this, the man shook his head violently. "He understands," Congreve said. "He's telling the truth. He swears it."

"Good. Now that he's in a talkative mood, I want to know when he received final payment for the Borzoi and when it's scheduled for delivery. I also want to know how many subs he's sold, the total number, and I want to know what type of boats they were. Diesel, nuclear, everything. Would you ask him that, please?"

Congreve extracted this information and relayed it to Hawke.

"And one more thing," Hawke said. "Tell him that if either he or the little mad monk ever lay a hand on that poor girl Gloria again, the sharks will be eating their balls for breakfast."

When the man shook his head again, Hawke withdrew his sword, wiped the bloody tip on the Russian's trousers, and stuck it back in his cummerbund. Then he turned and walked toward the portside rail.

Brian was waiting with a glass of port and Hawke's parrot resting on his forearm. The bird instantly flew to Hawke's shoulder.

"Call me old-fashioned, Brian," he said to his steward. "Politically incorrect, I'm quite sure. But, God, I hate dealing with Russians. They're almost as bad as the French." He took a swig of the ruby-colored wine.

"*Bad as French!*" Sniper screeched.

"Almost, Sniper old boy," Hawke said. "I said 'almost' as bad, didn't I, Brian?"

"Couldn't agree more, sir," Brian said, discreetly checking the automatic weapon strapped to his shoulder.

"Would you mind seeing these two infections safely back to Staniel Cay? Keep a gun on them."

"Will do, sir. I think—"

"*Hawke! Hawke!*" Sniper shrieked.

Hawke spun around. Rasputin, with a murderously mad gleam in his smoldering eyes, was plunging toward him. He had an ugly serpentine-shaped dagger raised above his head and he began screaming like a crazed banshee.

Hawke came close to freezing. Knives, he'd learned long ago, tend to have that effect on most people. But he feinted left and moved right with blinding speed.

He had exactly one second to get an arm up and ward off the downward slashing dagger. He felt the burn as the blade sliced his forearm open and saw bright blood splashing upon the teak decks. Ignoring the pain, he sucked in a deep breath and in an instant he had Rasputin's knife hand in his grasp and had planted one foot solidly on the deck. He pulled Rasputin forward and pivoted on his one planted heel at the same time.

The Russian pitched forward, grunting, losing his balance, and Hawke gathered himself, using Rasputin's own forward momentum to lift the shrieking Russian off the deck. Still gripping the knife hand, he pivoted once more and released his grip, flinging the man bodily into the air, out and over the yacht's waist-high gunwale rail.

With an inhuman wail, the man went pinwheeling into space, finally hitting the water some forty feet below with a great splash.

Hawke leaned against the bulkhead, calmly tying his pocket handkerchief around his blood-soaked forearm. "Cut me to the bone, the bloody bastard," Hawke said.

"Shall I ring the ship's surgeon, sir?" Brian asked, returning his weapon to its holster. Hawke had dispatched the Russian with such alacrity he hadn't needed it.

"Not now. I've suffered worse in a nasty badminton match. Ambrose, please ask Mr. Golgolkin if his comrade down there can swim."

Ambrose and Golgolkin had their backs to Hawke, both peering down over the side of the yacht. Someone flipped on a spotlight and trained it on the Russian. They could see him thrashing about in the water and the disturbance was attracting the attention of the sharks congregated at the bow.

"I say, did he survive the fall?" Hawke asked.

At the sight of the fins slicing through the water in his direction, the floundering Russian started screaming.

"Apparently, he did," Hawke said, answering his own question. He stepped to the rail and glanced down. He was pleased to see all the dorsal fins, circling, closing.

"Brian, let the sharks get a little closer and then have

someone open the closest starboard hatch and pull the little bugger in."

"They're pretty close right now, Skipper," Drummond
said. "Especially that big white-tip."

"Not close enough," Hawke replied.

He turned to Congreve.

"Ambrose, perhaps someone could give Comrade
Golgolkin here a towel or something to press against his
wound. It's nothing serious, unfortunately, just a scratch.
And I suppose we can return this to him now."

Hawke pulled the confiscated automatic pistol from
his pocket, released the cartridge magazine, and tossed
the clip overboard before handing the empty gun to
Golgolkin.

"You're quite welcome, I'm sure," Hawke said, having
heard no expression of thanks for his kindness.

The bearded Russian was speechless. Goggle-eyed, he
was leaning over the varnished teak rail, watching the
sharks circling ever closer around his hapless colleague.

"Will that be all, Skipper?" Brian asked.

"I think that's quite enough excitement for one
evening, don't you? If our chief bosun is still sober when
he returns to the boat, you might ask him to have my seaplane fueled and ready for me first thing. File a flight plan
to Nassau, I want to be airborne by dawn's early light."

"Aye, sir."

"After you've seen our guests safely ashore, you might
call my pilots in Miami and tell them I want the
Gulfstream to meet me in Nassau, tanks topped off and
ready for wheels-up at noon. I'm taking her into Reagan
Washington."

"Aye, aye."

"*Aye, aye!*" squawked Sniper.

"Ah, Sniper, my brave fellow. You deserve a treat. Brian, a lid of our best Beluga for old Sniper?"

"Done," Brian said, smiling.

"Oh. And tell Miss Perkins down in the ship's office to have Stokely pick me up in D.C., and book me a quiet table for two at the Georgetown Club at eight."

"Done," Brian said. "And your usual suite at the Hay-Adams overlooking the White House?"

"Not necessary, thanks. I spoke with Pelham. Apparently the new house is ready for occupants."

Brian saluted and headed aft to make the arrangements.

Hawke noticed that the fat Russian, still looking down over the rail, appeared to have been eavesdropping on his conversation with young Drummond. Nosy, he decided, very nosy.

"Ambrose, do you have a second?" Hawke asked, and he and Congreve walked to the top of the steps leading down from the bridge deck, moving out of earshot of the Russian.

"Well done," Congreve said softly. "He wants his money."

"He's bloody lucky he's got his life," Hawke said. "Tell that socialist disease that anyone who lines his pockets putting nuclear weapons in the hands of terrorists takes his chances with me. He's already used up one. And one is about all he gets. Bagged his bloody limit."

"We'll get them off the boat, Alex. But I would definitely increase the security on and around the yacht, starting tonight. Round the clock. These chaps are beyond unsavory."

"I agree. I'll have a word with Tommy Quick. Double the watch. This *Telaraña*. I seem to have heard the name. Spanish, isn't it? Something to do with spiders?"

"The spider's web, actually."

"I've always been petrified of spiders," Hawke said, shuddering. "Strange, isn't it? Ever since I was a boy. No idea why, of course. Spiders. Horrid little buggers."

"Let's have a nightcap up on deck, shall we?" Ambrose said. "And you can finish the gripping saga of that scourge of the Spanish Main, the blackguard Blackhawke."

"Pirates' lore. Most appropriate after a splendid evening of saber-rattling and plank-walking," Hawke said. Motioning his friend up the stairs, he said, "After you, Constable."

17

· · · — — · · ·

Once Hawke and Ambrose had made themselves comfortable up on deck, Hawke continued the story of his illustrious ancestor.

The old pirate, upon hearing that the king's men were in the courtyard, now knew he was not to be spared the hangman's noose. Collapsing back upon his tattered cot, he uttered one word, "Lost."

The parson knelt on the cold stone beside him and put his hand out to the man. "Repent with me now, and make your final journey with peace in your soul. I beg of you to—"

"Innocent!" Blackhawke bellowed. "How does an innocent man repent? The king himself long encouraged piracy to fill his coffers. Now that damnable East India Company decides pirates are discouraging the mercantile trades, and suddenly our heads are on the block!"

"Alas, 'tis true."

"My friends at court, my crew, one and all betray me to save their own skins! It's these foul traitors must repent their treachery, not Captain Blackhawke!"

"Alas, 'tis true twice over," the parson said. "Let us go now, and speak with the Lord."

On their way to the courtyard, the parson took the hapless pirate into the prison chapel for one last chance at redemption. They sat for a moment in the gloom on a long hard pew facing a single coffin draped in black. As was tradition, the doomed prisoners had been forced to sit before the symbolic coffin, quite empty, for hours each day, supposedly doing their penance.

Thick incense floated to the high, vaulted ceilings, but it couldn't mask the pervasive stench of urine rising in every dark corner; nor could the chants and mournful prayers of the condemned hide the sounds of those wretched souls fornicating on the back benches.

Blackhawke stared silently at the draped coffin, quietly sipping his grog.

"It's no use, Parson," he said finally. "It ain't in me, repentance. Nary a bit of it. I'll step off into the next world and take me chances as I am." He pulled the spyglass in which he'd hidden the map from his cloak and slipped it into the parson's hands.

"This glass is all that's left to me in this world," Blackhawke rasped. " 'Twas a gift from my wife when first

I went to sea. Now I want her to have it as a poor remembrance of her husband. I beg you to see that it makes it safely into her hands. I've four gold doubloons sewn into me coat here that are yours, if you'll give me no more than your sacred word. It's my last wish."

"Consider it done, Captain," the parson said. And Blackhawke ripped open the seam in his coat, withdrew the doubloons, and slipped them to the fellow.

The parson and the pirate emerged into the courtyard.

"I warn you, Parson," Blackhawke said, angrily eyeing the crewmen who'd betrayed him, some of whom were already in the cart. "I warn you this. An unarmed man full of vengeance is the most dangerous of men. I warrant I'll rip their treacherous hearts out!"

But in the event, riding in the king's cart, Blackhawke merely drank grog all the way to the dock. He was simply too tired and too weak and too full of rum to wreak his vengeance. He was thus oblivious to the merry shouts and taunts of the crowds lining the streets leading to the River Thames. By the time he and the other condemned arrived at the place of execution, the parson had to help the old man stagger up the steps to where the hangman waited. The notorious pirate captain would be the first to go.

He stood, with the noose finally around his neck, and looked out over the noisome crowd. He had arranged for some few remaining friends to stand below the gallows and witness his departure. Theirs was a mission of mercy. Since the drop itself seldom did the job, his mates were there to leap up, grab his heels, and yank down to end Blackhawke's agony quickly.

As it happened, the rope parted, and Blackhawke tumbled to the ground with little more than a bad rope burn round his neck. The dazed man had to be carried once more up the steps to repeat his agonizing departure.

By now, however, the rum fog had dissipated a bit, and it was a much-sobered Blackhawke who had one final revelation. Standing once more upon the precipice, he felt suddenly alive, breathing, conscious. Even the sting of the rope burning around his neck was something to be cherished, and, oddly, the crowd ranged below him now seemed to be cheering. A joyous sendoff for one last epic and uncharted voyage! Yes!

His mind allowed him to stand once more on his quarterdeck, shouting orders fore and aft. Lines cast off, sheets loosed, sails filled with an evening breeze. Bound for the far horizon. Men scrambling like monkeys in the rigging, all color and glory. Bound for that fat yellow moon floating just over that far, far horizon.

Farewell.

Well. This is it then. Torches burning along the riverbanks. The dusky glow of London Town shimmering across the water. Lovely night. Been a good life, hasn't it, after all? Strongly lived. Well fought and well rewarded. Left the treacherous Caribee and tedious humdrum of the New World's penny-pinching merchants far astern, hadn't he?

Been a young man then, still, when he'd taken up the pirate's adventuresome ways. Loved the endless roll of the boundless blue sea, he had, really. Loved every league and fathom of her, for all his life.

A small sigh escaped his lips and his mates below drew forward, hushed now. All the crowd below quiet now. He would go into the next world unarmed. But he was unafraid and had no doubt he'd conquer the next as he'd done the present.

He'd given some serious thought to his parting shot, looking for a defiant farewell, and he uttered those words now, raw and raspy, but still strong.

"The man without sword is oft the deadliest enemy," Blackhawke bellowed. "Hear me, Death, and lay on!"

There was a resounding huzzah from below.

He brought the curtain down on this world, squeezing his eyes shut and remembering just as hard as he could:

> *And the cannons' thunder, too, and the blood, and the plunder. Loved it all and no regrets now, none save the sweet wife's face hanging out there in mid-air now, beckoning, all her tears falling like soft rain on the upturned faces below. His wife, his children, lost to him, too, and all that buried booty and—*

He sucked one last draught of sweet air into his lungs and then—stepped off into forever.

The next morning they hung Blackhawke's corpse from a post on the riverbank, in plain view of the passing river traffic. It rotted there for some months, sloughing off flesh, blacker and smaller with every sunrise, a stern and daily reminder of the fate awaiting those foolhardy enough to consider the pirate's adventuresome ways.

In the end, there was little left of Blackhawke but legend. That, and his sun-bleached bones, tinkling gaily in the wind off the river.

* * *

Hawke was silent a moment, having finished his tale. He drained his port, then he stood and raised the empty glass to his friend.

"Hear me then, Death, and lay on!" Hawke said, and flung his glass far out into the nighttime sky.

"Hear! Hear!" Ambrose said, and, getting to his feet, he flung his glass over the rail as well. "Now we've sent Captain Blackhawke off to his reward, I'm for bed myself. Good night, Alex. Sleep well."

"Good night, Ambrose," Alex said. "Thanks to you, old soul, I'll no doubt be dreaming of pirates tonight."

But of course he dreamt of them every night.

18

• • • — — • •

At six the next morning, a crewman on the bridge initiated a program that caused the entire stern section of *Blackhawke* to rise upward on massive hydraulic pistons. It revealed a yawning, cavernous hangar, where Hawke garaged a few of his "toys," as he called them.

The deck and bulkheads of the hangar were brilliantly polished stainless steel and contained only a tiny portion of Hawke's permanent collection. Among them were the 1932 British Racing Green Bentley, supercharged. A C-type Jaguar, winner of the 1954 Le Mans race, and Alberto Ascari's Mille Miglia–winning Ferrari Barchetta.

Then there was the seventy-foot-long *Nighthawke,* an offshore powerboat capable of speeds in excess of one hundred miles an hour. Hawke had made many a narrow escape thanks to *Nighthawke*'s powerful turbocharged engines.

One of Hawke's favorite toys, however, was the shining silver seaplane now being positioned at the top of the ramp. Its lovely streamlined appearance looked like something Raymond Loewy himself might have designed in the early thirties. At a signal, the plane was lowered to the foot of a ramp that stretched directly into the sea. In seconds, the small plane was bobbing merrily on the mirrored surface of the blue water.

The name *Kittyhawke* was painted in script just below the cockpit window. And, under that, a painting of a very pretty young bathing beauty. Sutherland and Quick stood at the foot of the ramp, each holding a mooring line attached to the plane's pontoons.

Hawke and Congreve stood watching the operation. Hawke was wearing his old Royal Navy flight suit. It was his standard wardrobe whenever he flew the seaplane. He was literally rubbing his hands together in keen anticipation of the flight to Nassau.

"Fine morning for the wild blue yonder," Hawke exclaimed, taking in a deep breath of salt air.

"Lovely," Congreve replied, expelling a plume of tobacco smoke the color of old milkglass.

"Now, listen, old boy. I want you to have a bit of fun while I'm gone. Do some more snorkeling. Get some sun. You look like an absolute fish."

"About that treasure map. I do hope—"

"The box is open on the library desk. If you have to lift it out, there are tweezers in the drawer."

"I'd like to include Sutherland in my research. He might prove extremely useful."

"Smashing. Spent some time heading up your cartography section, didn't he? Best of luck. Who couldn't use an extra few hundred million in gold?"

"Should be good fun."

Hawke zipped up his flying suit and put a hand on Congreve's shoulder.

"I've left you all the notes I've made over the years. A lot to plow through. All those rainy afternoons at the British Museum digging up contemporaneous maps and manuscripts and what-not."

"Really? I always imagined you whiling away those hours in a pub somewhere, huddled in a dark corner with a beautiful married woman."

"Indeed? Well. Some excellent volumes of eighteenth-century history and cartography in the library, as you know. I've made a fair bit of progress, but, of course, I don't read Spanish as well as you do."

"I was wondering—" Congreve said, and then looked away.

"Yes?"

"I wonder—well, you said you'd been in these islands before," he said, still not looking Hawke in the eye.

"Yes?"

"Well, I was thinking perhaps that voyage you took might itself have been some kind of treasure-hunting expedition. If the map has been in your family for generations, it might be that—"

"I really have no idea," Hawke said, his face clouding up. He stepped onto the plane's pontoon. "I told you. I was so young. I don't remember anything."

"Of course. You said that. Sorry."

"I'm off, then."

"Please give Victoria my best."

"Oh, I will indeed," Hawke said, merry blue eyes and a smile returning to his face. "And mine as well, I should hope."

"Safe journey," Congreve said. Hawke patted the rosy cheek of the painted bathing beauty for luck and climbed up into the cockpit. He pulled the door closed after him. The window on Hawke's side slid open, and his curly black head appeared.

"Back in a few days, I should think," Hawke shouted. "I'll ring you right after my meeting at the State Department. Have some fun, will you? Play some golf!"

"Golf!" Congreve exclaimed. "There's not a golf course within a hundred miles of this bloody place!"

Hawke smiled and pulled the window closed. He looked at the preflight check he'd strapped to his knee. God, he loved this airplane! Just the smell of the thing was enough to make him feel sharply alive. Since arriving in the Exumas, he'd made good use of the little plane, taking her up for early-morning explorations of the surrounding islands.

There were a few loud reports as *Kittyhawke*'s Packard-built Merlin 266 engine fired, and a short blast of flame erupted from the manifold. The engine was a custom version of the one that had powered the Supermarine Spitfires that had won the Battle of Britain.

As the polished steel propeller slowly started to spin, Congreve turned to Ross, who was now standing beside him, holding the plane's mooring line.

"What's the weather like between here and Nassau?" he asked his Scotland Yard colleague. "I saw a nasty front moving toward the Bahamas on the weather sat this morning."

"Should be ideal, then," Ross said, smiling with evident fondness for Hawke. "You know the skipper. Even as my squadron commander, when we were flying sorties in Tomcats, he was always frustrated he never got to be one of those hurricane hunter chaps. He does love the eye of the storm."

"No," Ambrose said with a puff of smoke, "the eye of the storm is far too quiet for Alex Hawke. He loves the storm."

Ross quickly checked the plane's exterior controls over, then gave Hawke the thumbs-up. He tossed the last mooring line out toward the pontoon where it was automatically spooled aboard.

The engine noise increased as Hawke ran up the motor. Testing his flaps, ailerons, and rudder, he turned the plane's nose into the wind. With a sudden roar, the plane surged forward. Congreve, who hated flying contraptions, had to admit the silver plane looked splendid, catching the sun's early rays on its wings as it darted across the glassy blue water.

The plane lifted, did a quick looping turn, dove back over *Blackhawke*'s stern, waggled its wings in salute, and was gone.

Into the "mild" blue yonder, Congreve thought, furious with himself for not coming up with the joke a few minutes earlier.

As it happened, there would be nothing mild about it.

Hawke gained a little altitude, climbing into his turn northwest. He would be flying right over Hog Island, home of the most famous pig in the Caribbean. The big hairy sow, named Betty, was completely blind and had been the island's sole inhabitant for years. Hawke had discovered her only a few days earlier, shortly after *Blackhawke*'s arrival in these waters. He, Tom, and Brian had been bonefishing the flats just off the small island's sandy white beach.

Betty lived on the generosity of the many tourists who would take their boats in near shore. She would come running out of the dense thicket of scrub palms at the sound of their outboard engines and plunge into the sea. She'd swim out toward the cries of the children and their families, who'd always bring Betty's favorite meals, which consisted of apples, oranges, or potatoes, Hawke had noticed that day, watching the tourists.

Betty would swim right up to the side of the boat, sniffing, and take the food from the delighted children's hands. Since then, Hawke himself had fed her many times and developed a great fondness for the old sow. On his morning sorties in *Kittyhawke,* he now made a great fuss of "airlifting" supplies in to Betty. In fact, he had a big canvas sack of apples in his lap at this very moment. And he was just coming up on Hog Island.

His method was always the same. Go in low on the first pass so Betty could hear his engine and know breakfast was about to be served. Then he'd bank *Kittyhawke* hard over and fly back out to his original position. By the time he got turned around, he could usually see Betty running through the scrub palms toward the water.

That's what he did this morning.

He lined up on the island, staying low. The sunlit turquoise water racing beneath his wings was beautiful.

Because of the hour, he was flying directly into the rising sun. There she was, he could make her out, still deep in the bush, trotting along. Odd, she'd usually made it to the water at this point.

He slid back his portside window and felt the sudden rush of air and the explosion of engine noise inside the cockpit. He held the sack of apples outside the cockpit, ready to release at just the right moment. Steady, hold your course, nose up, you're coming in a bit low, and— bombs away! The apples tumbled into the sea. Hawke was laughing, looking ahead for Betty to emerge, when he saw a man all in black stand up in the midst of the scrub palms. What?

The man raised something to his shoulder and seemed to be pointing it directly at Hawke. Then the most amazing thing, Betty bursting from the palms directly behind the fellow and smashing him to the ground! He scrambled to his feet, kicking wildly at the relentless pig and aiming once more at the onrushing airplane.

Bloody hell. He could even see the man's face now. Rasputin? Yes. Wild-eyed, grinning like a monkey.

Hawke yanked back on his stick just as he saw a puff of white smoke at Rasputin's shoulder. The plane's infrared detector warning sounded instantly, telling him what he already knew.

There was a heat-seeking missile screaming toward him, locked on. The bloody Russian had fired a Stinger at him! There it was, Christ, he could *see* the bloody thing hurtling right toward his goddamn nose!

This little chap is really starting to piss me off, Hawke said to himself. His forearm still burned where the Russian had stabbed him with the dagger. He instantly went to full throttle, feeling the full thrust of the Merlin engine kicking in, and banked hard left, then hard right, jinking violently. He had the *Kittyhawke* right down on the deck and his wingtips were brushing the tops of the scrub palms every time he banked her.

His enormous burst of acceleration had confused the missile, and he saw the little silver killer scream beneath his fuselage, missing him by maybe a foot. Maybe less. He didn't have time to congratulate himself. He knew, even now, the Stinger would be correcting, arcing around and coming at him from behind.

His missile alarm warnings confirmed his fears. Still locked on.

Even for a fighter pilot, the inside loop at low altitude is easily one of the most dangerous maneuvers you can attempt. A flawless execution is critical. It was also, he knew, the only chance he had. He leveled his wings and pulled straight back on the stick. *Kittyhawke* responded instantly, going into an almost vertical climb. The g-forces were enormous, and Hawke was shoved back into his seat, hearing the constant wail of the alarm telling him the missile was still locked on.

At the top of the loop, the hard part started. You had to keep the aircraft with her belly skyward as you came over the top and started your descent. He strained around in his seat, looking for the Stinger. It was sticking right with him.

As he nosed over, the g-forces increased. And so did the airspeed, because he had the plane in a vertical dive, screaming down toward the scrubby little island. This was the most dangerous part, the part where you could easily "red out," as pilots called blacking out.

He smelled the fire before he saw it. He heard popping noises behind him, electrical, and smoke started to fill the cockpit. The missile must have clipped one of the transponders dangling from the belly of the plane. Now, in addition to the Stinger, he had an electrical fire on his hands.

Well, the fire would have to wait. He just hoped it would wait long enough.

"Bastard," he shouted, craning his head around and seeing the missile gaining on him. The ground was rushing up so fast, he could literally see crabs scurrying across the sand. Do-or-die time. If he was to have any chance at all, he had to wait until it was too late to pull out.

Then one of two things would happen. He would be obliterated. Or he wouldn't.

Now! He hauled back on the stick and accelerated out of the dive. He'd come within mere feet of the earth and the plane was slicing through the tops of scrub palms. As long as he didn't hit anything solid before he got a little altitude—

WHUMPF!!!

The Stinger hit the earth and exploded.

Hawke, busily avoiding the taller palm trees by banking hard left and right, managed a quick look over his shoulder toward the rear of the small cockpit. Flames were licking at the back of his seat and the smoke was starting to burn his eyes. The fire hadn't waited. It was seconds from spreading out of control.

He had to get to the fire extinguisher mounted very inconveniently on the portside bulkhead behind him. The fire was directly between Hawke and the extinguisher.

It's these little design flaws that make life so interesting, Hawke thought, struggling out of his shoulder belts. He leveled *Kittyhawke*, flipped on the autopilot, and climbed out of his seat.

There was nothing for it but to wade into the flames, grab the Halon extinguisher, and use it before he was incinerated. The legs of his vintage flight suit caught fire instantly, and he ripped the suit off with one hand while stretching out his other to grab the Halon.

He put out his flaming jumpsuit, then emptied the canister's contents into the heart of the blaze. Wonder of wonders, it actually worked! The fire was out as quickly as it had started. Now all he had to do was open the cockpit windows on both sides and get all the bloody smoke out of the plane. And hope the fire hadn't damaged any of his critical controls.

Climbing back into his seat he saw that, while all the hair on his legs was singed off, he wasn't badly burned. He flipped off the autopilot and banked hard left. He'd make a pass over the island and see if he could spot the bastard who'd almost killed him.

Flames and black smoke from the crashed Stinger had already climbed into the sky, and a brush fire had started to spread at the heart of Hog Island. The Russian was nowhere to be seen. But Betty, thank God, was now safely offshore, swimming blindly around in a sea of apples.

Hawke allowed himself a deep sigh of relief.

Betty had saved his life. If she hadn't knocked the little cretin down and he'd gotten that first shot off, Hawke would surely be a dead man.

"Toast," as the Americans would have it.

19

•••—••

"If you'll join me in the library, Inspector Sutherland?" Congreve said, after Hawke was safely airborne and they had entered the hangar elevator. "Scotland Yard, Caribbean Section, namely you and me, suddenly has a great deal of work to do in the next few days."

"Yes. These Russians are a bad lot, sir."

"Oh, it's not the Russkies we're on to. That's purely Hawke's affair for the time being."

"What then?"

Congreve touched the button for the main deck and said, "Oh, we're on to much more thrilling stuff, I assure you."

"Really? Such as?"

"Pirates. Golden doubloons buried under silver moons. Skulls. Crossbones, and dead man talk. All that sort of thing."

"Sounds fairly exciting."

"It does have that potential, yes."

The elevator came to a stop and the door slid open. As the two men walked toward the ship's library, Congreve said, "Do you remember hearing stories about Blackhawke the pirate in your childhood?"

"Of course. Everyone did. Silver skulls braided into his beard, as I remember. Fond of decapitating chaps and hanging their heads in the rigging as a warning sign."

"That's the fellow. It may surprise you to learn that our dear friend and benefactor Alex Hawke is a direct descendant of that notorious pirate. Alex has acquired a treasure map from his grandfather drawn by Blackhawke himself just before he was hung for piracy and murder."

"Astounding! I like this already," Sutherland said, following his superior into the library. He was literally rubbing his hands together in anticipation.

"The map is in that box on the table. Have a look."

Sutherland went to the table and peered into the open box. He pulled back a chair, sat, and stared at the contents for several long moments before speaking.

"Good Lord, Ambrose, you can still read the thing," Sutherland said, excitement in his voice.

"Astounding, isn't it? Over three hundred years old and entirely legible." Congreve put his old leather satchel on the table beside the box and pulled out a thick file, yellowed with age.

"What's that?"

"It's an old CID file, Ross," Congreve said, looking at the man thoughtfully. "A cold case, almost thirty years old now. Murder. An unsolved double homicide, in fact." Congreve looked away, and pulled a pipe from his tweed jacket.

"Is something wrong?" Sutherland said, looking at his superior, for clearly there was.

"It's a delicate matter," Congreve said, tamping tobacco into the pipe's bowl. "I'm probably one of the few people left alive who even know of this file's existence."

"Well, sir, if you'd rather I not—"

"No, no. Sit, please. I need your help here, Ross. But I must ask for your absolute assurances that this matter will not be discussed outside this room. And that includes the owner of this vessel. Am I clear?"

"Certainly. You have my word," Sutherland said, puzzled. He simply couldn't imagine any secrets between Hawke and his lifelong friend Congreve. "I will not discuss anything you share with me with anyone."

Congreve looked at the man carefully. He was one of the best of the Yard's new generation, that much was certain. And the young fellow had enormous respect for Hawke, his squadron commander in the Navy and the man who literally saved his life during the Desert Storm affair. Still, it was a risky business.

"Well, good," Congreve said finally, and opened the file. "You see, Ross, I suspect that the contents in this file and the map in that box are connected in some way."

"A three-hundred-year-old map and a thirty-year-old murder case? Connected?"

"Yes, I rather think they are."

He pushed the file across the table toward Sutherland.

"You're free to read it in its entirety after we're done here. You will see that the murders took place aboard a yacht moored in these very waters."

"And the victims?"

"The mother and father of Alexander Hawke."

"Good Lord," Ross said, taking a deep breath. "Any witnesses?"

"Just one. A seven-year-old boy. Alex Hawke himself."

Well after midnight, Congreve and Sutherland were still in the ship's library.

Three meals had been brought in, served, and removed. The desk and two tables were piled with books, folios, maps, and satellite photographs of the region. Ross had ordered the sat photos printed on the bridge that morning and delivered down to the library.

Ross had also scanned the pirate's crude drawing of the island into his computer, enhanced it, and had it blown up. It was now taped to the wall above Hawke's desk. The sat photos, too, were taped to the wall, surrounding the computer's version of the pirate's drawing.

He had been on his feet for hours, poring over the photos with a magnifying glass, comparing them to the three-hundred-year-old drawing. So far, he'd seen nothing in the Exuma chain of islands that remotely resembled the island in the drawing. He was exhausted, but determined not to give up until he'd cracked it, a trait that had stood him in good stead at New Scotland Yard.

Congreve, meanwhile, had pulled up a chair next to the gas fire that was lit in the small fireplace. The cold front he'd seen on the satellite that morning had moved down through the Bahamas to the Exumas. The fresh salty breeze now flowing through the open portholes was actually chilly. Most refreshing, he thought. A welcome respite from the brutal heat he'd experienced since his arrival.

He was puffing contentedly on his old brier pipe, working his way through the voluminous notes relating to the search for the treasure. He was also combing a small stack of ancient and crumbling leather-bound ship's logs and histories of the Caribbean. Occasionally, he would emit an "a-ha" or a "well, well, well," but, to Sutherland's frustration, he never elaborated on the source of these exclamations.

"Do you fancy some tea, Ross?" he asked as the ship's clock on the mantelpiece struck one.

"Yes, please."

Congreve pressed the button on the remote that summoned the steward and said "A-ha," for perhaps the tenth time since supper. Ross sighed, put down the glass, and collapsed in the chair opposite Congreve.

"A-ha *what* exactly?" he asked.

"I am referring to this Spanish corsair that Blackhawke mentioned in his final message to his wife. This 'Andrés Manso de Herreras' specifically," Congreve said. "I was beginning to doubt his existence, but here he is all right. He's mentioned by name in this ship's log. Penned by a contemporary of de Herreras. A Captain Manolo Caracol who was then sailing for the Spanish crown."

"A-ha," Ross said, peering excitedly at the ancient book written in a fine Spanish hand. "Well, that's quite good progress, isn't it, Chief? And what does it say exactly?"

"Well, according to Manolo Caracol's log, this fellow de Herreras wreaked a good deal of havoc in these waters. He was a Spanish privateer, born in Seville, who lurked about in the Windward Passage. His specialty was intercepting his colleagues, those headed for Spain loaded to the gunwales with gold. He'd relieve them of their cargo, slit a lot of throats, set them afire, and send them to the bottom."

"Testy bloke," Ross allowed, feeling some excitement for the first time that evening. "Suddenly, Captain Blackhawke's letter appears to be more than the rum-sodden ramblings of a condemned man. The thing actually smacks of authenticity now, wouldn't you agree?"

"Yes. Hmm. Let me quote this chap Caracol:

"On the seventh of September of this year of our Lord, 1705, the villainous Manso de Herreras sailed from Havana Bay, embarking on a voyage to the Isle of

Brittania. I witnessed this myself. My bosun and I stood on our foredeck and watched his departure in wonder. The sun struck gold on his stern. It was a sign. His barque, the Santa Clara, was so full of gold, she was nearly foundering at the harbor mouth."

Congreve paused and puffed thoughtfully on his pipe. "Is that it?" Ross asked. "Read on, read on!"

"Yes, of course," Congreve replied. "I was just thinking that if de Herreras was bound for England, why then would he—at any rate Caracol continues:

"My bosun, Angeles Ortiz, said de Herreras was bound for London Town, where he planned to deposit the vast quantities of his ill-gotten gold in the Bank of England. Still, we were glad of seeing his stern lights and all our ship's officers raised a tumbler at table that night in hopes that we'd seen the last of him."

"But," said Sutherland, "according to Blackhawke's document here, Manso de Herreras never made it to England. He was done unto as he had done unto others apparently."

"Precisely."

"And Blackhawke's letter to his wife indicates he captured the de Herreras flagship and buried the plunder on something called Dog's Island."

"I'm not so sure of that," Congreve said, rubbing his chin. "I was just thinking that, in his letter, Blackhawke claims to have encountered de Herreras's *Santa Clara* off the island of Hispaniola, am I right?"

"Yes," Sutherland said, sipping the tea the steward had

brought in. "That's right. And if the Spaniard was bound from Havana for England, fully loaded, his fastest route would be to head straight for the Straits of Florida. Or take the safer route through the Windward Passage. So, what was he doing down off Hispaniola?"

"According to the letter, it was September," Congreve said, taking a sip of tea.

"Hurricane season."

"Hmm. The Spanish ship could easily have been blown off course and ended up down there. And Blackhawke only encountered him by sheer luck."

"And," Sutherland said, "once Blackhawke had claimed this prize, he would be carrying an enormous amount of booty around with him. One would think he'd want to get it ashore and buried as quickly as possible."

"Exactly my thinking, Sutherland," Congreve said, rising from his chair and going to one of the maps taped above the desktop. He stood there with his back to Sutherland, small puffs of white smoke rising above his head like Indian smoke signals. He seemed to stand there for hours, puffing away, hmm-ing and a-ha-ing till Ross could stand it no longer.

"Find anything?" Sutherland asked his colleague's back.

"Perhaps," Congreve said. "Do you play much golf, Ross?"

"Golf?" Sutherland was dumbstruck. He knew his boss at the Yard hated any physical activity. Still, he was a fanatic about the sport of golf. Ross couldn't imagine a less appropriate time to discuss it. "Complete duffer, but I do enjoy an occasional round, Chief."

"Pity. Marvelous old game. I myself am somewhat

obsessed with it, I'm afraid. Having never managed a hole in one at my age often keeps me awake at night. I dream about . . . never mind. Come over here a second, will you?"

Sutherland went to stand beside Congreve. The chief was standing before the oversized printout of what historically had been the island of Hispaniola. Now, of course, the western end of the island was called Haiti. The eastern and much larger portion was the Dominican Republic.

"Alex, naturally enough, has been looking for a *small* island," Congreve said, staring at the image on the wall. He had a small laser pointer in his hand.

"Yes, well, Dog Island would certainly lead one in that direction."

"But I have a hunch we should be looking for a *big* island. This very one, in fact," Congreve said, and the red pinpoint of light moved across the map. "*Here*, to be exact. This bit of coastline on the island of Hispaniola."

"But Blackhawke called it Dog's Island," Sutherland said. "Wouldn't he have called it by its name at the time? Hispaniola?"

"One would assume," Congreve said. "But look. A careful reading of the passage has him saying '*that* Dog's island' and referring to its teeth as being 'sharp enough to rip you to bits' if you try to get ashore. He even gives his wife a stern warning. *Cave canem!*"

"Sorry, my Latin's a little rusty."

"Beware of the dog," Congreve said. "I wonder if the 'dog's teeth' might not be the vicious outcroppings of jagged coral along this coast. Sharp enough to rip the bottom out of any boat attempting to land there."

Pointing his finger at the southeastern tip of the Dominican Republic, Congreve said, "I'm talking about this bit of coastline here, Ross. There's a town here called La Romana. It's a sugar town. Thousands of acres of sugar cane. A huge refinery. Some thirty thousand employees in the fields. All owned by one family, the Hillo family."

"I've heard of them, certainly, but what does all this—"

"Please. Patience," Congreve said. "Two brothers control this vast sugar empire. The world's largest, in fact. Pepe and Paquiero Hillo. Both world-class sportsmen. Polo, hunting, and game fishing. And, of course, golf."

"Golf."

"Yes, golf. And here, just east of La Romana, they built one of the most famous golf courses in the world. It takes its name from the name the ancients gave to the rocks that line this treacherous stretch of coastline."

Congreve turned to Sutherland and smiled, raising his teacup to the bewildered man standing beside him.

"They named their golf course *Dientes de Perro*," Congreve said.

"Which means?"

"Which means, my dear Inspector Sutherland, the Teeth of the Dog."

He picked up a black marker and put a large X on the Hillos' golf course.

"By God, I think you're on to something," Sutherland said with a broad smile.

"Might be," Congreve said, puffing away, his blue eyes alight with satisfaction. "Just might be."

20
·· · — — ··

Stokely Jones was waiting for Hawke just outside customs. Stoke, a former NYPD cop, had been with him ever since Hawke's kidnapping five years ago. Gangsters from New Jersey had carjacked Hawke's Bentley at a stoplight on Park Avenue, shot his chaffeur, and abducted Alex at gunpoint. Stoke had climbed six flights of burning stairs to rescue Hawke from where the kidnappers had left him to die. The top floor of an abandoned warehouse, a blazing inferno in the Greenpoint section of Brooklyn.

Thanks largely to Stoke's determined police work, Hawke's two kidnappers went off to spend life sentences in a maximum security New Jersey charm school, and the ten million in ransom was recovered from a motel room in Trenton.

Stoke was standing there, a huge grin on his broad face, holding up a sign that said "Dr. Brown." It was their code at airports and hotels. "Dr. Brown" meant no immediate security issues.

"Dr. Brown has come to town!" Hawke said, dropping his small duffel bag and flinging an arm around the man's massive shoulders. To say that Stoke was about the size of your average armoire would be an understatement.

Stoke had managed to have a fairly checkered career in his young life. A judge in the South Bronx had given him two choices. The slam on Riker's Island or the U.S. Navy.

Stokely Jones had joined the latter, eventually winding up in San Diego at the Navy SEAL Training Center. Out on Santa Catalina, where the SEAL teams practiced using their munitions, he discovered a love of jumping out of airplanes, swimming huge distances underwater, and blowing things up. He became an expert in underwater demolition and search-and-seizure operations.

Stoke ended up as the legendary leader of the legendary SEAL Team Six. Six was the most elite and deadly of the SEAL teams, a top-secret counterterrorist unit founded by another Navy legend, the baddest of the bad, Richard Marcinko.

Needless to say, when Stoke left the Navy and joined the NYPD, he was one of the toughest rookies ever to walk a beat. He was still massive, and still took exceedingly good care of himself. He worked for Hawke, but in his heart, he was and always would be a Navy man.

"My man," Stoke said, "look at you! Got yourself a tan! Why, you brown as a berry! What you been doin' down in them islands?"

"Let's just say that in the course of my current assignment, I was able to catch the occasional ray," Hawke said, laughing. He picked up his bag and followed Stoke through the revolving doors.

"Well, get ready for changes in latitude, bossman," Stoke said over his shoulder, " 'cause you 'bout to freeze your skinny white ass off!"

He knew it might be a bit cool, still the sting of icy air took his breath away. December in Washington was usually just wet and chilly, but this was seriously cold weather. Under his flight suit, which had burned up in the fire, he'd been wearing nothing but khaki shorts, a Royal Navy T-shirt, and flip-flops. Mistake.

Flip-flops weren't all that ideal for icy puddle-hopping,

Hawke discovered following Stoke through the maze of snow-laden cars in the parking lot.

"So. Tell me. How was your flight, boss?"

"A little unexpected turbulence on the first leg. I'll tell you all about it later."

"So we going straight to the State Department," Stoke said. "Conch called on the car phone and said it was urgent. Said bring your ass over there as soon as humanly possible."

Stoke unlocked the doors to the beat-up black Hummer and climbed behind the wheel. For a Hummer, the car was deliberately unassuming. The fact that there was a turbocharged four-hundred- horsepower engine up front and that the entire body of the car was armor-plated was hidden by a disguise of dust and dents. The banged-up Virginia vanity plates on the Hummer read:

HUM THIS

Hawke opened the passenger side door and climbed in. He was hugging himself, shaking with cold. "Right, then. State Department," he said, his words forming puffy white clouds of vapor that hung before his face. "And step on it."

"You got it," Stokely said, downshifting and roaring out of the parking lot.

"Any danger of getting some heat in here, Stoke?"

"Chill a minute, brother," Stoke said.

"Oh, I *am*, I am chilling. I can assure you that much," Hawke said, his teeth literally chattering.

"Hell happened to your arm?" Stoke asked, noticing the bandage.

"I cut myself shaving," Hawke said, and Stokely just looked at him. Man said some crazy shit sometimes. Funny, but crazy.

"Good old Foggy Bottom, coming up," Stoke said, stepping on the gas.

"Well," Hawke said, settling back in his seat now that a blast of hot air was coming up from under the dashboard. "You look chipper, Stoke. Fine fettle, I must say."

"Hell does that mean, 'fine fettle'?"

"It means you look fit, Stoke, that's all. In good form. Are the decorators all out of the new house?"

"Yeah, they out. None too soon for me, I'm telling you something. I ain't had lots of experience with no decorators, but what I just had is plenty. Kinda shit we talk about at lunch? You ever heard of cerulean blue, boss? Me, either. But it's serious blue. Nothing candyass like robin's egg blue, you understand. Cerulean blue is darker, more like cobalt when it's done. Anyway, that's your bedroom."

"Cerulean."

"That's it, boss. But this is one prime piece of real estate you got now. Man, wait till you see it. I still haven't figured out all the security shit."

"That's reassuring. You being chief of security and all that."

"No, man, I got most of it down. But this is some major high-tech shit you got goin' on now. Hell, we got so many TV monitors 'round that house, our *monitors* has monitors! Know how they call the house The Oaks?"

"That's been its name for two hundred years."

"Well, my thought is we oughta change it. We oughta call it The Monitors. Got a hell of a lot more monitors than we got oaks."

"It's a thought."

"So. Whassup? We chillin' 'round here tonight or you flyin' back to the Bahamas or wherever?"

"Spending tonight here," Hawke said. "First night in the new house. I hope Pelham has seen to the flowers. Vicky will probably be—joining me there tonight."

"Vicky? You still messin' with that chick? Man, you are something else."

"In what sense?" Hawke asked as Stoke turned into the underground garage. At the security booth, the guard leaned into the car, saw Hawke holding up his pass, and, smiling, waved them in.

"In the sense that you don't ever understand nothing about women." Stoke pulled the Hummer into a space and shut it down. "For instance, you got a perfectly good woman upstairs waiting for you, totally in love with your ass. Now, you chasing around with Vicky."

"So?"

"I don't know. What's going on with Conch?"

"What do you mean?"

"I mean, well, maybe you still working in there, too, is all I'm saying."

"I'd never do that, Stoke," Hawke said, reaching for the door handle. "It wouldn't be chivalrous."

"Chivalrous? Oh, yeah. I forgot. Wouldn't be chival-rous."

"Are you coming in?"

"No, I ain't coming in that building. That place spooks me. All them chivalrous white people running around wearing them little polka-dot bow ties and shit. Place is spooky."

"Matter of fact, I'm meeting a couple of spooks. That's why I'm here," Hawke said, smiling at Stokely. "I'll be about an hour, if you want to go get yourself something to eat."

Stoke watched Hawke walk away.

Spooks?

Is that what the man said? Wasn't very damn chivalrous, now, was it?

21

Spooks, here I come.

Hawke was still grinning at Stoke's obvious misinterpretation of the word when the elevator arrived. He showed his badge to the stoic marine twins at the metal detector, and passed through into the elevator.

Reaching the top floor, the very kingdom of spookdom, Hawke returned the salutes of two more marines standing duty by the double doors to the secretary's outer office. Both wore odd expressions, he thought, until he looked down at his own wardrobe.

Marines, apparently, were unaccustomed to visitors wearing flip-flops.

"Ah. Yes. Just flew up from the Bahamas," he said as one of the marines pulled the door open. "Called the secretary from the plane. Wanted me to come directly from the airport. No time to change, you see."

Entering the outer office, now feeling self-conscious about his appearance, he thought he saw a familiar face behind the reception desk.

"Sarah?" he said hopefully. Sarah? Sally? "It's Alex Hawke. Remember me?"

A pretty, heavyset woman in her mid-forties looked up into his face. "Good Lord," she said. "I mean, why, Lord Hawke! Well. What a surprise! I certainly don't have you down in my book this early! Wonderful to see you, your lordship!"

Hawke started to say something, then bit his lip. He'd always found his title a little embarrassing and off-putting. He allowed no one to use his title except his butler, Pelham, who threatened to quit if he could not use his employer's proper title. Still, this was hardly a time to press the issue.

"And you as well, Sarah," Hawke said. "Now, look at you. You've changed your hair. It's most becoming, I must say."

"And look at *you*," Sarah said, fighting the pink flush she knew was rising up her throat. "You look—"

"Dreadful," Hawke said. "I know. Sorry. I just flew in, actually. Your boss insisted I come here straightaway so I had no time to, you know, tidy up."

"They must be expecting you, Lord Hawke," Sarah said. "Please go right in."

The double mahogany doors swung open and Hawke strode into the secretary of state's office.

"Hello, good looking! *Bienvenidos!*" the secretary said, moving toward him with her slender arms outstretched. She was tall and elegantly dressed. Something from Paris, Hawke guessed. Her glorious hair fell in a blue-black curtain to her shoulders.

Consuelo de los Reyes, only in office a few months, was already the most photographed secretary of state in history. You were just as likely to see her on the cover of *W* or *Vanity Fair* as on the cover of *Time*. Alex embraced his old friend and inhaled the familiar perfume.

"The new secretary, herself. You look absolutely gorgeous, Conch," Alex said.

"And you look absolutely ridiculous, Hawke."

Despite the wardrobe, she still found him impossibly attractive. Six-three and right around 180 pounds. The wavy black hair, going the slightest bit gray at the temples. The bushy black eyebrows over those intense blue eyes. The imperiously straight nose above the firm lips, the constant hint of mischief in the grin lurking around the mouth. In that cursory appraisal, she instantly remembered why she'd fallen so hard.

"Reporting as ordered, sir." Hawke grinned, executing a snappy salute. "Straightaway from the airport. Your assistant said you told her to, quote, 'get his ass over here.' "

"Yeah, well, pardon my effing French. I haven't got all that bureaucratic protocol crap down yet, but I'm working on it."

"Suggestion. Don't ever get it down."

Conch smiled. "Bingo. So you flew up here in that get-up?"

"The marines outside considered it quite a fashion statement. Not the foggiest what that statement is, nonetheless a statement."

"Let's see," she said, rubbing her chin and eyeing him carefully. "I would call it Haute Margaritaville, as a matter of fact. Cute. Wildly inappropriate, but cute."

The secretary was a huge fan of the American singer Jimmy Buffett. She'd gotten Alex hooked on him to the point where he now played Buffett CDs aboard his yacht and in his planes constantly. His current favorite, he noticed, was now playing softly in her office. "Beach House on the Moon."

"Do me a small favor, Conch?"

"Name it."

"Turn up 'Beach House' just a smidge?"

"No way," she whispered. "And, please. I know it's difficult but try and act professional. I'm the secretary of state now, Alex."

Hawke smiled at her. "Oh, right. I forgot."

"Yeah, well. Next time you see your pal the president, tell him to stop playing grabass with me every time I'm alone with him in the Oval Office, okay?"

"Yes, Madame Secretary."

The secretary's family, de los Reyes, was one of the oldest sugar families in Cuba. They'd lost thousands of acres when Fidel entered Havana, and the secretary's father had moved his whole family to Key West. Bought a large Victorian just across the road from Truman's Little White House. Consuelo had grown up a true citizen of the Conch Republic, bonefishing, drinking beer, swearing like a sailor.

After earning her doctorate in political science at Harvard, and before entering politics, Conch had taken a few years off. Returning to her beloved Florida Keys, she'd become one of the best bonefishing guides in the islands. Hawke had spent a week under her tutelage at Islamorada Key and fallen for her almost immediately.

In addition to being the most beautiful woman he'd

ever known, she could spot the mere shadow of an elusive bone sliding over the shallows at sixty yards. After a glorious week in the Keys, fishing the flats, drinking beer, and listening to Buffett while the sun went down, he was hooked. That was all long ago, but it was a time neither of them had forgotten, nor were they likely to forget.

Conch took Hawke by the hand and led him across an expanse of richly colored Aubusson rug to the large windows overlooking the Lincoln Memorial. It was still snowing, but you could see the majestic structure where Lincoln sat.

"I see you've moved your office," Hawke said.

"I did," she replied. "To be able to see my hero over there. He helps me, Alex, I promise you. Now, let me introduce you to my colleagues."

They entered a small anteroom the secretary often used for meetings like this one. On a large silk brocade sofa, two men unfamiliar to Hawke were seated, sipping coffee. Both stood up as they approached, and Consuelo did the introductions.

"This is Alexander Hawke, gentlemen. An old fishing buddy of mine. Alex, this is Jeremy Tate from the CIA and Jeffrey Weinberg, the deputy secretary of defense for nuclear matters. Both of them have been wetting their pants at the idea of meeting you."

Both men uttered small coughing noises at this remark and stuck their hands out.

Alex shook hands with Weinberg, then Tate. The CIA chap had small eyes set in a porcine face. Aggressive type, Hawke thought, withdrawing his hand from Tate's grip before any fingers were broken. Weinberg was tall, thin, and bushy-browed, looked like a rumpled academician from Harvard come to Washington with the new administration. Which is exactly what he was.

"What's this? The latest from Savile Row?" Tate said, smirking at Hawke's odd outfit. "I've always admired the British flair for understated elegance."

Hawke had taken an instant dislike to the man. He ignored the comment and turned to Weinberg.

"What, exactly, do you do, Mr. Weinberg?"

"He's a bomb baby-sitter," Tate said.

"That's not far from the truth," Weinberg said, smiling. "I keep track of all our nuclear weapons, making sure every single one is under the command and control of the president."

"Don't fall for this false modesty bullshit, Alex," Consuelo said. "He also monitors every single nuclear weapon possessed by any nation on earth. It is his primary task to identify and locate any weapon that may have fallen into the hands of terrorists. He's the one that noticed a Borzoi had disappeared."

"And once you've located them, what then?" Hawke asked Weinberg.

"I develop techniques and strategies to seize or neutralize such weapons. I believe the use of a nuclear weapon is a sin against humanity. I'm the lucky guy in charge of global sin prevention."

"I think I may have found you a whole boatload of sinners, Mr. Weinberg," Hawke said. "Shall I begin?"

"Yes, of course," Secretary de los Reyes replied. "Sit down, please, everyone. Coffee, Alex?"

"This Fiji water is fine, thank you," Hawke said, pulling up a side chair and sitting down. He looked at each of them in turn before he started speaking.

"Yesterday afternoon, on Staniel Cay in the Exumas, I met with two Russian arms dealers. Based on information I've gathered since receiving the assignment, I felt they might be very helpful," Hawke began. The CIA fellow pulled out a notebook and pen and started noisily turning the pages of his book. Hawke stared at him until he looked up. "Ready?" Hawke asked.

"Sure. Sorry," Tate said, but he didn't look it.

"Their names are Golgolkin and Bolkonski. The former being the one who did all the talking. Both are ex-Navy, Soviet Submarine Command at Vladivostok, childhood friends, classmates at the Academy. Am I going too fast for you?"

"No, no," Tate said. "Go ahead."

"I was shown a portfolio of weapons for purchase which I can describe in detail should anyone want to hear it. Soviet scuds, scud launchers, SAM-7's, hovercraft. All the usual hardware and materiel, I can assure you."

"Submarines?" Weinberg asked.

"No. I had to make that request specifically," Hawke replied. "I told them I was interested in purchasing an Akula-class bomber."

"You mean 'boomer,' " Tate said.

"No. I mean bomber. You call them boomers. In the Royal Navy, we call them bombers."

"Whatever. And what did the Russkies say?" Tate asked.

"They said they had an Akula. 1995-vintage Typhoon. Fifty million, half up front, half on delivery. Six months to get the vessel seaworthy and assemble a trained crew. Then delivery to the specified location."

"I'm wondering," Weinberg said. "Did you get any sense at all for whom they might be working?"

"None," Hawke said. "I got the feeling they were independent agents. Of course, I could be wrong. Obviously, there's some kind of infrastructure behind them. What they do is a bit more complicated than selling used autos."

"What happened next, Alex?" the secretary asked.

"I told them I really wasn't interested in the Akula I. I really wanted a Borzoi. They denied any knowledge of such a craft. After a bit of unpleasantness, they admitted the possibility that such a submarine might be purchased. I invited them aboard *Blackhawke* to continue negotiations. You're looking for a Borzoi, these are your guys, all right."

There was a heavy silence in the room. The secretary of state looked at Weinberg and mouthed the word *bingo*.

"*Blackhawke?*" Tate asked.

"My yacht," Hawke said.

"Of course," the CIA man said. "Your *yacht*."

"Quite. I invited them to join me for dinner. I showed them the money provided me by your CIA station man in Nassau. After dinner, I invited them on a tour of the yacht. It was then that I offered them an immediate five million in earnest money if they met my conditions."

"Good strategy, Alex," the secretary said. "Bait the hook immediately."

"Thank you. I told them I wanted a guaranteed six-month delivery. I wanted to personally inspect the boat before any commissioning took place. And, finally, as the secretary and I discussed, I said that I wanted to speak directly to their last purchaser as a confirming reference."

The two men and Consuelo de los Reyes leaned forward to hear what he had to say next.

"How did they respond?" the secretary asked.

"They refused to reveal any names, of course. But, after a little, how shall I put it, *prodding,* they reconsidered."

"Tell me. What did you find out, Alex?" the secretary asked, lines of anxiety forming around her eyes.

"That payment for the last submarine Mr. Golgolkin sold was wire-transferred to Golgolkin's numbered account in Switzerland—"

"When would that have been?" Weinberg asked.

"He claims about six months ago."

"Shit," Tate said. "It's on its way."

"Maybe," Weinberg said. "Maybe not. Things happen to schedules. Anyway, please continue, Mr. Hawke. This is very good stuff indeed."

"According to our boy, Golgolkin," Alex continued, "the money was wired from a bank in Miami. The Sunstate Bank."

"Were you able to get the account name?" Weinberg asked. He was leaning forward, excitement plain on his face.

"As a matter of fact, I was. The money was wired from an account in the name of *Telaraña.*"

"*Telaraña,*" the secretary said, standing and moving to the window. "Unbelievable!" She gazed out at the swirling snowfall. "Look out this window, Mr. Tate. See it? There goes your pan–Islamic jihad theory."

Jeremy Tate frowned and sat back in his chair. It occurred to Hawke that he seemed almost disappointed to discover that the combined nations of Islam weren't purchasing a weapon capable of killing millions.

"You've heard of this *Telaraña,* I take it, Madame Secretary?" Weinberg said. "I have not."

"Oh, yes," she said. "You're damn right I've heard of *Telaraña*. A coterie of generals at the very top of Castro's ladder. Three brothers, all dirty. Cocaine cowboys. I ordered our Cuban station to get all over them like white on rice, starting six months ago when we started getting sporadic tips of a possible coup. They take their name from a small island fortress they've been pouring tens of millions into. *Telaraña*. It means 'the spider's web.'"

"Sounds like these guys wouldn't be much of an improvement over the status quo, Madame Secretary," Weinberg said.

"Remember the old Cold War expression about dealing with the Russians?" de los Reyes asked. "'Two steps forward, three steps back'? Should *Telaraña* successfully topple Castro, we would be looking at three steps backwards followed by three hundred steps backwards."

"How'd you get all this stuff out of them?" Tate asked.

"Let's say the Russians were encouraged to be forthcoming in our conversations," Hawke said. "I didn't hurt them, just scared them a bit. I might add that they didn't take it very well."

"What do you mean?" the secretary asked.

"I mean this little chap Bolkonski, a dead ringer for the mad monk, Rasputin, tried to kill me. Twice, actually."

"Both unsuccessful attempts, obviously," Tate said.

Alex looked at the man and held his eyes for a long moment before speaking. "This *Telaraña*. Anyone you know personally, Conch?" Alex asked.

"Not personally, no," the secretary replied. "It's basically the mafia. The Cuban-version mafia at any rate. The personal narcofiefdom of Cuba's top generals. They've built a huge military installation on an island just off Manzanillo. *Telaraña* is built on the site of one of the rebel general's *haciendas.*"

"But of course you knew that," Hawke said, smiling at Tate.

"All right, all right," Conch said, quickly riding over the obvious animosity between Tate and Hawke. "Here's what we're going to do. I want immediate U-2 and Predator surveillance flights over the entire southwest coast of Cuba. I want a twenty-four-hour bird in the sky snapping pictures and gathering thermals of the *Telaraña* complex."

"No problem," Weinberg said.

"How many guys do we have on the ground in Cuba, Jeremy?" she asked Tate.

"A ton in Havana," Tate said. "Out in the sticks, *nada.*"

"Rectify that. Like, today. I want our people fucking crawling all over Oriente province."

"Right. And I'll get us on the president's calendar immediately," Tate said.

Conch looked at him until he literally squirmed.

"Unless, of course, you'd rather handle that one personally, Madame Secretary?" Tate said.

She ignored him. "Good job, Alex. The president will be delighted to get this off his 'to do' list."

"This Borzoi, it's that bad, huh?" Tate asked.

"Our worst nightmare. Borzoi is huge," Weinberg said. "She carries forty warheads, twenty on each wing. All sharp angles and planes, so no round surfaces to bounce back radar or sonar. Coated stem to stern with a three-foot-thick coating of some new absorptive substances the Russians developed. Vastly superior to the old Anechoic rubbercoating."

"What's that do?" Tate asked.

"Well, it means she's virtually invisible to sonar, radar, you name it. She's also got what's commonly called a 'decoupling' coating, which dramatically reduces the amount of sound she puts into the water. She was going to be the Soviets' last-ditch effort in an Armageddon showdown with the U.S. Navy."

"A desperate come-from-behind finish," Tate said, rubbing his chin.

"And now this nightmare contraption is in the hands of some very unstable Cubans," Conch said, getting to her feet and walking over to the window overlooking Lincoln's memorial. "Sweet Jesus."

Snow had become a hard sleeting rain beating against the windowpanes of Dr. Victoria Sweet's two-hundred-year-old brick townhouse. In her ground-floor office, a crackling fire kept the chill outside at bay. It was late afternoon, and the gray light was fading rapidly from the skies of the nation's capital, especially the snowy, tree-lined streets of Georgetown.

Still, the woman lowered the light from the red-shaded lamps by the couch where the man was lying, and said, "Enough light?"

"It's fine, thank you."

She pulled a chair closer to the couch and sat down, crossing her long legs. There was the faintest whisper of silk on silk as she did so.

"Comfy?" she asked.

"Quite."

"Then let's begin, shall we?"

"Yes, Doctor."

"What would you like to talk about today?"

"My addiction."

"Addiction? I wasn't aware that you had one."

"Neither was I. Until quite recently, that is."

"Are we talking about drugs? Food? Alcohol?"

"We are talking about sex."

"Sex?"

"Yes. I've discovered I'm a sex addict."

"I see. And how did you come by this amazing discovery?"

"I'm constantly overwhelmed with . . . thoughts. Day and night. I can't sleep at night. I can't function by daylight."

"These thoughts. Can you describe them?"

"Some of them. Others—"

"All right. Let's begin with the ones you're comfortable describing."

"Well, a recent one, then. I'm in your office, lying on the couch, and there's a fire in the fireplace. It's early evening. It's sleeting outside, you can hear icy pellets beating against the windowpanes and—"

"Wait a minute. *My* office?"

"Yes."

"And where am I? Am *I* in your dream?"

"Yes. You've turned the lights down, so most of the light comes from the fire. I can see its shadows flickering on the ceiling above my head."

"And where am I?"

"You've pulled up a chair next to the couch. My eyes are closed but I hear you. You've crossed your legs. I hear a rustle of silk when you do it and open my eyes. I try to catch a glimpse of—"

"Yes?"

"You know. When you cross them, I try to see."

"What I'm wearing, you mean. Underneath my skirt."

"Yes."

"And in the dream, do you see?"

"No. I see nothing."

"But sometimes I do this. Is that part of your dream, too? What do you see then?"

"I see everything."

"In these dreams. Do I ever unbutton my blouse like this?"

"Yes. Just like that."

"Remove it? Drop it to the floor? Like this?"

"Yes."

"And you can smell my perfume when I bend over you, can't you."

"Yes. I breathe it. Deep into my lungs."

"Perhaps I kiss your mouth. Like this?"

"Yes."

"And touch you . . . here."

"Yes."

"And how does it make you feel?"

"Like I'm drowning. Like falling."

"I've missed you, Alex. So much."

"Be here, Doc."

"Yes. I'm here. I'm here now."

22

Victoria Sweet took one last look in the mirror in her front hall.

Hair? Check.

Makeup? Check.

Dress? Check.

Jewelry? Check.

Sanity? Well, maybe not, but what the hey? She was in love. She and Alex had spent a wonderful hour together earlier, and, already, she was aching to see him again. Getting dressed, she had imagined him standing before his mirror shaving, perhaps even feeling just the way she was feeling.

"Ta-da," she said to her reflection, as she slipped into her warmest winter coat and opened her front door. Stokely was out there at the curb with the engine running and, hopefully, the heat on. It had stopped sleeting finally, but the temperature was dropping.

She somehow managed to negotiate her icy walkway without ending up ass over teakettle. And there was Stokely standing on the curb, holding the passenger side door open. Holding the door open? It was *not* a Stokely thing to do.

"Evenin', Miz Vicky," he said in his best *Driving Miss Daisy* accent. "Y'all lookin' partickly fine, this evenin'. Yas'm. Y'all in partickly fine fettle *tonight* all right."

"Fine fettle?" she said, climbing in. "Let me guess where you came up with *that*." Stokely smiled, shut her door, and went around to the driver's side. He eased his big frame behind the wheel.

"*Fine* fettle, yes indeed!" he said.

"Okay, Stoke," she said. "What's all this stuff about?"

"What's all *what* stuff about?" He cranked up the Hummer and pulled out into the snowy neighborhood street. It was mercifully warm inside the bizarre vehicle.

"Oh, holding my door open," Vicky said. "All this 'shufflin' shoes and silver trays' stuff."

"Actin' on orders, is all," Stoke said, pulling away from the curb. "Bossman say jump, old Stoke, he leaps around like a long-tailed cat in a room full of rockin' chairs!" Stoke slapped his knee. "Yassuh!"

"Are you on some kind of medication, Stoke?" Vicky asked, grinning at him. "I can tell, you know. I'm a professional."

"Alex, he says, 'Stoke, you be nice to Vicky,' is all I'm sayin'," Stokely said. "So, I'm bein' nice to Vicky."

"Funny, I thought you were always nice."

"Try to be, mostly. But the boss, now he thinks I need *noodging*. That's what folks call encouragement in New York."

"*Noodging.*"

"That's it. He asked me put on this damn sport coat, just for you. Sharp, ain't it? Boss looks sharp tonight, too. Got on his tux. Man is fixated with tuxedos. Hell, wouldn't surprise me he wore one he was taking you to KFC."

"I know. Weird. Do you think he's weird?"

"Hell, everybody's weird. You ought to know that more than most folks."

Vicky nodded her head and said, "I mean, do you think he's a little bit . . . abnormal?"

" 'Course he's abnormal! Normal folks is a dime a dozen. Now, maybe I ain't the sharpest knife in the drawer, but I do know one thing. Alex Hawke is a fine man. Maybe the finest I ever knew. Rich as he is, that man will do *anything* for *anybody* at *any time*. You know what I'm sayin'?"

Vicky was silent the rest of the way, lost in thought. Stoke had taken a series of turns that brought them to the entrance of the Georgetown Club. A doorman stepped out from under the canopied walk and opened Vicky's door.

Before she got out, she said, "Thanks, Stoke. I wasn't trying to get you to say anything negative about Alex, you know. I love him, too. I just thought you could help me understand him a little better."

"I know what you're sayin'. He does act funny sometimes, way he dresses and talks and shit. Part of that whole English thing, I guess. But I think it all comes down to this. That boy is *chipper*."

"Chipper?" Vicky said, shaking her head. "Yeah, now that you mention it, he *is* chipper."

She blew Stoke a kiss and turned away to go inside. It was freezing out in the wind.

"I'm going to tell you something, Vicky," Stoke said then.

"Yes?"

"I seen 'em come and I seen 'em go. Women been chasin' Alex all his life. Ain't no thing. He never cared about one of them. Until you, I mean."

"Thanks, Stoke," Vicky said.

"See, you figured the boy out. You want to catch Alex Hawke, rule number one is you don't chase him."

"Nobody's chasing anybody here, Stoke," Vicky said. "Believe me."

"Yeah, I guess that's right. Must be the reason why he's so happy these days."

The maître d' didn't bother to look up as she approached his podium. He was new, she saw, and didn't know who she was. When he deigned to lift his head from his reservations book, he was somehow able to look down his nose at her at the same time. Even though Vicky was a good foot taller than he was.

"*Oui?*" the man said, assuming she was French for some unknown reason.

"I'm meeting someone," Vicky said. "He may be waiting."

"The name of the reservation?"

"Hawke. Alexander Hawke," Vicky said, and started a mental countdown to see how long it took the name to have its predictable effect. One point five seconds.

"*Ah, mais oui, mademoiselle! Monsieur Hawke. Oui, Monsieur Hawke, il attenderait au bar. Mais certainement!*" the man said, bowing from the waist.

He had metamorphosed from an imperious little snob into a groveling little toad in just less than three seconds. It wasn't even a world record.

"You prefer smoking or nonsmoking?" he asked.

"You're new. You probably never heard what my father said about smoking sections in restaurants?"

"*Mais non, mademoiselle.* He said?"

"He said having a smoking section in a restaurant was just like having a pissing section in a swimming pool."

He looked at her for a second, not sure if this was funny or serious.

"Monsieur, il est là," the man finally said, pointing in the direction of the bar. "You go through the door and—"

I've known where the bar is a lot longer than you have, buster, Vicky wanted to say, but she merely plucked the menu from his chubby little fingers and headed happily for the bar.

She'd been wondering why Alex had chosen the Georgetown Club. Alex had no idea how happy the choice had made her. It was her favorite restaurant in all of Washington. She still recalled the countless hours she'd spent here alone with her father, Senator Harlan Augustus Sweet. There were fireplaces in every room, all ablaze on a cold, snowy night like this. Large, overstuffed leather chairs were scattered everywhere, and the dark paneled walls were adorned with gilt-framed English landscapes and foxhunting scenes.

Coming here as a little girl had always felt like sneaking into the secret world of men. There was the intoxicating aroma of fine whisky and illegal Cuban cigars, and the clink of ice in crystal glasses. There were whispered stories she was too young for and the raucous laughter at their completion.

"Cover your ears, Victoria" was the way she knew when one of *those* was coming.

Her father, the retired United States senator from Louisiana, had been a much loved figure in these rooms. He loved a good story and could tell one better than any man. He could also drink most of them under the table and frequently, to her mother's dismay, did just that.

If the senator wasn't at his office or on the Senate floor, he was on the Chevy Chase golf course. If he wasn't on the golf course, he was here, holding down the bar at the Georgetown Club.

And his curly-haired daughter had always been the little princess by his side. Now she squeezed her way through a press of loud, cigar-smoking lobbyists and politicos and saw Alex waiting for her at the cozy little bar.

23
•••—•—••

Fidel Castro had gone pale as death.

He had not said a word in the last hour, which was fine with Manso. He still had his big black Cohiba stuck between his teeth, but had never gotten around to lighting the trademark cigar. He sat hunched against the window, staring down at his green island. His silence had become as ominous as the furious diatribe that preceded it.

Through the forward cockpit window, you could see lush mountains and valleys rushing beneath your feet. To the south, you could already see the blue waters of the Guacanayabo Bay, now tinged with the gold of the setting sun. Endless echelons of whitecaps were rolling in, row after row breaking upon the white beaches. He was almost home.

Beyond, Manso could see a pale green hump of land lying about a mile off the town of Manzanillo. The island known as *Telaraña*. He could only imagine the state his men on the ground must be in, seeing the approach of

the familiar olive-green chopper. It would signal the end
of all their endless planning and plotting. Events now
would take on a life of their own. Every move they made
would write a line in history.

Manso himself would be happy just to get this goddamn machine on the ground. His nerves were like
strings of barbed wire running from the base of his skull
down his arms to his fingers. He had a death grip on the
control stick of an aircraft that demanded a light touch.

In the last half hour, Manso had lost anything even
resembling a light touch. The chopper was pitching and
yawing as he corrected, overcorrected, and then over-
compensated for every correction.

It's like flying in combat, Manso tried to tell himself;
you have to keep your wits about you. Steel your nerves
and fly the plane. He had many happy memories of his
days as a *narco*, flying for Pablo. The Colombian army
and the *americanos* had shot up his planes many times. He
always counted the holes in his wings and fuselage once
he'd returned to one of the cartel's secret airstrips.

All the pilots considered their drug runs "combat." In
their minds they were at war with the *norteamericanos*.
The gunpowder their planes carried was white and it
killed an enemy not only willing to die, but to pay outra-
geous fortunes for the privilege. In their jungle hideouts,
they would laugh at the stupidity and poor marksman
ship of the U.S.-sponsored government soldiers.

This was just another combat mission, he told himself.

But what about when your adversary was seated only
two feet away?

"Save yourself, Manso, my son," the leader said, breaking the silence. "Tell me where this bomb is hidden, and I

will put a stop to this insanity. I will see to it that you and your family are allowed to leave the country safely."

"Too late, *Comandante.*"

"You can buy a fancy mansion in Miami and fill it with whores, just like Batista."

"It's too late for these lies, *Comandante.*"

"Lies? No. Not to you, Manso. I have always treated you as a son. I am not a father who would harm his son. No matter how disgracefully he would betray me."

"I am sorry for so much pain between us. But our country has suffered much pain in much silence for long enough. Something had to be done. Someone had to do it. I am only sorry that it had to be me."

"What exactly is it you think you're doing, Manso? Do you even know the answer to that question?"

"I am taking the first steps toward saving what is left of our beloved Cuba, *Comandante.*"

"So the son stabs the father and anoints himself savior. It's too biblical for words. Even in Hollywood they would call this shit."

"Your life will be spared. And, of course, your son, Fidelito. I promise you that. I have bought a beautiful *finca* for you in Oriente."

"You promise *me*? Your life is as worthless as your promises. You were *never* a revolutionary. You have no political philosophy, no idealism. Money is your religion. You are nothing but a highly paid killer, a terrorist. And you should kill yourself before I do. I guarantee it will be less painful."

"I learned much from Pablo during my time in the jungle, *Comandante.* Terrorism is the atomic bomb for poor people. It is the only way for poor people to strike back. The old experiment must make way for the new. The old one is over."

"For *you* it is, I can promise."

"We will be landing at *Telaraña* in twenty minutes. My guard will escort you to the main house. I have set up a television studio at *Telaraña, Comandante,*" Manso said. "After you have had some refreshments, you will be escorted to the station where you will address the nation."

"You will be hunted down like a dog and killed like one before the eyes of your family."

"You will tell them that the *revolución* has been a great political success. But, sadly, you have come to believe, not an economic one. So, after great thought, and with the good of your country at heart, you have decided to step down. It is time for a new generation of leadership."

"*Leadership?* This is a farce!"

Castro turned toward Manso and spat in his face.

Manso ignored the saliva dribbling down his cheek and said calmly, "*Sí, Comandante,* spit. Spit until you are dry. It's the only weapon you have left."

"Fool. I have the hearts of my country. I have my army. You are a dead man when this is over."

"The few remaining officers loyal to you will be imprisoned. My men are prepared to seize control of all telephone, television, and radio stations. It will happen as soon as you address the nation and announce that you are stepping aside. When I said the word *mango* over the radio, the wheels started turning."

Castro reddened. That particular song not only mocked him and his green fatigues, it said that though the mango was still green it was ripe and ready to fall down.

"And as for the hearts of our country," Manso continued, "their hearts have too long been the prisoners of their stomachs. I will feed one and so win the other."

"You are nothing. No one. I made you. I will unmake you. The country will spit you out. And then spit on your grave. Just as I spit on you now." Castro unbuckled himself, leaned over, and spat on Manso again, square in the face.

"No, *Comandante,* they will not," Manso said, ignoring the attack once more. "The entire country, like the army, is successfully brainwashed. You have erased cause and effect in the mind of the populace. You have achieved a magnificent success in that regard, no one will dispute. The result is a total lack of loyalty. Of values. Of beliefs. We could install an illiterate *jinetera,* a stupid whore, as *presidente* and the whole of the country would bow down."

"It sounds like exactly what you intend to do, Colonel Manso de Herreras. It sounds as if it is *you* who is to be the new *presidente.*"

Manso knew better than to rise to the bait.

"After you have told the nation your decision, I will speak. I will tell the people that our new government has your blessings. That we remain united against the Americans. I will name the new *presidente.* We will then be giving the *americanos* exactly thirty hours to lift the paralyzing blockade and evacuate every last soul from Guantánamo Naval Station."

"And why the hell should they listen to you, little pissant?"

"I have initiated certain reprisals if they do not."

"Idiot! The *americanos* will take any provocation as a declaration of war. They will bomb our country into a fucking parking lot. Do you understand *nothing?* Does your pitiful memory not even stretch back to the year oh-two, when the Amerians flattened what was left of Afghanistan? The Soviet traitors have left us completely exposed and vulnerable! The *americanos* have been *praying* for just such an excuse as yours!"

"The Americans will not touch us."

"May I ask why not?"

"We have purchased a weapon that will prevent any thought of reprisal. Borzoi. The most lethal submarine ever built. It was constructed by the Russians in total secrecy in the last years of the Cold War. It utilizes the American stealth technology and is completely invisible to sonar and radar. Twice the size of conventional subs. She carries forty ballistic missiles."

Castro was struck speechless.

"And we have cultivated new, powerful allies," Manso added.

"My brother Raul's trips to China?" Castro sputtered. "You are beyond stupid, Manso. You believe *anything* my brother says? The Chinese don't give a rat's ass about Cuba. Or Raul either."

"How do you know the Americans would not prefer our new government, *Comandante?*"

"You have betrayed us to the Americans?"

"My brother Carlitos and I have many friends in America, from our days working for *el doctor* Escobar in Colombia. Carlitos is a very powerful player in that world, you know."

"Carlitos is a drug-addled lunatic. Out of control. And Pablo Escobar's Mafiosi friends in America, what's left of them, are nothing but pitiful gangsters. Powerless, castrated eunuchs who sell their stories to the magazines and movies."

"Ours will not be the first government to include a few sympathetic outlaws, *Comandante*. In fact, one of them has just purchased the Hotel Nacional. He intends to create a beautiful new casino like the one of *Señor* Meyer Lansky. Our new government will welcome these investors with open arms."

"Infidel! You will have no government because you won't live long enough to preside, you filthy—"

Castro must have pulled his revolver from its holster because he now had it jammed into Manso's temple.

"It is a fitting way to end the struggle, Manso," Fidel said, his voice barely under control. "I kill the ignoble traitor who would murder our noble *revolución!*"

He pressed the gun to Manso's temple and pulled the trigger.

"The gun is empty, *jefe*," Manso said. "Don't waste your time."

Castro heard the hammer's harmless click five more times before he screamed in frustration and threw the useless weapon at Manso's head, barely missing him.

"How?" he asked.

"Don Julio," Manso said. "Your beloved manservant. This morning, very early, before we left for the dedication, he removed the cartridges while you were 'busy.' "

"Don Julio! No! He, of all men, would never betray—"

"You, of all men, should not be surprised at who any man will betray for the right amount of money, *Comandante*."

Castro lunged for the control stick and wrested control of the cyclic from Manso. He shoved it forward.

"I will go down then, Manso. But we go down together!" Castro screamed over the jet turbine engine's roar.

The helicopter instantly went into a precipitous dive. Manso screamed and fought for the cyclic. But Castro had a death grip on the control stick. The old man was ready to die, Manso could see it in his eyes. The green mountains rushed up to meet them as the chopper began its sickening death spiral.

24

Hawke was standing at the bar with a martini glass in his hand. The other hand was stuck in the pocket of his dinner jacket. Unlike those of most men she knew, Alex's hands were always naturally quiet. A good sign. A sign of inner calm, she thought.

He looked pretty good in his tuxedo. Very Mel Gibson, she decided, with his black hair slicked back in waves from his forehead and the deep tan he'd acquired down in the Caribbean. He didn't see her coming.

She planted a big wet one on his unsuspecting cheek.

"Hey, sailor," Vicky said, taking the stool next to him, "buy a lady a drink?"

Hawke smiled, and said, "Name your poison, darling."

"Yours looks lethal enough. My daddy called those 'see-throughs.' I'll have one, too," Vicky said. "Used to be, Daddy never would drink liquor he couldn't see through. Now, all he drinks is bourbon. He says gin brings out unpleasant qualities in a man. 'Loudmouth soup,' he calls it. And when he flew on an airplane, he always took a flask."

"Why?"

"He said he just plain didn't trust airplane gin."

"My beautiful girl."

"Yes?"

"Did you come here with him very often?"

"Yes. All the time. It's my most favorite place in Washington. That's why I was so surprised when you suggested it."

"I hoped you'd like it. Does your father get to Washington much?"

"I wish. Ever since he went back home to Seven Oaks, it's been tough to get him out of his rocker on the front veranda. He's got some old hunting dogs and he likes to stomp around his fields with them, looking for quail or pheasant. That's about the extent of his current travels."

"I've never been to Louisiana," Hawke said. "Perhaps we could go down and visit him sometime."

"I'd like that very much. You'd love Seven Oaks. It's smack dab on the Mississippi River, on the River Road, about twenty miles south of Baton Rouge."

"It all sounds very Scarlett O'Hara."

"A whole lot of good things in the South have gone with the wind, but not Seven Oaks. I had a heavenly childhood. There's a reason for all those stories about the Mississippi. It's a storybook river. Daddy loved politics, but he hated living in Washington. He once said that if he owned Washington and Hell, he'd rent out Washington and live in Hell."

Hawke smiled and reached across the table to squeeze

Vicky's hand. Seeing her here where she'd had so many cheerful hours with her father was wonderful.

Hawke signaled the bartender and ordered her drink.

"I'm very happy to be here with you tonight," he said, putting his hand to her cheek and caressing it.

"Funny, I was just thinking the same thing," Vicky said, trying to hide the effect his touch had on her. Her martini arrived and Hawke raised his glass.

"Who shall we toast?" Vicky asked.

"Let's see. How about Tom, Huck, and Vicky? Or was it Becky?"

"You are a total and complete piece of work, you know that, Hawke?" Vicky said, laughing. She clinked her glass against his, and said, "Cheers. I need this."

"A brutal day at the office, Doc? Anything you can talk about?"

"A new patient," Vicky said, swirling her olive around in the vodka. "Poor guy. He's suffering from an addiction. Incurable."

"Really? Odd. I should think you could cure anyone of anything. I read in *The Washingtonian,* the magazine so prominently displayed all over your reception room, that you are considered one of the best doctors in town."

"Some addictions are best left untreated. Let me borrow your pen, honey."

Hawke pulled a slim gold pen from his inside pocket.

"Thanks," Vicky said, and began scribbling all over the menu. Female behavior at times *was* mystifying, as he'd told Stokely on the way in from the airport. But then again, as a woman, he supposed she was entitled.

"*Monsieur* Hawke," the obsequious little maître d' said, "your table is ready."

He followed Vicky into the small dining room, unable to take his eyes off the movement of her body under the swishing red silk skirt. Pleats. What *was* it about pleats?

When they'd been seated, the waiter arrived. He was an ancient white-haired gentleman wearing white gloves.

"Why, good evening, Mr. Hawke! You too, Miz Vicky," he said. "Lord, I haven't seen you since you was a little thing. Look at you! You grown into a beautiful woman."

"Herbert! I can't believe you're still here."

"I can't either, Miz Vicky. I just turned ninety-two years old today and still going strong."

"Happy Birthday! Alex, Herbert was a great friend of Daddy's and always took care of me when I came here."

"I imagine he did," Hawke said, rising to shake the old fellow's hand. "He's certainly taken good care of me. Happy Birthday, Herbert."

"Thank you, suh. You know, Miz Vicky," Herbert said, "this old place ain't ever been the same since your daddy left town. I still remember him playing the piano and telling his jokes. Have everybody in the place laughing."

"And you used to let me slide across the parquet dance floor in my socks. It was just like ice skating."

"Lord, we had us a good time, didn't we?" Herbert said, a smile lighting up his soft brown eyes. "Can I bring you all something more to drink?"

"That would be great, Herbert," Vicky said. "Two Ketel One martinis straight up, please."

After the elderly waiter left, there was a long silence in which Hawke simply sat there staring at her. Vicky was not one easily embarrassed by silences at the table, but the intensity of his stare finally got to her. She noticed that he still had his right hand stuffed into the pocket of his dinner jacket.

"Gun in your pocket, big boy? Or, you all just happy to see me?" she asked, unable to think of anything more original.

"No gun," he said. "Just this." He pulled a small black velvet box out of his pocket and placed it on the table. He saw the look in her eyes, and said, "Don't worry, Doc, it won't bite. Open it."

She reached for the velvet box. "Oh, Alex, I—"

"Miz Vicky?" The waiter had somehow reappeared at their table.

"Yes?" Vicky said. "What is it, Herbert?"

"My apologies for disturbing you all," Herbert said, "but there is a telephone call for Dr. Sweet. The gentleman said it was urgent."

She looked at Alex. "Oh, Alex, I'm so sorry. I have to take it. It could be one of my patients, an emergency."

"Of course you should take it," Alex said, standing up as she pushed her chair back. "I understand completely."

"Order me something yummy, will you? Whatever you're having."

Alex picked up the menu she'd been scribbling on at the bar. For a moment he couldn't figure out what she'd been writing and then he saw it. She'd been correcting all the French errors. There was a note at the bottom, in French, addressed to the maître d'. It suggested that he take a crash course at the nearest Berlitz school before handing out any more mangled menus.

Alex smiled. He'd taken an instant dislike to this new chap they'd put at the gate. Disliked him despite the fact that Hawke was quite sure he wasn't remotely French.

"That was quick," he said, standing when Vicky returned and took her seat. She picked up the little black box she'd left on her empty serving plate.

"Hmm," she said, looking from the box to Alex and back to the velvet box.

"Yes, hmm," Alex replied.

"Weird. There was no one there, Alex," she said, smiling and brushing a wing of auburn hair away from her eyes.

"No one there?"

"No."

"Well, they'd hung up, then?" Hawke asked, lines of worry suddenly furrowing his brow. "Been disconnected."

"I don't think so, Alex," Vicky said. "I could hear breathing at the other end. It's so strange. I was thinking, none of my patients would have any idea of how to reach me here. I've got my cell phone, but of course you can't have it on in here."

"I'm sure it's just a mistake."

"It didn't sound like a mistake, Alex," Vicky said. "It sounded horribly deliberate. Almost like—"

She never finished her sentence.

A brutal explosion rocked the room. The sound and force of the shock wave hit instantaneously. Watches and clocks stood still. Time itself stopped and was exploded into countless pieces of flying glass, masonry, and human agony.

Alex found that he was no longer seated at a small, round table talking to Vicky. He seemed to be on his back, staring up into a roiling white fog. A fog that smelled more like harsh, choking smoke. There were cries and moans coming from all around him. He was aware of a jabbing pain in his shoulder and tried to roll away from it.

It got worse. He seemed to be lying on a bed of broken glass and cutlery. He held his hands up before his face and saw that they were sticky and bright red. He felt it might be a good thing to get out of there. He just wasn't sure where he was. He heard a woman's voice nearby, whimpering. He recognized it. It was Vicky.

"Doc?" he said, but there was no reply.

The acrid smoke was so thick now, he couldn't see where any of the cries were coming from. He couldn't see anything at all.

He got to his hands and knees and started crawling over the glass in the direction he thought her voice came from.

"Vicky," he shouted. "Vicky!" That's when he heard her.

"Alex, it hurts," the voice said. "I'm cold. Where's Daddy? Where's my daddy?"

And then the voice stopped.

25

• • • — — • •

"Christ, it's hot," Congreve said to Sutherland. "Hotter than the bloody Exumas, if that's not a physical impossibility."

"You could probably take off that blue blazer without offending the local citizenry," Ross said.

Ross wasn't exactly sure what an actual "harrumph" sounded like, but it had to be something similar to what emerged from Congreve's direction.

It was ten o'clock Saturday morning. The temperature had already climbed into the nineties.

They were in Nassau. And time had not been kind to Nassau.

An invasion of giant cruise ships, disgorging their legions of T-shirt shoppers, had laid waste to old Nassau Town. Straw markets and lazy little shops on Bay Street had been replaced with cheap souvenir emporiums full of worthless gewgaws. American fast food outlets had replaced the clubby little Bahamian restaurants. Every-where he looked, Ross saw to his dismay that the island had succumbed completely to the dollar.

"Well, Ross, you were quite right. This *is* a lovely spot," Congreve said, straining to be heard over the angry buzz of motorbikes careening through the crowded streets. He and Ross were negotiating their way along Bay Street, dodging the hordes of invading Americans as best they could.

Inspector Sutherland had flown them up at first light in Hawke's little seaplane. Mechanics aboard *Blackhawke* had worked through the night to repair the damage done by the missile and the ensuing fire. Ross had risen at dawn, gone to the hangar for an inspection, and pro-nounced *Kittyhawke* airworthy.

"Must you fly so bloody low over the water, Ross?" Ambrose had asked, once they were airborne. "We're not exactly a pair of jet jockeys sneaking in under the radar screen, after all."

"Sorry, Chief," Ross had said, pulling back on the stick

and gaining altitude. "I thought you might actually think it was fun."

Fun? There was nothing remotely *fun* about being sealed in an aluminium tube that might plunge from the heavens into the briny depths at any moment.

Now, having made it to Nassau alive, the two Scotland Yard detectives were decidedly lost. The house they were looking for was supposedly on this small street. They'd turned right off of Bay Street onto Whitehall Road as directed. After the blistering sun and crowded sidewalks of Bay Street, they found themselves plunged into shade. The road was choked with overhanging banyan trees. Birds of every hue sang from the branches. Multicolored oleanders and orchids and falling blossoms of frangipani filled the air with narcotic fragrances.

"I've never ventured into an actual South American rainforest, Sutherland," Congreve announced, "but I imagine it to be a vast sunny plain compared to Whitehall Road."

The trip to Nassau had been planned the evening before. The two detectives had spent a long frustrating day with the files pertaining to the murder of Alex's parents.

The CID files had yielded a few names of officers and detectives who'd worked the case here in Nassau, but all of them seemed to be either dead or retired. Endless phone calls, countless dead ends. They'd almost given up the angle when Ross had noticed a faded signature at the bottom of the police report.

"Hold on, what's this?" Ross asked.

Congreve leaned over to take a look. "Just some ordinary policeman by the looks of it. The signature is so smudged and faded, you can't even make it out. Believe me, I've been over it with a magnifying glass a thousand times."

"Well, it's our last shot. Let's see if we can't enhance it enough to get something out of it."

Ross scanned the document into the computer. He then used a program called Photoshop to enhance the entire image. After long minutes of fiddling with it, and endless hemming and hawing by Congreve, he had it. A legible signature suddenly appeared.

Officer Stubbs Witherspoon.

The signature belonged to an obscure member of the Nassau Constabulary, probably now dead or long retired.

"Here's a thought, Ross. Why don't we just ring Nassau directory information? Maybe the old fellow still has a listing." In short order, they had Witherspoon's home number from Bahamian information. Both holding their breath, they dialed the number on the sat phone.

Someone picked up the phone on the first ring and said, "Stubbs Witherspoon."

Mr. Stubbs Witherspoon, upon hearing what the English detective was interested in, had immediately invited them to Nassau. He had told Congreve to look for number 37 Whitehall Road. He had said it was a pale pink house, with blue shutters and that he'd find an arched gate covered with white bougainvillea. It had all sounded simple enough when Congreve had been standing on the bridge of *Blackhawke* writing it down.

Now he and Ross had been up one side of the street and down the other three times.

"If you wish to pay a visit to someone in this road,

you'd better arrive armed with a machete," Congreve said, using his sodden handkerchief to mop his brow.

"Perhaps we should go somewhere and ring him up, Chief," Ross said. "It's already gone half past ten."

And that's when a woman magically appeared from the dense shrubbery pushing a baby carriage.

"I wonder if you might help us," Congreve said. "We're in a bit of a fog here, you see. We're looking for number 37 Whitehall Road. Can you possibly steer us in that direction?"

"Why, number 37 is right here," she said, smiling. "You standing right in front of it! See? Here's the gate!" With a great laugh, she pulled back a massive portion of green shrubbery and revealed an ancient arch covered in white bougainvillea. "Mr. Stubbs, he live in dere. Always has."

"Most kind of you, madam," Congreve said, tipping his hat once more. "You've been most helpful. I wish you a pleasant morning."

Ambrose and Ross pressed through the thick foliage and emerged into a lovely, well-tended garden. At the end of a short pathway stood a small pink house with blue shutters. There was an ancient white-haired man sitting on the covered porch in a rocking chair. A sleeping dog of no recognizable breed was at his feet.

"Scotland Yard!" the old fellow shouted as they made their way up his walkway. "Always get your man! Even if you do it half an hour late! Ha!"

He laughed and rose a bit unsteadily from his chair.

"I believe it's the Mounties who always get their man," Congreve said, climbing the steps and shaking the frail brown hand of Stubbs Witherspoon. The man had extended his left hand. Congreve saw that the right sleeve of his simple linen shirt hung empty from his shoulder. Somehow, the poor fellow had lost his right arm.

"My apologies for the lateness of our arrival. I'm afraid we were unable to locate your gate. May I present Inspector Sutherland, also of Special Branch at New Scotland Yard."

"You're a hard man to find, Mr. Witherspoon," Ross said, shaking hands. "Sorry we're late."

"Well," Witherspoon said, "you know, I thought about that after we hung up the phone. And then I thought, good Lord, if Scotland Yard can't find me, no one can!" He laughed again, almost doubling over. "Why don't we just step inside?" Witherspoon asked. "I've made some iced lemonade and the fans in there keep it nice and breezy."

They followed Witherspoon inside and he disappeared through a swinging door, presumably leading to the kitchen. The shuttered living room windows were all thrown open and yellow hibiscus branches were drooping inside at every window. You could hear the trills of song-birds in the trees outside as well as the yellow canary in the cage standing in the corner. Witherspoon returned from the kitchen carrying a large frosted pitcher.

"Let's all take a seat," the old man said, pouring lemonade. "This is my rocking chair. I like to rock."

"Well," Congreve said, "we're honored to meet you, Mr. Witherspoon. As I said last evening on the telephone, Inspector Sutherland and I are looking into a very old murder case. An unsolved double homicide that took place here in the islands back in the 1970s."

"Yes. Lord and Lady Hawke," Stubbs said. "Brutally murdered aboard their yacht *Seahawke*. Well, that was a bad one, I'll tell you. One of the worst I ever saw. I just joined the force at that time, no big cases under my belt. Until that one."

"Can you tell us about it, Mr. Witherspoon?"

"Better than that. I've got the entire Hawke file right over there in my desk. I dug it out last evening after your call. Sip your lemonade, I'll get it, I'll get it. Soon come."

"*I like to rock,*" Ross whispered under his breath, and Congreve broke into a big grin.

Witherspoon returned with a large cardboard box held tightly to his chest with his left hand. He sat down and looked at his two guests.

"Before I show you the file's contents, may I tell you gentlemen something? I may have still been wet behind the ears on that case, but what I did know was the name of the man responsible for the murders aboard the yacht *Seahawke.*"

"You know his *name?*" Congreve said.

26

"Hey."

"Good morning, Doc."

"What time is it?"

"I think a little after seven—wait, don't get up. You're supposed to stay in bed until the doctor comes."

"Oh. That's right. I'm in the hospital."

"Good. You haven't lost your remarkable powers of perception."

"Oh. God. I've got a terrible headache."

"I should imagine you do, darling."

"Did I have a lot to drink last night?"

"You were working your way through two rather large vodka martinis."

"That's all? Wow, what a hangover. It feels like I really got bombed."

"Bombed?"

"Why aren't you laughing? You don't get it?"

"Feeling sluggish. Slow on the uptake."

"You look awful. Have you been sitting there in that chair all night? Doesn't look very comfy."

"Me? No, no. I raced home straightaway after you were admitted to the hospital. There I cracked a bottle of champers, soaked in a long hot bath, shaved, and jumped right back into this bloody tuxedo."

"That's funny, too."

"Really? Why is that funny, too?"

"Because you're always saying 'bloody this' and 'bloody that.' "

"And?"

"And this time, your tuxedo really *is* bloody. Get it? Ouch, that hurts."

"Stop laughing. You'll kill yourself."

"I feel fine. Can I get out of here?"

"The doctor's coming by at eight when he does his rounds. I think he'll let you make a run for it if you can convince him you're feeling well enough to walk."

"What are my chances for escape?"

"Fairly good, I should say. You've suffered a mild concussion. Under those lovely bandages, you've got a number of stitches on the top of your head. Assorted contusions, scrapes, and scratches. Otherwise, fine fettle."

"How about you? Are you in fine fettle?"

"I got a fork through the hand. That's about it."

"Next time you invite me to dinner, let's order in Chinese."

"Brilliant idea. Chopsticks being a lot less dangerous than salad forks. Are you hungry? Your breakfast is on the tray in front of you."

"I can't even look at food. What's this little box thingy?"

"The nurse put it on the tray with your cereal. You were clutching it in your hand when they wheeled you into the Georgetown University emergency room."

"What is it?"

"It appears to be a small black velvet box."

"What's in it?"

"Perhaps you should open it. I gave it to you last night, before we were so rudely interrupted."

"I'm terrified of men bearing small black velvet boxes."

"Go ahead and open it, Doc. It's something I want you to have."

"Oh, Alex."

"Yes?"

"Alex, it's lovely."

"It's quite an old locket, actually. It, well, it belonged to my mother."

"It's the most beautiful thing anyone's ever given me."

"You can open it up, too. There are little heart-shaped pictures inside."

"Oh, look! It's—"

"Hard to see, I know. On the left side of the heart is my

mother and me. On the right, that's me and Scoundrel. He was a fine old dog."

"How old are you in the pictures, Alex?"

"Not more than five or six, I shouldn't think. Those were taken in England. On the beach below my grandfather's house on Greybeard Island. It was summer. Just before a bad storm. See the waves breaking?"

"Alex, I don't know what to say. It's—"

There was a knocking at the door then, just as Alex was bending over the hospital bed to kiss Victoria.

Stoke was standing in the doorway with a huge bouquet of yellow roses.

"Man, I can't leave y'all alone for twenty minutes y'all don't manage to get y'allselves all blown to shit and back."

"Hi, Stoke," Vicky said. "Those are beautiful. Thank you."

"Mornin', boss," Stoke said, handing the flowers to Vicky. "Be glad you alive, my brother. You front page news."

"Oh, God, just what I need," Hawke said, giving Vicky a kiss on her bandaged forehead and taking the *Post* from Stokely.

What he did not need at the moment was publicity. He started skimming the long article.

"It was a bomb, all right, boss," Stoke said. "Plastic. C-4. Joint was so full of dignitaries it's hard to say who it was intended for."

"Anybody killed?" Hawke asked.

"Lots hurt. Just one killed. An employee. Some cat who'd only been a waiter there for about seventy years.

Five hospitalized including you, Vicky. Your name is in there, too, boss. Says you were treated and released."

"Any group claiming responsibility?" asked Hawke.

"Nope, nobody. Hell, half of Washington was in that joint last night. Target could have been anybody. The police think it was PLO, Hezbollah, or the Mujahideen, though. Least that's what my D.C. boys are sayin' privately."

"Not a particularly bright idea on the part of our Arab friends, blowing up a Washington restaurant in the middle of peace talks," Hawke said.

"Well," Stoke said, "no actual fingers are pointed yet. Naturally, FBI, CIA, NSA, all them initials are in there now, poking around. But I hear the focus is on the PLO."

"Why the PLO?"

"Remember that Israeli commander who bombed the shit out of Arafat's West Bank headquarters last month? Boy had himself a reservation at eight o'clock. Bomb exploded at eight-thirty right beside his table."

"Was he hurt?" Alex asked.

"Lucky for him, he hadn't showed up."

"Alex?" Vicky said softly from her hospital bed.

"Yes?"

"Do you remember that urgent phone call for me?"

"Of course, Vicky."

"When Herbert showed me which of the telephone booths to take it in—"

"Yes? Go on."

"Well, I'm sure this doesn't mean anything. But when I sat down to take the call, I felt something with my foot. There was a black briefcase. It was on the floor, tucked under the little shelf where the phone sits."

"And?"

"When there was no one on the line, other than the breathing, I mean, I hung up. I picked up the briefcase figuring someone had forgotten it."

"What did you do with it, Vicky?" Alex asked, looking at her intently now.

"I handed it to Herbert on the way back to our table. A couple of minutes before—"

Alex and Stokely stared at her.

"Oh my God," she said.

"Don't jump to any conclusions, darling. I'm sure it's just a coincidence. We don't know anything about that briefcase. Now, eat your breakfast. You're getting up and out of here. Stoke, could I speak to you out in the hall for a second?"

"You think it was for *Vicky?*" Stoke said as soon as they were out in the hallway, out of earshot. "Don't make no sense at all."

"It could have been for anybody."

"Yeah. Could be political, could be mob stuff, type of clientele they got."

"The doctor said Vicky could be released this morning if she's feeling all right. I want to get her out of here."

"Say the word. What are we doing?"

"I'm going back into the room to calm Vicky down. I want you to get my pilots on your mobile and tell them to light the candle on the G-IV, we're getting out of town."

"Pilots know where they supposed to be flying to?"

"Nassau. Tell them to have my seaplane meet me at the Atlantis Marina. The doctors told me last night that

Vicky was going to need a couple of weeks' rest. And she owes herself some holiday time anyway. No better place to do that than a few weeks in the Caribbean aboard *Blackhawke*."

"How else can I help out, boss?"

"We'll figure that out when we get down there."

"We? You mean *I'm* goin'?"

Hawke nodded. "Yes. Please help Vicky get checked out of here. Then you go to her house and help her get a few of her things together. Maybe she could rest for a couple of hours. Then pick her up and meet me at the plane. Say three hours, max."

"Got it, boss. What you up to on this fine morning?"

"I've invited the secretary of state for an early breakfast at the new house. I've barely seen it myself."

"I better call Pelham and tell him to turn the perimeter alarms off. I showed him how to do it, but you know how he is. Boy is definitely not a techno-geek."

"Pelham is the definition of old school, all right. I've got to go, I'm late already. I hope the secretary isn't bringing those damn spooks with her."

Stoke decided it probably wouldn't be chivalrous to call his boss on that one. Best let that one pass.

"That bomb that got that waiter, boss?"

"Yes?"

"Decapitated his ass."

"Did they print his name?"

"Yeah. Cat named Herbert Carrington."

"Bloody hell," Hawke said, and walked back down the hallway toward Vicky's hospital room.

"The man that died last night," Hawke said, crossing

to her bed and taking her hand. "It was your friend. Herbert Carrington. I'm so sorry."

"Herbert?"

Vicky looked up at him with tears in her eyes.

"It was his birthday," she said. "Ninety-two years old and still going strong."

27

The Russian chopper plunged from the Caribbean heavens, falling, sideslipping, and twisting all at the same time. The instrument panel was a blurred nightmare of wildly spinning needles. The terrain warning alarm was howling. The screaming tail rotor blade was about to go. Without that blade, the chopper was lost.

They were moments from entering the "crescent of death," namely, the failure of forward velocity and total loss of control of the helicopter. Lose your tail rotor and the chopper begins to rotate. Because of gyroscopic action, it begins to swing like a pendulum. Your chances of crashing vertically, coming down on your skids, are reduced dramatically. Which is bad because, as Manso well knew, you might actually survive a vertical crash. But if any part of its main rotor blade touches solid ground, the chopper would just do a flaming cartwheel into the jungle.

All these thoughts went through Manso's head. In seconds it would be beyond man's, or machine's, ability to recover. They were plunging down through two thousand feet, with maybe a minute to live.

Castro's hold on the control stick was unshakable. For an ailing man in his late seventies, his grip was iron.

Manso had no choice.

He pulled the slim stiletto from the sheath attached to his right leg. He showed the Maximum Leader the blade, giving him just enough time to register what was about to happen to him and release the control stick.

"Let it go!" Manso shouted. "Now!"

"I don't negotiate with traitors!" Castro shouted back, thick white spittle forming at the corners of his mouth. "Fuck you!"

When Castro did not remove his hand, Manso jammed the blade down into his muscular thigh with all the force he could muster. Blood spurted from Castro's wound, spraying the instrument cluster and the leader's fatigues. It wasn't mortal. Manso had deliberately avoided the femoral artery. Still, sticking a blade in a man's leg down to the bone takes a lot of the fuck-you out of him.

Castro howled in pain, releasing his hold on the control stick. He looked down at his bloody leg in shocked disbelief. Manso yanked the knife out of the leader's thigh and threw it clattering to the cockpit floor between his foot pedals.

He then grabbed the blood-covered control and hauled back on it, twisting hard left. The chopper kept plunging for a few desperate seconds as Manso worked the controls, cursing and praying at the same time. There was now a big green mountain in his immediate future. With seconds to live, he wrestled the beast, twisting, tugging, pumping. His only chance was to drop the helicopter as rapidly as possible. And hope to come down vertically.

Suddenly, he felt it responding and stabilizing. He had it under control. Still breathing hard, he banked and started climbing, with the mountain still looming massively before him. Too late? His skids were brushing the treetops as Manso held back on the stick, holding his breath, his heart exploding in his chest. He was waiting for the shuddering crunch of the undercarriage hitting solid wood, which would bring him crashing into the face of the mountain.

It didn't happen.

He gained a few hundred feet of breathing room, banked hard right, and found himself in clear air. He took a peek at Castro. The man was obviously in shock. He was losing a fair amount of blood and had gone a deathly shade of gray. His eyes were cloudy, out of focus.

"*Comandante,* I will radio for emergency medical to stand by for our landing. Press your finger into the wound. Hold on. We should be on the ground at *Telaraña* in ten minutes."

He got on the radio and made the request.

"Everything okay up there, Colonel?" the tense voice in his earphones said.

"*Sí! Viva Cuba!*" Manso responded.

Castro was silent and remained so for the short balance of the flight. Ever the survivor, he'd wrapped his own belt around his thigh and cinched it tight, staunching the bleeding.

The sun was dipping below the western horizon when Manso flared up and prepared to land. A large concrete structure, only recently completed, stood astride a wide river, flowing out to the sea. Now the giant structure was bathed in pure white light. Manso had not seen it since its completion and the mere sight of it gave him enormous satisfaction.

To a spy plane or satellite it could be anything. A convention hall, a movie theater. Better yet, a ballet theater. The Borzoi ballet. This huge building would house the world's largest and deadliest submarine.

An encircled red H, newly painted on the broad, flat roof of the building marked the helicopter landing pad. As Manso hovered over it, he could see a squadron of heavily armed men forming up into a solid perimeter around the pad.

Manso turned to Castro.

"On behalf of our entire crew, let me be the first to welcome you to *Telaraña, Comandante,*" Manso said when the skids were solidly down. "You will notice a few changes since your last visit." The Maximum Leader grunted but said nothing. Two soldiers approached the helicopter at a run from either side as Manso shut down the engines. They pulled open the doors and the pilot and his passenger stepped out onto the brilliantly illuminated pad. Castro limped some twenty yards, head held high, glaring at the soldiers who ringed the chopper. No one around the perimeter said a word.

"Lower your weapons!" a defiant Fidel Castro shrieked at the soldiers. "I said lower your fucking weapons!"

Without a word, and only out of respect, every soldier lowered his gun.

"*El jefe* needs immediate medical attention," Manso said to his brother Juanito, who had come forward to embrace him. "He has lost a lot of blood."

"*Sí, mi hermano,*" Juanito de Herreras said. "The emergency medics are on the way. Welcome and well done."

Juanito called to Castro. "There is someone most anxious to speak to you, *Comandante,*" he said. "Here he comes now."

The formation of soldiers parted and allowed a man onto the pad. He strode toward Manso, Juanito, and Castro, smiling. He was young and handsome, and bore a striking resemblance to someone Castro had not seen in over thirty years.

"*Comandante,*" Manso said to Castro, "may I present the new *presidente* of Cuba?"

"*Bienvenidos,*" Fulgencio Batista said.

It was the grandson of the man Castro had overthrown more than thirty years earlier. The new *presidente* was to be Fulgencio Batista's *grandson!*

Fidel Castro shot Manso a look of palpable hatred.

This was simply more irony than he could stand.

28

•••——••

Gomez ducked inside the cool gloom of St. Mary's Cathedral. It was the Naval Air Station's oldest and most beautiful church.

It was four o'clock in the afternoon, hot as hell out in the sun, and he was supposed to be at the pistol range. He'd slept in all morning, then had a long liquid lunch and decided to blow off target practice. Brewskis and bullets don't mix, he knew that much. Hell, he had a couple of missing toes to prove it.

He'd been blowing off a lot of stuff lately. He'd even spent another few nights in the brig after a stupid fight he got into with a noncom who'd called him a dumb spic in the mess hall. He couldn't remember who'd started it, but he'd finished it. Look at it this way. He went to the brig. The noncom went to the infirmary. So, you gotta ask yourself. Who won?

Gomez walked quickly up the left side of the nave and entered the confessional booth. As soon as he was seated, the small partition opened and he could see the silhouette of Father Menendez through the screen.

"Father, forgive me, for I have sinned," Gomez said. "It has been six months since my last confession."

Gomez took a deep breath and tried to get his act together. He realized that he was literally shaking. He shook out a few Tic Tacs and popped them into his mouth. He probably smelled like a goddamn brewery. His mouth was dry as dust, too. He'd woken up feeling like a lizard lying on a hot rock.

"Have you had sex outside of your marriage?" the priest asked.

Sex?

Sex had been one of the last things on his mind for nearly a month. But this Menendez, he always wanted to hear about sex. He steered every confession that way. He always asked if you had "spilled your seed."

Gomer was worried about much more important things than screwing some *chiquita* and spilling any goddamn seed. Rita had sent him to church to talk about his drinking. His "violence." What lovely Rita peter maid didn't know was that his drinking was the result of a few *underlying problems.*

Problem, name it. Solution, beer. Secret of a happy and successful life.

The nuns at the Catholic schools he'd gone to in Miami always said you should treat your body like a temple. In the last few months, Gomez had been treating his more like an amusement park. And, lately, the combination of beer, Cuban rum, and tranks he'd been on was starting to get to him in some fairly scary ways.

He put his hands together as if in prayer and squeezed them between his knees to stop the shaking.

He began his confession.

"Father, I—" He stopped. "Father, give me a second—please. I'm praying."

And the truth of it was that he was praying.

At six o'clock on that very morning, Gomez had been sitting in his small kitchen with a gun in his mouth. He was staring out the window at the sunrise. He'd been up all night. There was an empty rum bottle on the kitchen table. A lamp cast its yellow glow on an unfinished letter to Rita and a picture of him and his family.

The barrel of the gun in his mouth tasted like the Hoppe's gun oil he remembered as smelling pretty good when he was a kid. Didn't taste all that great, however. Felt like his teeth were coated with it. Pretty goddamn ironic. This was the exact same revolver his grandfather carried at the stupid Bay of Pigs. Grandpa gave the gun to Gomez upon his graduation from St. Ignatius High School. The pistol held six bullets. Gomez had loaded one bullet into the cylinder and spun it a few times.

He had already pulled the trigger four times unsuccessfully.

Click. He pulled it again.

Nada.

How lucky can one guy get? Five pulls, five misses? *Five out of five? Nada?* Come on. Nobody got that lucky. Maybe somebody up there was trying to tell him something, he told himself. The hell you going to do when you get a message like this, he'd like to know. He took the gun out of his mouth and put it down on the kitchen countertop. He reached over to the little TV and snapped off CNN, which he'd only been sort of half listening to, anyway. Something about Cuba.

The sun was up now.

Everybody in the house was still asleep. He could use a couple of winks himself, couldn't he? Maybe feel better when he woke up. Unless he dreamed about that damned teddy bear again. The big white one standing in the corner in the little pink room with the white lace curtains.

Goddamn teddy bear was driving him crazy. Ever since the birthday party. He'd imagined it would be easy, handing the bear to the little girl. Walking away. It wasn't like that. Oh, no. She didn't let him just walk away.

Little Cindy had laughed when he tore the paper off and showed it to her. Her eyes were wide open, just looking at that bear like it was her favorite present of her whole life or something. She'd stood up on her tippy-toes and given Gomer a big smacker. She hugged that bear to her chest and never let go of it all afternoon. Even though it was almost as big as she was.

Then, when it was finally time to go, Ginny Nettles, who was Fightin' Joe's wife and the kid's mother, had come up to him. Thanked him for his generosity. Said what a wonderful present it was, how it was just what Cindy wanted. Told him she'd like to have Amber and

Tiffany spend the night at their house with little Cindy. His own daughters. Right there in the Nettles kid's room.

Sleeping right there in the same room with the big white teddy bear.

And the *bad* thing, the *really* bad thing, was he'd said to her, "Sure, why not?"

Nothing had happened, of course. That's not how it was going to work. That was definitely not the Big Plan. Still, he never felt right about himself after that night. He would lie there next to Rita, wide-awake, thinking about how he'd let his two kids sleep in that kid's room with the bear. He tried to get his mind off of it. Think about his million dollars waiting for him in Switzerland. Growing like mushrooms in the dark. A dark vault. With a big white bear in the corner, its eyes glowing bright red.

Rita had finally thrown him out of the house three days prior to this little visit with the padre.

He'd come home pretty messed up that night and she'd gotten more pissed than he'd ever seen her. Gave him living hell. So he'd smacked her a couple of times to shut her up. Nothing serious. No *stitches,* for chrissakes. No broken anything. Nothing to get your panties in an uproar and kicked out of your own friggin' house over.

She'd be sorry. Wait till she found out how rich her soon-to-be ex-husband was. That would be something. He could see himself driving up in a brand new Corvette Z06, telling her about the bank in Switzerland, the money. But, hey, just stopped by to say good-bye. See ya.

Hey, way cool plate for his new 'Vette.

SEE YA

He was now living on a pullout sofa. In the upstairs apartment of his buddy Sparky Rollins, one of the guards up on the tower. It wasn't so bad. He could watch dirty movies on TV. Drink all the beer he wanted. Eat stuff with his hands. Burp, fart, leave the toilet seat up. Hang at the USO until closing time. Nobody ragging his ass all day and night, right? Not a bad life.

Want to hear something funny? Kind of life he was living? He woke up one morning, went into the head to pee, and noticed his pecker had turned orange. Talk about freaked out! He was dialing 911 when he remembered. He'd fallen asleep watching *Debbie Does Denver* or *Tina Does the Tri-Cities* or one of those—*and he'd been eating Chee-tos!* Yes!

Mystery of the orange pecker disease solved, Sherlock. Life was good.

So why had he snuck back inside his house last night? He'd used the key under the mat to let himself in through the kitchen door. Opened a bottle of Mount Gay and had a few. Gone and got his gun out of the garage and stuck it in his mouth. Pulled the trigger five friggin' times. Man. Click. Click. Click. Click. Click. You talk about dodging a bullet.

After he decided not to pull the trigger that one more time, he'd put the gun down and started crying. Staring at the picture of his kids. Watching the sunrise. Crying like a goddamn baby.

He'd gone upstairs to Rita. Gotten down on his knees beside the bed and begged her to take him back. Said how sorry he was and how he'd never hit her again. She said she thought he was sick. Crazy in the head. She'd made him swear to go to church and talk to Father Menendez about whatever it was that was wrong with him. He'd wanted to crawl in bed with her so bad he'd said yes.

And here he was, just like he promised.

"Father, I'm afraid I've done a terrible thing," Gomez said in the confession booth. "I don't know if treason is a mortal sin or not, but it's a bitch all right—sorry, I didn't mean to say that word—it's a real bad thing, I know that."

"Tell me your sins," the priest said.

For about half a minute, he actually thought he was going to be doing just that. And that's when he forgot about the bear with the bomb in his belly and thought about the million dollars again.

"Sorry, Father, I guess I'm not feeling all that great right now," he said. "I'll catch you later."

He stood up and left the confessional, hurried out of the church, and got in his broiling car.

Christ, he could use a cold one, he thought, starting the Yugo. He'd seen a cool Corvette ad in one of his magazines. Showed a guy in a red 'Vette, and in big type it said, "Know that warm feeling of belonging you have owning a Yugo? We don't either."

29

"You say you know the name of the murderer?" Congreve said, staring at Stubbs Witherspoon in disbelief.

The elderly gentleman had returned to the table with an ancient cardboard box containing the Hawke file. He removed the cover and pulled out a pale blue folder.

"No. I said I know the name of the man *responsible* for

the murders, Chief Congreve," Witherspoon said. "I will come to that. Please bear with me."

The old man put his hand on the blue folder. "These are the crime-scene photographs," he said. "Before I show them to you, could you indulge me a moment? I'm a little curious about Scotland Yard's interest in a thirty-year-old murder case."

"Of course. I should have explained that earlier. Have you ever heard the name Alexander Hawke?" Congreve asked.

"Yes. That was the child's name. The sole witness," Witherspoon replied. "The husband was Alexander. An English lord. The wife, of course, was Catherine, although everyone called her Kitty. A famous actress. She was one of the truly great beauties of that era. An American, from the south. New Orleans, I believe."

"Yes, it was a famous marriage on both sides of the Atlantic. The sole issue of that marriage is my employer as of this moment. I met young Alex Hawke over twenty years ago. A famous jewel robber was holed up down on one of the Channel Islands and I was hot on his trail. I found him on the same island where Alex was living with his grandfather, Lord Richard Hawke. A brilliant detective himself, he helped me solve the case. And his grandson has been like a son to me ever since."

"So the reason for your interest in the case is personal?" Witherspoon asked.

"Entirely," Congreve said. "I should explain that I am mostly retired at this point. Although I do maintain an office in the Special Branch, I work, as I said, primarily on assignments for Alex Hawke himself. As does Inspector Sutherland here, who is on loan from Scotland Yard."

"So, Mr. Hawke has decided to reopen the issue of his parents' murders?"

"No! Alex Hawke has no idea I'm even looking into this. In fact, he has no memory of the actual murders—"

"Which he witnessed," said Witherspoon, shaking his head sadly. He poured each of them some more lemonade.

"Which he witnessed," Congreve said. "He has those memories buried very deeply in his mind. He has, in effect, erected a wall of denial around them. He never, ever refers to that terrifying chapter in his life. But, I think it haunts him to this day. In fact, I know it does. It is a source of enormous pain."

"You want to exorcise your friend Alexander Hawke's old ghosts, Chief Congreve?" Witherspoon asked.

"I'd like very much to somehow put his mind at rest, yes," Congreve said. "That's why we're here in Nassau. If we could solve this thing, even bring the murderers to justice, it might offer him a bit of peace."

"I see."

"You should probably know that Alex Hawke is one of the wealthiest men on earth," Ross said. "He controls a vast business empire. You may have heard the name of the holding company. Blackhawke Industries."

"They own a shipping company based here in Nassau, I believe," Witherspoon said.

"Not to mention the banks and brokerages," Congreve said. "Blackhawke's central operations are run out of London, but the reach is worldwide. Because of this, he has tremendous contacts at the highest levels of every major corporation and many governments."

"In recent years," Congreve added, "he has been doing

a lot of work with both the British and American governments. Because of who he is and whom he knows, he has
been invaluable to both governments in certain delicate
matters."

"One such mission for the Americans has brought us
to your beautiful islands, Mr. Witherspoon," Ross said.
"But my superior and I are here in Nassau completely
unofficially. We are looking into these murders on our
own."

"I think I understand now. Thank you," Witherspoon
said, holding the blue folder in his hand as if he were
unsure about sharing it.

"We are eager to hear what you have to say," Ross said.

"Well. I told you that I know the name of the man
responsible for the murders. That is true. His name is
revealed in these photographs." Witherspoon slid the file
across the table to Congreve.

Only the birds outside and the whir of the fan could
be heard in the room. The minutes stretched out as
Congreve studied each black-and-white photograph and
then handed it to Sutherland, who did the same.

The old policeman rose from his rocker and crossed
the room to stand at the window. He had no need to see
the photographs again. He had been first to board the
yacht when it arrived in the harbor. The first police officer to view the crime scene. The image of that stifling
room and what horrors lay inside it would be engraved in
his mind forever.

A small, bright green bird alighted in the yellow hibiscus outside his window. The bird turned its darting
glance this way and that, finally settling its tiny black eyes
on the old man standing in the window. Stubbs

Witherspoon willed the vision of the little bird to drive the other vision from his mind. It almost worked.

When he finally turned away from the window, he saw Congreve slumped in his chair, staring down at his hands, which were folded in his lap. Tears were streaming down the Englishman's face. He made no effort to wipe them away.

Inspector Sutherland was gathering the photographs and returning them to the folder. His eyes, too, were red. It occurred to Witherspoon that these two men had been looking at the nightmarish pictures not with their own eyes, but through the eyes of a seven-year-old boy. A boy, now a man, whom they both deeply admired, perhaps even loved.

"Would you like to take a little walk in my garden?" Stubbs Witherspoon said, putting his hand on Congreve's shoulder.

"Yes," Congreve said, composing himself. "Indeed, we should both like that very much."

"Come along then," the old fellow said, picking up his folder, and they followed him outside onto the porch.

"Those plants are quite amazing," Sutherland said, pointing at a bizarre group of palms. "Nothing like that in an English garden, Mr. Witherspoon."

"Thank you. Birds of Paradise. And that tree? That's what I call a 'Tourist Tree.' "

"Why is that?" Congreve asked.

"Just look at de bark of it, mon! It always red and peeling!" Witherspoon said with his merry laugh. "Real name of it is Gumbo Limbo. You see that other tree over there past the Tourist Trees? That big old Calusa tree?"

"It's lovely," Congreve said.

"Alex Hawke and his grandfather helped me to plant that tree."

"You don't say?" Congreve said. "How extraordinary!"

"Not really. I had just bought this old place at the time. I invited them for luncheon one day, just before they flew back to England. Considering the circumstances, we had ourselves a fairly jolly good time, I remember. Little Alex and my dog Trouble, he was the grandfather of old Roscoe over there, runnin' all over the place, chasing Trouble's little red ball." The three men walked out into the yard. There were a few wooden chairs under the Calusa, and they all sat down in the quiet shade of its branches.

"Of course," Congreve said quietly. "You would have interviewed little Alex in the course of your investigation."

"Oh, I wasn't the lead investigator. Far from it. But I loved that little fellow. I took some little toy or something to that hospital room every single day," Witherspoon said. "I sat by his bed most of the time. But I wouldn't call it investigation. Just keeping him company. Poor boy Alex, he couldn't talk at all at first. When his grandfather got down here, well, he started to come back a little."

"No memory of the crime, even then?"

"None at all. The first time I saw him he kept repeatin' somethin' over and over. *Three knocks.* He never would explain it, but I figured it out eventually."

"Three knocks. What do you think it meant, Stubbs?" Congreve asked, leaning forward in his chair.

"I think it was a code. Between him and his father, I mean. See, little Alex was locked in that locker from the *inside*. And the key to the locker was found in Alex's pocket."

"So his father, probably having heard someone up on deck, had hidden him in the locker, then given him the key and told him to lock himself inside," Ross said.

"And told him not to come out for anyone unless he heard three knocks on the door," Congreve concluded.

"That's just the way I saw it," Witherspoon said. "His father, he died with his back to that door. Wasn't any way anybody was going to get through him to that child."

"How do you know that?" Ross asked.

"If you look closely at the photo of the bulkhead wall where the door was, you'll see two deep holes on either side of the door. Those holes match the two knife wounds that penetrated the victim's hands."

"He was *nailed to the wall?*"

"He was crucified. As I said, the photographs reveal the name of the man responsible for the murders," Witherspoon said.

"The method of killing then?" Congreve asked.

"Yes. You see, that kind of mutilation—the throat slit with the tongue drawn out through the opening and left hanging on the chest, for instance—"

"The infamous 'Colombian necktie,'" Ross said, and Witherspoon nodded at him.

"We had a reign of terror down here, early in the seventies and into the eighties," Witherspoon said. "Anti-British feelings in the islands. Then, anti-American. It was also the beginning of narco-terrorism. Everywhere in these islands were the narco-traffickers and *sicarios,* or the assassins. Most learned their trade at the foot of a vicious Colombian drug king we called *el doctor.*"

"And that's the man you think is responsible for the Hawke murders?" Congreve asked.

"Yes, sir. I'm sure of it. Whoever killed Alex's parents, he worked directly for a man named Pablo Escobar."

"Escobar is dead, as you know, Chief," Ross said to Congreve. "Tracked down and assassinated in Medellín in 1989 by a team of Colombian special forces. No one will admit it, of course, but there were Americans involved, Delta Force black ops."

"So the murderers are Colombian," Congreve said.

"No," Witherspoon said, "I think they were Cuban."

"Please explain," Ross said.

"Three Cuban boys on a murderous rampage. I think the killings occurred in the Exumas. That's where *Seahawke* was last seen, moored in a little cove near Staniel Cay."

Sutherland and Congreve looked at each other but said nothing.

"But the style of the thing, it was pure Colombian. So, I went down there to Staniel Cay myself," Witherspoon said, "on a tip from a friend of mine, a young policeman down there by the name of Bajun. He said there had been three Cuban boys, brothers, who'd been working odd jobs in the Exumas. Bartenders, paid hands, fishermen, you know."

"Yes, go on, please," Congreve said, plainly excited.

"They attracted Bajun's attention, he told me, because they all wore expensive gold jewelry. Colombian jewelry. He thought they were *narcos* killing time between drug drops, and he had his eye on them."

"So. Not Escobar himself. But three Cubans who might have been working for him at the time," Ross said, mulling it over. "Entirely plausible."

"That was our thinking, me and Bajun. We dusted the murder scene for prints but our techniques were pretty primitive back then. We did find three sets of footprints, in addition to the victims'. All had bare feet. So, there were three murderers. And the three Cubans disappeared the same night that the yacht did. Never seen again."

"What happened then?" Congreve asked, leaning forward and rubbing his hands together. A chill of excitement had made him forget all about the tropic heat.

"Nobody paid me no mind. I didn't have too much credibility at that time. And we had a backlog of cases two miles long. So I went out on my own. I tried the Americans first. The CIA station chief here at the time was an acquaintance of my father's. His name was Benjamin Hill.

"Now, Ben knew that I knew the CIA and the U.S. Army were all over Colombia. It was the worst-kept secret down here. They had the Medellín cartel under daily surveillance. But, of course, Ben couldn't admit to anything, even though he wanted to help. Officially, the Americans were not in Colombia, so I hit a stone wall."

"What did you do then?" asked Ross.

"Simple. I emptied my savings account and borrowed some money from my father. Then I went down to Colombia," Witherspoon said. "I had a good description of the three brothers from Bajun. And a warrant based on the evidence we had gathered in Staniel Cay. I poked around a little. 'Bout a week. People smile in your face, shake they heads. Got nowhere. Finally, I met with the chief of police in Medellín. I showed him the police sketches I'd had done of the suspects."

"Sorry to interrupt," Congreve said, his words tinged with excitement. "You still have those sketches?"

"Of course. Anyway, I got nowherc with that damn man. It was clear the chief down there was, like most everybody in those days, in Escobar's pocket."

"May I see those sketches?" Ambrose asked.

"You can have them," Witherspoon said, taking the tattered sheaves from his folder and handing them over.

"And that was the end of it, then?" asked Congreve, studying the rough caricatures.

"Not exactly," Witherspoon said. He stood up from his chair and gazed up into the sun-dappled branches of the Calusa tree, the empty flap of his sleeve floating in the breeze.

"That last night in Colombia after I met with the chief of police," he said, continuing to gaze upwards, "an automobile packed with one hundred kilos of dynamite exploded right outside my hotel. The entire front of the building collapsed into the street. Six people were killed. There was a young mother and her two infant children, just entering the hotel when the bomb—all I lost was my right arm."

"It was not your fault, Mr. Witherspoon," Congreve said to the old man, putting a hand on his bony shoulder.

"*It wasn't?*" Witherspoon said.

30

· · · — · ·

"Welcome home, m'lord," Pelham said, swinging open the wide mahogany door at the entrance of Hawke's new Georgetown home. He'd heard the familiar roar of Hawke's motorcycle outside and made his way across the black-and-white checked floor of the foyer.

Hawke shut down the motorcycle and reluctantly

climbed off. He loved firing up the old Norton Commando and was glad of any excuse to use it. After leaving Vicky's office the previous afternoon, he'd had only an hour or so in his new home. In the splendor of his cerulean blue bedroom, he'd had just time enough to call his decorator Le Coney in New York, thank her for the splendid job, then hop into a shower, a dinner jacket, and then out to the garage and onto his Norton for the short sprint around to the Georgetown Club.

"Hullo, Pelham, old thing," Hawke said, mounting the stone steps and smiling at his butler. "Glad to see you're still among the living this morning."

"As Alfred Lord Tennyson put it so succinctly in his poem 'The Brook,' I go on forever, m'lord," the aged butler said, with a slight bow.

Pelham Grenville had to be nearly a hundred years old. He still had a good head of thick white hair, an imperious nose, and twinkling blue eyes. He wore spotless white gloves, a cutaway jacket, striped trousers, and a stiff white tie at his throat every day of his life.

He'd spent the majority of that lifetime working for one member of the Hawke family or another. Though he was in fact a thoroughly professional butler, the family had long since ceased to think of him as a servant. He was a member of the family. He was Pelham, that charming fellow who kept successions of Hawke properties, town and country houses, well oiled. And, until they could be shipped off to Eton or Harrow or, later, Dartmouth, he also kept generations of Hawke children on the straight and narrow.

Pelham had insisted on coming over to Washington to supervise the restoration and decoration of The Oaks.

Hawke didn't have the heart to say no. With Hawke away on business, and with only the odd aging aunt or cousin dropping by for tea, there was certainly not much activity in the London house in Belgrave Square. Besides, he enjoyed Grenville's company enormously.

Hawke gave Pelham a stern look.

"Now, none of this bowing and scraping stuff to anybody over here," Hawke said, as the butler took his overcoat. "This is America, Pelham. Land of freedom and equality."

"Please," Pelham sniffed. "I've been in service for over eighty years. I hardly need—good heavens! Look at you, m'lord, you're all bloody."

"Must have been someplace I ate," Hawke said, smiling at his own little joke. "Do I have time for a quick shower?"

"Very little, I'm afraid," Pelham said. "Madame Secretary just rang. She's on her way."

"Is it that bloody late?" Hawke said, looking at his shattered watch. He'd been unable to tear himself away from Vicky's bedside and forgotten all about the time.

"I tried your mobile, but as usual it wasn't turned on."

"Well, yes, there's that. I wonder if you could possibly get the secretary some tea and apologize for me, will you? I'm going to have a scrub and put on something clean."

"Indeed, sir. Your current appearance leaves a great deal to be desired. One might use the word 'frightening.' I've taken the liberty of laying out one of your favorite gray Huntsman suits," the butler said. "And may I suggest a tie? A nice Turnbull Navy foulard should do quite nicely. After all, your guest is a personage of great—"

But Hawke was already halfway up the sweeping marble staircase, mounting the steps three at a time.

"Lord Hawke is bloodied but unbowed, I see!" the old fellow muttered under his breath.

"Indeed, I am!" Hawke shouted back over his shoulder.

Ten minutes later, he'd showered and, ignoring the wardrobe laid out by Pelham, donned a pair of faded Levis, Royal Navy T-shirt, and an old black cashmere sweater. If Conch saw him in a coat and tie, she wouldn't recognize him.

Entering the library, he found Consuelo de los Reyes sitting by a crackling fire, sipping a can of Diet Coke through a straw, and staring at the television.

"You're here!" Hawke said. "Sorry, I didn't—"

"I figured out how to turn this damn thing on. Hope you don't mind."

She was watching herself on CNN Newsbreakers. Hawke couldn't help smiling at Conch's television appearance and demeanor.

Very genteel. Black dress, pearls. And, Hawke noticed, a marked absence of the usual stream of four-letter words that flowed so naturally from the mouth of the American Secretary of State.

"Does that dress make me look fat?" Conch asked.

"No dress makes you look fat, Conch."

Today, Conch had on a tight pink cashmere sweater. It was a sweater he remembered quite well. It buttoned up the back. Or unbuttoned, as the case may be. Beyond the tall crystalline windows on either side of the hearth, a snow-covered Washington basked in the brilliant morning sunlight.

"Well, you're my first guest," Hawke said, pulling up a chair by the fireside. "I guess since you found the house for me, by all rights it should be you." Conch owned the house just across the street and had first shown Alex the pretty Georgian brick home he now owned.

"Good God almighty, Alex," she said, reaching over to flip off the television and looking around. "You've turned the old dump into Brideshead Manor."

"Decorators certainly captured the English Country look in this room, didn't they?"

"Feel like I'm sitting in the middle of a goddamn Polo ad. Like Ralph's going to walk through the door any minute and plop down amidst the chintz with a couple of springer spaniels."

Hawke smiled. Conch's tastes ran to bamboo, rattan, and mounted blue marlins, even in Georgetown.

"Dreadful business last night at the Georgetown Club," he said. "I've just come from the hospital."

"Hell of a fright, buster. I got a call during dinner with the president. The Georgetown Club! We'll nail these guys, whoever they are. And then we'll nail the sonsabitches' balls to the walls, believe me. Tell me about it. What happened to your hand?"

"Just a salad fork through it, Conch. I was lucky."

"And Victoria?"

"I would say that she is *extremely* lucky."

"Meaning?"

"This may be difficult for you to believe, but—" Alex broke off what he was saying when Pelham suddenly floated into the room.

"I've laid a breakfast out on the table there, m'lord," he

said. "Fruit, cereal, coffee, tea. Muffins with your favorite strawberry jam. Please ring if you need me. Otherwise I shan't disturb you further."

Hawke smiled as the butler withdrew, pulling the double doors closed, and said, "At any rate, I know it's preposterous, but I think it's possible that bomb was meant for Vicky."

"Oh, Alex, get serious. Why in hell would anyone—"

"The bloody Cubans, perhaps. After all, that submarine was purchased by this *Telaraña* bunch. Could be trying to scare me away."

"Alex, if they really wanted to, why not just kill you?"

"Too much bad publicity? I don't know. Look, I'll be honest. I gave those Russians a fairly rough go of it. Forced them to divulge who bought the Borzoi. They were terrified of the possible repercussions. In order to cover themselves, they'd go straight to the Cubans and tell them about my keen interest in their activities. So, I expect the new Cuban government aren't exactly happy with me at the moment."

"Big-time CYA."

"Sorry?"

"Cover Your Ass. Your Russian friends are covering theirs with the Cubans," Conch said. "That's precisely what your little arms-dealing buddies *would* do. Go to the Cubans, tell their sob story, blame everything on you. Cuban Secret Service does a little backtracking and ends up in Kuwait City, where the first deal fell apart. CIA just received word that your friend Cap Adams just turned up dead. Sorry."

"What?"

"London Metro Police found him last night in his

apartment in St. John's Wood. No apparent cause of death. Pathologists using an electron microscope detected a minute pellet of Ricin in his thigh muscle."

"Ricin?"

"Toxic albumin found in castor beans. Remember the famous 'Umbrella Murder'? A KGB thug with a trick umbrella assassinated an inconvenient Bulgarian named Marlgov on the Waterloo Bridge way back in '78. Ancient history to us, but apparently not to the Cubans. Kudos to your British forensic boys for getting to the bottom of this one so quickly."

"Kudos all around. Hope someone gets word of their brilliant success to Cap's wife, Anne, and children in Arlington. Christ. I've got to call Anne."

"Stick with Vicky a moment, Alex. What makes you think Vicky might be the target?"

"She was called to the phone by the waiter just minutes before the explosion. When she got to the booth, there was no one on the line. Just breathing. There was a black briefcase on the floor. Thinking someone had simply forgotten it, she gave it to the waiter on her way back to the table."

"And it exploded in his hands minutes later," the secretary said, shaking her head. "I'll get this info to the lead team right away."

"Thanks."

"Alex, the reason the president asked me to stop by this morning is Cuba. What we don't need at State right now is another hotspot right on our doorstep. That island is coming to a fast boil. I'm going to need a little help with this one."

"Whatever I can do. Tell me."

"As I told you, rumors of a coup have been circulating for a while. Now, a televised speech Fidel was scheduled to make last evening was canceled at the last minute. It's not at all like him. I've got a shitload of HUMINT pouring in through our Cuban desk at the Swiss embassy in Havana."

"HUMINT?"

"Sorry. Human intelligence. State Department speak for spies. I try like hell not to talk like that, but sometimes . . ."

"Castro's had a rough go of it with Parkinson's, you know. Relapse?"

"Possible. But we know he'd had a major recovery after the pope's last visit. We get weekly medical reports on him from a doctor on our payroll. He's down, but he's not out by a long shot. Tough old bird. And every male in his family lives to be at least a hundred."

"So. What's next?"

"I'm going from here right back to the White House. We've had contingency planning for a Cuban overthrow on the books forever, as you can well imagine. We're moving to the implementation stage right now."

"Any news on the submarine front?"

"You bet. Here, look at these," de los Reyes said, and handed Hawke a bright red folder full of black-and-white photographs.

"Where were these taken?" Hawke asked, flipping through the pictures.

"Predator spy photos, taken yesterday. About an hour after you identified the purchaser as *Telaraña,* we got a Predator in the air out of Gitmo. Look. There's the southeast coast of Cuba. That's the town of Manzanillo.

On Guacanayabo Bay. There's *Telaraña,* that small island off the coast, do you see it?"

"Yes," Hawke said, rising and taking the pictures to the window where the light was stronger. "A lot of construction. Looks like barracks, warehouses. And, here, mobile scud launchers."

"Yes. We think they're recently purchased massive numbers of Russian scuds. There's also a large white structure at the mouth of the river, do you see that?"

"Yes, it looks huge. What is it?"

"Navy at the Pentagon says it's some kind of amphitheater. I think it's a submarine pen disguised to look like a public building. Certainly wide enough for the beam of a Boomerang. We really don't know, Alex," the secretary said.

"The plot, as they say, sickens. The new Cuba—a dog or a rat in every pot and a half-billion-dollar invisible nuclear submarine in every garage."

"Alex?" Something in her tone had changed.

"Yes?" He looked into her incredibly beautiful brown eyes for an extra second and then turned back to the window.

"Look at me."

"Bad idea."

"Turn around and look at me."

"Terrible idea, Conch."

As a charter member of the bad idea club, he knew one when he saw one coming. And his intense desire to unbutton that tight pink sweater was definitely not a good idea. He didn't need this now. Especially now, in fact. He was in love. And the woman he loved was lying in the hospital. Christ.

"I can't do it, Conch. I won't do it," he said. He heard a rustle of papers and folders being gathered up behind him. When he turned around, she was headed for the door.

"Conch?"

She paused and turned to look at him. The expression on her face was all business.

"The president has asked me to form an emergency task force to deal with this," she said. "I've asked the two men you met in my office to head it up. He sent me here to ask you to be part of the team."

"Consuelo, you know I'm always at your disposal. But if you look carefully at my résumé, you'll see the telltale notation, 'Doesn't work well with others.'"

"I expected that. But this is obviously a matter of enormous consequence to the president. We simply cannot have this goddamn thing floating around out there, a couple of miles off Miami Beach. He is deeply appreciative of your stunning success in the Caribbean. Hell, we all are."

"He was kind enough to call."

"You found out who bought it. Now all we've got to do is find and neutralize the sonofabitch. I promised him I'd secure your help. See it through to the end."

"Really? That's a fairly staggering thing for you to do, Conch."

"Isn't it? I take so much for granted. I just never learn."

"Conch, listen. I was a sorry little shit, dreadful. Forgive me one day?"

"Yeah, well, I hated the way we ended. You caught me looking, I'll give you that much. No warning signs. Nothing. It really hurt, okay? I felt like you never even gave me a chance. Gave us a chance."

"Yes. Well, if you really think about it, we never—"

"Please shut up, Hawke. You're really crappy at this kind of stuff."

Alex had no reply for that.

"What's your schedule look like?" she asked, all business once more.

"I'm headed right back down to the Exumas. Vicky's had a mild concussion and could use a couple of weeks away from her office anyway. I'm taking her to the islands for two weeks aboard *Blackhawke*."

"Lucky girl."

"I'm flying down this afternoon. When I get there, I'm your man. Whatever I can do. Just don't drag me into another one of those bloody task force meetings."

"Remember what you did at the last one?"

"No. I try to forget these things."

"Halfway through, you stood up and announced that, while you were enjoying the meeting immensely, you had to leave because you had a leg of lamb in the oven."

"Ah, yes. Mustn't overcook lamb. Quite a good one, wasn't it?"

"Okay, my man." The secretary of state grabbed her coat from the back of a chair and headed for the door without looking back.

"'Bye, Conch."

"Scoot over and borrow a cup of sugar anytime," she said, pulling the door closed behind her.

31

• • • — — • • •

Manso and his two brothers, Carlos and Juanito, stood together at the very end of a long jetty. Waves were breaking over the rocks, soaking the three men to the skin. There was no moon and no stars, only the raging sea. It was a miserable Cuban night. It was a magnificent Cuban night.

Manso, shivering in the cold rain, was aglow inside. He'd done it. They had all done it. The country would soon learn that a new Cuba was about to be born. Right now, looking at their exuberant smiles, he felt like this small band of brothers were the three happiest men in all of Cuba.

They stood on the concrete jetty, just at the base of a newly installed red channel marker. Every three seconds it flashed, splashing the three men with brilliant red light. A green marker flashed at the end of the other jetty, a halo of light some two hundred yards across the mouth of the river in the darkness.

It was almost midnight and raining hard, but they didn't care. In the long, tortuous history of their country, this was a moment of historic importance. The de Herreras brothers were euphoric as they peered through the slashing rain, out across the black water.

"Anything?" Manso asked.

"I thought I saw something," Carlos said, "but I think it's only salt water in my eyes." He took a swig from a silver flask and stuck the container back inside his jacket.

"You're going to see something, *mi hermano*," Juanito

said, laughing and clapping him on the back. "You are definitely going to see a great big something!" All three men had night-vision binoculars hanging from their necks.

Nothing.

"The television was a disaster," Manso said, after a few more moments of scanning the black horizon with his binoculars. "He was a wild man, even with the sedatives. I had the announcer say that he was rescheduled for tomorrow. I don't think he's going to cooperate."

"Who cares?" Carlos asked. "He's irrelevant. Right now, all the Cuban people know is that he missed a telecast. Unfortunate. But remember that they saw him at the Yacht Club only this morning. The *Granma* reporter was there, so it will be in the paper. If he ultimately refuses to go before the cameras, so what? You and Fulgencio will announce the change of government and that's the end of it. Everything else is accomplished."

"It's better if Fidel does it, Carlitos," Juanito insisted. "Easier for all of us. In the long run, the people won't care. But, for now, I—"

"Listen. I have an idea," Manso said. "I was talking after supper to the video technician. He tells me we can make him say whatever we want."

"Of course we can always do that." Carlos laughed. "Rodrigo and his silver scissors can make anyone say anything."

"I don't mean that way, Carlitos," Manso said, looking at his crazy brother Carlos with eyes like black stones.

"You mean there is another way?" Juanito asked.

"There is a way to digitally alter his speech and lip movements," Manso said. "As long as it's kept very short."

"How short?" Juanito asked. "You mean, like, 'I quit, here's the new guy'?" He laughed and took another pull on his flask.

"My God, look at that," Carlos said. "Look!"

"Turn on the lights!" Manso said. Carlos flipped a switch mounted on the base of the channel marker and massive banks of floodlights above them lit up the storm-torn night.

All three raised their binoculars and aimed them in the direction Carlos had pointed.

"There!" he said. "See it?"

"Where? Oh . . . Mother of Christ!"

Out of the sea came the head of the monster, black and knife-edged, its V-shaped snout spewing not fire but boiling white water as it rose ever higher into the rain-whipped skies. It was a dull deadly black, looking like some evil engineer's nightmare machine. There was in fact no more efficient killing device on earth.

"I told you you were going to see something, my brothers!" Juanito shouted. "Oh, my God, look at this thing! Have you ever seen anything so huge?"

The deadly thing was still rising, a froth of white water pouring off the sleek, sharp-angled sides of its twin swept-back hulls and diving planes. Then that amazing snout came crashing down into the sea and the submarine surged toward the jetties. It was immense.

Water broke over her V-bow. They heard an alarm and saw something rising slowly from the forward-most part of the hull, another sharply angled shape with faint lights glowing from within. Then the structure was looming above the decks, and they understood at once that this was the retractable conning tower. After a moment, they could see the small black silhouettes of men begin to appear at the very top.

A powerful searchlight on the sub's tower was illuminated and swept back and forth across the river's entrance.

Manso couldn't make out any faces, of course, the men were just black figures at this distance, but he knew the identity of one of them. Then he caught a face in his powerful night-vision glasses.

"Commander Nikita Zukov," Manso said under his breath. "Welcome to Cuba. We've been expecting you."

The three brothers embraced, rain splashing on their faces. It was a moment they seemed to have been imagining forever. But their imaginations had been capable of nothing so grand as the events of the day and this sight and this historic night.

The mammoth black-winged creature from the deep was now entering the mouth of the river. It was the most stunning thing Manso had ever seen. He waved at the men atop the conning tower and they returned his salute.

"Well, my brave brothers, I have a question for you," he said, gathering them together. "Walk with me."

Arm in arm, they started walking back along the jetty, toward the sub pen. They wanted to be inside the newly constructed pen with the construction crews and all the on-shore support teams when the sub made its dramatic appearance.

"Just one little question," Manso said, looking back at the sub sliding majestically toward them.

"Sí, Manso?" they replied in unison.

"I want to know, my brothers, exactly how does it feel to be a super-power?"

Laughing, the three men raced ahead of the submarine back towards the pen. The huge doors were sliding open, revealing the cavernous interior. Light poured out and so did many of the workers, charged with excitement at the sight of the approaching sub.

It was hard to say who was more excited, the Cubans or the Russians. There were over a hundred Russian electronic engineers, machinists, plumbers, electricians, and various nuclear technicians. They'd been working side by side with the Cubans for months, building the necessary machine and tool shops it would take to support such a sophisticated nuclear submarine.

As the giant sub finally eased into the wide mouth of her slip, there was a deafening roar as the men surged down the floating docks running along each hull, cheering wildly.

Commander Nikita Zukov stood atop the towering sail of his submarine, surveying the sea of activity taking place all around him. He had his hands over his ears to block out the terrible sound. It wasn't the sound of the arc welders or the steelworkers still putting the finishing touches on the sub pen that bothered him. It was a small orchestra struggling through yet another rehearsal of the Cuban national anthem.

The band was practicing for the dedication ceremony. They stood at the end of a long concrete pier, only twenty feet from where the sub was moored. Commander Zukov thought that if he had to listen to one more stanza, he might well go insane.

"Not bad, not bad," Admiral Carlos de Herreras said in Spanish. "I think by the time of the May Day ceremony, they'll be perfect." Zukov, who spoke fluent Spanish, looked at the man to see if he could possibly be serious. He was.

Zukov's father had been a Soviet navy "adviser" to Cuba and had married a Cuban woman. So he'd grown up in a house where everyone spoke both Spanish and Russian. Born in Havana thirty-five years ago, he had not been in Cuba in many years. He was ten years old when his father had taken the family back to Moscow. He was accepted at the Naval Academy at eighteen, and became a submarine officer, gaining command of his own boat by age thirty.

Zukov's Cuban background accounted for the fact that he happened to be standing here instead of any of a dozen former Soviet sub commanders vying for the job. He knew the language and the culture. He knew and loved the people. He had served his country with great distinction. And he'd never forgiven the politburo for their betrayal of his homeland. And his navy.

"The band, they sound pretty good to you, Commander?" the Cuban admiral asked him.

"Symphonic," Zukov replied, straining to be heard over the orchestra, the arc welders, and the steelworkers.

A crew was already painting the sub's new name on both the starboard and portside flanks of the gleaming black hull.

Zukov recognized the new name instantly.

José Martí.

Named in honor of the great patriot who had liberated Cuba from Spain after a long bloody war, the *José Martí* was a splendid symbol of the new Cuba. The excitement inside the submarine pen verged on hysteria.

Flags and bunting hung from every corner of the building in preparation for the celebration of May Day, the great Communist holiday, just three days hence. The mood inside was frantic, but festive.

One man had started whistling the "Mango" melody and soon the whole construction and support battalion was singing the ironic lyrics at the top of their lungs.

> *The mango, the mango, even though it is green, it is ripe and ready to fall . . .*

Mercifully, the swelling voices drowned out the band.

Admiral Carlos de Herreras, CNO of the Cuban navy, and his two brothers had boarded the sub soon after Zukov guided it expertly up the narrow shoaled river and into its slip. After the sub was properly moored and her propulsion systems shut down, Zukov had welcomed them aboard. He had offered them some chilled vodka in the wardroom, then given them the official guided tour, stem to stern.

Although their questions were outrageously naive, it was obvious the Cuban officers were more than delighted with their new toy. They were giddy with excitement, and hurried from one end of the boat to the other, laughing with glee.

The Cubans were especially excited, he noticed, when they entered the starboard hull compartment where, in their silos, twenty gleaming warheads sat atop twenty ballistic missiles. Over on the port hull, a matching set of twenty more. With forty warheads, you could blow up the world. No one had yet told Zukov what his first mission would be, and he had only a rough idea of the primary targets. But the very thought of going to war in such a magnificent machine sent an electric charge racing through him. A feeling he hadn't experienced since the glory days of the Cold War.

The commander's Russian crew of one hundred thirty men, all former submariners under his Cold War command, were also in a jolly mood. All of them were now, like Zukov himself, mercenaries. And all of them, after a frozen winter in Vladivostok, were equally ecstatic at the very idea of a shore leave on the beautiful tropical island of Cuba.

For Zukov, this return elicited deeper emotions.

Zukov had been deeply humiliated when the Soviet empire collapsed. As a naval officer in command on an Akula, he'd spent his entire life playing undersea cat-and-mouse with the Americans. Endless days and nights rehearsing for a war that would never get fought. He'd spent months under the polar ice cap, stalking the SSN *George Washington,* praying for any excuse to engage. Once he had tracked the carrier *John F. Kennedy* for weeks, staying dead astern of his prey, so that the signature sound of his screws went completely undetected by enemy sonar. All this, at a time when the ultimate weapon, his new command, Borzoi, was still on the drawing boards.

Like many of his warrior comrades, he was bored to stupor with the decade or so of "peace" following the collapse of the Soviet Union in 1991.

On a purely personal level, Commander Zukov was happy just to return to his homeland. Memories of his beautiful birthplace haunted him still. On a professional level, he was ecstatic at the prospect of killing a whole lot of Americans.

He sensed in the wild-eyed Cuban admiral, Carlos de Herreras, a kindred spirit. He'd seen the man in the missile compartment out of the corner of his eye. He had been rubbing his hands together gleefully, almost maniacally.

Bloodlust. He knew it well, for it coursed through every vein in his body.

32

"Hey, Doc, you awake?"

"Alex? Yes, I guess so. What time is it?"

"I don't know. A little before midnight, I think. Sorry. I just need to—no, don't turn on the light. It's all right."

Alex had temporarily given Vicky her own stateroom in the vain hope that she might get more rest the first few days. He'd promised himself he'd stay away from her for at least three days. He hadn't even made it through the first night.

"Alex, your hand is freezing. You're trembling. What's wrong?"

"I don't know. I'm sorry to bother you. I got up to use the loo and—sorry—can I climb in with you?"

"Of course you can, darling. Here, let me move over."

"Thank you. Oh, God, you feel warm."

"You're trembling all over!"

"I know. It's the strangest thing. I think I passed out. I went to my stateroom right after we—we said good night. Went right to sleep, too, out like a light. Something woke me up. A bad dream maybe. Anyway, I was looking in the mirror over the basin and then—I woke up on the floor."

"You fainted?"

"I don't know. I remember I felt really odd, looking at my face in the mirror. As if it weren't me. Or, it was me, but only vaguely. I didn't recognize myself. So, I—"

"Is this the first time this has happened? Close your eyes a second, I'm turning on the light. I need to look at your pupils."

"Yes. I mean no, not the first time. Ouch. That's bright."

"It is, or it isn't the first time?" she asked, examining him. His eyes, normally a hard blue, now looked breakable, like china.

"I'm not sure. A few days ago, just before I flew up to Washington, I was standing up on deck. Just looking at the stars. Thinking about you, actually. How much I missed you. And then, my breathing went all arsey-versey and my heart sort of went pounding off the rails and—"

"Is there a physician here on board the *QEII?*"

"Of course."

"I want you to see the doctor first thing in the morning, Alex. No excuses."

"Why? Hell, I just fainted, Vicky. I'm fine. See? I'm not even shaking anymore. This is just an elaborate ruse to come down and bother you. Check out which nightie you're wearing. Good selection."

"I'm sure it's nothing serious. But you do need to see him. Get a complete blood workup done. He may want you to have an MRI."

"It's a she."

"What?"

"The ship's doctor. He's a she."

"Of course. Your nurse-uniform fetish. God, how stupid of me."

"What do you think is wrong with me, Vicky? Brain tumor?"

"I think you're fine, darling. I think you've had a panic attack."

"Panic? Over what? I've never been happier."

"I don't know. You're not really my patient, remember?"

"We'll fix that."

"You said you had a bad dream, Alex. Can you remember anything about it?"

"No. It's a very bad dream."

"Tell me about it."

"May I have a sip of your water? Thank you. Well. It's always the same at the beginning. I'm locked inside a small—I've never told anyone this before, Doc."

"It's all right, Alex. Tell me."

"Can we just make love again instead? I'll tell you first thing tomorrow."

"No."

"All right, all right. It's frightfully mundane. I'm locked in a small room. A closet of some kind and—why am I talking about this? It's only a stupid childish dream."

"Dreams are important because they offer clues to our deepest feelings."

"You sound just like a bad textbook, darling. 'Our deepest feelings.' Well, in my case this shouldn't take long because deep down I'm a very shallow person."

"Tell me the goddamn dream, darling."

"Yes. Anyway, in my dream, I'm locked inside a small closet. It's insufferably hot and foul-smelling. There's a small hole in the door, and I can see into the next room."

"What's in the other room?"

"Nothing. But there's a hole in its ceiling. And I know something bad is coming down through that hole. That's the feeling I have. *A bad thing is coming.*"

"Is it always the same bad thing?"

"Yes. It's—it's a spider. It wants to kill me. It wants to kill everybody."

"And you're powerless to stop it?"

"Um, yes. I am."

"Because of the locked door?"

"Because I'm so little. And the door. Yes, it's locked. I'm hiding so the spider won't find me."

"How old are you in the dream?"

"I don't know. Six or seven maybe."

"What do you do? Where are your parents? Can't they help you?"

"I don't have any bloody parents. I never had any! I was raised by my grandfather!"

"Alex, calm down. It's all right."

"Sorry. There's no one in the closet but me. I'm all alone. I've always been alone. I want to scream. But I can't because then the spider will hear me and find me. After a while, I don't care. I want to open my mouth and scream and scream but nothing comes out."

"Alex, you're shaking again. Are you all right?"

"No. I'm not all right. My dreams, my life. Sometimes I can't tell the difference. I always seem to be somewhere on the road between Heaven and Hell, and I never know which way I'm headed."

"Oh, Alex."

"You know—I really don't want to talk about this, Doc. Drop it, all right? I'm thirty-seven fucking years old. I managed, somehow, to make it this far through my life without a lot of psychobabbling doctors digging into my past, and I'm not bloody well about to start digging into it now."

"Why are you so angry?"

"This is my life you're poking around in. I'm a private person."

"I'm just trying to help. You came to me, remember?"

"Right. My mistake. Sorry. I don't need any bloody help. I'm sorry I disturbed you. I'll go back to my bed now, thank you very much. Good night."

"Alex, you need to talk to someone. Maybe not me, but someone."

The door slammed and he was gone.

"Good night, Alex," Vicky said, and turned out the light.

She lay staring into the darkness for about ten minutes, arranging and rearranging her pillows. There was no possible way she could go back to sleep. She'd been in bed for the best part of forty-eight hours. She felt great. Mild concussion? Obvious misdiagnosis. Minor concussion, that was this doctor's second opinion.

She flipped on the light, got up, and pulled on a pair of khaki shorts. Then the white T-shirt with the big black hawk that the captain had given her when she'd first come aboard. She caught a glimpse of herself in the mirror. She'd completely forgotten about the bandages around her head.

Pulling open a drawer, she grabbed the lovely Hermès scarf that Alex had found for her on New Bond Street in

London. Dolphins and whales. She wrapped it around her head and went off in search of the nearest stairwell.

She hadn't been on the yacht long, but she already knew where to find Ambrose. She knew his habits well enough to know that right now, he was sitting out on deck under the stars, probably at the business end of a vintage cognac. It was Ambrose, after all, who'd introduced her to Alex in London. There'd been a dinner dance at the home of the American ambassador. Vicky was a guest there because the current ambassador to the Court of St. James, Patrick Brickhouse Kelly, and his wife had been great friends of her father's.

And, besides, she had a new children's book out called *The Whirl-o-Drome* that had won all sorts of English literary prizes and was all the rage in London. She'd found herself invited to countless dinner parties because of it.

Alex was the guest of honor that evening, and she'd been seated next to him. He was devastatingly good-looking, and she was sure this seating had been carefully arranged. When the beautiful man proceeded to ignore her all through the first course, she'd turned once more to the charming older man on her left, Ambrose Congreve, and asked if he knew why the rude guest on her right was ignoring her. He said he happened to be the man's closest friend and would be happy to assist.

He scribbled something on the back of his engraved place card, and handed it to Vicky. It was folded and said "Alex Hawke" on the outside. She tapped the rude man on his shoulder and handed it to him. He read it, looked pale, and then said to Vicky, "Excuse me, I'm a dreadful bore. But I would be twice honored if you would do me the singular honor of the next dance."

Ambrose would never tell her what he'd written on the place card. But when she'd turned and asked the gorgeous man if "twice honored" meant two dances, well, that was the beginning of everything.

In the event, the three of them spent the next two weeks in a merry whirlwind of pub crawls, parties, and weekend trips to lovely old country houses. She and Alex spent the last weekend alone at his rambling home, Hawke's Lair, deep in the Cotswolds. They had, of course, fallen deeply in love by then. And Ambrose had become a frequent companion as well.

So she knew Ambrose's nocturnal habits. Now, he'd most likely be up on the topmost deck in the open stern lounge. It was his favorite haunt and he'd nicknamed it the Fantail Club. He'd be smoking his pipe and having his Hine cognac, which is exactly what she wanted at the moment.

She emerged into the cool night air. The stars were so bright she wished she'd brought sunglasses. Seated at the rounded banquette in the curvature of the stern were two familiar silhouettes. Their heads were bowed together, deep in conversation, and neither saw or heard her barefoot approach.

She bent and kissed the nearly bare pate.

"Ah, the very lovely Doctor Victoria Sweet!" Ambrose said, standing up. "Up for a midnight stroll round the decks, no doubt? The sharp sea air? Smashing idea!"

"I couldn't sleep a wink," Vicky said. "Hello, Ambrose. Hello, Stoke."

"Evenin', Doc," Stoke said. "Sit down, girl. We've got us a fine night goin' up here. Hell, you sit up here long enough, you bound to see meteors, comets, sputniks, and at least three or four shooting stars. Leastways Ambrose sees 'em, but then he's on his fourth star and his fifth brandy."

"I don't want to sit," Vicky said. "I feel lucky to be alive. I want to have some fun. Go somewhere and dance by the light of the moon. Isn't there someplace where a girl could get you two to dance and buy me a seriously good rum drink?"

"Staniel Cay Yacht Club fits that description," Ambrose said. "Amen Lillywhite, the barman there, serves a notable concoction called the Suffering Bastard, which I've found to be extremely serious."

"Let's go, then!" Vicky said. "How do we get there?"

"Ain't far. See all them Christmas lights hanging in the trees on that island over there? Only a couple of miles. We could swim it," Stokely said. "But Mr. Congreve, he old-fashioned. He likes to take the launch."

"Can we go, Ambrose? Will you and Stoke escort me?"

"Of course, my dear, we would be delighted. Stokely, would you please ring down to Brian at the launch deck and arrange a transfer?"

"It's all happening as we speak," Stoke said.

"Should we see if Alex would like to join us?" Ambrose said.

"Yes, of course," Vicky said. "Might cheer him up. He's having an awful night."

"Ah. A bad night," Ambrose said, looking at her. "Bad dreams, no doubt." Vicky nodded.

"That old joint going to be jumping long about now," Stoke said. "There's a junkanoo on tonight. You listen very carefully, you can almost hear the music floating over the water."

"Junkanoo? What's that?" Vicky asked.

"Junkanoo's where a cat can get so rum-brained his eyes and his brains stop communicating to each other and the cat don't know half how ugly the person he dancing with is," Stoke said, getting up and going over to the intercom phone. "That's junkanoo," he said over his shoulder. "Might cheer us all up. I'll go arrange the launch."

"Sounds pretty good to me, Stoke," Vicky called after him.

33

· · · — — · · ·

"Tell me about Alex's bad night," Congreve said quietly, once he and Vicky were alone. Stokely had gone below to arrange the launch and they were still sitting under the stars.

And she did.

"You say 'panic attacks,'" Ambrose asked, concern furrowing his brow. "How many?"

"I'd say this is his second or third," Vicky said. "He passed out tonight. Not good. I'm hoping they *are* panic attacks, Ambrose. We could be looking at something serious."

"How serious?"

"If I had to hazard a guess, epilepsy. Possibly meningitis. Worst-case scenario, a cranial tumor. I want him to get a complete blood workup tomorrow."

"He seems in perfect health."

"*Seems* being the operative word given his symptoms."

"Stick with panic attacks a moment," Congreve said. "Alex was in these islands once before. When he was a very small boy. A terrible thing happened. His parents were murdered in cold blood."

"Good God. He's always been so circular and oblique about his childhood. I just assumed he'd been adopted and didn't want to talk about it. I didn't ever push it."

Ambrose looked at her closely and made a decision. Discretion here was pointless. She was a doctor. And Alex was in love with her.

"It's worse, Victoria. Alex was an eyewitness to the murders. He has buried this horror successfully for most of his life. I think returning here, to the exact place where it happened, is bringing the submerged images floating to the surface."

"How horrible."

"Unimaginable."

"All I want to do is help him, Ambrose," Vicky said.

"That's all any of us want to do, dear girl. You can perhaps bring some of your professional gifts to bear. I know that some of your work involves children with problems. I am certainly trying to utilize my own experience."

"Meaning?"

"Meaning, my dear, that I've been trying to solve these blasted murders for nearly three decades. On my own, of course. The case was consigned to the Yard's dead file long ago. Sometime in the early eighties."

"Does Alex know what you're doing?"

"On some level, perhaps. We've never discussed it."

"Do you think it's wise? Proceeding without his knowledge, I mean?"

"It was the only way. Recently, I've made some considerable progress. If I begin to get close, really close, I'm going to tell him everything."

"Be careful how you do that, please, Ambrose."

Congreve gave her a look suggesting impertinence on her part.

"Sorry. That was very stupid of me. From what I've seen you are the very soul of delicacy and discretion. Shall I go fetch Alex and we'll all go to the junkanoo?"

"By all means, dear girl, by all means!" Ambrose said, and Vicky raced down the wide and gently curving set of steps that led to Alex's quarters in the stern.

As predicted, the Yacht Club was a seething organic mass of sweating, writhing bodies. Flaming torches mounted high on the walls painted the intertwined mass below with flickering yellows, blacks, and oranges. On a small bandstand toward the rear, a trio of dreadlocked Rastafarians was deep into some vintage Marley.

The atmosphere was a potent admixture of sweat, heavy rhythm, and sweet-smelling ganja; the whole crowd looked explosive, as if you threw a match at them, the junkanoo might blow sky high.

Vicky and her two escorts fought their way to the bar and miraculously found three stools side-by-side. Alex, despite Vicky's pleadings, had begged her to go on without him. He even asked her to keep an eye on Congreve lest his old chum be "overserved," as sometimes happened. His mood seemed much improved, and Vicky finally relented, leaving him to a good night's sleep.

A bare-chested bartender appeared and was introduced to her by Ambrose as Amen. It was instantly apparent to Vicky that Amen and Ambrose seemed to go way back. Ambrose ordered them two Suffering Bastards, and Stoke ordered himself a caffeine-free Diet Coke. The drinks arrived immediately and Vicky took a deep pull on the straw.

It was a potent elixir, a potion easily underestimated by Vicky, who, despite her self-diagnosis, was still suffering the aftereffects of the explosion.

Polishing off this delicious poison, she debated ordering another and quickly gave in. As Amen served her, Vicky surveyed the overheated scene and said to no one in particular, "This place reeks of sex."

Stoke laughed and said, "How would you know that, Doc? Little sleepy-time-down-South gal like you?"

She sipped deeply from the cocktail and regarded Stoke with laughing eyes.

"Just because I know what something smells like, doesn't mean I know what it looks like."

Stoke laughed again, and she noticed that a beautiful dark-skinned girl seemed to have appeared at Stokely's side and he had his arm around her waist. She looked very soft and shy, and had a wonderful smile.

"This is Gloria," Stoke said, and Vicky shook her hand. "We met this afternoon down by the beach. Girl was fishin' and obviously didn't know what she was doin', so old Stoke, he gave her some professional fishin' lessons. Gal was in serious need of instruction. Girl caught herself a fine fish after that. Big damn fish."

"How big?" Vicky asked, smiling.

He held his hands about two feet apart and Gloria laughed.

"Is Stokely a friend of yours?" Gloria asked Vicky, with the tiniest bit of suspicion in her eyes.

"Shoot, he's a friend of everybody's," Vicky said, sipping her drink. "But I'm pretty sure he likes you a whole lot better than the rest of us." She giggled at that, which was odd because it wasn't even slightly funny.

"I work here," Gloria said to Vicky. "Tonight's my night off, but if there's anything you need, please let me know."

"I know what I need," Stoke said. "I need to go fishin' in the moonlight!" Gloria laughed.

"You tink they bitin' tonight, Mr. Jones?" Gloria said.

"I hope so," Stoke said. "Long as they ain't bitin' too damn hard."

Laughing, the two of them quickly disappeared into the crowd.

"How about a dance, Constable?" Vicky said to Ambrose, who was swirling his drink around his glass with his finger.

"I have the notion under serious consideration. I was thinking of perhaps climbing up onto the bar," Ambrose said, "and demonstrating the traditional Highland Fling. Do you think that's unwise?"

She didn't get around to answering because a very handsome boy, blond and deeply tanned, held out his hand to her and asked her, with his eyes, to dance. She smiled apologetically at Ambrose and plunged into the throbbing tumult holding the boy's hand. She must have danced far too long with the pretty little boat boy, because when he returned her to the bar, Ambrose had deserted his post.

She finally spotted him in a far corner of the room,

dancing with a tall blonde. Because of the press of bodies, it would take an hour to get over there and ask him to take her home.

She looked at her watch but somehow couldn't see what time it was. Her watch seemed to be shimmering, hazy. Couldn't be that late anyway, she thought, and called Amen over to order another of whatever they were called.

"Good evening," a man said, suddenly appearing on the stool next to hers. "I buy you drink?"

He had a thick accent, Hungarian or something Slavic, she decided. Russian? Dark hypnotic eyes and long straight hair pulled back into a ponytail. Thin face, long nose, all dressed in black. Exotic. Interesting. A little scary, but interesting.

"I have one very strict rule," Vicky said, smiling at her new friend. "I only drink when I'm alone, or with somebody. So, I guess I'll accept."

It was one of Alex's old jokes and she laughed even though he didn't. She thought she was funny and if nobody else did, so what? He just kept staring at her with those crazy eyes. Good thing she couldn't focus very well because she'd swear he was trying to hypnotize her.

"What's your name?" Vicky asked him.

"I'm Grigory."

"Nice to meet you, Grigory. I'm drunk." She giggled and stuck out her hand. He shook it and his hands were hot and moist.

"You stay here, on this little island?" he asked, leaning toward her. He was stirring his drink with his long white finger.

"Me? Oh, hell no. I'm on the *QEII* out there."

"I beg your pardon?"

"The *Elizabeth, Mary*, some old queen. See it out there, all lit up?"

"Oh. Such a beautiful yacht. To whom does it belong?"

"Oh, a friend of mine."

"Not Alexander Hawke?"

"You know him?"

"Not well. Only by reputation, of course. He is famous, you know."

"Really? For what? Oh, thanks, Amen. Cut me off after this one, okay? I've bagged my limit. Sorry, what did you say, uh, Grigory, is it?"

"Is not important. You and your friend are here long?"

"A week or two, I think."

"That long? How boring. Whatever will you do all day?"

Boring? His eyes were boring into hers. Is that what he meant? Boring? No. He wanted to know what she was going to do all day. That was it. Well, something exciting and glamorous, that's for sure. What? This European sophisticate expected something exotic, she was pretty sure about that.

"Well, I don't know, exactly," she said finally. She was having trouble remembering why she was even here. "Oh, I know! Tomorrow afternoon, we're going to a place called Hog Island. Doesn't that sound like fun? There's a blind pig there named Betty. Have you heard of her?"

"Oh yes, she's quite famous in these islands. Well, good-bye. My pleasure speaking with you, Miss—"

"Sweet," she said. "Like sugar."

The strange man was gone. Poof, like in a horror movie. She scanned the dance floor for Stoke, but everyone looked the same. She thought she saw Ambrose chatting up the blonde in the far corner but he was a bit blurry. She felt uneasy. She looked for Amen. Maybe some coffee would be good. She called him but he couldn't hear her above all the hubbub.

Suddenly, she needed air.

She climbed off the stool, pressed herself into the writhing mass on the dance floor, and headed for the door, smashing through the bodies, desperate for a gulp of fresh air. She was outside. She seemed to have acquired a glass of delicious dark rum. The moon was so bright, it seemed like another day had begun.

Steps led down to the beach. She walked along the surf and found a little stand of palms with a great view of the harbor. Soft, powdery white sand in the moonlight. *Blackhawke* all ablaze out on the horizon. She sat beneath the whispering palms, sipping the rum, enjoying herself immensely, finally drifting into a lovely tropical dream.

Stokely and Ambrose, having searched most of the island, finally found her on the beach about half an hour later, sound asleep under a coconut palm. Stoke threw her over his shoulder and they carried her back to the waiting launch.

"Girl fell asleep," he said to Brian, who was driving the boat. "Long day. Needs a good night's rest and she'll be good as new."

Vicky woke briefly, said something incomprehensible, and then collapsed with her head on Ambrose's shoulder. She snored deeply all the way across the bay.

Stoke was right.

It had been a long day. But the long days were really just beginning.

34

At eight o'clock in the morning, Commander Zukov was summoned to the main *finca* to breakfast alone with General Manso de Herreras. Two heavily armed guards posted outside the dining room waved him inside. Manso was seated at the huge table all alone, drinking a solitary glass of fruit juice. A place setting of solid gold had been set opposite the general and he motioned for Zukov to sit down. He did so, but waved away the approaching waiter. The general stared at him for an eternity before speaking.

"This fucking Russian who sold me the submarine. Golgolkin. You know him?"

"Yes, slightly," Zukov said. "Black Fleet. Vladivostok. At one time, a promising officer."

"Then?"

"The cliché Soviet scenario. Peace, vodka, and women. One night he surfaced without periscope surveillance and struck one of our own destroyers in the South China Sea. Considerable loss of life. That was it."

"He has come here, the idiot, begging for his life."

"General. Tell me. What has he done?"

"Done? Put everything in jeopardy! Everything! Met with some fucking Englishman named Hawke in the Exumas a week ago. Trying to peddle the second Borzoi, I hear. The Englishman apparently asks a lot of questions and Golgolkin gives a lot of answers. My sources in Washington say the Englishman was in the American capital the very next day! Bastard! I initiated reprisals against this Hawke, using Golgolkin's contacts at the Russian embassy. But they, too, were disastrous."

"What will you do?"

"What I always do. Go through, not around."

"I will deal with Golgolkin. He is an embarrassment."

"No. Bring him to me. I may have one last use for him."

Zukov opened the door to the fat Russian's room without knocking. There were three naked girls in his bed. One leapt up, a short, chubby little thing with enormous breasts bouncing, and ran to the bathroom, slamming the door behind her. Zukov couldn't tell if she was laughing or crying.

"The majordomo told me you were ill and could not come down for your breakfast," Zukov said. "You were missed."

"I am better now," Golgolkin said, the two men speaking in Russian. Leaning back against the pillows, one fat pink arm around each of the two girls, he said, "Room service."

"Fidel is scheduled to go before the cameras in three hours. He is refusing to step down. Two of the brothers want to shoot him."

"I have bigger problems," the Russian said, and drained a beaker of orange juice and vodka.

"Yes, you do, comrade. *El nuevo comandante,* General Manso de Herreras, wants to see you. Now."

"Where is he?"

"I'm to bring you to him. You'd better tell your little playmates goodbye and come with me."

"Comrade Zukov, I need help. I have made a mess of

this. I am probably a dead man. But you owe me, Zukov. You have a submarine under your feet again, thanks to me."

"I will do what I can, Comrade Golgolkin. That's all I can promise. I work for the Cubans, now, not the Russians."

"That fucking Englishman Hawke is responsible for this mess! He made me tell. It wasn't vodka talking. I swear it. I was going to die. He was going to kill me and Grigory without a thought."

Zukov looked away from the pitiful spectacle on the bed. He had other things on his mind.

"Get dressed. He's waiting. I'll be outside."

Golgolkin sighed, climbed out of the bed, and pulled on a bathing suit imprinted with cartoon exploding Cuban cigars. He saw his soiled white *guayabera* on the floor at the foot of the bed and he shouldered himself into it. Fear was rising in his stomach and the sour taste of it overpowered the vodka and orange juice he'd been drinking since sunrise.

Golgolkin did not expect to see the sun set on this day. He turned to the two girls remaining in his bed.

"If I'm still alive at sundown, we'll go for a nice swim," he said, patting them both on their heads. He smiled and walked out into the sun. Zukov was just outside his door, leaning against the balcony rail of the *finca,* smoking a yellow cigarette.

"Want one?" he asked, offering the pack. "Egyptian Deities. You can only find them here."

"It may be time for me to start smoking," Golgolkin said. "Life being so unpredictable, eh, comrade?" He took one. Zukov thrust his lighter at him and the man flicked it, lighting the cigarette. The lighter was solid gold, with a ruby hammer and sickle, and Golgolkin turned it over in his hand, the sun striking the red stones.

"There was one pretty good Marx, you know, comrade. Julius Henry Marx. Groucho," Golgolkin said.

"Follow me," Zukov said, and strode off, making his way through thick stands of palm trees toward the beach. Golgolkin struggled to keep up, huffing and puffing his cigarette. Most Muscovites find it hard to learn to walk in sand, he'd noticed. Not Zukov.

"Where are we going?"

"To the beach," Zukov said, expelling a cloud of smoke that wafted back. "You see that big yellow *finca* over in the trees? With all the guards? That is where they are holding Fidel and his son Fidelito. The Maximum Leader's future, too, is very uncertain at this point."

"There is no need to torture me, Zukov."

"Cheer up, comrade. The odds are in your favor. Two out of three brothers want to kill Fidel. Only one wants to shoot you."

They arrived at a small crescent of a bay, rimmed with palms leaning almost horizontally out over the surf. Manso sat with his back against one such tree, quietly smoking a cigar. He had his old machete next to him, the blade buried halfway in the sand.

"Please sit," he said, and Zukov translated the Spanish into Russian.

"Cohiba?" he asked, pulling a crocodile cigar case from his shirt pocket and offering it to both men. *"El jefe's* favorite."

"No, gracias," Zukov said for both of them. Golgolkin's complexion was already green enough from the cigarette. A cigar would not help.

"Comrade Golgolkin," Manso said, leveling his eyes at the arms dealer. "I am sorry to hear that you are not feeling well."

The Russian nodded. He bent over and placed his hands on his knees. He seemed incapable of speech.

"This should help," Manso said, and he picked up a large ripe coconut lying in the sand directly in front of Golgolkin.

"The *macheteros* say the milk of the coconut has miraculous powers," Manso said. "It can cure practically anything. All you have to do is cut its head off and drink. Like this."

As Zukov translated this, Manso tossed the coconut high into the air, waited for it to begin its descent, and then whipped his machete from the sand. The blade of Manso's machete caught the sun as it slashed the falling fruit in mid-air, neatly clipping off the top third of the coconut. Manso caught the coconut itself in his free hand, splashing some milk into Golgolkin's lap.

"Cures everything except, of course," Manso said, getting to his feet and handing the dripping coconut to Golgolkin, "a stupid fucking cowardly heart. Drink!"

"Colonel, please! I beg—"

"Shut your mouth. I said drink!" Manso stepped behind the Russian and held the machete at his throat. A thin red line of blood appeared where the knife pierced his flesh.

"Drink!"

Golgolkin looked at Zukov, pleading with his eyes, and said nothing. He splashed some coconut milk into his trembling mouth.

"You must be curious, comrade, as to why you are still alive, no?" Manso said, releasing him.

Golgolkin, his head lowered, whispered yes.

"You were incredibly stupid to come here to *Telaraña*, Golgolkin. One wants to say suicidal."

"I-I wanted to warn you about the Americans. Prove my loyalty. And this man, Hawke. Help you to—"

"*Silencio!* First, you betray me to this fucking Englishman," Manso said. "Then you and your personal geniuses at your Russian embassy in Washington somehow bungle a simple assassination. You blow up a fucking waiter instead of the target, but still manage to bring both the CIA and the FBI down on our heads. And your response to all this? At an exact moment in time when everything for my country, I mean everything, hangs in the balance? Climb in bed with some whores and get drunk."

"In fairness, Colonel," Zukov said after translating. "He was—"

"Fairness? Don't be ridiculous. I am not finished with this cowardly pig. Is he still listening to me?" Manso forced more coconut milk down the gagging man's throat. "Does he listen?"

Zukov nodded as a red-eyed Golgolkin swallowed, heaved, and sputtered, spewing the whitish liquid on the sand and making mewling noises at the same time.

"He's listening."

"Tell him I am giving him one final chance. One. Does he understand?"

"He says anything, Colonel. He will die trying anything to redeem himself to you."

"Yes, he probably will. Listen extremely carefully. I want this Alexander Hawke neutralized. His nose out of my fucking business. My people in Washington say Hawke has returned with his woman to the Caribbean."

Golgolkin uttered something in guttural and unintelligible Russian.

"He wants to kill this man Hawke for you, Colonel," Zukov said. "He swears that he will bring you his head or die in the trying."

Manso threw down the coconut and looked up into the whispering palm fronds, composing himself.

"I'll have Hawke's head. Believe me, Zukov, I will. But, for the present, no. Hawke has too many friends in Washington, including the White House. I don't care how it's done, but I want this Hawke out of the picture until the time is right for his execution."

"There is another plan. Rodrigo's. He says some kind of a kidnapping—"

"Rodrigo has told me this new plan. Execute it. He has a genius for these things, Commander Zukov. He is my most trusted and valued comrade. Keep him close by you."

"*Sí, Comandante.* He is waiting now aboard the *José Martí.* We shove off for the Exumas in three hours. Immediately after the dedication ceremony."

"You will not fail me. Nor will Rodrigo. Do you understand me, Zukov?"

Zukov nodded his head.

Manso stuck the machete back inside his belt. As he turned to go, he slammed his fist against Golgolkin's nose. The sound of the small bones breaking and the resulting gush of blood made him smile for the first time all morning.

"Won't you join me, Commander?" he asked Zukov. "On this lovely morning?"

Manso and the Russian submarine driver strode off through the palms, leaving Golgolkin blubbering in the sand. They headed in the direction of the large yellow *finca*. *El jefe* would be coming around by now. After last evening's heavy sedation, Manso had ordered the doctors to give him a cocktail injection of methamphetamines at sunrise.

"I must speak of something delicate. I can count on your discretion?"

"It goes without saying."

"It is regarding my brother, Admiral de Herreras."

"*Sí, Comandante?*"

"He is—how to say it—unpredictable. You would do well to keep an eye on him. I have told Rodrigo the same thing."

"I understand perfectly."

"The navy is his. The *José Martí* is yours. You understand me?"

"*Sí, Comandante.*"

"The Cuban naval officers you've interviewed, they are ready to go?"

"They have much to learn, but they are eager."

"These are your orders," Manso said, withdrawing a folded sheaf of papers from his pocket. "The Borzoi shakedown cruise now becomes your first active mission as a commander in the Cuban navy."

"*Muchas gracias, Comandante,*" he said. "I can never thank you enough for this great opportunity."

"I leave you to the final preparations for your fabulous submarine's first real sea duty. I am going now to have a word with *el jefe.*"

Manso turned to go, stopped, and looked Zukov in the eye.

"One more thing," he said. "I never want to lay eyes on that fat Russian traitor again. I would dearly love to lop off his ugly head. But he knows this Hawke, and he knows his boat and its location. Use him on your mission, if you can, and then feed him to the fishes. Or I'd be happy to introduce him to Rodrigo and his little silver scissors."

"He may prove useful," Zukov said. "Either way, you will never see him again, General."

Manso walked away, whipping his pistol out of his holster. A magnificent weapon. It was a Sig Sauer nine-millimeter, plated in solid gold with pearl handlegrips. It had been a gift from Escobar. All the pilots had received one on the final Christmas. He had not killed anyone with it yet. Out of habit, he checked the clip to see if it was loaded.

It was.

He found *el jefe* sitting on the side of his bed with his head in his hands. His breakfast tray, untouched, sat on a table by the open window. Manso pulled up a chair and sat facing the old man.

"*Jefe,*" Manso said, "I have something to show you."

The *comandante* looked up at him, his eyes shot red with blood.

"I have nothing left to see," he said.

"No. You have this left to see." Manso handed him a yellowed manila envelope, tied with string.

"What is this?"

"Open it."

His fingers were shaking as he untied the string that sealed the flap. He was muttering something under his breath but Manso didn't bother to try to understand. He was watching the old man's eyes as he pulled out a sheaf of faded brown-and-white photographs.

"Mercedes Ochoa," *el jefe* said.

"You recognize her."

"Of course."

He held the picture up close. Manso had looked at the picture a thousand times. As a boy, it hung on the wall above his bed.

The two young lovers were standing arm in arm outside the camp in the Sierra Maestra. The woman so young, so beautiful. Beaming in the bright sunlight of a jungle clearing. So proud. The man smiling, too, and powerful. A conqueror emerging from the jungle, poised on the verge of perfect vengeance. A victor's eyes, even before the fight.

"There are other pictures, *Jefe*," Manso said. "Keep looking."

Fidel looked up and saw that Manso had the golden gun aimed squarely at his heart. He looked at all the pictures. He sighed and laid them carefully on the bed.

"So, it's true then," Castro said.

"You knew all along?"

"I suspected."

"My mother was nothing to you. Just another tissue you used and threw away."

"That is not true."

"Liar."

"Think what you want. Shoot me now. But spare Fidelito."

"Ah, of course. Your *real* son."

"I ask you to spare his life."

"For the good of the country, then, I want you to say to the cameras all the words I have written. Then, if you still want to die—"

"You will grant your father's last wish? The son will live. The father will die. Do you swear it?"

"I swear it, Father."

35
●●●—●●

Rafael Gomez was on the floor playing dolls with his daughters when the telephone rang.

Rita picked it up on the third ring. She was in the kitchen making Gomer's favorite Sunday supper, *arroz con pollo.*

"It's for you, honey," she said. He noticed she'd started calling him "honey" and "baby" again. Pretty good progress. He'd cut way back on the suds factor. *Nada* on the vodka. Came straight from duty to the house with no detours to the USO. No hanky-panky with Rita under the covers yet, but he was getting close. Second base maybe, rounding for third.

Life was good when you were a millionaire. Even if you couldn't spend it, you knew it was there. "Who is it, sweetie?" Gomer asked. "We're pretty busy with Barbie and Ken down here. They won't put on their bathing suits and we're all going to the beach."

"Who is calling, please?" he heard Rita ask, the phone cradled under her ear, stirring something garlicky in a big pot.

"It's Julio Iglcsias," she said, covering the mouthpiece and making a face.

"Oh, okay. Good. I'll take it up in the bedroom. Thanks, hon."

She gave him a look as he got up and left the kids on the living room floor. That was okay. Plenty of quality time on the way. He was going to make them all so rich it didn't matter. In the bedroom, he plopped down on the bed and picked up the phone.

"This is Elvis," he said.

"*Hola,* the king himself. I am honored."

"What's up, Julio?"

"It's Iglesias."

"Sorry. Listen, Iglesias, I'm kinda busy right now, so—"

"Oh. You're busy. Well, in that case—"

"No, no. I just meant, well, it's a little hard to talk now, you know?"

"It's a little hard to talk to you anytime, Elvis. Is your wife giving you our messages? We haven't heard shit from you in over a week."

"Maybe because there's nothing to say."

"Everything is okay?"

"Everything is perfect."

"You are ready?"

"Does a bear shit in the woods?"

"*Perdón?* What?"

"It means of course I'm ready. The bear is ready." Gomer, thinking about the big white teddy bear, couldn't help laughing at his own bear joke.

"Well, good, really good. Because, to tell you the truth, Elvis, we're getting kinda close here."

"Close?"

"*Sí, amigo,* close."

"Like, uh, how close are we getting?"

"I think the cockaroaches should be all packed and ready to check out of the motel. You understand what I'm saying?"

"Yeah. I understand. It's checkout time."

"*Sí.* But not tonight. When I have the exact checkout time, Julio or I will call you. You have the RC?"

"Yeah, the RC, it's out in the garage."

"You remember what to do when you get the call?"

"I hit the little button on the left and when it starts to blink I put in thirty hours."

"*Perfecto.* You are not so stupid as Julio thinks you are."

"You tell Julio I'm happy to kick his sorry ass any time he's ready."

"I am kidding you, Elvis. Relax. You sound so tense."

"Tense? Why should I be tense? I kill a coupla thousand people every day."

"You sound like you have second thoughts, *señor.* Perhaps we should talk about this. You know, the money, it is not released to you until we are satisfied you have accomplished your mission. You know that?"

"I don't have the money? What the fuck are you—?"

"I didn't say that. You have it. But you can't get to it until I give you the account password. It's a numeric code that allows you to withdraw. See what I mean, Elvis?"

That's when Rita stuck her head in the door.

"Honey—dinner's ready. Can you get off the phone, please?"

"Yeah, I'm just—gimme a sec, okay, sweetie? I'm just finishing up here."

"As long as you've got him on the phone, tell Julio I loved that old album he did with Willie Nelson," Rita said, and slammed the door.

Christ. This spy stuff was tough. He looked at the phone in his hand and saw that it was shaking again.

"Listen, Iglesias, I've done my part. Your bug bomb is hidden where nobody on earth could find it. You call me, say the word, and the bugs will vacate that fucking cockaroach motel like Chinamen with their pants on fire in a fuckin' firecracker factory."

"*Bueno, bueno.* I'm sure you will not let us down. After all, you have a lot to lose, *señor.*"

"I ain't jeopardizing a million bucks, pal, believe me."

"I'm not only speaking of money, *señor.*"

"What the hell—?"

"If you do not do exactly, I mean, exactly, as I say—if there is even a hint of stupidity or cowardice or duplicity, you will lose a lot more than money, *Señor* Gomez."

"You want to tell me what the fuck you're talking about?"

"You have an Aunt Nina in Miami. She won't suffer. A nine-millimeter to the back of the skull. They'll find her someday, stuffed in a rental car trunk at the bottom of a canal somewhere in the Everglades."

"Are you—"

"Then, of course, there is Rita. She will be last. Before she goes, she will witness the deaths of your two young daughters. Their names, let me look at my notes, yes, their names are Tiffany and Amber. First Tiffany, then Amber, then Rita. They will all die slowly. Have you got all that, Elvis?"

"I think you guys are smoking something, right? Just screwing around with me to—"

"Good luck, Elvis. I just want you to know what you're dealing with here. We're watching your every move. Be a good boy. We will be in touch very shortly."

"Oh, man. Fuck me," he said, and put down the phone. "Fuck me all to hell."

Gomez went down the stairs and out to the garage. He reached up to a high shelf and pulled down a big old Maxwell House can half full of nails and stuff. There was a half-full pint of Stoli inside, too. He sat down at his workbench and tipped the bottle back.

Good old Vitamin V. Yeah, it helped. Steadied his nerves. If he was ever going to get the goddamn million dollars, staying steady was critical.

Not to mention keeping his goddamn family alive. God, you mind your own business, join the Navy, get married, and then wake up one day and find yourself mixed up in all kinds of shit. Everything goin' along just fine and then, whammo.

36

He had the little sloop close-hauled, on a reach out across the sparkling blue bay. There was a freshening breeze blowing out of the northeast and he had *Kestrel* heeled hard over, making a good eight knots through the water, bound for Hog Island. Ahead, a vicious riptide flowed out to sea between Hog and its nearest neighbor, a small island called Pine Cay. He needed to tack the boat just before he entered the rip and then it was an easy downwind run up into the Hog Island lagoon.

"We're going to come about in a few seconds," Alex said.

"Is there anything I can do to help?" Vicky shouted from her perch on deck just aft of the mast. She was slathered in oil, her face to the sun, long tresses streaming behind her. She was wearing a bright red two-piece bathing suit with a see-through linen top over it and she had simply never looked more beautiful.

"You can get ready to duck," Alex said, with as much nonchalance as he could muster at the moment. *Kestrel*'s boom was solid spruce and nearly as thick as a telephone pole. And in this strong breeze, it was going to come screaming over the deck when he tacked the boat. Alex knew how hard the wooden boom was. It had slammed him unconscious once during a violent storm in the Azores, putting him out for three hours.

Vicky scrambled to get back down into the cockpit, but she slipped on the steep pitch of the wet deck and screamed, grabbing a stanchion at the last second.

"Hang on, darling," Alex said over the wind. "Hold on to something. Always."

"One hand for yourself and one for the boat," Vicky said. "Temporary lapse of nautical memory."

Kestrel was not big, only about twenty-six feet overall, but she was beautiful, with white topsides, teak decks, and a lovely old mahogany cabin top. A Sitka spruce mast soared overhead flying a snowy white mainsail and a big Genoa jib, now filled with wind.

There was nothing much below save a V-berth forward, a small head, and an alcohol stove. When Alex had the boat in England, he sometimes took short cruises around the Channel Islands, the places where he'd grown up. Then he'd sleep aboard the little boat and do all the cooking on the small stove. Now he kept *Kestrel* stowed in a sling inside *Blackhawke's* massive hangar deck.

"How fast are we going?" Vicky cried, arching her back and letting her long hair trail over the gunwale.

Alex didn't reply, he was looking aloft at the slight flutter of luff in the mainsail. He hauled in on the mainsheet. Vicky could not tell if he was still angry with her after last night's conversation. He'd been very charming all morning, and she thought he was probably embarrassed at his outburst.

He'd knocked on her cabin door at eleven, carrying a tray with tomato juice, lemon wedges, aspirin, and Alka-Seltzer. There was a silver vase with three yellow roses. Her favorites.

"Look alive, matey! We shove off at noon sharp," he'd said after delivering the goods and just before pulling her cabin door closed behind him.

She'd downed all three hangover potions and staggered to the shower, letting the steaming hot water work its wonders. By noon, she was in reasonably good shape. The prospect of a quiet picnic on a desert island lifted her somewhat soggy spirits.

"All right," Alex now said, "we're going to come about now and tack for Hog Island. Get ready to duck when I tell you."

"Ready, Skipper," Vicky said, nervously eyeing the big wooden boom that would soon come swooping across the decks.

"Ready about?" Alex cried.

"Ready about," Vicky replied. She uncleated the mainsail sheet, as Alex had taught her on the sail across the bay. After the tack, she would haul in on the sheet and take a few wraps around a winch on the opposite side. She'd done a little sailing with her father on the Potomac, and it was coming back to her. Alex seemed surprised she knew a sheet from a halyard.

"Hard alee!" Alex said, and put the tiller hard over, swinging *Kestrel*'s bow up into the wind and then over onto a dead run straight for the small island. Alex eased the main and jib sheets and the little sloop surged forward.

Vicky had ducked just as the thick boom came slashing over her head. Pine Cay was now on their starboard side and looked quite beautiful. The entire island seemed to be covered with tall Australian pines. She could almost hear the wind whistling through the swaying trees. It looked enchanting and she found herself wishing it were their destination. "Hog" wasn't nearly as romantic-sounding as "Pine."

Hog Island, in fact, was distinctly unlovely. She could make out some scrub palms along the shore and the backbone of an old wooden boat half-sunk in the sand.

"What a pretty little island that is," she said, pointing at the one called Pine Cay. "Maybe next time we could have our picnic there?"

"Yes, darling," Alex said. "Next time. Hog Island may not be the prettiest, but it's the only one inhabited by a blind pig."

Alex freed both halyards and dropped the mainsail and jib to the deck. *Kestrel* ghosted up into the little crescent of a lagoon. Nearing shore, the boat slowed and Alex scrambled forward to the bow. He picked up the small Danforth anchor and flung it overboard.

"Sorry, but we'll have to anchor out here. It's as close in as I can get with our deep keel. Go ahead and swim ashore. I'll follow with the picnic basket."

"That's a big roger, sailor boy," Vicky said. She climbed up onto the top of the cabin house, removed the linen top she'd been wearing over her bikini, and gracefully dove over the side into the crystalline blue water. Alex noticed she swam with long powerful strokes. She reached the shore in seconds and ran from the surf, sprinting across the hot sand.

She stretched out on the white sand in the shadow of the half-buried fishing boat and watched Alex wade ashore. He was struggling through the surf, trying to balance the wicker basket he held on his head.

"Come on, MacArthur, you can make it!" she shouted.

Alex emerged grinning from the surf and ran to her. He placed the picnic basket beside her and ran his fingers through his damp black hair.

"Would you mind unpacking everything?" he asked. "I want to go check on something."

"Looking for Betty?"

"No, Betty will arrive as soon as she smells food. I'll be right back."

She opened the basket and pulled out a blue and white beach towel. There was a large H with a small crown above it embroidered on the towel. Spreading it on the sand, she began to unpack the basket. She pulled out a bottle of still-cold Montrachet, a baguette of French bread, and several kinds of cheese. She wasn't very hungry following her night on the town, but the wine certainly looked good. Where was the corkscrew?

Alex walked along the shoreline until he spotted it. A lone blackened palm standing amidst the charred and scrubby vegetation. He walked inland and soon found the crater the surface-to-air missile had made when it crashed. It was about six feet across and three feet deep. He sifted through the sooty palm fronds and twisted shards of metal until he found what he was looking for.

A jagged piece of the missile with identifying marks. The piece was badly burned, but he could see something stamped into the metal. It wasn't a Stinger after all. It was a Russian bloc SAM-7. The section in his hands looked as if it might have been one of the fins. With any luck, it might be enough for the "bomb baby-sitter," as Tate had called the deputy secretary of defense, to help put the pieces of this puzzle together.

"Well, that was certainly mysterious," Vicky said when he returned. "Marching off down the beach, clearly a man on a mission. What's that?" she asked, looking at the piece of black metal in his hand.

"Piece of evidence," he said.

"Really? Of what?"

"Attempted murder," Alex said, and knelt down on the blanket. "I think he would have got me, too, if Betty hadn't rattled him."

"Betty rattled a murderer?"

"This piece of metal is all that's left of a SAM missile a chap fired at me the other day. Betty knocked him down once, but he still managed to get a shot off."

"Hold on. Someone actually tried to blow you out of the sky? You've got to be kidding me!"

"Vicky, I sometimes get involved in negotiations for a third party. As frequently happens, one party feels my demands are unreasonable. They'd like me out of the loop."

"So, they tried to *kill* you? Alex, does this have anything to do with that briefcase?"

"That possibility is under investigation. Meanwhile, I thought it best we make *Blackhawke* our address for a week or two."

"Keep us out of the loop," Vicky said, looking at him evenly. "You said *us.*"

"It's me they're after. Would they try to get to me through you? I'd be less than honest if I said no."

After considering this for a few moments, she smiled and kissed him on the cheek. Then she spread some Brie on a piece of the baguette and handed it to him. "Eat up. Wine?"

"Yes, please," he said, eating the bread and holding out a wineglass.

She filled his glass with the cold white wine. It was wonderful with the bread and cheese. She'd already had two glasses herself. After feeling absolutely horrible all morning, she was now starting to feel pleasantly indolent and relaxed. The sun and salt were beginning to work their way into her. The idea of two weeks like this was beginning to seem perfect.

It was the first time she'd seen Alex in a bathing suit. He looked good, she decided. Especially the legs. His body was hard and maybe too lean but for the bundled force gathered at his upper arms and shoulders. He caught her staring at him and brushed some sand off her cheek with his hand.

"You were a very naughty girl last night, Victoria."

"I was not."

"Yes, you were. And I've half a mind to give you a good sound spanking."

"Only half?"

"Shh, here comes my savior! Betty! Over here! Get out the oranges. Those are her favorites."

Vicky could hear the big pig meandering through the scrubby palms. The pig made loud snorting sounds as she emerged onto the beach and headed in their direction.

"She's huge," Vicky said, shrinking back from the beast. "And hairy. I thought pigs were soft and pink. And small."

"Betty is a very well-fed animal. She has many admirers. Hold out an orange in your hand. She'll take it from you."

Vicky did, and Betty immediately gulped it down whole.

"Terrible manners," Vicky said.

"She's a pig, for heaven's sake." Hawke patted Betty's snout affectionately. "A blind pig at that, aren't you, Betty?"

"A blind pig who saved your life, apparently."

"If not for Betty, I would now be, to use a favorite Americanism, toast,"Alex said while he patted and nuzzled the pig.

"I know you two are close, but is Betty going to be joining us for the entire picnic?"

"No. She just wanted to stop and say hello. Watch this."

Hawke grabbed the sack of oranges and apples, got to his feet, and strode down to edge of the surf. Betty followed him. Hawke threw all the oranges out beyond where the waves were forming, and all the apples, too. Betty trotted out through the surf, swimming just as a Labrador might, her nose leading her to the nearest oranges.

Hawke looked back and smiled, then sprinted through the sand and returned to Vicky.

"That ought to keep her busy for the better part of an hour," Hawke said, dropping to the towel.

"More wine?" Vicky asked.

"No, thanks. Wine and sunshine make me sleepy." He lay back on the towel and closed his eyes.

"Me, too," Vicky said, lying down beside him. "It is a lovely little bay."

"Isn't it?" Alex said, yawning. "I call it the Bay of Pig."

Vicky smiled. She rolled toward him, then propped her head up on her hand and stared at this man she'd come to love. He'd closed his eyes and there was a contented half-smile on his face. His thick black hair was wet and shining. His chest, beaded with salt water, was rising and falling rhythmically. What saved him, she thought, was that he had no idea how good-looking he was.

She sat up and unhooked the top half of her red bathing suit. Then she put her hand over his heart.

"Are you asleep?" she asked.

"Yes."

"Then I don't suppose you would mind terribly if I licked your shoulder?"

"What?"

"You heard me. Just a lick, lollipop. I love salt. I think I don't get enough of it, the way I eat. It's essential to the body's fluid balance, you know. Sodium. Chloride. Yummy."

"Lick away then, darling. Dine to your delightful sufficiency."

"Thank you."

"How am I?" he said, after a few moments of feeling her tongue dart about his neck and shoulders.

"Yummy," she said. "Can't get enough."

"You could always pour some olive oil and vinegar into my hair and make a small side salad to go with the entree."

"I'll stick with the main course, thank you."

"Suit yourself, then."

She started with his shoulder but soon moved to his chest and then to his belly. She immediately noticed a marked increase in his breathing rate.

"Sorry to bother you. I wonder if you would mind pulling down your bathing suit?" she asked, brushing the tips of her white, coral-tipped breasts across the deeply tanned skin of his belly.

"My bathing suit?"

"Here, I'll help you."

She took the bow of little white strings that held up

his navy blue bathing suit in her teeth and pulled them apart.

"There you go," she said. "Now, will you please pull it down?"

"Why should I do that?"

"Because you're my lunch and you're covering up my favorite part. The *piece de résistance.*"

He pulled both knees to his chest, lifted himself off the towel, and removed the bathing suit in one motion.

"Well done," she said.

"Happy now?" he said.

"Oh my, that does look good," Vicky whispered in his ear, and then her lips were everywhere, causing him to arch his back upwards involuntarily as he felt her mouth close around him.

They made love there on the beach with the blind pig swimming to and fro in the blue sea, chasing the apples and oranges. Vicky was astride him, riding, rocking, her hair matted to her forehead with the heat of both sun and passion, her eyes locked on his right up until the instant when she cried out and arched her back, raising her arms to the sky with both hands outstretched, reaching for something she'd never quite touched until this very moment.

She lay in his arms for a time, her head on his chest, listening to his heart pumping, feeling him fall slowly away from inside her and drift down into what she hoped was the bliss of a peaceful dream.

He began to snore softly. She got up and put on her bikini, looking down at him, smiling. Then she dropped to her knees once more and stroked the damp black ringlets of hair on his chest.

"Alex Hawke," she whispered to him, "you can't hear me, but you know what I wish more than anything? I wish I'd become a surgeon instead of what I am. I wish I could take a little scalpel inside that brain of yours and find the exact little furrow of gray matter where whatever hurts you is hiding. Snip, snip, snip, I would cut it out. And you'd never have those terrible dreams, ever again."

She sat up and brushed the hair back from her eyes. She sucked deep gulps of tangy air deep into her lungs, feeling totally invigorated, bristling with sharp, kinetic energy. She got to her feet and stood there, shielding her eyes with her hand, scanning the blue horizon. A flock of white seabirds was circling the pretty little island of pines beyond the channel.

Pine Cay, Alex had called it. It couldn't be more than a mile from where she stood. She was a strong swimmer. A competitive swimmer. She could swim across and explore the pine forest while Alex slept. She could probably be over and back before he woke up, he was sleeping so soundly. The water was such a lovely shade of light blue it seemed to be begging her to plunge in.

She swam out toward the delicious river of dark blue that ran between the two islands.

Alex had no idea how long he'd been asleep.

He sat up with a start, realizing Vicky was no longer beside him. He looked around, but didn't see her swimming or anywhere along the deserted beach.

He called out her name. No answer.

He leapt to his feet and ran along the line of scrub palms. Maybe she went exploring. He called her name repeatedly, thinking, she's barefoot. Why would she go back among the rough and prickly palms?

His heart started pounding. That's when he heard something that sent an arrow of fear through his heart.

Alex . . . Alex . . . Alex!

Faint. And coming from the sea.

He ran to the water's edge, desperately scanning the rolling waves for a sight of her. There. A faint smudge. It had to be Vicky. She was halfway across the pass between the two islands! In the very middle of the vicious riptide rushing toward the open sea!

He made a running dive and started swimming as hard as he could, cursing himself furiously for not warning her about the current. Stupid! He never dreamt that she'd go out that far, but remembered how enchanted she was with the pine-forested island. That had to be it. She'd decided to swim over and—

He stopped swimming and raised his head. He could barely make out the dim shape that had to be her.

No . . . no . . . no . . .

Her voice was weaker now, a faint *no* repeated over and over. She was telling him to stop. Telling him the current would only take him as well. He plowed ahead another fifty yards, feeling the swift pull of the running tide taking him into its grip.

He swam harder. He was strong. Stronger than this bloody current that was stealing Vicky away from him. He swam until the muscles in his legs and arms were burning and then he swam harder still.

Another look. There. She was much farther away now. He saw her go under. Then surface again. He swam toward her, heedless of the wicked pull of the water.

Raised his head, gasping for air. A sick, hollow feeling began to steal its way inside him. For every ten yards of progress he gained, she was being swept away another thirty.

He plowed forward, refusing to acknowledge it was hopeless now, unwilling to give up. He swam another thirty yards, feeling himself right on the periphery of where the rip was strongest. He raised his eyes, stinging with a mixture of tears and salt, and looked again.

"I love you!" he cried out, praying she might yet be able to hear him.

He saw her just that one last time, briefly, being pulled past Pine Cay now, and then he saw her go under. Waited. Fought the tide. Waited for that dear little head to surface, please, just once more and maybe he could get to—somehow get to—God—just to see her again . . .

He knew then that she was gone. Simply. Irrevocably. Gone.

He lifted his face to the heavens and screamed mercilessly at God.

Alex Hawke turned and swam as hard as he could for *Kestrel*. The edges of the rip had him, fought him, but not hard enough to overcome his rage. In minutes, he was climbing aboard the sloop. He ducked down through the companionway to the small navigation station.

There was a satellite phone hanging above the notebook computer with the GPS system.

Ambrose was on the sat phone speed dial.

He picked up on the first ring.

"I need immediate help," Alex said, gasping for breath. "Immediate! I need our main launch in the water headed out the cut between Hog Island and Pine Cay. At least two divers aboard. I need you to call the Bahamas Air-Sea Rescue Command at Harbor Island. Tell them we need search-and-rescue choppers out here now."

"Alex. Calm down. What's going on?"

"It's Vicky, goddammit."

"What's wrong, Alex?"

"She's gone. Swept out in the riptide. I don't know! Maybe we can save her! Christ, just get some bloody help out here, all right?"

"We're coming," Ambrose said, and hung up.

Alex scrambled back up on deck and hoisted the main and the jib. He weighed his anchor and headed the sloop out into the cut, his eyes fixed on the area where time and speed of current might have put her since he last saw her.

His eyes were burning. He was praying for that little brown smudge he'd last seen drifting away from him.

Praying to see it again. Simply praying for it to still exist.

37

Reel Thing, a brand-new fifty-foot Viking sport-fishing boat, was swinging on her anchor in the dark of a small cove. It was a hot moonless night, and only the lights of a few dim stars were visible. The cabin lights were all off below and above decks, and the sounds of the Allman Brothers came softly from speakers mounted throughout the boat.

The owner, Red Wallace, and his best fishing buddy, Bobby Fesmire, were sitting in the stern drinking Budweiser in the dark. Red was the biggest Ford dealer in South Florida. Bobby was his sales manager. Red and Bobby went way back. They'd gone to Florida at Gainesville together, pledged Kappa Alpha together, and played on the national championship Gator football team together. Both of them still wore their big gold NCAA rings with all the diamonds on their pinky fingers.

They took this little fishing trip to the Exumas as often as they could, which was once every two or three months. Sometimes they took clients so they could write it off, most often they'd bag the clients so it was just the two of them.

Tonight, they'd moored the boat in a small cove, ringed with mangroves. The wind was out of the east, so *Reel Thing* had her stern toward the small opening to the channel. Not that there was anything to see, but it gave them a view of the heat lightning blooming on the horizon.

"Know what heat lightnin' is, Bobby?" Red asked.

"Yeah. Lightnin' that comes from heat."

"No, it ain't. It's ordinary lightnin' comes from so far away, you can't see nothin' but the reflection of it. Ain't no such thing as heat lightnin'."

"Why the hell d'you bring it up then?"

"Just tryin' to educate your dumb ass, is all."

"I ain't so dumb."

"Only guy I ever knew saw a family reunion as a chance to meet girls."

"You sayin' it ain't?"

"Bobby, we had a class of five hundred and thirty-seven seniors graduate."

"Yeah?"

"You did not graduate in the top five hundred and thirty-six."

"And your point is? Grades don't mean nothin' in my book. Look at us. We're doing pretty damn good, I'd say. Couple of dumbass crackers sitting on top of the whole damn world. Look at that ring. What's it say?"

"NCAA National Champions."

"Bet your ass."

Earlier that afternoon, Bobby and Red had given up on marlin fishing and found a little cove to put up for the night. At sunset they'd sat out on deck, drinking beer and casting into the mangroves. Didn't hook a snook or any other kind of damn fish for an hour or so and gave up when it got too dark to see.

They had two big sirloins sitting out on the counter down in the galley but they'd pretty much forgotten about them. They'd wolfed down some boiled shrimp earlier. Good shrimp, too, from the Publix supermarket down the street from the Bahia Mar Marina in Lauderdale.

Red and Bobby had been down here scouring the Exumas and Bahamas for fish for about ten days. Red had been wearing the same T-shirt every day. It said, "My Drinking Crew Has a Fishing Problem."

That sentiment pretty much summed up the entire voyage. They hadn't caught a hell of a lot of marlin, but then again, as Red had often pointed out, they hadn't caught a hell of a lot of hell from their wives either.

Red, who was sitting in the fighting chair on the stern, took a big swig of his Bud and said, "Bobby, lemme ask you another goddamn question. How many fish we catch this week? Total."

"Three," Bobby said. "Maybe."

"And how many beers you reckon we've had all week?"

"Hundreds. Maybe a hundred and fifty."

"So, let's go with a hundred and fifty. Now let me ask you another question. How many times does three go into a hundred and fifty?"

"Shit, I dunno. What do you think I am? A human calculator?" Bobby burped deeply and tossed his empty over his shoulder.

"Hell, Bobby, it ain't like I'm asking you to divide goddamn Roman numerals! It ain't rocket surgery! It's simple damn arithmetic. You're a car salesman. You ought to be able to do the calculation. Three goes into one-fifty, lemme see now, fifty times."

"Sounds about right."

"My point is, we've achieved about fifty-to-one beer-to-fish ratio. And I think that's pretty goddamn good, considering."

"Considering what?"

"Considering the fact that I like Budweiser a hell of a lot better than I like fish. I'm going to tell you a secret I've never told anybody else. I can't stand the taste of fish. Hate it. You ever tell my wife, Kathy, that, I'll whup your sorry ass."

"Well, that's good, Red, that you don't like 'em," Bobby said. " 'Cause if them damn helicopters and search-and-rescue boats are back here in the morning, your chances of catching any marlin'll be about the same as they were today. Shitty."

"I was monitoring channel sixteen earlier, up on the flybridge. I think they gave up on whoever or whatever was missing out there. We should be all right for tomorrow."

"Maybe."

"I will eat a tuna fish sandwich," Red allowed after a long silence. "Long as it's got a lot of mayo. Mayo I can eat out of the jar."

"Hell, I've seen you do it."

"How many times America save France's ass, Bobby?"

"Least twice. And what'd they ever do for us?"

"That's my point. The frogs invented mayo. In my book that just about evens things up."

"Good point."

"Hell, Bobby, I'd eat a mud sandwich, you put enough mayo on it. Hey. You hungry?"

"Could be. You want, I'll go put that cow meat on the griddle?"

"I could eat—damn, it's late—what the hell time is it?"

"Gotta be getting close to midnight," Bobby said. "You want yours rare or—holy goddamn Christ! Red, what the hell is that?"

"Hell is what?"

"Look out there in the channel! Off to starboard. See it? Looks like the whole damn ocean is exploding!"

Red leapt out of his fishing chair and ran to the stern rail. Bobby was right. Something was going on out there. "Sonofabitch! Hand me them damn binocs, Bobby! Hanging right there by the tuna tower ladder."

Red put the binocs to his eyes and couldn't believe what he was seeing. The sea was exploding. About a thousand yards off the *Reel Thing*'s stern, out in the middle of the dark deep channel.

"Shitfire, Red! Lemme see."

He handed Bobby the binoculars.

"Jesus," Bobby said. "What is it, Red?"

"Whale? How the hell do I know? What am I, a god-damn oceanographer?"

A huge mound of boiling white water was growing in the midst of the inky waves of the channel. It became a mushroom shape, rising and growing, and then the roil-ing sea did explode and a massive sharp-edged black snout emerged, surging majestically into the midnight sky at a forty-five-degree angle. Black and white seawater was pouring off her sleek dark sides in sheets.

"Well, I'll be damned, Bobby," Red said, passing him the binocs just as the strangely shaped hull finally broke the surface.

"A goddamn living breathing submarine!" Bobby said.

Red looked at it, shaking his head in wonder.

"You ever seen a submarine look like that, Bobby?"

"I ain't never seen a goddamn thing looked like that. Sweet Jesus. Looks more like a UFO than a submarine."

The thing was still rising at an impossible angle. Then the triangular-shaped bow came crashing down into the boiling sea and the bizarre craft began a slow turn toward one of the many islands on either side of the channel.

Red couldn't believe his eyes. The hull was in the shape of a giant delta wing and what looked like some kind of weird conning tower was now rising from the apex of the two hulls. The sub was literally as broad abeam as an aircraft carrier.

"That's the biggest, craziest-looking damn submarine I've ever seen," Red said. "Hell, it looks like one of them stealth bombers and it's as big as a goddamn battleship!"

"It ain't natural-lookin', Red," Bobby said, staring at it.

"Something spooky about it. Like it's from goddamn Mars or something."

"Shitfire. Aliens in submarines," Red said. "What's next?"

"Yeah. You always wondering 'bout flying saucers. Well, maybe here's your goddamn answer!"

Water broke over the huge sub's bow in great white torrents, and, with the binocs, Red and Bobby could make out the silhouettes of three small figures appear atop the now fully exposed conning tower. Someone raised a fluttering flag to the top of a tall post capped by a red light.

A powerful searchlight on the sub's portside was switched on and swept the sea immediately around the sub. Just when the broad white beam was about to reach the opening to the little cove where *Reel Thing* was moored, it stopped and started back the other way. Deep in the cove, they would be pretty hard to see anyway.

"Look at the flag. It ain't Russian, is it, Red?" Bobby asked. "I mean, it is one of ours, right?"

Red had the binocs trained on the conning tower.

"Naw, it ain't Russian," Red said, studying the flag. "Then again, it ain't American either."

"Well, what then? Mars?"

"I seen that flag around here before. I just don't exactly remember which one it is. Jamaica?"

Bobby spewed beer all over the deck, he was laughing so hard. "Jamaica? Jamaica! They ain't got any damn submarines in Jamaica, Red."

"Well, you're so smart, go down in the cabin and bring me up that atlas. We'll look her up. Use a flashlight. And turn off that damn stereo, too. Maybe we're not supposed to be seeing this."

Bobby went below to get the book and Red stood staring at the sub, transfixed by it. He knew subs were down here in the Caribbean; hell, they were everywhere. But he'd never dreamed of eyeballing one up so close. Especially such an otherworldly machine.

The sub's searchlight flashed three times, two short and then one long. Then it was extinguished. Some kind of signal? Had to be.

In the last long flash of the searchlight, he'd seen three people come out of the woods on one of the little islands, just to the west. They were dragging a big inflatable across the beach, with an outboard on the back. Red saw them put it in the water. Then he heard the engine sputter and start, and then the raft was moving at high speed toward the submarine.

Drug deal. Goddamn drug deal. Colombians, probably. Shit, he should get on the radio and call the Coast Guard. It was a good thing that searchlight hadn't spotted them. But what if it was some kind of naval exercises thing? Top secret experimental shit. A joint U.S. war games thing with some allied country. Hell, where was Bobby with that atlas?

"It's Cuban," Bobby said, coming out of the dark cabin. He had the book in his hand. "I looked it up."

"Cuban?" Red said. "Cubans ain't got any goddamn submarines."

"Yeah, well they do now. Look on page sixty-two," Bobby said, handing Red the book and the flashlight. Before Red could make a move, Bobby started climbing like a drunken monkey up the ladder of the tuna tower.

"Bobby, goddamn you! What the hell you doin'? Come on back down here!"

Bobby, upon reaching the top of the tower and laughing like a madman, turned on the powerful spotlight and aimed it right at the submarine's conning tower.

"Jesus Christ, Bobby! They'll see us!"

"See the flag?" Bobby shouted down. "Now turn to page sixty-two and look at the flag. Then tell me it ain't Cuban!"

Suddenly, the sub's searchlight flashed on again. This time it didn't stop short of the *Reel Thing*.

Red put his hand up to his eyes. The light was blinding. He didn't know what the hell was going on but he did know one thing. He was getting his brand-new goddamn fifty-footer the hell out of there. Colombians and Cubans didn't much care for Americans and vice versa. He had a twelve-gauge Remington above his bunk, but the rusty old pump action wouldn't do much against a goddamn giant submarine.

He ran inside the darkened cabin and cranked up the twin five-hundred-horsepower Cummins diesels. Then he got on the radio to Bobby up on the tower.

"Bobby, now you listen to me. I don't know exactly what's going on, but something tells me we ought to skedaddle on out of here on the double. You get your ass down on the bow and get that anchor aboard. Right now. You hear me?"

In five minutes, Bobby had hauled the anchor aboard. Red went back on the stern and looked for the sub, but they'd turned the searchlight out and all he could see was blackness. Shit. Were they just waiting for him to come out?

Back at the wheel, he flipped on the flashlight and looked at his chart. He'd keep all his running and navigation lights off, run out of the cove fast as he could, put her hard over to port, and head for open sea. Full throttle. He wanted as much water between him and that damn sub as he could get.

Reel Thing was capable of a top speed of thirty-five knots. Once safely outside the cove, Red leaned hard on the throttles and headed for the wide open spaces.

Man, what an adventure, he thought, popping a Bud. He turned on his radar, fishfinder, and GPS and was comforted by the green dials lighting up and showing his position and speed. He looked for a blip of the sub on the radar screen. Nothing.

He considered calling the Coast Guard on sixteen, then thought better of it. It was, after all, none of his damn business. He just wanted to get back to Lauderdale and sell a few more goddamn Explorers. Now that most folks had forgotten about that goddamn tire fiasco, he was selling cars again.

Reel Thing was up on a plane, throwing masses of white water to either side of her bow. After a few minutes of high speed and cold beer, Red started to calm down. He throttled back a little. The engines were brand-new and he knew he shouldn't be running them at such high RPMs. Hadn't seen the sub on the radar anyway. Lost the sucker.

Then he had another thought, not as comforting. *Hadn't seen it on the radar because it had submerged.*

"Whoo-ee," Bobby said, lurching into the cabin, spilling beer on the carpet. "That was something."

"Why the hell'd you turn that light on, Bobby? Goddamn. All we had to do was sit there and mind our own damn business."

"I wanted to show you that Cuban flag, amigo. That's all. What the hell's wrong with you? Big old sub scare your ass?"

"Hell no."

"Then what'd you run away for then?"

"Bobby. Do yourself a favor. Shut the fuck up."

"Uh-oh. He's mad. Well, guess what. I'm going back up top that tuna tower, put on some Waylon, and have a couple of cold beers. So I won't be in your goddamn way, oh mighty Captain . . . Kangaroo."

Bobby pulled a six-pack out of the fridge and slammed the cabin door shut behind him.

Red settled back in his captain's chair, eased the throttles until they were at cruising speed, and picked up the sat phone. It was only around midnight. Maybe Kath would still be awake and they could have a little chat. He'd tell her he was all fished out and headed home. Tell her about the amazing encounter with the submarine.

He started to punch in his home number.

"Uh, Red?" he heard Bobby say over the speaker.

"What the hell you want now?" But he didn't like the sound of Bobby's voice as he finished dialing up his number on the sat phone.

Kath picked up on the first ring. Her voice was sleepy. He'd woken her up.

"Hey, Red, you might want to—"

"Hold on, Bobby, I'm talking to my damn wife! Hey, babe, sorry to wake you. How you doing?"

"You might want to come on up here, little buddy." Bobby's voice on the speaker.

"Sleepy," Kath said. "It's almost two in the morning, Red."

"Red? You coming?"

"Sorry, hon, my watch must have stopped. Hold on. I won't be a sec," he said into the phone.

Then, into the mike, he said, "Come up there? Goddammit, Bobby! Why the hell would I do that?"

"Something weird going on out here. I don't know what it is. Off our port beam. Long white thing in the water. Like a trail. Headed in our direction. Looks like it's coming right at us."

Red was just sober enough to understand this instantly.

"Honey, something crazy's going on," he said to his wife. "Lemme check it out. Hold on."

He dropped the phone and ran to the portside window. A trail of white, maybe a hundred yards away. He had time enough to say just one word.

"Shit."

The Soviet Mark III torpedo was traveling at a depth of thirteen feet. It was running at over sixty miles an hour and leaving a huge white wake. The nose of the torpedo was packed with enough explosive to level a city block.

It took only seconds for the torpedo to reach its target. It hit the *Reel Thing* dead amidships.

Red, Bobby, and the *Reel Thing* vanished. They had been atomized.

In Fort Lauderdale, Red's wife hung up the phone, having heard a fragment of loud noise and then silence. She shook her head, thinking of how much fun Red and Bobby had on these little getaways. Then she rolled over and went back to sleep.

The fire caused by the explosion was climbing into the blackness of the night sky. It was visible for four miles.

Less than a mile away, a man with his eyes glued to the periscope lens of the *José Martí* witnessed the destruction with grim satisfaction.

Commander Nikita Zukov of the *José Martí* removed his eyes from the rubber eyepiece of the periscope and allowed a wry smile to cross his face.

A fishing boat. He'd just sunk a stupid fishing boat.

He shook his head and flipped up the handles on either side of the periscope. There was a hiss of hydraulics as the tube slid into the deck. Then he turned to face his new crew of would-be submarine officers.

"Direct hit," he said nonchalantly in Spanish. "Target destroyed."

The Cuban officers standing around him in the dim red glow of the sub's control room burst into applause. They brought the scope back up and each took a turn at the eyepiece, watching the orange sky lit by fiery debris falling into the black sea. They were laughing, shouting "bravo," and clapping each other on the back.

Zukov stood back and watched them in disbelief. The former cold warrior could not decide if he was amused or humiliated by this scene and what had just precipitated it.

His first kill. After a brilliant twenty-year career. His first kill was a fifty-foot sport-fishing boat festooned with outriggers and fishing rods, instead of cruise missiles and eight-inch guns. With a crew of perhaps two men aboard.

The communications officer monitoring all radio transmissions announced that only one call had gone out from the boat and it wasn't a mayday. The *Martí*'s position had not been revealed before she had sunk them.

Good.

Two American fisherman. Aboard a rich man's fiberglass toy. Nothing to write home to Moscow about, but it was perhaps a start. First blood, at any rate.

Two figures stepped out of the shadows. It was Admiral de Herreras and the Russian Golgolkin, who'd stood silently by while the officers celebrated.

"May I have a look?" de Herreras said.

Zukov stepped back and let him use the periscope. The admiral studied the flaming debris pool for a moment, then swiveled the eyepiece ninety degrees left and stopped, grunting with satisfaction.

"Comrade Golgolkin, have a look. Is that it?"

Golgolkin put his eyes to the rubber cups, sweat stinging his eyes. His hands were shaking badly and he couldn't seem to focus the blurry image.

"Is that it," the admiral shrieked, "or is it not?"

Golglolkin nodded yes and stepped away from the periscope.

"So. Our next target, Commander Zukov," de Herreras said, grinning with satisfaction. "Have a look."

Zukov put his eyes to the scope and focused. It was beyond ridiculous. Impossible. A large private yacht, huge, over two hundred feet. Brightly lit. With a massive British flag fluttering in the breeze at her stern. Zukov took a deep breath, remembering Manso's admonition on the beach early that morning.

"It's not possible, Admiral," Zukov said.

"Why not? Comrade Golgolkin here has just informed me that *Blackhawke* is the ship of the man who betrayed us to the Americans. My sources in Washington say he's aboard. I wish to destroy him."

"A small fishing boat is one thing. Accidents happen. But this. The loss of life. It would be considered an act of war by the British, Admiral! A huge international incident! Surely you don't want to—"

"I am the fucking chief of naval operations, let me remind you! Are you refusing a direct order, Commander?"

"Sir, in good conscience I cannot—"

The Cuban admiral unfastened the leather holster that held his sidearm and raised the pistol. It was a silver-plated Smith & Wesson .357 magnum.

"I asked you a question, Commander. Are you refusing a direct order?"

"I am."

The explosion was instant and deafening inside the cramped control room. A fine red mist erupted from the back of the Russian commander's skull as brains and bone spattered all over the periscope. He swayed on his feet for a second, then collapsed in a heap on the deck. All of the men, both Russian and Cuban, looked on in horror.

"I am a firm believer in summary justice," the admiral said. "The man was a traitor. I am now in command of this vessel and I want that boat sunk. Is that clearly understood?"

No one said a word. The silence was as deafening as the gunshot. The already fetid air reeked of cordite and the coppery smell of blood. The Cuban admiral stepped over the body and stared hard at the shocked faces of his crew.

Golgolkin leaned back against the bulkhead and breathed a sigh of relief. Only an hour earlier, he had slipped into Zukov's quarters and rifled through his orders. Zukov had orders to kill him once the mission was completed. Now that Zukov was dead, perhaps he was safe. He stepped back into the shadows, removed a silver flask from his pocket, and drained it.

"I want someone to take a bearing on this target and sink it," the admiral said, his face turning bright red. "Now!" he bellowed.

No one moved or spoke. After an endless minute, an officer who had been standing by the ballast control panel stepped forward. He moved slowly through the reddish smoky light, eyes riveted on the Cuban with the pistol in his hand. He dropped to his knees beside the fallen captain.

There, kneeling beside his oldest and dearest friend, he looked up at the glowering admiral with tears of rage in his eyes.

"I am the boat's executive officer, Comrade Admiral," he said in Spanish. "Vladimir Kosokov, second in command. This man you have murdered was my boyhood friend in Cuba. I have been his XO in the Soviet Navy for ten years."

"Very well. I order you to sink that vessel!" the admiral roared.

"In my cabin are orders given me by Commander Zukov. They come directly from General Manso de Herreras. They are explicit, Admiral. They say that if anything should happen to Zukov, I am to assume command, offload you at Staniel Cay, and return the submarine immediately to base."

The Cuban regarded him in shocked silence. His own brother! Manso would pay for this humiliation.

"Fine. You can die beside your traitorous friend."

"I would be honored. But I must warn you. This is the most advanced submarine on earth. And I am the only one aboard now capable of getting it safely home. And the only one who knows the codes for fire control sequencing of all weapons. Kill me, and you render the submarine useless. And condemn every man on this vessel, Russian or Cuban, to certain death."

The admiral raised his pistol once more, his countenance aflame with righteous anger. The crew waited in silence for their death sentence, every eye focused on the finger that would squeeze the trigger.

A tall, thin man emerged from the shadows, shot out his hand, and gripped the admiral's wrist.

"Give me the gun, Carlitos," the man said quietly, and the admiral, eyes blazing, did as he was told.

It was the man the crew had been whispering about during the entire voyage. The man who seldom left his cabin and never spoke. The new Cuban head of state security. Rodrigo del Rio.

The man with no eyes.

38

· · · — · ·

Alex Hawke sat on the edge of his bed, smoking a cigar and staring at the black telephone. There was a half-empty bottle of scotch whiskey beside the phone.

He shook his head and tried to clear it. This morning, he had awoken in this very bed in the rapturous state of a man in the midst of a love affair. Now he felt as if he had been broken into infinitely small pieces, starting with his heart.

The Bahamian Air-Sea Rescue Teams had called off the search after twelve hours. Hawke, having failed in his pleas to get them to continue, had stayed aloft in his seaplane for another few hours, sweeping in low grid patterns over the empty moonlit waters. Finally, just after midnight, he'd landed in the lagoon and taxied up to the ramp at *Blackhawke*'s stern.

Ambrose and Stoke had been standing there, waiting for him. They started to say something, but Hawke interrupted.

"How?" he said, staring at them angrily, for that's what he felt now, anger superseding his sadness. "How could one man be so bloody stupid as to allow anyone to swim out into that bloody current? Without a warning? Not a word! How? Answer me!"

Ambrose and Stoke reached out to him but he brushed past them. He paused and turned to face them.

"Here's the bloody answer! I might as well have drowned her with my own hands! What's the difference? Murder is murder!"

He climbed four flights of stairs and went straight to his stateroom, where he had remained. He called the bridge and told the captain to call him on the direct line if there was any news. Then he turned off the main phone and opened a bottle of whiskey.

In that way, he had spent an hour or so, drinking and staring at the phone to the bridge, willing it to ring. It didn't. There had many knocks at his door and he'd ignored them all. At some point, Ambrose had slipped an envelope under his door but he'd ignored that as well.

Somehow, later, he heard the ship's bell chiming. Four bells. Two o'clock in the morning. Alex rubbed his eyes and looked at his watch. Two A.M., which would make it maybe midnight in Louisiana.

He picked up the half-empty scotch bottle and climbed the stairway leading up one deck, making his way along the companionway to Vicky's stateroom. Save the low thrumming of generators, the ship was dead quiet. There were a few crewmen about, armed, looking out over the rails to sea. They kept the underwater flood-lights on all night now, and monitored the video cameras installed below the waterline twenty-four hours a day.

There was a man out there somewhere who clearly wanted to kill him. Little did that man know his target was already dead.

Her room was just the way she'd left it, hats, blouses, scarves, bathing suits, straw hats, all strewn about the bed. He sat down amongst these things, not quite sure why he'd come here. Unable to stop himself, he picked up her pillow and pressed it to his face. The scent of her perfume, of course, still lingered there.

God.

Then, through eyes blurred with tears, he saw the address book on her nightstand and remembered why he had come here. He opened the book to S and didn't find what he was looking for. He turned to D and there it was.

Daddy. And a 225 area code. Louisiana.

Even the sight of her handwriting in the address book was unbearable. When he thumbed through its pages, a small envelope fell out. It had his name on it. It wasn't sealed.

Inside were two tiny photographs. The ones that had

been inside his mother's locket. Then he remembered. She'd vowed to wear the locket always. She must have removed the pictures that morning, not wanting to harm them, realizing they'd be going for a swim on the island.

He remembered the golden locket hanging from her neck, suspended between their bodies, swinging to and fro in the rhythms they were creating, the two of them there on the sand beside the ripples of pale blue waters that lapped the sand. And the swift dark blue waters farther out.

He uttered the one oath he'd always considered himself too much of a gentleman to say and reached for the receiver. He began punching in the number he'd found in the book. He lost track of the number of times the phone rang before anyone picked it up.

"Hello?" a sleepy Southern voice finally said.

"Is this Seven Oaks plantation? LaRoche, Louisiana?" he asked.

"Yes, suh, shore is."

"This is Alexander Hawke calling. I'd like to speak to Senator Harley Sweet, please."

"Might be asleep out on the porch, suh. Too hot to sleep indoors, but the senator, he's not a believer in air-conditioning."

"I'm sorry to disturb him, but would you please tell him it's extremely important?"

"Well, if you say so, suh, I surely will do that. Will you hold the phone? I'll go see if I can rouse him up."

Alex waited, rubbing his eyes, staring at the framed picture of Vicky and him on her nightstand. They had their arms around each other, standing beside the Serpentine in

Hyde Park. When the deep voice suddenly came on the line, it startled him.

"This is Harley Sweet."

"Senator, we've never met. This is Alexander Hawke calling."

"Alex Hawke! Well, it's mighty fine to finally hear your voice, son. I've been hearing an awful lot about you from my little girl."

"That's why I'm calling, Senator. I'm afraid I have some horrible news. There's been an accident."

"What do you mean? Is Vicky hurt?"

"Senator, I'm afraid Vicky has been lost."

There was a long silence, and Alex just held the phone to his ear, numb, staring at her face in the picture.

"Lost? You mean dead? Tell me exactly what happened, Mr. Hawke."

"We, uh, we went for a picnic this afternoon on a small island. Just Vicky and I."

"Vicky is my only child, sir."

"I know that, Senator. I must tell you that I'd far rather be dead myself than giving you this news."

"Go on, son. Tell me about it."

"We had a small lunch. After we'd eaten, we both fell asleep on the beach. When I awoke, I didn't see her. I thought perhaps she'd gone off exploring the island. I didn't see her swimming, so I looked up and down the beach. I—"

"Please continue, Mr. Hawke. I'm sure this is difficult for you."

"Sorry, sir. I heard a faint cry coming from the sea. There is a deep channel a few hundred yards offshore. It runs between the island where we'd gone and another island about a mile away."

"Yes?"

"I could see her. It was Victoria. She was almost two thirds of the way to the other island. I could see that the, uh, current had her. The riptide."

"What did you do, Mr. Hawke?"

"I swam for her, of course. I tried to keep her in sight. It's a riptide that runs to the open sea. It was moving very swiftly."

"You were unable to reach her?"

"I'm a good swimmer. I swam as hard as I could. She was calling to me, saying no, telling me to go back, I think. She might have realized it was useless at that point. I—"

"You gave up."

"No, sir, I did not. I swam out into the rip. When I looked up, I realized that for every ten yards I was gaining, the tide was opening the gap between us by thirty or forty yards, maybe more."

"You lost sight of her?"

"I saw her go under. I swam for her. She came up once more and called out something, but by then she was too far away."

"And then?"

"I watched her go under. She never came back up."

"My baby is gone?"

"I had Bahamas Air-Sea Rescue and my own men on the scene within fifteen minutes. We continued the search for eight hours without any—without any sign of her, sir."

"I understand."

"I've ordered the search to resume at first light, Senator. I'm going back out in my own plane as well."

"I'm certain you're doing all you can, Mr. Hawke. I appreciate your efforts on my daughter's behalf. If you'll excuse me now, I'm going to hang up the phone."

"Senator, I cannot possibly tell you how grievously sorry I am. This is all my fault."

"Vicky was a very powerful swimmer, Mr. Hawke. All-American at Tulane. She swam all the way across Lake Pontchartrain when she was thirteen years old. She knew what she was doing. The idea that a current might be too strong would never occur to her."

"But I should have—"

"My daughter would not have wanted you or anyone else to die needlessly. If there'd been a prayer of you reaching her, I'm sure you . . ."

"I couldn't, sir. I couldn't."

"Son, listen to me. I've never had the pleasure of meeting you, but if my daughter cared for you, you must be a good man. Vicky grew up in this old tumbledown place. It was just the two of us. Her momma died in childbirth."

"I'm sorry, sir."

"That was a long time ago. There's a big live oak out at the end of our drive. Sits on top of the levee and you can see clear to the other side of the Mississippi from the topmost branches."

"Yes, sir."

"Victoria loved that old tree. Called it the Trinity Oak because it had three big old branches. She'd spend all day up on the highest branch, reading her books, writing her poetry. It's where she felt closest to God."

"Yes, sir."

"I'm not a religious man, Mr. Hawke. But my daughter was. So, I want you to find my little girl. I want to lay her down to rest in her sacred place, that little churchyard that is in the shade of old Trinity."

"I'll do everything I can to find her, sir," Hawke said.

"I believe you will. Goodbye, Mr. Hawke. And don't drink any more damn whiskey. I find too much of it only makes things worse."

"Yes, sir. Good-bye, Senator."

Hawke hung up the phone. He couldn't bear the scent of her, the sight of her things, a second longer. He rose and wandered back to his own stateroom where he collapsed upon the bed. He stared at the ceiling, trying to make Vicky's face go away. He could see her perfectly. Her beautiful auburn hair was matted to her forehead. But she wasn't above him. She was below him. About fifteen feet down in the green water, her arms and legs spread out. Not moving. Drifting and—

Sometime later, there was a squawk from Sniper on his perch, followed by a knock at the door. "Yes? Who is it?"

"It's Stokely, boss," said the muffled voice outside.

"What do you want?"

"Can I come in?"

"Sure," Hawke said, and sat up, drying his eyes on his shirtsleeve. "Why not?" he said, opening the door. He padded back to his bed, leaning his head back against a large white pillow.

"How you feelin'?" Stoke asked, pulling up a chair.

"Ask me something else."

"I don't mean to bother you. You hurt. You on the

bench. You sidelined. Ambrose sent me down here to check on you. Man thinks you should eat something."

"He sent you down here to tell me that?"

"No, boss. He wants you to come up to the bridge. The radio guy or whatever picked up something on the satellite TV. News show off the Cuban television. Ambrose taped it and wants you to see it."

"I can't believe I'm hearing this. What is it? A fucking cricket match?"

"Naw, it ain't no crickets. It's Castro. He's on the Cuban TV station. Something going down in Cuba. Ambrose said you need to see it is all I'm sayin'. I wouldn't have bothered you for nothing but—"

WHOOOOMPH!

The sound of an explosion, muffled and distant but still enormous, reverberated throughout Hawke's stateroom. The crystal decanters and glassware on the bar tinkled but didn't fall.

"Holy Christ, now what?" Hawke said, and picked up the direct line to the bridge.

"What the hell was that, Captain?" Hawke asked when *Blackhawke*'s skipper picked up.

"We're looking at it now, sir," the captain said. "An explosion about two miles off our port beam. We had them on radar. They were headed northwest at about twenty knots. Small yacht, fifty feet or so."

"No SOS prior?" Hawke asked.

"No, sir. They just blew sky high. I've ordered the launch lowered. The second officer is on with the Coast Guard now, apprising them of the situation. I'm sending Quick and the launch over to look for survivors. Not much hope by the looks of it, I'm afraid."

"I'm coming right up."

"Very good, sir."

"Come on, Stoke," Hawke said.

When Hawke reached the bridge, he could still see the fire two miles distant. Congreve and the captain were both standing just outside the wheelhouse on the starboard bridge wing with their binoculars trained on the scene. Alex and Stokely stepped out onto the small bridge deck. The smell of burning fuel had already drifted toward them.

"Sorry to bother you, Alex," Ambrose said, handing him the binoculars. "But I had no choice. A military coup in Cuba, apparently. Now this poor fellow out there seems to have blown himself up."

"A Cuban coup. Is that good news or bad news?" Hawke said, raising the glasses to his eyes. There was nothing left of the yacht but flotsam and jetsam floating in a spreading pool of burning fuel.

"I'd say a rogue military government with a ballistic submarine was bad news," Ambrose said.

"Is Castro dead?"

"No. I don't believe so. Not yet anyway. I taped the broadcast. Whenever you're ready."

"What do you think happened to that yacht, Cap?" Hawke asked, still looking through the binoculars.

"Hard to say, sir. The most likely scenario is an electrical fire in the engine room. Raged out of control and both fuel tanks exploded."

"That's what I was thinking. Poor chaps never knew what hit them. Jesus Christ. Welcome to life aboard the yachts of the rich and famous. It's been one bloody rotten day in Paradise, gentlemen."

"Indeed it has, sir," the captain said. "On behalf of the

entire crew, we are all terribly, terribly sorry about your tragic loss, sir."

"Thank you," Alex said. "Please convey my gratitude to the crew for all they've done to help. If you could have my seaplane ready, I'm going back out at first light, Captain."

"Aye, aye, sir," the captain said, and returned to the bridge. Alex stood with his hands on the rail, gazing out at the distant fire on the black sea. There was a sharp line of pink and gold on the far horizon.

"Come look at the tape, Alex," Ambrose said, putting his hand on his friend's shoulder. "Then the doctor wants to give you something to help you sleep."

"I'm not going to sleep until I find her, Ambrose."

39
• • • — — • • •

"Well, I will say one thing," Hawke said. "That has to be the shortest speech Castro ever gave."

They had gathered in the ship's darkened screening room, scattered about on large, overstuffed leather chairs, to watch the tape originally broadcast on the Cuban National Television station.

"Please rewind it and replay with the sound turned down a little," Hawke said. "And if you'd be so kind as to give me a simultaneous translation, Ambrose? Needn't be word for word."

Castro appeared on the screen. He was seated at a small table, staring into the camera. He looked ten years older than his recent pictures, haggard and worn. There were deep black circles under his eyes, and his hands were shaking uncontrollably.

As Castro started speaking, Ambrose said, "He begins by expressing his enormous gratitude for the sacrifices the heroic Cuban people have made during the time of the struggle. He goes on to say that he knows it has been difficult for them, but that it was in service of a great cause. He says that the revolution, while it has been a great political success, has not been a great economic success."

"Fairly mild understatement," Hawke said.

"He alludes now to his health. Everyone knows of his recent illnesses. He says he has the will but doesn't have the energy to continue. He says he's stepping aside for health reasons and—he starts to say something else, and they cut him off."

"Health reasons meaning someone off camera has a bloody pistol aimed at his head," Hawke interjected.

"No doubt," Ambrose agreed. "A chap from the American State Department called. I told him you couldn't be disturbed. I spoke with him for a few moments. According to him, it's a full-blown military coup, all right."

"Who's this lovely ponytailed fellow we're seeing now?"

Ambrose took a deep breath. Whether he was prepared to admit it or not, Alex Hawke was finally confronting his demons face-to-face.

"This is General Manso de Herreras, Alex," Ambrose said. "Castro's right-hand man. Former minister of state security. Apparently he's just promoted himself to general. He's now head of all the armed forces."

"Man look just like a woman," Stoke blurted out in the dark. "Man look like he wearing makeup."

"What does the general have to say for himself?" Hawke asked, leaning forward in his chair and staring intently at the face on the screen. He'd seen something there, Ambrose quietly observed.

"General de Herreras says he is deeply honored that *el comandante* has elevated him to the great responsibilities of military chief and has placed such trust in him."

"Bullshit," Stoke said.

"Indeed," Ambrose continued. "He is proud to be part of a new leadership that will bring Cuba forward to her rightful place in this new century. The new government will announce many social and economic reforms in the coming days, weeks, and months."

"Could you freeze-frame this guy right here, Ambrose?" Hawke asked.

"Certainly."

The picture froze on a close-up of de Herreras. His heavily lidded eyes conveyed a cold ruthlessness that was startling.

"What is it, Alex?"

"I've seen this man before," Hawke said, pressing the fingertips of both hands against his eyes and heaving a deep sigh.

"Are you all right, Alex?" Congreve asked.

"Perfect."

"Manso de Herreras. It must sound familiar?" Ambrose said.

"Yes. That must be it. De Herreras. Name of that chap in Blackhawke's letter, isn't it? The one carried all that buried booty we're trying to find."

Then he got to his feet and went to the rear of the room where a steward poured him a cup of hot coffee. He then walked forward again until he was about four feet from the large screen, staring up at the face frozen there for two long minutes.

"Are you all right, Alex?" Congreve finally asked, imagining what dreadful thoughts must be going through his friend's mind. Hawke didn't reply and, after a few seconds, Ambrose said, "Alex? Everything all right?"

"Couldn't be better," Alex said, his eyes never leaving the screen.

"Shall I continue to pause?"

"No," Hawke said. He returned to his chair and collapsed into it. "I've seen enough of this bloody bastard for now. Please roll the tape."

"This part is interesting," Ambrose said, hitting the Play button once more. Alex had clearly made the Manso connection. But he was not yet ready for a psychological showdown.

"What does he say?"

"He says never again will Cuba need to rely on the strength of false allies who promise much and then disappear. Cuba's own might will be felt by anyone who threatens her self-interest."

"We certainly know what he means by that," Hawke said. "That bloody submarine. He's taken delivery, or he wouldn't tip his hand."

Ambrose continued translating.

"Cuba will no longer tolerate the injustices it has suffered at the hands of the Americans. He is demanding that the American blockade of Cuba be lifted immediately. He is also declaring that the U.S. Naval Station at Guantánamo is an insult to Cuba's sovereignty that will no longer be tolerated. America will be given a deadline to evacuate or face extreme consequences. Further statements on these matters will be issued by the new government tomorrow."

"Jesus Christ," Hawke said. "A rogue state with an invisible submarine bearing forty MIRV nuclear warheads ninety miles from Miami."

"Chilling thought, isn't it? Here he introduces the new president of Cuba," Ambrose said, as a new face appeared on the screen.

"Who the fuck is that guy?" Stoke said. "Looks like goddamn Zorro in a three-piece suit."

"That," Ambrose said, "is *el nuevo presidente de Cuba,* Fulgencio Batista. Grandson of the man Castro overthrew some forty years ago."

"Where'd they dig him up?" Hawke asked.

"Grew up in Spain. Went to Harvard College, and then Wharton School of Finance. Renounced his U.S. citizenship and took his family to Cuba six months ago. Prior to that, he was a partner at Goldman, Sachs on Wall Street. Had a farm in back-country Greenwich, Connecticut, and played golf every Saturday at the Stanwich Club."

"Really? From partner at Goldman to president of Cuba? Bad career move," Hawke said. "What's Batista Junior got to say for himself?"

"More glowing rhetoric about a new day dawning."

"That's it?" Hawke asked.

"Basically."

"And the forces loyal to Fidel?"

"Most likely executed or imprisoned. If you can still find any."

"The Cuban people themselves? What's the reaction?"

"Alex, after forty years of lies, fear, and torture, these people don't believe a word anyone says. Anyone. They don't trust their own children. Life will just go on. I guarantee you, they won't even discuss these political events with their closest friends. Someone might chat up his own mum if he really trusts her, but that's about it."

Hawke flipped a switch that slowly brought up the hidden ceiling lights. He swiveled his big leather armchair around and faced Ambrose, Stokely, and Sutherland, who were all scattered two or three rows back.

"How do you know so much about this band of brigands, Ambrose?"

"The secretary of state also called immediately after the Cuban broadcast. We had a long chat. You were sleeping. I told her about the tragic events of the day. She asked me to convey her deepest sympathies. She didn't want to disturb you, but asked if you'd call as soon as you'd seen this tape."

"I've seen it."

"There is going to be a meeting tomorrow afternoon. She's assembled a team to deal with the crisis. You're not going to like this. They're all aboard the aircraft carrier *John F. Kennedy,* currently en route to Guantánamo. The meeting is at five P.M. She knows that you won't want to come but insists you must."

"Why, may I ask?" said Hawke, plainly infuriated. It was precisely what he'd told Conch he did *not* want to do.

"Apparently the British minister for Latin American affairs went directly to the president. He says that since it was a British citizen who 'cracked this thing wide open,' namely you, he wants the British represented. The president elected you."

"Well, he simply ain't going," Stokely said. "We going back out to look for Vicky. He's taking his plane, I'm taking the Zodiac. Soon as it gets light."

"The meeting aboard the *Kennedy* isn't until five tomorrow afternoon, Alex," Ambrose said.

Alex muttered, "Bloody hell."

"She predicted you'd say that. Also, she herself may arrive late due to an emergency planning session the president has scheduled at the Little White House in Key West. She'd like you to be on the *JFK* as her safeguard in case, she said, 'anybody has any really stupid effing ideas' close quote."

Hawke pressed his fingertips to his eyes and leaned back in his chair.

"I suppose I have to go, damn it to hell," he said after a few long moments. "Ross, can I land a seaplane on a carrier deck?"

"I don't see why not. *Kittyhawke*'s pontoons have retractable wheels. All it doesn't have is a good, sturdy tailhook. I'll have one installed immediately."

"Good. Ross, also, please have the radioman send a message to flight ops aboard the *Kennedy*. Advise them they're going to have an unusual little visitor dropping in tomorrow afternoon."

"Aye, Skipper."

"How long until sunrise?" Hawke asked.

"A few hours."

"All right," Hawke said, getting to his feet. "At first light, I'm going back out to find Vicky. Ambrose, would you mind taking a little walk with me aft?"

"Not at all."

Once the two men reached the stern they stood side

by side at the rail staring at the glassy water stretching to the horizon. Hawke finally broke the silence.

"I saw something, Ambrose. On the wall at the club."

"Yes?"

"I know it means something. I know I should understand it. But I can't—I can't see. Or I won't see. Am I making a complete fool of myself?"

"No, Alex, you're not."

"Anyway, see if you can make something of it for me, will you?"

Alex pulled an old Polaroid snapshot, yellow with age, out of his pocket and handed it to his friend.

"I'll be happy to see what I can come up with, Alex."

"Thank you, Ambrose. You are the most wonderful friend a man could ever ask for, you know."

He walked away without waiting for a reply.

40

· · · — — · · ·

Ambrose had awoken to the heartbreaking sound of Hawke's little airplane coughing and sputtering to life. When the noise came to resemble a screaming banshee outside his window, he sat up in bed, yawning, and pulled aside the curtain of the small rectangular port. He watched the silver plane lift off the water and climb into the nighttime sky.

Ambrose was keenly, painfully aware that Alex must know his search for Vicky's body was hopeless. He also knew that Alex would be up there all day, flying every square mile of ocean within and beyond the search area, praying to find this woman who had seemed to offer him, finally, peace and passion.

He rolled over and tried to go back to sleep.

It was useless.

He picked up the brier pipe from his nightstand and jammed it between his teeth. It was both a comfort and a stimulant to thought. He realized despite the tragic events of the day, he was still poking around the edges of the thing that had haunted him for thirty-odd years.

He had slept fitfully, tossing and turning in his bed, unable to erase an image that simply would not go away. The image he saw was black-and-white and compelling. A simple composition. A story. A very old, sad story.

There were three figures in the foreground. A snow-storm of confetti and silver streamers filled the air. The photo was blurred as if some reveler had jostled the photographer at the moment the shot was taken.

Happy New Year.

A beautiful blond woman in a white sarong, diamonds sparkling around her regal white neck. A brilliant tiara in her hair. The woman had a flute of champagne in her raised hand and was smiling. Her other arm was thrown carelessly around the shoulders of a very fat young man with a bald, bullet-shaped head. A heavy golden crucifix was suspended from the thick gold chain around his neck.

There was another man in the foreground of the image. Tall and strikingly handsome in a spotless white dinner jacket, he stared directly into the eye of the beholder. The sober eyes were not amused. Fixed, impatient, not smiling.

For him, at least, this was not a very happy New Year. Why?

Because the woman has had too much bubbly? Been too friendly with the bald-headed chap, perhaps. Said something indiscreet.

Ambrose sat bolt upright. He took a deep breath and looked out his oval port window. Overprinting the rippling black water, he saw the lingering image still, and now he had it.

The beautiful woman in Alex's blurry Polaroid was Alex Hawke's mother. The man in the dinner jacket was Alex's father. And the fat youth with the golden cross? His large chunk of the puzzle was rapidly fitting into place, too.

Three Cuban boys on a murderous rampage.

Alex Hawke had handed him a key to the puzzle he'd been trying to solve for over thirty years.

Ambrose picked up the phone and called Sutherland's cabin, waking him from a dead sleep. He told Ross to meet him on the bridge deck in ten minutes. Then he called Stokely and delivered the same message. He got up, padding quickly across his small cabin. He opened the door to the tiny head and stood before the sink, gazing at his haggard reflection in the mirror.

He was busily brushing his teeth when the magnitude of what was happening struck him like a blow to the head. He was standing at the very brink of solving the insoluble. The mystery surrounding the events aboard the yacht *Seahawke* that had occurred over thirty years ago.

Dressed, he shoved his service revolver, a pre-war nickel-plated Webley-Scott, into the side pocket of his favorite tweed jacket and headed for the bridge.

Sutherland and Stokely were already there.

"We're going ashore," Ambrose said. "Ross, please ask Tom Quick to select four of his best crewmen and arm them with automatic weapons. Stokely, do you need a gun?"

"I am a gun," Stoke said, dead serious.

"Good. We might well put your talents to use then. Have everyone meet at the launch as quickly as humanly possible."

"What is it, Constable?" Sutherland asked.

"Our first stop will be a surprise visit to Mr. Amen Lillywhite. If we find out what we need to know, there will be a second surprise party, quite possibly a highly charged affair."

"We'll be ready at the launch in ten minutes," Sutherland said, and picked up the ship's phone to begin assembling his team of raiders. It took less than a minute.

"Ross, do you have the Streetsweeper aboard?"

"Certainly."

"Bring it," Ambrose said, and left the bridge.

The Streetsweeper was Ross's invention. It was a pistol-gripped, sawed-off shotgun capable of firing fifteen twelve-bore cartridges in less than twenty seconds. He had used it with much success in some difficult operations. He would carry it in addition to the matching flat Wilkinson throwing knives strapped inside each forearm.

Half an hour later, the launch arrived at the Staniel Cay docks. The small raiding party was armed to the teeth. It was just past four in the morning, still dark, and the entire island seemed to be sleeping. They still had the cover of darkness on their side. After disembarking,

Ambrose posted one man on the dock to cover their escape if necessary.

The six remaining men moved swiftly toward the old club, bristling with weapons. All they knew was what Stokely had told them on the ramp. It was going to be a search and seizure, and it was most likely going to be a hot one.

The door of the club, not surprisingly, was open. There was a man sleeping atop the bar, snoring loudly. Ambrose considered waking him and reminding him of the club rules but disturbing him seemed unnecessary. He moved to the wall of photographs adjacent to the bar, pulling Alex's Polaroid from his pocket and gazing up at the montage of overlapping snapshots. His eyes went to the upper left-hand corner where he'd seen a grouping of shots that had the appearance of being taken in the late seventies.

Two days ago, this had been a solid wall of photographs. Now, quite a few obvious patches of crumbling stucco revealed that a number of them had recently been removed. He looked at the picture in his hand, then placed it inside his jacket pocket. Satisfied, he turned to Sutherland and Stokely.

"All right, then. Two doors either side at the top of these stairs. Amen's room is on the right," Ambrose said. "At least, I saw him enter that room two nights ago. Ross, you and Stokely come with me. Tom, you and your fellows please remain down here unless you hear something disturbing upstairs."

Ambrose was first up the steps. He waited for his two colleagues outside the bedroom door. Then he pulled out his revolver and stood back as Stokely kicked the old wooden door open. The force of his kick knocked the door off its hinges and sent it flying into the room.

A startled Amen sat bolt upright in his single iron bed, his eyes wide with surprise and fear.

"Good morning, Mr. Lillywhite," Ambrose said, and walked straight toward him, his gun aimed at the naked man's heart. Stoke and Sutherland stood just inside the doorframe, their weapons at the ready.

"What the—"

"Please be silent and listen," Ambrose said. "I'm going to ask you a few very important questions. If I hear the right answers, no harm will come to you. You should know that I am a policeman and so are these gentlemen."

Ambrose opened the small black leather case and showed the man his warrant card. "Are you ready?"

Amen, eyes on the gun, nodded his head.

"Good," Ambrose said. "What is your name?"

"Amen, sir. Everybody knows that."

"Your full name, please."

"My name is Amen Lillywhite," Amen said. "Named after my father."

"Mr. Lillywhite, the very first time I visited this establishment, I noticed a number of particularly interesting snapshots on the wall downstairs. Some of them appeared to have been taken at a New Year's Eve party in the early seventies. Tonight, I return only to find that many, if not all, of those particular pictures, have been removed. Any idea who might have taken them? Or why?"

"I don't know," Amen said. "I swear. So many pictures up there, I didn't even notice they were missing."

"You don't have them?"

"No, sir. I don't."

"I believe you. Next question. Who is the owner of this establishment?"

Amen Lillywhite leaned back against the stained wall and shook his head.

"I am investigating a murder case for the Criminal Investigation Department of Scotland Yard," Ambrose said. "If you withhold either evidence or information pertaining to this crime, you're going to prison for a long, long time. Again, who is the owner of this club?"

"I don't know anything. I just work for the man is all."

"Give me his name. Now." Ambrose pulled the hammer back on his revolver. It made a big impression.

"Don Carlo, that's what he's always been called 'round this little island. Just Don Carlo."

"Did he remove the pictures?"

"I guess maybe he wanted some pictures taken down. Two days ago, Gloria ask me why Don Carlo seemed so upset about some pictures on the wall. Said he noticed one was missing. Said somebody had taken one. He told her to take some other ones down and burn them all out in the trash pit."

"Did she do it?"

"I don't think so. Don Carlo beat her up pretty badly one time she wouldn't, uh, well, you know what I'm talking about. Ever since then, she don't ever do what he say, less he standin' right there watchin' over her. Prob'ly, she hid the pictures in her room."

"I hope so, for her sake. Destroying evidence related to a homicide investigation is a very serious offense."

"Yes, sir. I understand."

"Good. How long has Don Carlo owned this club?"

"I guess thirty years or so. As a young man, he work

for me tending bar. Only a month or so. Then he left without a word. One day he shows up again with a big wad of cash money and buys the place from my boss, Mr. Daniel Staniel was his name. Don Carlo, well, he's what you call an international businessman. Big man. To him, this old club ain't nothin' but a hobby, like a—"

"Front for an international narco-terrorist operation. What is this man's nationality?"

"You mean—"

"What is his country of origin?"

"You mean, where he was born, that would be Cuba. He and his brothers are big shots there. Military."

"Their names?"

"Don Manso is one. The other he just calls Juanito."

"Ah, yes," Ambrose said, barely suppressing an urge to shout with joy at the mention of these two names.

Ambrose removed an envelope from his jacket and took out three folded and yellowed sheets of paper. He selected one and showed it to Lillywhite.

"Is this the man now known as Don Carlo, who worked for you thirty years ago?"

Lillywhite narrowed his eyes and said, "Yes, sir, that's him."

It was the police sketch Stubbs Witherspoon had given Ambrose on Nassau.

"Is this man on this island now?"

"Yes, sir. He live here most of the year. Spends a lot of time up in Cuba, too. But the man here now. Showed up yesterday."

"Where does he live? His house, where is it?"

"Other side of the island. Over on the ocean side. Big place."

"Guards?"

"Yes, sir. All the time."

"Does the house have a name?"

"Finca de las Palmas."

"Describe it."

"Big white place. High stone walls all around it. Main gate at the top of the steps up from the beach road. Where de guard house is. Some big wooden gates round dere on de west side wall. House sits in a pine forest up high overlooking the sea. Nothing else round that place, sir."

"Where is Don Carlo's room?"

"I ain't been up there. But I think it's third floor, over-looking the sea. He got a long balcony where I think he sleeps sometimes. Anyway, I've seen him up there in his pajamas, entertaining, you know? Fancy black iron railing up there."

"Does he have a wife? Children in the house?"

"No, sir, he do not have no wife, no children."

"There's an old schoolbus parked outside the club."

"Yessuh."

"Run?"

"That's my mother's bus. She hauls kids to school in it every day. Calls it her bread and butter."

"You have keys?"

"Yes, sir. 'Course I do."

"Get dressed. You're coming with us."

"I ain't done nothin', sir, but tell you the Lord's honest truth."

"I'm taking you into protective custody until I can determine the truth of that statement."

"Don Carlo, he see me with policemen, I'm dead."

"He won't get the chance to see you, Mr. Lillywhite. I'll see to it that he does not. No harm will come to you or any member of your family."

"You got to mind yourself with Don Carlo, Mr. Congreve. Real careful. Man is crazy. He 'bout bad as they get down in these islands. And they can get very bad."

Lowering his weapon, Ambrose walked toward the empty doorframe, paused, and looked over his shoulder at the man still lying on the bed.

"You're dealing with Scotland Yard, Mr. Lillywhite. Bad is our bread and butter."

41

• • • — — • • •

Gomez felt as if he must have died and gone to heaven.

Not only had his wife taken him back into her bed, she'd gone to acting like a bitch in heat. Right now she was sitting astride his chest, panting, her hands planted beside his ears, slapping her big breasts back and forth across his cheeks, pausing every now and then to let him nurse hungrily at her swollen nipples.

It wasn't all good behavior that had led Gomer to this blissful new state of affairs. He'd been a very bad boy.

His buddy on the guard tower, Sparky Rollins, told him a shipment of generic Viagra had arrived last week at the Gitmo PX. Cheap. And, goddamn, it worked. Man, did it work. Not only for him, but, he discovered, for Rita as well. He decided not to tell her about it. Just let her get a taste of the new and improved Gomer for a few days. Show her that the big dog was back.

And once you let the big dog out, well—

She'd been surprised at his new ability and, after a few nights, even a little friendly. She wasn't exactly all the way to the moaning and groaning stage, but she was allowing him to do what he wanted to do. Certainly better than the frigid ice bitch she'd been for months now.

He hid the pills from her way at the back of the top shelf of the little closet where she stashed the clean bath towels. The shelf was so high, she couldn't reach it, even with the stool. But he could. And, like clockwork, he'd climb up there every night before dinner, take down the jar, and pop a couple. An hour later, stand back, baby, nobody knows how big this thing's gonna get.

Couple of nights ago, climbing down from the stool in the bathroom with the plastic jar full of little blue pills, he'd had another one of his brainstorms.

What if he crushed up a bunch of them little blue wonders and sneaked them into the spaghetti sauce? Or soup or whatever the two of them were eating for dinner. Then just sit back and see what happened. Hell, couldn't hurt. Not like he was putting poison in her food or anything.

It was like Spanish fly. Hell, he must have gone through a ton of Spanish fly when he was a kid. Problem was, nobody knew if it worked or not. It sure didn't seem to work for him, but who knew? Other guys seemed to be getting lucky all the damn time.

This stuff definitely worked. Made her stone crazy in the sack. Couldn't get enough of that big old dog, that was for sure.

She was moaning now, calling him names, words coming out of her mouth he'd never heard any woman say, begging for it, and she was going to get it, by God. Right friggin' now! Oh, yeah—

A tinny rendition of the *William Tell* Overture started up on the bedside table. Shit. His cell phone. Nice timing, dickhead, whoever you are. He let it ring a couple of times, thinking whoever it was would give up and call back later. Groaning, he entered her and that's when it hit him. What if it was—?

He reached for the phone, not missing a beat.

"Hello, Elvis," said the familiar voice.

"Hey, how you doin', amigo? Long time no see. Um, listen, could you call back in about—"

That's when Rita whupped him up the side of his head so hard it knocked the phone out of his hand. He rolled out from under her and onto the floor, reaching around for his phone, hearing the tinny little voice coming from it. He grabbed it and said, "Sorry, baby, I—"

"Goddamn you!" Rita screamed, and in the moonlight he could see her grab the damn lamp off the table and rip it out of the wall, throwing it right at his head. He ducked, but it still hit his shoulder and hurt like hell. He stood up, rubbing his arm, and noticed he was still hard as a rock. Damn, this stuff was good!

"Listen, baby, I'm sorry. I just thought it might be an important call and—"

"Your little friend Julio Iglesias, maybe?" she snarled at him. "Or maybe it was Madonna. Or Mariah Carey. Get the hell out of here! Get out of my sight, you bastard."

He was about to plead with her, beg, but then he

thought, wait, it was *them*. Well, they'll call back. Like any second now. He'd better get down to the kitchen and be there when the phone rang.

"Chill, baby, I'm sorry," Gomer said, pulling on his jockeys standing on one leg. He stuffed the cell phone inside the waistband of his jockeys. "I'll go. You try to get some sleep, baby. You'll feel better and—"

Something else was hurtling at him through the darkness. Clock radio? He pulled the door shut and heard whatever it was shatter against the thin wooden door. He ran down the narrow stairway that led to the kitchen, Rita still hollering upstairs. Jesus H. Christ, this spy shit was tough on a marriage.

Now, there was a good question. Everybody knew that Jesus' middle name started with an H. But how many people knew what the H stood for? Huh? How many?

Henry? Harold? Howard? Jesus Howard Christ. Didn't sound right. Screw it. Leave that one to the nuns and the Bible experts.

He opened the fridge, one eye on the wall phone, thinking they might try that number, and grabbed a cold Bud. Popped that tallboy while he was in the laundry room, digging around in the dryer. He found a nice clean T-shirt and a pair of jeans.

He was zipping up his jeans, damn, he still had a friggin' woody! Jesus, this stuff was—he suddenly felt something vibrating on his pecker. What the—? His cell phone. He had switched it to vibrate. Felt pretty damn good, he was thinking, reaching down and pulling his cell out, not bad at all. Pick up the wall phone and call his dick a few times.

"Hello?" he said, putting the cell to his ear.

"Fuck you doin', Elvis, hanging up on me?"

"I'm sorry, man, see my old lady, she—"

"Tell it to somebody who gives a shit. We've got business to discuss, Elvis. Urgent business."

"Okay, well, who is this? Who'm I talking to?"

"Julio."

"Julio, my man! Whassup?" Gomer asked, trying to sound like he had his shit together and was ready for action. He'd had a few beers, but he'd learned one thing. You had to be sharp on the phone with these dudes.

"Listen carefully. It's checkout time at the Roach Motel, Elvis. We just got the call. You know what you have to do?"

"Checkout time! Aw-right! My man, it's about time! Let's get it on! Let's rock and roll!"

Gomer noticed his breathing was getting shallow and his mouth had gone dry like that old iguana, one who'd been lying on a rock out in the sun too long.

"You got the RC, Elvis?" Julio was asking him.

"Some in the fridge. Why?"

"The radio control box, you dumb shit."

"Oh, yeah. That. Just kidding around. No. Not on me. I mean, I know where it is."

"You remember how to work it?"

"Tell me again."

"Are you drunk, Elvis? Tell me the truth, right now. If you are, you're dead. You and your whole family, understand? Dead meat."

"Hell no, I ain't drunk, Julio! I swear it! I had two beers with dinner and I've been screwing my brains out for two solid hours! Jesus! Calm down, all right?"

"I'm glad to hear it. Now, listen to me, *compadre*. You go get that little bug box. You remember the little window with the red numbers?"

"Of course. Jesus. I'm not stupid. You're talking to a petty officer third class here, pal."

"Is it armed?"

"Uh, it says 'armed,' yeah."

"*Bueno*. Now, you push the button on the left side. The numbers should all come up 0000. That's step one. Step two, you push the button on the right. The numbers will start going up. Push the button again when they say 3000 exactly. The numbers will stop."

"Okay, I'm with you," Gomer said. He was scribbling furiously on Rita's grocery store pad, trying to keep up. "3000. What if I go too far, you know, by accident?"

"No problem. Push the right button again and it will zero you out. Then you just do it again."

"Cool. So I can't mess up. Then what?"

"What time you got?"

Gomer looked up at the big kitchen clock, then at his watch.

"Exactly ten o'clock P.M."

"Okay. Once you're programmed, you don't do anything, *anything*, until midnight. At the stroke of twelve, you push the left and right buttons at exactly the same time. You got that? Exactly the same time."

"That's it?"

"That's it, *señor*."

"What does that do, pushing both buttons?"

"Starts the countdown to checkout time at the old cucaracha motel. Thirty hours. The numbers will start rolling backwards."

"Holy shit, then what?"

"Then you are a very rich man, Elvis. At ten or fifteen seconds after midnight, your cell phone will ring. You make sure you've got it on you, charged up, and turned on. Got it?"

"Yeah. What do I say?"

"You answer, 'Roach Motel.' A voice will ask you if there are any vacancies. If you have successfully initiated the countdown, you say, 'No vacancies for thirty hours.' Then you hang up."

"No vacancies for thirty hours. I got it. Then what?"

"One more little thing, amigo, one more thing and then you are a very, very wealthy individual."

"What?" Gomer asked, feeling a little chill.

"You have to deliver the RC to one of the guards at the Cuban checkpoint. That's the only way we can confirm that you have fulfilled your mission. And the only way you get the password to your Swiss bank account."

"What? The Cuban side? How the fuck do I do that?"

"You told us you had a good friend at one of the American towers."

"Sparky Rollins?"

"Exactly. He'll let you through, no questions, right? You said he was your amigo, the one you did all that time in the brig with?"

"Yeah. I guess. What if he doesn't just happen to be on duty tonight?"

Christ, he was starting to shimmy and shake like a goddamn Mexican jumping bean.

"You ever hear of wire cutters, amigo?"

"Aw, shit, Julio," Gomer said. He felt like he was going to start bawling. "There's a goddamn minefield out there!

You guys know that. How the hell do I walk across that?"

"Very, very carefully, amigo. You got a million dollars at stake. You got to think positive. You got to watch your step, man, you'll make it. *Vaya con Dios.*"

"But what about—hello?" The line had gone dead. Shit. He stared at the phone in his hand. It was shaking so bad, he didn't trust himself to put it in his pocket. He set the phone on the counter and took a big swig of the Bud. He wiped his eyes with the bottom of his T-shirt.

Stay cool, he told himself. You can pull this off. This is the big one. But you got to stay cool. Stay focused. Focused on what? The Big Plan, of course! He'd been so nookie crazy lately that, until Julio's call, he'd almost forgotten the Big Plan. The money, dickhead. The million dollars over there in goddamn Switzerland, that's what he had to focus on.

And the box. Had to focus on his little pal RC. Good thing he'd been smart enough to write it all down. He looked at the pencil scribbles on the grocery pad. They were kinda blurry because of his sweaty hand, but he could make them out. He folded the paper and stuck it in his jeans pocket.

Then he grabbed another Bud and headed for the garage. The phone! He'd need the cell phone! He grabbed it off the counter and stuck it back down into his underpants. Safer that way. He ducked out the screen door that led to the little backyard.

It was raining. Hard. He hadn't even noticed. Thunder, lightning, the whole weather thing. Christ. His backyard was underwater. He splashed the few short steps to the garage and stood under the eaves, breathing hard. Why? What was the problem? The minefield? Yeah, that was a problem. A bona fide bitch. Would he try it for one million big ones? Bet your ass.

So, what then? There was something missing in the plan, that's what. He couldn't put his finger on it, but he would. He just needed a little Vitamin V to calm his nerves.

He stepped into the dark garage and reached up to the shelf where he hid the bottle of Stoli inside an old coffee can. Can was there but it felt too light. He peered inside. Nothing but a few rusty nails. Goddamn kids. Or maybe Rita. She was always sneaking around, looking for his bottles. Now he'd have to drive over to the PX and buy a fifth of the Stolmeister. No biggie.

A thought. He better program the little RC Cola thing before he dipped into the sauce. Smarts. Total concentration. That's what it took in this modern world of high-tech espionage.

He opened the trunk and lifted the spare. The little bundle was right where it was supposed to be. The RC wrapped in one of his old T-shirts. He lifted it out, carefully, carefully, and moved from the car to his work bench and pulled the cord on the hanging work light.

He unwrapped the bundle. He smiled when he saw the little red letters saying ARMED. He stuck his hand in his jeans pocket and pulled out the directions he'd written in the kitchen. Took a deep pull on the old brewski. Smoothed the scrap of paper out on his worktable and went to work.

Unbelievable. How good he was. He had it programmed in thirty goddamn seconds. Just seeing the 3000 flashing made him smile.

Who wants to be a millionaire?

Rafael Gomez, that's who. Yeah, baby.

Then he leaned in through the driver's window and put the little box on the front seat. He got in and started the piece of crap Yugo. He looked at his watch glowing in the dark. He had an hour and forty-five minutes to relax and enjoy himself. Couple of drinks, calm down, and think.

Because there was still a part of the plan he hadn't wanted to deal with, but now he had to face it head on.

The problem he had to figure out, now that he'd programmed the goddamn thing was, once he'd pushed the two buttons, what the fuck did he do then?

He got behind the wheel and started the car, thinking hard as he could about the one thing he'd been trying so hard not to think about.

Namely, how did he make sure his family got the hell out of Dodge before the fit hit the shan when all them damn roaches checked out? That was the one-million-dollar question, all right. Had to work on that one.

Good news was he had thirty whole hours to figure that beauty out. Give a man with his kind of brainpower that much time, he'd be more than likely to come up with the goddamn secret of life!

He put the car in reverse and backed out of the garage. He'd start to figure something out, once he sloshed a couple of cold vodkas down the pipe. Another family emergency in Miami? Would that work again so soon? Probably not.

He backed into the street and put the car in first, splashing through puddles, tearing up his street at a pretty good clip. He could afford to speed. Weren't too many MPs cruising around in their Humvees this time of night. And after all, he was on a pretty tight deadline.

As he drove with his left hand, he unwrapped the bundle. The RC felt cool to his touch on the seat beside him. He looked down at the red window that was flashing ARMED and then 3000, back and forth. So, he was ready. Focused.

He pulled into the PX parking lot. Something was wrong. All the windows were black. Goddamn. Sunday night. He'd totally forgotten. PX was closed on Sunday night. He pounded on the steering wheel. Now what? Here's what. Go around the back, break a window in the door, and let himself in! Hello? Duh!

Steal a Stoli for Jesus!

The hootch would be locked up behind the metal gate back of the bar. Nothing serious. He had a tool kit in the trunk. Wirecutters, everything. He could jimmy anything. Hell, probably jimmy the back door at the White House *no problema* if he had to. He'd always been good with tools. Good with anything. He saw the little box winking at him. Bad if somebody took his little friend RC while he was on a mission. Real bad. He decided to take it with him along with the tool kit. Swig of Bud, toss the empty in the backseat, and it's party time, pretty mama!

"RC call home" popped into his mind and he giggled.

He climbed out of the car and turned his face up into the falling rain. He opened his mouth and let the sweet water fill it. So this was what life was like on top of the world.

Christ, it was great to be rich. Don't let anybody kid you.

Sweet.

42

· · · — — · ·

"Call the ball, *Kittyhawke,*" squawked the irritated voice of the air boss in his headphones.

Calling the ball.

That's what the U.S. Navy carrier pilots called it.

If the ball showed green, you were coming in too high. Red, too low. A line of white lights was what you wanted to see.

He watched the lights at the after deck flash green, then red, then green as his little plane bucked the thirty-mile-an-hour headwind. On final approach, what you were mostly worried about was a stall, and Alex was definitely worried. His jumpsuit was wet with the sweat of his adrenaline boost.

He'd already had two unsuccessful attempted landings.

A stall now would be catastrophic.

His headphones squawked again.

"You've got to land here, son," the air boss said. "This is where the hot chow is."

The carrier had turned into the prevailing wind. It was traveling at flank speed to give maximum wind over the deck, helping pilots to reduce their landing speeds. From experience, Alex knew that wind, wave, air, and skill must be in total sync for him to get home.

Alex had lined up once more, approaching the fantail of the heaving 1,000-foot steel runway of the U.S. aircraft carrier *John F. Kennedy* from astern. The 82,000-ton *Kennedy,* or "Big John" as she was called in the service, had a four-and-a-half-acre deck. Because of the heavy rolling swells, the huge flight deck was lazily rolling ten degrees side to side, but it was rising and falling with the wave action, causing twenty- to thirty-foot surges of the deck.

A carrier landing like this in his old Royal Navy Tomcat was one thing. All those thousands of pounds of thrust gave you a lot of control. A lot of options. Too low? Pull up. Too high, nose her down. Miss the wire? Power out at full throttle. His little seaplane was a different matter entirely. He'd already been waved off twice. The landing signal officer he'd been arguing with on the radio had finally told him to please just go home.

He'd considered just landing alongside the carrier and letting them send a launch to pick him up. The giant swells took that idea out of his consideration set fairly quickly. There was no going home, either. The cold front had moved in solidly and the conditions had worsened to the point where flying back to the Exumas was not an option. He told the LSO he was coming back around. His earphones crackled again.

"*Kittyhawke,* you're three-quarters of a mile out. Call the ball."

"Roger. Got the ball," Hawke said.

He felt the little plane shudder as he lined up on his target. Wheels down, full flaps, tailhook down, prop pitch into full low, adjusting his trim tabs to get *Kittyhawke* into proper trim. His fuel was at total rich mix for maximum power recovery. He knew he'd have to dump the plane down hard to have any chance of his tailhook catching the wire. There were four arrester wires on the deck. Catching one of them would be his only chance of stopping short of the water at the other end of the carrier.

"*Kittyhawke,* you're way below glide path. Pull up!"

"Roger," Hawke said. "No problem."

In fact, it was a problem. He didn't think there was any power left in the old Packard-Merlin engine. He was pitching and yawing and the headwind was killing him. Somehow, he had to get his nose up. This was his last shot. He hauled back on the stick. What the hell. He was going in one way or the other.

He'd gotten his nose up a little but the deck was still rising, lifted by the enormous swells. Christ. Fall, damn it, fall! Sweat stung his eyes. It was going to be very, very close.

At the last second, he saw the deck pause majestically and finally begin its long slow fall. He'd timed the swell perfectly. That's the only thing that saved him. The deck began to drop at precisely the right instant. He cleared by maybe a couple of feet and he banged the little plane down hard. It bounced and jarred him and he said a little prayer, instantly realizing he had another problem. He might just bounce right over all of the four arrester wires.

In his old Tomcat jet fighter, he'd had sufficient power for a bolter. Go to full throttle in a touch-and-go and power out if you miss the last wire.

He didn't have that option in *Kittyhawke.*

Then he felt the wheels hit the deck again. In a second, he was thrown forward against the restraints of the seat harness as *Kittyhawke* wrenched to a violent and welcome stop. Second-best feeling in the world, he thought, smiling at the old carrier pilot's expression. He'd hooked the fourth and last of the arrester wires.

"Throttle back, son, you're not going to make this boat go any faster," the air boss said in his headphones.

Embarrassed, Alex realized he was still at maximum power. He eased his throttle down to idle.

"Bingo," the air boss said, from his control station just above the navigation bridge up on deck 010. "Welcome to the *Kennedy, Kittyhawke*. We were beginning to wonder."

"Third time's the charm," Hawke said, a lot more coolly than he felt. He taxied over to the nesting place that a yellow-jacketed crewman, an aircraft director, was now waving him into.

"Yeah," the air boss said. "Just a walk in the park, *Kittyhawke.*"

Breathing a sigh of relief, Hawke reached over and shut down his engine. There were a couple of wheezing gulps from the old Merlin and then it died quietly.

Climbing out of the plane, he saw the red-shirted "crash salvage" personnel sitting on their white fire-control tractors. They were all staring at him, shaking their heads and smiling, a few actually applauding. Refueling crews in purple jerseys and ordnance men in red were all smiling and looking his way, too.

He could hardly blame them. Clearly, the entire landing ops crew were happy to have this particular landing experience behind them. So was he.

He kissed the forehead of the little bathing beauty he'd had painted on his fuselage and jumped from the pontoon down to the deck. He looked up at the carrier's massive superstructure. From the keel to the masthead at the top, it was as tall as a twenty-three-story building. He then cast his eyes along the row of F/A-18 Super Hornets lining the deck. He saw the legendary logo on their tails. The Black Aces squadron seemed to be in final prep for a night exercise.

Downtown Havana, Hawke thought. And if not tonight, probably sooner rather than later.

Walking across the broad flight deck, he realized that it had been a long time since he'd been aboard a carrier. Since those balmy days in the Persian Gulf in fact. He sucked a draught of the sharp sea air down deep into his lungs. It felt good. Finally, after a remorseful day of endless crisscrossing miles of empty sea, something finally felt good.

Twenty minutes later, he'd tossed his duffel bag into a small cabin in the visiting officers' quarters, changed from his flight suit to khakis, and was now in the wake of a bustling admiral's aide escorting him down a long corridor through "officers' country" to the commanding officer's wardroom.

The first face he saw when he entered the room was Tate's, the unpleasant CIA chap he'd encountered at the State Department. Tate's thin, bloodless lips curled into something slightly resembling a smile and Hawke nodded in his general direction.

But he was relieved to see the face of Jeffrey Weinberg, the deputy secretary of defense, among the eager military and civilians ranged around the big square mahogany table. Alex imagined Cuba on a silver platter in the center of the table. Ranged round the platter, the long knives of the Pentagon. The bomb baby-sitter certainly had his work cut out for him.

Hawke had never seen so many ribbons, decorations, or so much brass on so many puffed-up navy blue and khaki chests in his life. And he was a man who'd seen a lot of both.

There were two empty chairs. One had a small blue

flag in front of it. Hawke took the other one and collapsed into it.

"Sorry I'm late, gentlemen," he mumbled, opening the big black three-ring binder in front of him. As he did, the door to the wardroom opened and an aide stood back as the commander in chief, Atlantic Fleet, ramrod straight, marched into the room.

He was a tall man, at least six-five, with keen gray eyes set wide in a deeply lined face, and snow white hair cut very short in the classic Navy "whitewalls" fashion. He was leathery, tough, and weathered from a lifetime at sea. He gazed around the table, sizing up his team.

Alex knew him and liked him. Born in Hyco, Texas, the CINCATFLT had been first in his class at Annapolis, a Rhodes scholar, a fine athlete, and still a young man for his exalted rank. He was in his prime and clearly at the top of his game.

"I'm Admiral George Blaine Howell. I'd like to welcome each and every one of you aboard my flagship. We're a little proud of the *Kennedy*, and we hope your stay aboard her will be both comfortable and productive." His eyes stopped when they reached Hawke, and he was clearly surprised to see him. Alex saw something you generally didn't expect in the eyes of the military. Sympathy.

"Commander Hawke. Good to see you again. We regret the tragic events of yesterday and especially appreciate your taking this sad time to be with us."

There were murmurs and head nods around the table.

"Glad to be aboard, sir," Hawke said. "Sorry to keep everyone waiting."

"A few of us were up on the bridge," Tate said. "You gave us all quite a thrilling air show."

Hawke looked up at the man across the table and glared at him, waiting for him to look away. He finally did.

"You're welcome to try your hand at a carrier landing anytime, Mr. Tate," Admiral Howell said. "I'm sure you'd find it quite exciting. Now, let's cut the bullshit and get down to business."

Howell opened the silver cigarette case in front of him, popped an unfiltered Camel in his mouth, and lit it. A steady stream of smoke escaped his lips as he started to speak.

"Everyone knows why we're here. These sons of bitches in Havana. A military coup in Cuba. Goddamn hoodlums, from what I hear. Drug dealers. Murderers. We don't know if Castro is dead or alive. Doesn't really matter much to me. One way or another we're going in there."

The admiral had reduced one cigarette to ash in less than a minute, and lit another.

"Thanks to Commander Hawke's efforts, we now know that we are confronting a rogue state quite possibly in possession of the most sophisticated and deadly nuclear submarine ever to roam the oceans. Somebody needs a clear and direct threat to American national security, this is it. The president has instructed this task force to negate that threat with a preemptive strike."

He paused, letting his eyes roam the table. "Since I'm in charge of this task force, that, gentlemen, with your help, is exactly what I intend to do. The U.S. Navy is going to find that submarine. We're going take it away from the Cuban rebels. Or we're going to sink it."

He looked around the table and said, "Last time we went into Cuba, it was a total ratfuck, dicked up in spades. We actually learn from history. Sometimes. So. Anybody got any bright ideas?"

"If I may, Admiral?" Weinberg said, getting to his feet.

"Of course," Howell replied as Weinberg walked over to a huge map of Cuba on the wall opposite Hawke. He picked up a laser pointer and flicked it on, aiming at Havana.

Alex settled back in his chair and tried to assume an air of composed, if not rapt, attention. It was now officially a "meeting." There were few things on earth Alex detested more than meetings. Within his own companies, meetings were strictly limited to ten minutes. Anyone who could not say a definitive yes or no to any question was forbidden to attend.

"Number one," Weinberg said, "we have to keep talking to these people, no matter how threatening, how belligerent they become. We keep them talking long enough to form and implement our strategy."

"Who does the talking on our side?" Admiral Howell asked.

"The president has suggested the secretary of state. Her Cuban heritage makes her ideal. Anyone disagree?" Weinberg asked. Howell nodded his approval. There was no dissent.

"Good," Weinberg said, "then she will be the gatekeeper for all information and intelligence we generate. She will lead our negotiations with the new regime. The secretary has asked me to apologize for her late arrival. She's coming from an emergency meeting with the president on Key West."

"That's one, what's number two?" the admiral asked, a wreath of smoke now encircling his head.

"Well. If you'll open your briefing books," Weinberg said, "you'll see that tab one contains a series of photographs taken by our U-2s and Predators over the last week or so. The photos are of an island here, off the coast of Manzanillo, on the southeast coast of Cuba. Please take a minute to study them."

"Never anything brief about a briefing book," Admiral Howell muttered, turning the pages, skipping ahead.

As the men leafed through their books, Hawke opened his case and withdrew a small package containing an audio cassette. The radioman aboard *Blackhawke* had handed it to him as he boarded his seaplane. He assured Hawke it would be interesting.

"The rebels' base of operations is called *Telaraña*," Weinberg said. "Tab two contains precisely detailed building-by-building layouts of the entire compound."

"How'd we come by that?" one of the admirals asked.

"Easy," Tate interrupted. "They recruit local labor, we supply it. We have at least three members of the construction crew on our payroll. The diagrams in your books are the product of their latest intelligence. Two, maybe three days old."

"Let's move on," Admiral Howell said.

"That large white structure you see at the mouth of the river," Weinberg continued, "is a submarine pen. Its dimensions tell me that it is precisely wide enough to accommodate the extraordinary beam of a Borzoi. Commander Hawke, would you like to speak to this?"

"Certainly," Alex said. "Six months ago, the Cuban rebels bought an extremely sophisticated Borzoi-class submarine from a pair of ex-Russian submarine officers, now arms dealers. Two Borzoi submarines were completed in late 1991 using purloined stealth technology. Borzoi utilizes a radical delta wing design, twin hulls forming a V-shape, twenty silos on each hull. It has a retractable conning tower for minimum drag whilst submerged. Fastest sub on earth, by a factor of three, biggest payload, virtually invisible to existing methods of detection."

"Don't tell me this thing can fly, too," Howell said.

"Pretty fair description of what she does underwater," Alex replied.

"Christ. Have they taken delivery?" Tate asked.

"I believe they have, yes," Alex said.

"Do you have any proof of that?"

"Perhaps."

"*Perhaps,* did you say?" the CIA man said, coating the word with gelatinous sarcasm.

"Yes, Mr. Tate, I said perhaps," Alex said. Before this was over, he and Mr. Tate were going to have a very private conversation.

Seeing the tension, Admiral Howell coughed into his fist, and Weinberg tapped the map with his pointer.

"We know they've built a sub pen, and we know they've purchased a Borzoi boomer," Weinberg said. "What we don't know is whether or not they've actually taken delivery."

"From the tone and manner of their opening salvo," Admiral Howell said, "ordering us out of Gitmo, I'd guess these boys were packing some serious heat. In all likelihood, the sub has been delivered."

"Perhaps," Alex said, looking at Tate, "you are right, Admiral. This little package might confirm your supposition. If I may?" The admiral nodded.

Alex pushed his chair back, got up, and walked around the table to Howell, handing him the small package.

"Audio cassette," Alex said.

"Of what, Commander?" the admiral asked.

"Admiral, my yacht is equipped with underwater towed array sonar. Since we frequent ports and coastlines where neither your Navy nor mine is welcome, we record everything we hear. If it's sufficiently interesting, we courier it to Washington or London. My radioman handed me that cassette this afternoon just before I took off. Your lads should give a listen to it. My man thinks our SONUS picked up the signature sound of a Russian Mark III torpedo's screws. But you fellows are the experts."

"Thank you," Howell said, and instantly an aide was at his side. He took the package and left the room.

"Commander," the admiral said, "when and where did your boy pick this up?"

"At 0220 hours, sir," Alex said. "It was recorded while we were lying at anchor one mile due west of Staniel Cay."

"What the hell would the sub be shooting at in the Exumas?"

"No idea, sir. A small American sport-fishing boat suffered a catastrophic explosion and sank at precisely the same time. I heard the explosion two miles away. Upon reaching the bridge I observed a fiery debris field. Why they'd waste a torpedo on such a target is beyond me. But I'm almost positive they sank that fishing boat."

"Shakedown cruise," the admiral said. "The Exumas aren't that far from the southeast coast of Cuba. Target practice. Tell your boy we appreciate his vigilance, Commander Hawke."

Hawke nodded.

"To continue," Weinberg said, "our mission objective is clear. We must neutralize or destroy that submarine and its missiles."

"I vote for destroy," Admiral Howell said, and everyone around the table chuckled. Weinberg smiled and resumed.

"If I know the president, Admiral, that submarine has an extremely short life expectancy," Weinberg said. "The president and his cabinet are meeting in Key West as we speak, formulating a precise response. There is a lot of pressure to invade coming from the Pentagon. I have my own opinions on that, however—"

"What is your opinion?" The question came from the lantern-jawed man two seats to Alex's left. General Charley Moore, U.S. Marines. There was no question about General Moore's opinion, Alex could see in the hard set of the cold blue eyes.

"This isn't Panama, General Moore," Weinberg said. "When we went in to extract Noriega, the Panamanians were dancing in the streets."

"That is correct," Moore said, leaning back in his chair with his fingers laced behind his head. "Hell, I put four of my boys on every street corner of every intersection in Panama City. The neighborhood women adopted every last one of 'em. Fed 'em so damn much, I had to put an ad in the newspaper begging them to stop. My troops were all outgrowing their uniforms!"

"That will not be a problem in Cuba, General Moore," Weinberg said, allowing himself a small smile. "I would like to say that the Cuban people are a nation of sheep. But that would be incorrect. They are a nation of ostriches. The state has them so thoroughly terrorized that—"

"Yes, but here's the real problem," Tate interjected. "In Cuba, you've got—"

"Mr. Tate, with all due respect, excuse me all to hell," Admiral Howell said. "But it's getting a little windy in here. Any damn fool can come up with the problem. I want the goddamn solution! Everybody's insights into Cuban and Panamanian politics are goddamn fascinating. But this is not the time for it. Now, I am a mission-oriented kind of fella. The president wants action now, not fucking *discourse*. Do I make myself clear?"

Alex breathed deeply and closed his eyes. Thank God, Howell was seizing control of this bloody thing. He had been on the verge of making some excuse and walking out. He could barely tolerate these saber-rattling ego fests when he was at his best. Today, with Vicky's loss spiking every thought, his tolerance was at zero.

Admiral Howell looked around the table, sucking down great volumes of smoke, waiting for a response.

"Find that sub, sink it, then invade the island, kill the bad guys, and put a decent, honest man in the president's office," General Moore said. Howell smiled.

"That's better. Thanks, Charley. The commander in chief gave us a job to do, and by God we're going to do it. He asked me if the Atlantic Fleet was ready. I said if anybody in Havana even sneezed in the wrong direction, my boys could send that country back to the Stone Age in about twelve minutes. Hell, I've got nine fighter squadrons right here on Big John! I'd just as soon take the goddamn Geneva Convention and shove it up Cuba's sorry ass. Now let's talk about that, goddammit."

Alex relaxed and took his mind somewhere else.

Doesn't work well with others.

That's what he'd told Conch. It was true. His idea of Hell was sitting in a room with any group that considered itself a committee. His grandfather had a saying: "Search every park in every city of the world and you will never, ever, see a statue of a committee."

As the meeting droned on, Alex stifled a yawn behind his fist and noticed a new sensation. Hunger. The food on American carriers was famously good. He hadn't eaten since the accident. After a dinner in the officers' mess, he'd try to get a good night's sleep in his little VOQ cabin. He'd take off at first light and resume his search for Vicky.

Tate was on his feet now, doing profiles on the new leadership of Cuba. Alex glanced up now and then, feigning interest. He looked up at the young face of the new president, Batista. Hawke wondered if he were the only one to find this ironic bit of history amusing.

He couldn't listen to Tate any longer. He pushed back his chair, starting to rise, and prepared to duck out of the meeting. But the face up on the screen now stopped him cold. He collapsed back into his chair, his eyes riveted on the image. A feeling swept over him, a feeling that everything inside him was shifting, starting to come loose. His eyes were burning and he massaged them with his fingertips, willing himself to control these sudden, swirling emotions.

Tate droned on, and soon had moved to a new character. Hawke, forcing himself to take slow, deep breaths, didn't hear a word he said.

"Excuse me," Hawke said, interrupting Tate midsentence. "I'm terribly sorry. I missed something. Could you possibly go back to the prior slide? Who was that man again?"

Tate couldn't resist an eye-rolling sigh as he hit the clicker and reversed the carousel to the previous slide.

"I'm frightfully sorry," Hawke said. "But who is this man again?"

"As I said, this is the man behind the military coup," Tate replied, a falsely patient expression on his face. "Formerly Castro's most trusted aide de camp. His name is General Manso de Herreras. Why? Do you have some information about him?"

"Yes, I do," said Alex Hawke, getting to his feet and gathering up his materials. He nodded to Admiral Howell and said, "Please excuse me, Admiral, I'm afraid I need to make an urgent phone call."

Howell nodded and Alex walked quickly to the door. The aide saluted and pushed the door open.

"Excuse me, Commander," Tate said, as Alex was halfway out the door. "But if you have any information regarding this man, I'd like to know what it is."

"I'm sure you would. But it's strictly personal. It's none of your bloody business, Mr. Tate," Alex said over his shoulder, not bothering to turn around before he walked out.

"Question," Tate said, sometime late in the evening, after the dinner dishes had been cleared and the men were sitting or standing around the officers' dining quarters in small groups. A blue haze of cigar and cigarette smoke hung just below the ceiling. There was the usual hubbub of conversation as port wine and Irish whiskey went round the admiral's table.

Hawke knew that no alcohol had been allowed aboard U.S. Navy vessels since the sail era. There were exceptions. A vessel returning from a vastly extended at-sea period was one. Big John had been steaming homeward from just such a period when this new crisis forced her return to the Caribbean. He'd been studiously avoiding the raucous chatter, preferring to nurse his vintage Sandeman port alone. He was thinking of turning in when Tate pulled up a chair next to him and tapped him on the shoulder.

"Yes?" Alex said, barely glancing up.

"You don't like me much, do you?"

"Let's just say I don't like the cut of your jib, Mr. Tate."

"Not that I give a shit. The point is, I have a job to do down here. For some reason, everyone in Washington thinks you can help. So. Why were you so interested in this Manso de Herreras this afternoon?"

"I think we covered that bit earlier, Mr. Tate," Alex said, staring into the man's bloodshot eyes, "when I said it was none of your bloody business. Now, piss off."

"Ah, but it is my business, isn't it?" Tate said, leaning in so that Alex could smell the scent of sweat and liquor pouring off the man. "Manso is the central figure in this little Caribbean drama. You clearly know more about him than you're letting on."

"Are you calling me a liar?" Alex said, looking up and glaring at the man.

"I'm calling you what you are, Mr. Hawke. A pompous aristobrit who'd rather keep his little secrets than assist his country's most valued ally in what has become a very, very dangerous state of international affairs."

Alex smiled, took a sip of his port, and turned to face Tate.

"Aristobrit? That's a good one, Mr. Tate. Do you duel?"

"Sorry?"

"Duel? Pistols at dawn? The Code Duello? An ancient custom for settling disagreements between gentlemen, which is probably why you're unfamiliar with it. Duels, unfortunately, seem to have fallen out of favor at about the same rate as gentlemen."

"I don't follow you," Tate said.

"Ah, hardly surprising. Let me help," Hawke said. Slowly setting his port glass down on the white linen tablecloth, he whipped his fist around and backhanded Tate hard across his right ear. Hard enough to snap the man's head back. Tate sat stunned, rubbing his bright red ear. His eyes blazed with hate, but Alex was amused to see that, in the general bonhomie surrounding them, their small tête-à-tête had gone completely unnoticed.

"That's how it works," Alex said, smiling. "You've been insulted. Dishonored. Do you now wish to avenge your honor?"

"You pompous shit, I'll—"

"Good. Now we have a duel," Hawke said, smiling pleasantly. He saw a fist headed his way and said, "No, no, not here, Mr. Tate. Bad form."

Alex's hand shot out and caught Tate's forearm mid-air, stopping the man's fist just short of his own temple.

"I'll kill you for this, you fucking English bastard," Tate said.

"Not here, old boy," Alex said. "This is the part where we step outside."

Still keeping the man's arm locked down on the table, Hawke reached under the table and used his free hand to grip Tate's testicles in a cruel vise. Tate winced and withdrew his arm.

"Good boy," Alex said, smiling. "As I say, it's customary to step outside to settle these affairs. May I suggest we leave these gentlemen to their port and finish this unpleasantness up on the flight deck? I don't think either of us will need a second, do you, old boy?"

"Shouldn't take me that long to kick your ass," Tate growled.

Hawke smiled, amused at the man's obvious confusion over the term "second."

"Good," Alex said. "Shall we go? I'm quite sure we shan't be missed, old boy."

"Don't call me old boy," Tate hissed, rising from the table.

"Sorry, old boy," Alex said, getting out of his chair and motioning Tate toward the door.

"Swords at dawn are out of the question, I suppose," he said. "More's the pity." He put his arm around Tate's shoulder and moved him through the crowd toward the exit. "It will just have to be the manly art of fisticuffs on the poop deck, old boy."

"I'll meet you up there," Tate said. "I've got to use the head."

"*A votre servis, monsieur.* I'll be waiting out on the fantail," Hawke said, and whistling a cheerful tune, he strolled off down the long companionway, up three flights of steps, and out into the salty air.

He found a place to sit, a small stepladder used by crews to reach the fuel ports on the Super Hornets.

"Hello, Hawke," a tall man said, coming toward him out of the covey of bedded-down F/A-18s.

Alex looked up, not recognizing the voice or the silhouette.

"David Balfour," the man said. "We were bunkmates in that hellhole hospital in Kuwait."

"Balfour?" Alex said. "Is that you? Good God, I thought you were dead!"

43
• • • — — • •

Stokely, barely able to keep his butt planted in his seat a third of the way back in the old bus, watched Ambrose Congreve bouncing around behind the big steering wheel and thought he'd bust a gut.

Man had on a tweed jacket with a little white hanky hanging out the top pocket, some kind of damn flannel trousers, and shiny brown shoes with little tassels dangling on the front of them. Best part, man had on uptown bright yellow socks, and his feet were flying back and forth mashing the clutch and brake pedals!

Stoke, like most everyone else on the bus, was dressed completely in black. All were wearing Kevlar vests. But not Ambrose. Had on a nice old gray woolly vest with leather buttons! Man was something else. Man on a mission, though, you had to give him that. Pipe jammed between his teeth, tearing up the deeply rutted sandy road twisting through the scrubby palm trees. Grinding gears, mashing on the brakes, flying over the hills.

Damn Mario Andretti of schoolbus drivers!

Just then the bus got airborne at the top of a big hill

and Stokely caught his first glimpse of the ocean. Which meant they were getting close.

Everybody on the team was quiet, holding on to keep from flying around inside the bus. In situations like this, Stoke knew, each man was thinking about his immediate future. Hell, he was too. Nobody really knew what they were up against. No time to even send a recon team ahead. Could be real easy. Could easily be real hard. When they went bad—like that time in Panama—well, best not be thinking about that.

Stoke checked his gear and ammo. In addition to the Heckler & Koch MP5 submachine gun hanging from a shoulder strap, he had his custom Beretta 92-SF in his thigh holster, along with ten clips of ammo. A hundred rounds of hollow-point HydraShok hot loads that could literally blow a guy's head off.

Lots of other goodies were hanging from his webbed belt. Dagger, flash-bang grenades, and thunder-strips to disorient the bad guys. And a secure Motorola walkie-talkie with a voice-activated lip mike and earpieces so he could communicate with Ross and Quick. He also had fifty feet of nylon climbing rope with a rubber-coated grapnel hook at one end.

He was pumped. Man. It had been a long time.

Stoke, Ambrose, and Ross, with the help of Amen Lillywhite, had quickly roughed out a plan. Amen had used a stick to scratch a diagram of the target house in the dirt parking lot outside the club. Ground floor, second floor, top floor. Big wide center stairway leading upstairs right from the front door. Hallways on either side leading to the rear.

Target's bedroom was on the top floor front, guard's

dormitories at the back of the first floor. A solid stone wall around the entire perimeter, ten feet high. Two ways in and out of the property. A guarded iron gate at the front. Two big wooden gates on the north side.

It was a basic snatch.

Surprise. Confusion. Overwhelming firepower. Float like a pissed-off butterfly. Sting like a badass bee. In other words, your basic SEAL behavior.

Ambrose saying the target must be taken alive.

Stoke saying that these things were entirely up to the target. Ambrose giving him a look. Not sayin' more, which was good.

The bus crested a hill, banged down hard, and Amen, sitting up front, said, "This'd be a fine place to stop, Mr. Congreve. This piney wood right here goes on down to the wall at the back of the house."

Ambrose mashed the brakes and the bus skidded to a stop at the edge of the pine forest. He pulled up the hand brake and turned around in his seat.

"This is where we disembark, gentlemen," Ambrose said. He pushed the handle that opened the door. "Check your weapons and ammunition. Stay low and stay silent. We will descend this hill in single file and regroup at the wall to the rear of the house. Mr. Jones will lead us in from there."

Mr. Jones? Nobody ever called him that. Still, man sounds like he knows what he's doing, Stoke thought. That was good. Rest of these guys, well, he wasn't used to working with amateurs. This Tommy Quick, of course, now he was a comfort. Had his Remington 700 sniper rifle with a bigass Star-Tron Mark scope on it. Guy was the best sniper in the whole U.S. Army. He could definitely come in handy. Still, this was definitely not your split-second-timing SEAL-type deal.

Hell, hadn't even had time to recon the place before going in. This would be a first, going in blind. Gain experience, that much was for sure.

"Lock and load, ladies," Stoke said, getting out of his seat and making his way to the front of the bus. He'd made sure the whole team was equipped with basically the same gear he had, minus the three walkie-talkies. "We going in to get this bad boy, truss him up like a Christmas turkey, and deliver his ass on a platter."

They moved swiftly down through the pines, their footsteps deadened by a thick carpet of pine needles. Stoke took the lead, Congreve was safely in the middle, and Sutherland, the trailman, brought up the rear. It took less than five minutes to reach the ten-foot stone wall that rimmed the perimeter of Don Carlo's estate.

Stoke held up his closed fist and the little band huddled around him. It was still pretty dark, but not for long. They had to move quickly. Stoke divided them into two squads. A Squad, led by Tom Quick, would go around the north side of the property. B Squad, led by Stoke, with Ross, Ambrose, and Amen right behind him, would go south.

Stoke would take out any guards at the front gate.

"Test, test, test," Stoke said into the tiny lip mike that he, Ross, and Quick were now wearing. "Everybody copy?"

"Loud and clear," Ross said.

"Ditto," Quick said. "Five by five."

Stoke looked at his watch and said, "A Squad, go!" Quick and his five men took off in a low, crouched run.

Stoke watched them disappear around the curved wall and then started with his team around the south side. Halfway, they came to a set of heavy wooden gates. He held up his hand and motioned for Amen to come forward.

"What's this for?" Stoke whispered to Amen, pointing at the gates.

"Way he gets his cars in and out," Amen said. "Two big Jeeps." Stoke pondered that a minute. Besides the bus, Stoke had only seen three or four cars on the whole island. All beat-up little taxis.

"Good," he said. "How much farther around to the guardhouse?"

"Another hundred yards, mebbe," Amen said under his breath.

"Tap me on the shoulder just before we get within sight of it, you understand?" Amen nodded.

"Hey, Ambrose," Stoke said, "you cool back there?"

"Never cooler," Ambrose said, smiling. Had to give the man credit, he wasn't lying. Seemed like the man had balls, after all.

Stoke hand-signaled his little team and they began to move forward behind him. Just when they had the ocean in sight, Amen tapped him on the shoulder, and Stoke dropped to his knees. The team came to a halt behind him. He pulled the Beretta from his thigh holster and fitted a silencer on the barrel. Then he crawled forward on knees and elbows, the pistol out in front of him.

Two minutes later, he was back.

"No sign of a guard in the window I can see," he whispered. "Just a blue TV light flickering. First time I ever seen a damn TV satellite dish on a guardhouse."

"Probably asleep, though," Amen whispered in his ear. "I'll go check. Guards all know me. If he's awake, I'll just hand him these. I do it all the time. Keeps peace in the family." He pulled a pint of Jamaican rum and a big hand-rolled spliff of marijuana out of his pants pocket.

"My brother," Stoke whispered to Amen. "You good, you very good."

Two minutes later, Amen came crabbing back along the wall, smiling his ass off. Stoke could already pick up the sweet smell of ganja drifting around from the guardhouse.

"What up?" Stoke asked Amen.

"One guy only in there," Amen said. "Usually, they two. Awake. Got headphones on, listenin' to his Marley tunes, watchin' TV. Gave me a big smile."

"Weapon?"

"Always keeps a machine gun layin' cross his lap."

"Quick?" Stoke said.

"Copy," he heard in his headphones.

"You guys in position?"

"Roger that."

"Okay," Stoke said to his team. "Nobody move. I'll be right back." He took off in a low crouch.

The guardhouse had three windows. One facing the ocean, two on either side. Long as he stayed low and quiet, no way the guy could pick him up. In seconds, Stoke was crouched just below the north-facing window. A cloud of pungent smoke floated out above his head. Beretta in his hand, he suddenly popped up and looked in the window, not four feet from the guy.

"Boo," Stoke said, smiling.

The guard looked up, big case of wide-eyes, the gun in his lap already coming up.

"Bad idea," Stoke said.

The Beretta spit twice and the man's shirt puffed inward and then outward as blood gushed from the sucking wound made by two shots to the heart. The man pitched forward from his stool. Stoke reached through the window and grabbed his gun just before it clattered to the stone floor.

He saw an old green metal panel on the wall. Lots of toggle-type switches. Not marked in any way. Shit. No way to know which was which. He saw Amen and Ambrose peeking around the corner of the wall and motioned them forward.

"Quick?" Stoke said into his mike. "Copy?"

"Copy," he heard in his phones.

"Guard is down at the front gate. Looks clear. Let's link. We're going in."

"Twenty seconds," Quick said.

Stoke turned and handed the guard's machine gun to Ambrose.

"We might come out this way, Constable," Stoke said. "We might not. But if we do, you got a great field of fire to cover our retreat from this guardhouse window." Man looked like he didn't find this plan agreeable.

"Listen to this very carefully," Ambrose said. "I've been working on this bloody case for thirty years. I'm going into that house and arrest that man either with you or without you."

Stoke looked at him for a long second, sizing him up.

"Let's go get him then, Constable," he said. He leaned back inside the guardhouse. The man on the floor was dead. He looked at the corroded control panel. Some of the switches had to be wired to some security system inside. Which ones? He felt a sudden heat on his shoulder and looked up. Goddamn. The sun had just broken the horizon. Way past time to move.

"Amen, do you believe in God?" Stoke said.

"I believe in Jah," Amen said. "Jah soon come."

"Thing is, this Jah of yours, he goin' to come a whole lot sooner you don't tell me the God's honest truth right now, my brother. Ready? Which one of those switches opens the gate? And which one shuts down the alarm system?"

"One on de far left is de gate. Middle one is the main alarm."

"You understand whose side you're on here, don't you, my brother?"

"I do, sir."

Stoke reached in and flipped the middle switch and the one on the left. If he heard any bells and whistles, he was prepared to shoot Amen on the spot, which he really didn't want to do, as he'd come to really sort of like the old coot.

He waited, the Beretta in his hand hanging loosely at his side.

The big black iron gates swung silently inward just as Ross and his team arrived. There were no audible alarms. Stoke waited a minute, his eyes focused on the house, looking for any sign of activity inside. Then he turned to Amen.

"Amen, you the man. Now you sneak back on up to the bus and wait twenty minutes. We don't show up, you go on home and get back in bed. We all thank you, brother."

He put his hand on Amen's shoulder. The man had been invaluable. Then he turned to the seven men who remained gathered at the gate. He felt dumb even asking the question, but under the circumstances, he had to do it. This was not exactly a highly trained SEAL squad that could perform like a bunch of deadly ballet dancers.

"Okay. Everybody know what they doin'?"

They all looked him in the eye and nodded. Good. They may not be cool, but they looked cool. He felt better. Anyway, what the hell. This one was for Alex. All the shit he'd been through, time he got a little back on the plus side.

"Let's book," he whispered, and stood back as they passed through the gates, fanned out into the pines, and started climbing. Stoke gave them twenty seconds and then he too started up the hill toward the house.

He started getting glimpses of the place through the trees. Huge. Towers, golden domes, damn house looked like Disney World might if it was on the Strip in Vegas. At the back of his mind was whether or not there was a silent alarm inside the house whenever the gate opened. That might make the whole thing way too interesting. Better not go down that road.

"Ross?"

"Copy."

"Out of the woods?"

"Edge. We have an open courtyard with a circular drive. Thirty yards to the front door."

"Sit tight. How's it look?"

"Quiet."

"Good quiet or bad quiet?"

"Good."

Stoke came over a rise and saw his whole squad crouching along the tree line, weapons ready. So far, nothing looked funky. He crept up and squatted beside Ross. He had the nylon climbing rope in his hands, swinging the hook and looking through the trees up at the third-floor balcony. Because of the thick woods, the house was still in shadow. But people might be waking up in there any minute now.

Middle of the man's circular driveway was this splashing fountain, all lit up. Three cars in his driveway, all bright red. Two Humvees and what had to be one of those Ferrari Testosterones. Where the hell you gonna drive a Ferrari on this island? Can't hardly keep a schoolbus on the road at more than twenty.

He looked at Ambrose and started undoing the snaps on his Kevlar vest.

"Since I'm going up the *outside* of the house, I won't be needing this," he said to Ambrose. "Best you wear it since you goin' *inside* the front door."

Ambrose looking at him like he'd lost his mind.

"I wouldn't be caught dead wearing that monstrosity," the man said.

"You sure as hell might get caught dead you not wearing it, Constable. Now put it the fuck on."

"I'm quite comfortable with what I'm wearing," Ambrose said.

"Ain't no time for this shit, Ambrose, know what I'm sayin'? Alex already lost Vicky. What I'm going to tell him I come back without his best friend, huh?"

Ambrose heaved a sigh and pulled the vest on over his tweed jacket, muttering to himself the whole time.

"Okay. Quick, get your boys through the woods to

the back of the house and wait for my go signal. Check?"

"Check."

"Ross, you and Ambrose wait here twenty seconds after I go. See me goin' up that wall, you haul ass for that front door. Stay low. Wait. You hear me tell Quick 'go,' that means I'm inside, and Quick's going inside and you and Ambrose blow through that front door. Then straight up them steps to that top-floor bedroom fast as you can, cool?"

"Cool," Ambrose said, smiling at him.

"I believe you are," Stoke said.

He gave Ambrose a punch to the shoulder right on his Kevlar vest, laughed, and took off, sprinting around the fountain like a running back. He looked in both Humvees and saw keys stuck in both ignitions. Man sure seemed lax about a lot of shit. In seconds, he was crouched beneath a window, looking up at the balcony. The sun's rays had just hit one of the tallest towers on the roof and were moving down toward the balcony. Shit.

He caught the balcony rail with the first toss of the rubber-coated grapnel hook on the end of his climbing rope. Didn't make a sound. He went up the wall hand over hand with the dagger in his mouth, just in case the man had decided to sleep out on his porch. Knife in your mouth like to scare folks shitless.

Peeking over the rail, he saw that the long terrace was empty. Just a row of louvered mahogany doors onto the bedroom, all closed. He hauled himself up and over and stood for a second, thinking it through. He turned to the rail, leaned over, and saw Ross and Ambrose scrambling around the fountain. He gave them five seconds, then started trying the doors, praying to find one open.

Third one was ajar. He pulled it open two inches and put his ear to the door. Snoring. Loud damn snoring. He started feeling lucky.

He slipped through the door and pulled it shut. Like stepping into a damn meat locker, it was so cold. Man had the AC down to fifty. He couldn't see shit for a couple of seconds, it was so dark. The snorer was to his left, maybe thirty feet away. To his right, same distance was a god-damn fire going in a fireplace. Had to be ninety outside and the man had a fire going!

Across the room, he could see light shining under a wide doorway. He started in that direction, not making a sound, and bumped into something hard. Banged his damn knee. It was some kind of damn chair, bolted to the floor. He felt the arms and back. Like a dentist's chair felt like. What the hell?

He moved through the darkness to the double doors most likely leading to the upstairs hallway. Tried them, both were unlocked. He cracked one door wide enough that Ross would see it, then he felt around on the wall for a light switch. Just before he pressed it, he whispered the word "Go!" into his mike.

He hit the switch, and the whole room lit up. Huge damn bed with a huge damn bald-headed man under some shiny black satin sheets. Man was on his back, had about twenty pillows behind him, propped up with a black and pink silk sleep mask over his eyes. Son of a bitch was still snoring!

That's when the first of many concussion grenades went off downstairs and the man sat bolt upright, lifted his cute little mask, and saw this huge black guy standing by his bed with a pistol aimed at his forehead.

"*Madre de Dios!*" he shouted. "*Qué pasa?* Who the fuck are you? What's going on?"

"Good morning, Doctor," Stoke said, a big grin on his face.

"Doctor?" the man said. "There must be some mistake. I'm not a—"

"You a pussy doctor, ain't you?" Stoke asked. "Otherwise, why you got that damn gynecological chair stuck in the middle of your damn room? Banged the shit out of my knee on one of your damn stirrups, Doc."

All hell was breaking loose downstairs, and just when he was starting to worry about them, Ambrose and Ross came through the man's bedroom door.

"I was just waking up the doctor here," Stoke said as Ambrose and Ross joined him at the foot of the bed. "See his chair? Man like to play doctor. Do pelvic examinations and shit." The man shifted under the sheets and Ross brought up the Streetsweeper and put it right on the target. Streetsweeper tended to get people's undivided attention.

"Take your hands out from under the sheets, very slowly, and cross them behind your head," Ross said. The man, who'd gotten real quiet, did like he was told, but who wouldn't, looking down the barrel of Ross's sawed-off weapon?

"Is this your man, Constable?" Stoke asked.

Ambrose stepped closer to the bedside and studied him, mentally adding thirty years to the face in the Polaroid photograph and the one in Stubbs Witherspoon's police sketch. It wasn't the face that did it so much as the eyes. One look at the eyes and you knew this was a killer. Wild, dark, killer's eyes. There was no question in Ambrose's mind.

He was face to face with the man in the New Year's Eve Polaroid. One of three brothers who'd slaughtered Alex Hawke's parents. He leaned in close to the fellow and spoke.

"What is your name, sir?"

The man stared at him in disbelief. This could only be the work of his brother Manso! He'd been set up. This was why he'd been forced off the *Martí*. Humiliated in front of his men. His treacherous brother would pay dearly for this. He would—

"I asked you your name!" Congreve shouted.

"I am Admiral Carlos de Herreras, *señor!* Commander in chief of the Navy of Cuba! This is an outrage! I demand that you—"

"Quiet."

Ambrose pulled out a little leather case and flipped it open, showing the man his warrant card.

"My name is Ambrose Congreve," he said in an even voice, full of measured intensity. "I am a special investigator for the Criminal Investigation Department of New Scotland Yard. In the name of Her Majesty Queen Elizabeth II, I am placing you, Carlos de Herreras, under arrest upon suspicion of murder. I order you to get out of that bed and come with me. Now."

"You will regret this, *señor*. We are the new ruling party of Cuba! My brother, he is the new—"

"Get out of that damned bed!" Congreve shouted, and ripped the sheets back. "As if I give a hoot in hell who you are! On your feet, Admiral, you're under arrest!"

The man sighed, major league all pissed off, slowly pulling his hands out from the pillows. Still had the little black and pink mask up on his forehead. Stoke was looking at Ambrose, smiling, about to congratulate him, when Ross shouted, "Stokely, watch out!"

Stoke turned but it was too late. The fat man's arm was extended toward him, a little black automatic in his hand. His thought was, shit, this is what happens when you go lending out your flak jacket. Then a sledgehammer hit him.

Stoke stayed on his feet long enough to see Ambrose raise and fire his weapon, hitting the suspect's gun hand before he could squeeze off a second shot. The fat man was screaming in pain as Stoke hit the floor.

Ambrose knelt beside him, stuffing his handkerchief into the wound. There was a tremendous amount of blood, but he was still breathing. Ross had the big man cuffed and was speaking into his mike. Stoke was fading in and out and Ambrose was feeling for his pulse when he heard Ross in his headphones say, "Tom, give me a sitrep."

"Still taking fire," Quick said. "I've got one man down."

"We're coming down the front way," Ross said. "Give us some cover."

Then Ross had his hands under Stoke's armpits and was pulling him to his feet.

"Come on, Stokely, we have to get you to a doctor now!"

"He's a doctor, ain't he?" Stoke said, grinning weakly at the fat man and getting woozily to his feet. His whole front was sticky with hot blood.

Ambrose led them out into the hallway and they headed for the stairs. Ross was in front with the Streetsweeper, supporting Stoke. Next, the prisoner, with

Ambrose's pistol jammed in his back. Ambrose could tell the firefight below was a lot less intense as they started down the broad marble staircase. He saw Stoke tighten his grip around Ross's neck to steady himself going down the stairs. He heard Quick shout a warning to Ross in his headphones. What the—

Suddenly, rounds whistled by his ear and over his head and he looked down to see three young chaps in T-shirts crouching at the foot of the steps, guns trained directly on them. One guy squeezed off another burst. He felt a sharp jolt of pain, clutched his chest, and fell back hard on the marble steps. Staring at the ceiling, Ambrose managed to move his hands and legs. God in heaven, he was still alive. But they were getting killed up here.

Ross didn't wait for another shot. His finger snapped shut on the trigger of the Streetsweeper, and it erupted in a rapid series of blasts that blew what was left of the three men right out the front door and down the steps to the driveway.

Ross stuck out his hand, and Ambrose grasped it, pulling himself to his feet.

"Hold on," Ross said to him, shouldering himself into the Streetsweeper's strap and getting his other arm under him. "We're going right out the front door!" They were going down the stairs fast. Then they were outside. Somehow, the sun had come up.

The front steps of the *finca* were slick with bodies and blood. Stepping over somebody's blown-off foot, Ambrose somehow managed to tell Ross what he'd seen on the way in. That there were keys in both Humvees. Blood was pumping out of Stokely, even with the handkerchief stuffed inside the wound.

Ambrose dredged up a strength he'd never known and jammed his gun into the back of the prisoner. The chap had been about to run for it.

"I'm all right," he told Ross. "Let's just get this bloody bastard the hell out of here!"

Then Ross was behind the wheel of the Humvee, the prisoner next to him up front. Ambrose climbed into the backseat and pressed his pistol against the back of the Cuban's head. He felt dizzy, and the sight of their prisoner still wearing black and pink silk pajamas, with the matching mask on his head, made him doubt his own mind.

Suddenly a new wave of chaps started coming out on the steps and seemed to be shooting at them. Then they started dropping to the ground, left and right. He thought he saw the sharpshooter Tom Quick in an upstairs window, picking them off with his sniper rifle, putting neat little black holes in people's foreheads.

"Hold on, Inspector," Ross said, and he mashed on the accelerator, the Humvee screaming around the fountain, heading for the wooden gates, and taking both of the gates off their hinges as they went crashing through.

"Okay, we have the suspect," Ambrose heard Ross say in his phones. "We have two casualties needing immediate medical attention. Get your guys the hell out of there! There are keys in the second Humvee at the front door. Use it!"

Two casualties? Ambrose thought. That meant he must be one of them.

That's when he felt a sharp pain in his chest and all the lights went out.

44

· · · — — · ·

Vicky had nicknames for most of her Cuban guards.

There was Ace, of the small black plastic comb, who was continually running it through his long black oily locks, swooping it up into an endlessly collapsing pompadour. And X-Ray, who was at least six-five and weighed maybe one hundred thirty pounds. Then there was Big Pimpin', so called neither because of his enormous size nor his scarlet pimples, which he had in pustulant abundance, but because he was constantly bragging about all the girls he was running in and out of the compound.

And, finally, the one she called Eyes Wide Shut. He was the putative leader of the four, and by far the worst of all. He had never hurt her, thank God, but he never took his eyes off her either. They had taken her bathing suit and jewelry away in exchange for a cotton shift she washed each day.

Eyes made her strip two or three times a day so he could search her. He would poke and prod, smiling all the while. He always found an excuse to get rid of the other three first. Sent them on errands, told them to take a break. Vicky was sure they knew what was going on. But they never said anything.

Eyes was the only one with a key to the manacles that shackled her to the bed. She had to ask his permission whenever she needed to use the bathroom. He always made her leave the door open. Once, when she'd stepped out of the shower, he was standing there in his trademark grungy sweatshirt with his pants down, erect.

"Aw, you think I'm supposed to get upset over a little thing like that?" she'd said.

Maybe he didn't understand what she'd said, but he understood what she meant. He never did it again. Then, of course, there were the Russians. The fat one. And the weird little one she vaguely remembered as having bought her a drink at the junkanoo.

So far, Eyes had kept the two Russians away from her. She'd learned from X-Ray that they were constantly offering the guards huge sums of U.S. dollars for an hour alone with her. Eyes, so far, had told them to stay away from her or he'd kill them. But you never knew just how long or how far his jealousy would stretch. She reassured herself daily that an ounce of flirtation equaled a pound of protection.

She was going to survive this. No matter what it took. No matter how long it took. At night, she thought of Alex. Worried about how what had happened added to the pain he was already suffering. And she thought of her father. She was all he had. If only there were some way to get word out. Bribe one of the guards? With what?

Eyes. If she could gain his trust, make him intimate promises she'd maybe never have to keep, he could get word out for her. He was both her principal tormentor and her only hope.

Little boys, big guns.

There were eight guards in all, working consecutive twelve-hour shifts. The night shift, she hardly dealt with. She'd talked the doctor who'd examined her that first night into giving her some heavy-duty sleeping pills. So, she either slept, or feigned sleep, from eight at night until eight in the morning when the night guards left. It made the time more bearable.

The guards were all killers and proud of it. She'd heard them bragging about kidnapping and torturing high-ranking journalists and politicians believed to be still loyal to Castro. Some spoke English, and she had three years of college Spanish, and when they got careless, they sat around saying things in front of her.

She listened to every word, and picked up a lot she wasn't supposed to know. Castro was a guest here. So was his son. So were the former officers of Fidel's secret police, army, and navy. It was a busy place. "The Hostage Hilton" was how she came to think of it.

Bit by bit, Vicky learned that there was a price on the heads of many people in Cuba. Millions of pesos for a long list of disloyal generals and journalists. Hundreds of thousands for certain "friends of Fidel" who were unfriendly to the new regime. Organized murder was about to become a booming business in Cuba.

Naturally, she didn't recognize the names, but some of the targets were apparently pro-Castro left-wing bigshots in Miami and New York, too. Meanwhile, an army of boys, just like the ones who guarded her, were roaming the island, murdering whoever got in their way. Cuba was now on the verge of becoming the new Colombia. Lawless. Murderous. Lost.

One afternoon, after Eyes had made her strip, he pointed his gun at her and said in good English, "If there is trouble, any kind of trouble, our orders are to shoot you first. You understand that, *chica?*"

She nodded. Since everyone thought she was dead, she wasn't too optimistic about a rescue attempt. Escape, yes, she was worried about how to do that. Very worried. Especially since the nightly screaming had started.

The guards called him Scissorhands.

He worked in a warren of basement rooms where all the interrogations took place. Late at night, she could hear the piercing screams. They said that when he looked at you, he had no eyes.

She'd overheard enough to know Scissorhands was not one of the top two or three generals who had overthrown the old regime. Apparently, his real name was Rodrigo, and she overheard someone say he was some rich nightclub owner from Havana. Scary-looking, because his eyes had no color. Another time, someone said he worked directly for the new military chief, General Manso something or other. This guy they all called Scissorhands, Rodrigo, was apparently the new head of State Security.

Scissorhands liked to attend interrogations just for fun. He wore a blood-soaked smock and carried a large pair of gleaming silver scissors in his pocket as he scurried from room to room during interrogations. "Snip, snip, snip," the guards would laugh whenever the screaming started.

She thought she was on the third floor of the prison. Blindfolded immediately after her abduction in the waters off Pine Cay, she'd not seen a thing until she was brought into the room she currently occupied. The windows were boarded shut. There were no newspapers. She was not allowed to watch TV.

All she knew, she got from careful listening. During the day, there were sounds of Jeeps and tanks and large numbers of troops going by under her window. So she was on a fairly main thoroughfare of some kind of military base, most likely the headquarters of the rebel general who had overthrown the old regime.

One morning, the thing she'd dreaded most actually happened. Someone came to take her away. Whether it was to be shot or simply "interrogated," she was sure it was not going to be a good morning. Still, she forced herself to stay calm.

It wasn't really a surprise. The guards had been acting strange all morning. Looking at her and then looking away. No Nintendo, no idle conversation. Just smoking and speaking quietly amongst themselves. Even the girl who came to clean each morning was acting strangely.

No one said a word. But she knew. Today was her day.

When the knock at the door finally came, Vicky was almost relieved. She heard the door open. When she looked that way, Ace pressed the barrel of his gun against her cheek, turning her head from the door.

Eyes unshackled her without looking at her. He wore a look of grim satisfaction. He grabbed her roughly by the back of her shift and held her while Ace tied a thick blindfold around her head.

Panic bloomed. She tried to pull away and heard the rip of cotton as the thin shift split down the back. She felt her heart thudding in her chest and her breath getting very shallow. She forced herself to breathe deeply and stay calm. The breathing helped a little.

Eyes and X-Ray steered her toward the door, Eyes managing to squeeze her breasts roughly as he did so.

The one who had entered said something in a raspy Spanish, and Eyes released his grip on her. She heard the door close behind her and knew she was outside and alone with this new raspy-voiced Cuban.

"*Buenos días, señorita,*" he said, and then, in perfect English, "I am Major Diaz. You are to come with me, please."

He held her arm lightly and led her down a flight of stairs. She was barefoot and she felt damp concrete underfoot. It had rained last night. If she was right about which floor she was on, three flights of steps would mean they were descending to the ground. One more would mean the basement. They reached a landing after three flights, turned right, and started down again.

"Where—where are you taking me?" Vicky asked.

"You'll see soon enough, *señorita,*" Diaz said.

They went through another door. Now they walked down a long corridor and suddenly there was shouting and whistling on either side of her. She heard what sounded like tin cups being banged on bars. It was not hard to imagine the row of cells on each side, or the prisoners' reaction to the woman in the torn shift.

They came to a stop, and Major Diaz said something to a guard. She heard a key turning in a lock, and then she was being pushed through an open door. A wave of cold air shocked her. The thin shift offered little protection. Air-conditioning. A new experience. A chilling experience, she thought, glad she still had a tiny reserve of humor in there somewhere.

"Just tell the truth," Diaz said, a harsh whisper in her ear. "And tell it quickly." He then released her.

"*Muchas gracias,* Major," a new voice said. "That will

be all." This new voice was velvety and musical. She didn't know if that was good or simply terrifying.

She heard Diaz walk out and the door close behind her with a solid thump. Thick door. Soundproof. She felt dizzy and disoriented without Diaz's hand on her shoulder. She had no choice but to stand and wait for whatever was coming.

"*Bienvenido a Telaraña,*" the man finally said. "Be seated."

"Where is the . . ." She reached out, feeling for any piece of furniture. "Where is the, uh, the—?"

"The chair? Ah. Three steps forward," the man said in his soft voice. Almost singsong.

She took three tentative steps, felt soft carpet beneath her feet, and put both hands out in front of her. She felt the wooden back of a chair, pulled it toward her, and managed to sit down.

"You may remove your blindfold," the man said.

Vicky did, blinking in the harsh light. There were two men in the room. There was one man in uniform sitting in a big leather chair behind a beautiful carved mahogany desk. Another man, tall and very handsome in a white suit, stood behind the desk, looking down at some photographs. Behind him on the wall was a large painting in a massive gilt frame. A museum-quality Goya. On the floor, a magnificent Aubusson carpet. She breathed a silent sigh of relief. This seemed an unlikely setting for all the midnight screaming.

Then the handsome man walked around from behind the desk and looked into her face, staring at her. "Good morning," he said in beautiful English. "I am so happy to meet you. My name is Rodrigo." He smiled down at her.

His eyes, she was shocked to see, were completely color-less. And in the breast pocket of his elegant white suit was a pair of silver scissors.

Vicky thought her heart would burst as the word exploded in her mind, Scissorhands.

"What is your name?" the uniformed man seated at the desk asked, and she squinted her eyes, trying to focus on him instead of the other one. She decided not to even look at the eyeless one. If she did, she'd never get through this alive.

She took a deep breath and composed herself. Somehow, she was going to make it out of here alive. She stared at the man behind the desk. He'd asked her a question. What was it?

Though he was seated, she could see that her inter-rogator was tall and thin. He wore an elaborate uniform, covered with decorations. He was handsome in a way, almost pretty. Long black hair, carefully swept back from his high forehead. Tied in a ponytail. Long black lashes and deadly gray eyes.

Spidery hands folded quietly before him on the leather top of his desk.

"I asked you a question. Your name?"

"Sorry. My name is Dr. Victoria Sweet. What's yours?"

"I am General Manso de Herreras. How are you being treated, Dr. Sweet?"

"Abominably."

Scissorhands smiled at this and walked back behind the desk. He perched on the edge and resumed leafing through his glossy eight-by-ten photos. From time to time he would look up at her with those monstrous eyes and smile at her.

"Sorry. We try to be accommodating. What kind of doctor are you?"

"I'm a pediatrician. I help children with neurological disorders. I also write books for children."

"Ah, a fellow student of human emotions. I've no degree, of course, I'm a lifelong military man. Yes, but a politician as well, and so a keen observer of the psychological."

"May I ask a question? Why am I here, General?"

"Ah. You would like to be the interrogator?"

"I'd like to know why I'm being held against my will."

"You ask the simple ones first, Doctor. Very well. You're here because you're a pawn."

"I'm a pawn?"

"Yes. The pawn resembles a queen perhaps, but she is still a little pawn. Does the little pawn play chess?"

Vicky sat silently for a moment, deciding how best to play this dangerous game. "Tell the truth, quickly," Major Diaz had said. For no good reason at all, she decided to trust him.

"You're holding me because you want to use me in some way. Probably to get to Alex Hawke," Vicky said, staring him straight in the eye. "How do you intend to do that?"

"Very good! We can make this short, then, although I am thoroughly enjoying our conversation."

"Short is good. That would include my stay here, General. When do I go free?"

"If you do exactly as I say, and the results are commensurate with your efforts, you will be released unharmed."

"I have your word?"

"What you have, my beautiful *señorita*, is no choice. Checkmate, you see?"

"I see. In that case, why don't we get started?"

"*Muy bueno.*"

The man opened a desk drawer and placed a cassette recorder and thick newspaper on top of the desk.

"Please bring your chair closer to the desk. You'll be more comfortable while you're recording."

She did as she was told and felt a wave of terror sweep over her. The photographs Scissorhands had been looking at weren't from his family album. They were pictures of women with fingers, ears, and nipples missing.

Vicky stifled the scream that was rising in her throat and forced herself to take deep consecutive breaths. She hardly heard what the man was saying.

"I have a statement here that I wish you to read into this microphone. State your name first and address this message to Alex Hawke. The statement simply says that you are a political prisoner. You have been taken hostage by the Cuban guerrilla group known as *Telaraña*. You may then use your own words. Plead your case to your lover. Tell him that your life depends entirely on how well your friend Hawke follows directions."

"What directions?"

"It is of no consequence to you. I will speak when you are finished. I want this man Hawke to use all of his connections in Washington, both at the State Department and the White House, to dissuade the United States from taking any preemptory offensive action against my new government."

"That's it?"

"Almost. Have you ever heard this Hawke mention a map? A treasure map, let us say?"

"No, never."

"It is not the reason he has returned to the Exumas after all these years?"

"It's a holiday, General. He likes to fish."

"Ah, well. If your memory doesn't improve, I'm sure you'll have a chance to discuss it in detail with this gentleman on my right. Meanwhile, I will conclude the tape by saying that if there is any rescue attempt whatsoever you will be shot immediately. How does that sound?"

He handed her a copy of today's *Miami Herald*. "You will then end this message by reading this front page headline and the date. So there will be no doubt on the other side. You understand?"

"Perfectly. Turn the thing on, please."

General de Herreras flipped a switch on the recorder. "One more thing," he said, pulling an envelope from inside his jacket and then sliding it across the desk toward her.

She opened the envelope and looked inside. It was the golden locket that Alex had given to her.

"This locket, it belongs to you?" he asked.

"It did," Vicky replied. "Once upon a time."

45

· · · — · ·

Gomer was sitting cross-legged behind the PX bar in total darkness. He was on the floor, a half-empty bottle of Stoli in one hand, his little pal RC in the other.

Any snoopy MPs who happen to walk by and peek in the windows, they wouldn't see nothing.

Mesmerized by the little red numbers on RC, reading 3000 now but not for long, he barely even noticed the sickly sweet smell of old spilled beer and booze or how grunged out the sticky floor was. He'd take a breath, though, and man, it was ripe. Like a skunk had taken a whiz back here.

He took another biting swig of warm Stoli.

Hell, he'd gotten shitfaced in a whole lot worse places than this! Besides his little sidekick RC, the only light came from a round fluorescent green clock on the wall. He could see it perfectly from right where he was sitting. Keeping track of time, man, that was critical at this juncture.

In between sips of Stoli, he was very busy, going over the Big Plan. In his mind, of course. Nothing written down. To make sure he had the BP down pat, he was reciting the steps aloud to himself over and over.

First thing, you press both buttons on RC at the stroke of twelve midnight. Keep an eye on the clock. That's why he'd strategically placed himself behind the bar so that he was hidden, but could still see the clock.

Okay, fifteen seconds after the Big Bug Checkout Countdown begins, his pecker starts ringing. Heh-heh.

No, no, he gets a call on his cell phone fifteen seconds after he pushes the buttons. He felt around down in his crotch area. Yep. Cell phone was right where he'd stuffed it. Not a lot of room down there where the big dog hangs, baby, whoo-ah!

Yes. Okay. Phone rings, he answers it. What does he say? Um, shit. What did Julio tell him to say? Roach Motel! Yes! He got it! He knocks back another biting shot of room-temperature Vitamin V as a reward. He practices:

"Roach Motel?"

And then the guy on the phone says . . . what . . . "Any vacancies?"

And he answers . . . lemme see . . . "No, no vacancies, not for thirty hours!"

Yeah, baby. He had the mother down cold!

Then what?

Oh yeah. He takes his little buddy RC and heads over to Sparky's tower station right on the no-man's-land fenceline. Gets Sparky to let him through. Then, if Sparky ain't on duty he—holy shit! The green fluorescent ring around the clock had caught his eye. He couldn't goddamn believe it!

The clock said it was twelve-fifteen!

He'd missed his goddamn deadline by fifteen minutes! Jesus. Sitting here thinking and drinking and what's he do? Just misses the most important deadline of his whole stinking life, that's all. Oh, man. Now what?

A million little green smackeroos sprout wings and fly somewhere over the rainbow, that's what.

Tears are streaming down his face as he gets slowly to his feet. Puts RC and the Stoli on the bar and wipes his eyes. All his life he'd thought he was so smart. And now he has to face the truth. He is just a dumbass *gusano* from Little Havana and he always had been.

He walked around the bar and pulled up a stool.

He'd kept his eye on that friggin' clock up there, he really had, and now he'd gone and—wait a minute. Hold the goddamn phone!

Now the clock says eleven forty-five! What the—oh, man. He was losing it. Almost. Sitting behind the bar, he'd been looking at the clock in the mirror! It said twelve-fifteen *in the mirror*. That was only the reflection. It was eleven forty-five in real life! He was okay! He was cool! He had fifteen whole minutes left! He was going to—ouch, there was a light shining in his eyes. He whipped around.

Somebody was shining a couple of flashlights through the windows at the front of the PX, rattling the front doors. Had they seen him?

MPs, had to be. Great timing, guys, really great, thanks a million, no pun intended.

He grabbed the Stoli and RC, ran back behind the bar, and dropped to his knees. He had to boogie on out of here but quick. He crab-walked the length of the bar and quickly reached the back door he'd jimmied open on the way in.

Two seconds later he was sprinting through the swirling curtains of rain toward his car. There was a Humvee pulled up right behind it, blue lights flashing. Goddamn. He looked back over his shoulder at the PX. Saw two lights flickering around inside. By the time those dumbass cops found the back door broken open, he'd be adios amigo.

He opened his car door and tossed the Stoli and the RC on the front seat. Then he jumped behind the wheel and twisted the key in the ignition.

Aw shit, not now. Piece of crap Yugo, come on! Start, goddammit! Rain must have blown up under the distributor cap, that was it. Of all the times to—wait. Better idea.

He grabbed his bottle and RC, jumped out of his car, and ran back to the MP's Hummer. Keys were in! Yes! There was a God!

He slammed the Humvee in gear, reversed, and saw the two flashlights bobbing through the rain, headed his way. Going to try and cut him off. No way, girls. He bounced back over the curb, put it in first, and stood on it, swerving up onto the grass, then back down the service driveway to the main drag, hauling complete ass. He looked at his watch. Ten minutes to midnight. He hung a Louie and headed for Sparky's watch tower, looking in the rearview.

Careening around the corner on two wheels, he was mystified to see another Humvee with its blue flashers going, blocking the street. Jesus H. Christ! He hit the brakes, skidded short of the two MPs standing there, and slammed it into reverse, knocking over some guy's arty-farty mailbox. Shit happens, neighbors.

Well, now, goddamn it all to hell. Here came the two Keystone Kops from the PX, running around the corner and blocking his "Escape and Evasion" maneuver. Held up his watch. Seven minutes. RC was on the seat beside him, thirty hours and seven minutes to payday. He just had to play it cool was all. The way he'd always played it, right?

The two MPs in front stayed put. Hands on their

sidearms, tough guys, watching too many episodes of *JAG* lately.

He craned his neck around and saw the two dickwads behind him coming toward his car. One guy stayed at the rear on the passenger side, the other one walked slowly up to his window. He rolled it down, nice and polite like, shoving the Stoli bottle under the seat with his right hand. He'd like to hide RC, but here was the guy shining some bright light right in his damn window.

Five minutes. He felt the Vitamin V pumping hot in his veins. Hell, any fool could stay cool for five more god-damn minutes.

"How we doin' tonight, sailor?" the MP said.

"Just fine," he said, giving the guy a big smile. He couldn't even see the guy's face, the light was so bright.

"What exactly you doing in the PX on a rainy Sunday night, sailor?"

"Just having a little drinky-poo, sir," he giggled. That's what Rita called cocktails when she was at somebody's house for dinner.

"Had quite a few, I'd say. Seein' as how you picked somebody else's vehicle to drive home in."

"No, sir, I have not been drinking quite a few. Only had one, sir. My vehicle wouldn't start is all."

"Keep your hands where I can see them."

"Yes, sir!" He'd been trying to slide RC out of the guy's sight.

"What the hell is that thing?"

"That'd be your portable CD player, sir," he said. Damn quick, too.

"Okay, very carefully, get your service ID out and hand it to me."

"Yes, sir. It's in the pantleg pocket of my fatigues. Right where I always keep it. 'Cause of the Velcro, you know. Okay?"

"Just show me the goddamnn thing," the MP barked at him. Touchy, touchy.

He reached down and ripped open the Velcro seal on his pocket. Pulled out his ID packet. An open pack of Rita's cigarettes came flying out, too, cigarettes spilling all over the floor. What the hell? Oh. She liked to wear his fatigues sometimes, when she went riding. So, that's where she'd been hiding them! She was going to get an ass-whupping for that all right!

Cigarette. That would steady the old nerves. He reached down and picked one up and popped it between his lips. Then he leaned over toward the MP's light, put the end of the cigarette right on the glass lens, and started to drag on it, trying to get the damn thing lit.

"Hell's wrong with your lighter, sir. Can't even get—"

It wasn't a lighter, he saw now, hell no, it was a damn flashlight. He'd tried to light his smoke on a flashlight! Sent a bad signal, probably.

"Step out of the vehicle, sir," the MP said. "Now!"

"Absolutely," he said, moving his foot off the brake and flooring the accelerator. He hit something, felt like a deer, maybe one of the damn MPs who wouldn't get out of his way, and then his new Humvee was tear-assing across a few lawns and driveways and drainage ditches. He had the ideal "Escape and Evasion" vehicle, all right.

There were a whole lot of flashing blue lights in his rearview now. Shit, looked like the whole damn military police force was on his ass. Too late, kiddies, too damn late! He knew a shortcut to Sparky's tower. He could be there in two minutes. He banged a wall hanging a hard right and banged walls a few more times going down the alley, sending trashcans flying left and right.

His watch said three minutes till twelve. He was going to make it, goddammit. He was going to pull this big bad mother out of the fire.

He burst out of the alley and there it was. Tower 22. Home of his best buddy, Sparky Rollins. All he had to do now was cross that baseball diamond and then a big open field and he was home free. No flashers in the rearview now. Good, they musta missed his shortcut. He accelerated across the diamond and decided to take out a row of bleachers down the right field line just for fun. Hell, it wasn't his Humvee.

Then he was tear-assing across the open field, friggin' airborne half the time. What a ride! His old heap would never have made it across all these damn flooded ditches and bushes and shit. To his left, he could see a train of blue flashers as the Humvees came to a stop in the parking lot of the baseball field. Then they too started racing across the diamond towards him. He managed a peek at his watch.

Thirty seconds.

He skidded to a stop a hundred yards from Sparky's tower, jumped out, and ran over to the base. Cupping his hands, he yelled up to the tower.

"Sparky! My man! Sparky, you up there?"

"Sparky's off duty tonight," a guy up in the tower yelled down. "Identify yourself! Who the hell are you and what the fuck are you doing?" Guy had an M-16 pointed right at him.

"I'll show you what I'm doing!" Gomer said, jumping back in his Humvee. "Watch this, asshole!"

He reversed back a hundred yards and stopped. The fleet of Humvees was racing across the field toward him, all fanned out, thinking about surrounding his ass.

He looked at his watch and saw the second hand coming around, come on, baby, come on, yes! He had the RC in his lap, staring at it. Twelve midnight on the button! Two buttons actually and he pushed both of them simultaneously just like Julio Iglesias had told him.

The red numbers instantly started rolling backwards.

The Big Bug Checkout Countdown had begun.

The whole U.S. cavalry was maybe two hundred yards behind him now and coming fast. He rammed the Humvee in first and floored it. He was headed straight for the fence, screaming at the top of his lungs. Glass was shattering and hitting him in the face and he realized the guy on the tower was shooting at him!

One of his own guys was shooting at him! Friendly fire? No such luck, pal. Court-martial time for somebody!

He was going eighty when he hit the wire fence. It slowed him down a little, and he took a lot of goddamn fence with him and he musta hit one leg of the tower by mistake because it looked like it was starting to topple over, but goddammit, he was headed for the promised land now!

He took a quick look over his shoulder. There was the guy on the tower, only now he was pinwheeling in the air, headed for the ground. He saw that all the Humvees had stopped short of the fenceline. Of course. You'd have to be crazy to drive across a goddamn minefield on a rainy night, right? He was peering over the top of the steering wheel, wondering if the mines would be like little bumps that he could steer around, when he felt his pecker humming.

He jammed one hand down inside his jeans and pulled out his cell phone, put it to his ear. Damn, it was hard to drive with one hand but what else were you supposed to do?

"Roach Motel," he said, realizing that his mind was totally clear but that he was screaming.

"Any vacancies?"

"No. No fucking vacancies for thirty hours."

"*Muchas gracias, amigo. Viva Cuba!*" the guy said.

Then there was a click in his ear and then a much louder noise, some kind of explosion, and he felt the entire Humvee lift into the air, seeming to break in half as it rose. Then it was falling end-over-end and he seemed to be upside down and there was this terrible ripping pain in both legs, hurt so bad he couldn't believe it and then—

He opened his eyes.

He was lying on his back in a ditch full of water. Rain was still falling hard, stinging his face. Stuff was on fire all around him. Shit, his own T-shirt was on fire! He scooped a handful of muddy water from the ditch and put it out. Had to get moving. Had to deliver the RC and get his money. He could even see the Cuban towers now, they all had their spotlights trained on him. He'd been so close!

He'd just have to walk this last part, that's all. He felt woozy, but he could do it if he could just get his legs to move. But he couldn't. Couldn't even *feel* his legs in fact. He reached down to where he thought they were and—

Oh, God. They weren't there. Just blood. And some

other stuff. What? Bones? Guts? Jesus. He was, what, cut in half? He was—

He felt something humming in his hand. He lifted his arm and looked at his hand. His cell phone! He still had his goddamn cell phone in his hand. He put it to his ear. He could call for help. He was going to make it. He—

"Hello, honey?" Rita said in his ear. It was Rita!

"Yeah, baby," Gomer said.

"You all right? I'm worried about you. It's real late. I know you've been drinking, but you come on home now and come to bed like a good boy."

"I can't, uh . . . honey, I can't move my . . . we were going to be so rich and . . . uh . . ."

"You still there? You don't sound so good, baby."

"Well, I'm not . . . all that good. I wanted . . . see . . . I've been meaning to tell you about the teddy bear."

"The teddy bear?"

"Yeah. The teddy bear's got . . . a tummy bug and—"

"Honey, just come on home, okay? You're not making a whole lot of sense here, okay? Mommy will make it all better."

"I wish I could, you know. I just really . . . really wish I could."

"Baby? Baby? Are you there?"

"I wish—"

"Baby? Baby?"

46

· · · — · ·

Alex was dreaming.

Sound asleep in the top bunk of his tiny berth, he was dreaming of his old dog Scoundrel.

They'd taken a small picnic supper to the edge of the sea. Scoundrel was plunging again and again into the waves, retrieving the red rubber ball. But now some terrible black storm appeared to be howling in from the sea, sweeping the little red ball farther and farther from the shore.

Scoundrel was at the water's edge, the waves lapping around his forepaws. He was mewling and barking, watching the red ball disappear over the horizon. The dog barked loudly, loud enough to wake Alex, who rolled over in his berth, clutching his pillow, mumbling something in his sleep.

He was so far down, he couldn't, wouldn't, come up.

Quiet, Scoundrel. Quiet.

But there really *was* a voice calling him to come and come quickly.

Someone really *was* grabbing him, a rough hand on his shoulder, calling his name loudly in his ear. Shaking him, telling him to wake up, wake up now, even though he knew it was still nighttime. He could hear the waves slapping against the hull of the ship, see the blue moonlight streaming through the porthole onto his bedcovers, and hear the faint sounds of activity up on deck.

"Rise and shine, Commander, wake up!" the young

crewman was saying. "It's 0600 hours, sir! You were meant to be airborne at this time! Sir!"

"What? What?" Alex said, sitting up. Scoundrel had been replaced by a sea of black dots, swimming before his eyes.

"0600, sir, you filed a flight plan for an 0600 hours departure. Flight ops has been calling, wondering where you are. We're getting ready to receive four squadrons. They'd like to get you out first. And this fax came in for you, sir, middle of the night. We didn't want to disturb you." He handed Alex a sealed envelope.

"Tell flight ops I'm on my way," Hawke said, and the aide slipped out into the brightly lit corridor.

He ripped open the envelope, pulled out the single piece of paper, and read it.

Alex,
    Events here require your presence. Urgent. Please contact as soon as you receive this message.
                        Best,
                        Sutherland and Congreve

Alex shook his head and tried to clear it. He stuck the fax into his pocket. He'd radio *Blackhawke* soon as he was airborne. His hand went immediately to his throbbing forehead. He remembered instantly. He'd fallen prey to the demonic whiskey gods once more. They'd had their way with him and now he must pay. Coffee. That was it. Coffee.

He rang for the aide, who, since this was Officers' Country, appeared instantly.

"Yes, sir?" the boy said as Alex, yawning, opened the door, still trying to rub the sleep from his eyes.

"May I please have a pot of hot coffee?"

"Certainly," the cheery young crewman replied. "How would you like it, sir?"

"Black. No cream, no sugar."

"Aye, aye, sir." The boy nodded and was gone.

Bloody hell, he thought. What a night. There was the single malt before dinner. Make that the double single malts. Then there was, of course, the claret, all the fine claret, with the perfectly cooked rack of lamb. Then there was the port wine. Ah, yes, the port.

An old Royal Navy expression his grandfather had used popped into his brain. He seemed to recall repeating it countless times last evening, to the evident amusement of the Americans.

"The port stands by you, sir," he'd said.

Which translated: "Don't hog the bottle, mister, I'm thirsty."

He had a dim memory of endless oceans of Black Bush whiskey and port wine, pounding against breakwaters he'd spent a hellish lifetime erecting in his mind. Elaborately constructed seawalls had been smashed to bits and ancient feelings had come pouring through. Along with them, he now remembered, came the long-buried memories.

God in Heaven, he thought, rolling his long legs over the side of the bunk and dropping to the floor. He'd had some kind of a breakthrough. The ghosts had come, yes, but it seemed he'd got the best of them.

The evening's events were all slowly coming back. What else? Ah. Something about challenging that noxious prick Tate to a duel. But the cove never showed. Hardly surprising.

Alex had found a perch on the fantail and waited, watching the billowing clouds drift past the moon, feeling the slow soothing roll of the deck. Feeling everything inside him shift, rearrange, and shift again.

Then Balfour had appeared. An American fighter pilot who'd become one of his closest friends during the Gulf War. During the course of their recuperation in a Kuwait hospital, he and Balfour had formed a close friendship. Then Balfour had taken a turn for the worse, and one day he wasn't there.

Sitting there on the *Kennedy's* fantail in the moonlight, Hawke had found himself doing something he'd never in his life done before. Opening his heart to another man.

God knows how long they sat there. He unleashed a flood of happy memories of his parents and those wondrous early years on Greybeard Island when the world was still a magical place. He spoke of Ambrose, and how his dear friend had tried to help him. And Vicky, of course, how he'd loved her and how he'd lost her.

Finally, exhausted, and miraculously unburdened, he stopped talking and just gazed at the stars, taking the peace and serenity they offered.

It was then that he realized he'd completely forgotten why he'd been sitting there on deck in the first place. Oh, yes, waiting for that insufferable man to come topside and have it out. He must have finally given up, said good night to David Balfour, and somehow made his way back down to his cabin. At least, that seemed to be the case, because it was morning and here he was!

Now, he straightened and touched his toes twenty times. Ouch. He dropped to the deck and did thirty very slow push-ups. His muscles were screaming, and his head was pounding. It had been a very long time since he'd experienced a hangover of this magnitude. Definitely Force Ten.

He stepped inside the tiny head and stood bracing himself, both hands on either side of the little stainless basin. He'd gotten himself bloody well drunk, he had. First time in recent memory. Not tipsy. Tanked. Snockered. He felt goddamn awful. He looked at his bleary, watery eyes in the mirror and was flabbergasted to see a faint smile there, lurking under the two-day beard he'd been meaning to shave off.

A *real* smile.

Actually, he didn't feel as bloody awful as by rights he ought to feel. Eventually, the sorrow over Vicky's loss would somehow be locked up in the strongbox of his heart. He'd locked up sorrow before, and, somehow, he would again. But this new feeling welling up inside had caught him entirely by surprise.

Strange, he thought, looking in the mirror again. He felt, what was the word? Light. He felt light. Exquisitely light.

No, a little better than that. Buoyant.

Alex knew himself well enough to know he was hardly the deep, introspective type. In his world, just as there was right and there was wrong, there were two distinct types of humanity. Those who float and those who dive deep. Alex, all his life, had happily tended to float. Diving was dangerous. And so this seeming sea change he sensed inside himself was all the more surprising and perplexing.

Shaving, he pondered the new experience of diving deep. What had happened? Vicky's death had affected him profoundly. But that wasn't the catalyst for these entirely new feelings.

No, it was seeing the face of the spider. That huge face up there on the screen in the wardroom; that's what had triggered it. He'd been painfully aware that every man in the wardroom was staring at him, but he didn't give a good goddamn. Some vague excuse, some innocuous justification, and he could have moved on. He could not do it.

He'd finally come face-to-face with the one unendurable truth that had ruled his entire life. It was so simple.

His father was never coming back.

He'd been waiting—

three knocks three knocks three knocks

—waiting for his father to return all his life. But his father was never coming back to save him. His father was dead. His mother was dead. He'd watched them die. Heard them die. At the hands of the deadly faceless spider who had haunted his dreams.

Only now, he'd seen the face of the spider.

He had locked on to those cold, dead eyes, and he knew. No more hiding, no more running away from the spider. Now, the spider would be running from him. The spider wasn't all-powerful after all. The terrified little boy locked in the dreadful closet was now a wrathful man bent upon a singular and terrible vengeance.

A man who could cry havoc, let loose his dogs of war, and conquer the spider. Find the spider and kill it, as slowly and as mercilessly as—

He splashed some cold water on his face and looked at his watch. Bloody hell, it was six-fifteen. The flight ops guys were going to be merciless up on the flight deck. They'd probably all turn out, just to see the little *Kittyhawke* attempt a takeoff. After the humiliation of two failed landings, he was determined to resurrect his once-sterling reputation.

He figured if he ran her up to full power and popped the brake, he could be wheels up in less than fifty feet. That would give the bastards a shock.

Just thinking about climbing into the cockpit of his little plane brought a huge smile to his face. He pulled on his faded green jumpsuit, zipped it up, grabbed his duffel, and ran all the way up five flights to the deck. When he swung open the heavy steel door and stepped out onto the sunlit flight deck, he felt as if he were stepping through the gates of Heaven itself.

The sky was pure and gold and blue. The ocean heaved gently, rolling the vast deck maybe five feet side to side. He noticed a destroyer had pulled up about a thousand yards off their port beam. Then, off the *Kennedy*'s stern he saw many, many more, destroyers, battleships, light cruisers, and in the far distance, the hulking black silhouette of yet another carrier and her battle group. Huge Sea King helicopters were circling overhead.

The massive wake of the *Kennedy* showed she was executing a hard tack westward, as were all the other ships of the Atlantic Fleet. West toward Cuba, no doubt.

He wound his way through the covey of F/A-18 Super Hornets to where his own plane was parked. Seeing the LSO on the fantail, in his yellow and black bumblebee costume, Alex waved a friendly hello and got one back.

There was a young green-shirted maintenance crew-man just climbing down from *Kittyhawke*'s portside wing. The boy stepped down off the pontoon, smiling, as Hawke approached.

"All fueled and ready, sir," he said brightly. He was a red-haired, freckle-faced kid, not even twenty, Hawke saw.

"Thank you," Hawke said, opening the hatch in the fuselage where he stowed his duffel. "Looks like a brilliant morning for flying!"

"Oh, yes, sir, Commander," the boy replied. "Especially in that airplane. I couldn't help taking a peek inside, sir. Hope you don't mind."

"Not at all," Hawke said. "What's your name?"

"Poole, sir. Richard Poole."

"I'm Hawke. Alex Hawke."

"I know all about you, sir. Your exploits over Baghdad are well known aboard this ship. But I've never seen anything quite like *Kittyhawke*, sir. First, I thought she was a converted Spitfire or an old experimental Grumman, but I see she's not. Who on earth designed her?"

"I did," Hawke said, grinning. "She's an exact replica of a toy seaplane I had as a boy. One of the early radio-controlled ones. That was the prettiest little plane I'd ever seen. Still is, but I can actually climb inside this one."

The sailor laughed. "She's designed after a toy?" he asked.

"Yes, she is," Hawke said, and stepped up onto the pontoon. "And she goes like stink, too. Same engine as the old Supermarine Spitfire Mark XVI. Packard-built Merlin 266."

"Man alive, that's one gorgeous machine, sir. So, who's the babe on the side there?" the boy asked, pointing at the smiling blonde painted just below the cockpit window.

"Why, that's my mother, as a matter of fact," Alex said with a big wide grin. "A pretty famous American movie star, actually, before she married my father."

"Wow," the boy said. "What was her name?"

"Catherine Caldwell," Hawke said. "She was from New Orleans. Everyone called her Kitty. Ever see the old film *Southern Belle?*"

"With Gary Cooper!"

"Right. That was Coop and my mother's last film together," Hawke said, climbing up into the cockpit and pulling the door closed. "She was nominated for the Academy Award. I was in England, but I saw her on the telly."

"Awesome!" the sailor said, gazing at the painted beauty on the fuselage.

"Awesome," Hawke agreed. "I was a very lucky boy to have had such a wonderful mother." He slid his Perspex window closed.

Time to fly.

47
• • • — — • •

Hawke donned his headphones and started his preflight routine, surprised to find himself still whistling an old hit tune he used to whistle as a boy. Couldn't remember the name. Theme song from one of his mother's many movies, he supposed.

"Good morning, Commander," he heard the air boss say in his phones. "You're late."

"Morning, sir, sorry about that," Hawke said, busily flipping switches. The big engine coughed a few times, then roared to life. Hawke craned his head around, testing his flaps, rudder, and ailerons.

"Doesn't matter, Commander. We've got an E2-C Hawkeye on final, vectoring in from Key West. The pilot asked me to hold you until they landed. Somebody from Washington aboard, I guess. Has an urgent need to talk to you, so sit tight."

"Roger that," Hawke said. "Permission to taxi out to the staging ramp and wait there?" Whatever Washington wanted, he wasn't going to give up his slot. He'd listen to whoever and whatever for five minutes, but then he was out of here.

"Roger, *Kittyhawke,* taxi to the hold."

"*Kittyhawke,* taxi and hold, roger."

Hawke throttled up and steered his little plane out to the staging area where a few F/A-18s were parked. Most of the squadrons of Super Hornets appeared to be long gone.

He heard a howl to his left and looked out to see the E2-C dropping in just off the fantail. The aircraft was in the classic "Turkey" attitude, so nicknamed because "everything is hanging down." The Hawkeye, an ungainly beast at best, provides the battle group with electronic surveillance and has responsibility for intercepting enemy transmissions. It carries more than six tons of equipment and is prop-driven.

Probably a bastard to land, Hawke thought, watching the pilot's final approach.

The Hawkeye flared up perfectly, snagged the third wire, and lurched to a stop. Instantly, swarms of blue-shirted plane pushers surrounded it. One of them wheeled a set of steps up to the airplane's portside and opened a hatch. A tall figure in a jumpsuit and helmet emerged, jumped down from the plane, and headed immediately toward *Kittyhawke*. Alex recognized that walk. It was Conch, all right.

She walked around the tail of Alex's plane and stood looking up at him for a few moments before she removed the helmet and shook her hair out. As if he didn't know who she was. He slid open his window and stuck his head out.

"Hi, Conch!" he said, smiling. "Imagine meeting you here!"

"Hi, yourself, sailor," she said. "Aren't you going to invite a girl aboard for a cup of hot java?"

"Absolutely," Alex said, reaching over to open the small door on the starboard side. "Come on around! Watch the prop wash, Conch, this isn't any little F-14, you know."

In a moment she'd climbed into the right-hand seat beside him, and he was pouring her some hot coffee from the thermos his new friend Poole had kindly left in the cockpit.

"All right," she said, "I know you're anxious to get out of here, but I'm very glad I caught you. I've been with the president and the cabinet in *Cayo Hueso*. Then a meeting with all the top members of the Cuban Exile Committee. We've got a nightmare scenario on our hands."

"What's going on?"

"A lot. First, Miami. It's like Dunkirk in reverse!" she

said. "There is not a single vessel to be bought, rented, chartered, or stolen between Key West and Jacksonville! It's amazing."

"What's going on?"

"Well, the Cuban community in Miami is getting ready for a big seagoing homecoming parade. They see themselves, flags flying, sailing right into Havana harbor, of course. They think a U.S. invasion is imminent. As soon as this unpleasantness is dispensed with, they think they'll just go home and it will be back to the good old days. They're exerting huge pressure on the president and the Congress to invade now."

"Will you?"

"No comment. Make your own determination. And there's another little wrinkle we just found out about at 0100 hours this morning. The Cubans have demanded the total evacuation of Guantánamo. They've given us thirty hours. The clock started at midnight last night. It's now, what, 0630 Monday? That gives us a little over twenty-three hours to evacuate thousands of women, children, and civilians."

"Surely you're not going to just do it, Consuelo?"

"I'm afraid we have no choice, Alex," she said, sipping her coffee. "The Cubans have managed to smuggle a weapon inside the base. We don't know if it's nuclear or biological, but it's serious either way. We're searching, but it could be literally anywhere. Unbelievable. The CO at Gitmo, Joe Nettles, ordered half of the CDC people in Atlanta down. They just arrived. They're turning the whole place upside down. So far, nothing."

"You have to assume they won't find it," Alex said. "Which is why the *Kennedy* seems to be steaming at flank speed toward Cuba. She's on a rescue mission, correct? Massive evacuation."

"We've got to get all those folks out of there. And we will."

"You don't think it's a hoax?"

"Hardly matters. Because there's only one way to find that out, isn't there?"

"Right, the bad way. Makes you long for the good old days of Fidel."

"Doesn't it? These de Herreras thugs are out of their minds. They're about to find hell and damnation raining down on their people's heads and wonder where they miscalculated. They're counting on that stealth sub to stay our hand but—"

"I want to help, Conch. Anything. I have a . . . personal stake in this matter."

"Personal?"

"Let's just say I have an old score to settle with this new dictator."

"Tell me, Alex. I'm your friend, and I need to know."

"Manso de Herreras and his two brothers murdered both of my parents one week after my seventh birthday. I saw them do it."

For the first time since he'd known her, Conch was speechless. Tears were forming in the corners of her eyes.

"I'm so sorry, Alex," she finally said.

"Well. I'll deal with it."

"Yes. I know you will." She took his hand and squeezed it. "You've been dealing with it for over thirty years, haven't you, darling?"

"Yes. By not dealing with it."

"How horrible for you. I always knew something horrible had happened, Alex. Deep and hurtful. There were rumors, of course. I just never had the courage to bring it up."

"Well, I must say I'm finding the ancient notion of revenge enormously satisfying so far."

"My poor dear boy."

"So, in the spirit of moving on, what's next on your geopolitical agenda?"

"Well, a lot. The Cuban rebels' new command and control center is on an island off Manzanillo. The one called *Telaraña*. Our first target. Soon as we've got everyone safely out of Gitmo, we turn that base into fine powder. The sub, now named the *José Marti* by the way, has returned to *Telaraña* from the Exumas. God knows what it was doing over there."

"My hunch would be a shakedown cruise with some Cuban Navy officers aboard?"

"Good guess. Anyway, we've got visual surveillance twenty-four hours a day. *Telaraña* now has its very own little spy satellite. This time, they were stupid enough to bring the sub in on the surface. Problem will be finding that thing underwater."

"How can I help, Conch?"

"The president sent me here to coordinate State and my task force with Admiral Howell and the Atlantic Fleet. I have an idea. How's this sound? We use *Blackhawke* as a decoy to get close enough to shore to insert two SEAL recon teams. Your yacht would arouse a lot less suspicion than one of our destroyers."

"Bad idea, Conch. They'll have patrol boats out obviously. They know me and they know who *Blackhawke* belongs to. I'm on their current hit list. Let me think about it. I may come up with a better idea."

"I'll be in contact. You'll get faxes of all the latest sat photos. Last item on my agenda. This is for you."

She handed him a small manila envelope with his name scrawled in black crayon on the outside.

"Nothing ticking inside," Conch said. "We checked. No anthrax powder either. It was blind-dropped yesterday at the American desk of the Swiss consulate in Havana, addressed to you. They flew it up to me at Key West."

"Strange."

"You've got a flair for understatement, Alex. Okey-dokey, big boy, I've got to run. These military types don't like to be kept waiting," she said, and she flung an arm around his neck and give him a peck on the cheek. Then she opened the door and stepped out onto the wing.

"'Bye, Conch," Alex said.

"You need anything, I'm your girl. Anything."

"Thanks, Conch."

"*De nada*. Every time we say good-bye? I deal with it."

She shut the door, and jumped down to the deck. Alex watched her walk away.

"*Kittyhawke*, you copy?" said the air boss in his phones.

"Copy," Alex said.

"Hey, listen, Commander, I hate like hell to bother you. But, if you're all through necking down there, you might wanna consider getting your little toy airplane the hell off my flight deck. I've got the entire Black Aces Squadron lined up two miles out dead astern. They had to get up real early this morning and they're probably coming home a little cranky. Might get fussy if anybody's in their way."

"Roger that, *Kittyhawke* taxi to position and hold for takeoff."

"I'm going to miss you, *Kittyhawke*. You brought a little excitement and romance into my otherwise drab and mundane existence."

"I'll miss you, too, sir," Alex said, and, shoving his throttles forward, taxied into position for takeoff. He kept looking at the envelope lying on the seat where Conch had left it.

Brakes full on, he ran his engine up to full power and waited for takeoff clearance. His curiosity finally got the best of him. He ripped open the envelope and shook it.

Vicky's gold locket fell out and landed in his lap.

"*Kittyhawke*, you're cleared for takeoff."

"*Kittyhawke* is rolling," Hawke said, staring at the locket.

Vicky was alive.

48

• • • — — — • •

During the short, uneventful flight down to the Exumas, Alex had raised Sutherland on the radio. By the time he'd landed on the mirrored surface of the bay and taxied up to *Blackhawke*'s stern ramp, he knew most of what had occurred on Staniel Cay the day before.

The news was staggering.

At first hearing, Ross's recount of the raid on *Finca de las Palmas* had been simply unbelievable. Alex had been incredulous, then shocked, then exhilarated by what they'd done. Only hours ago, he'd stared at the face of one of the three men who'd killed his parents. Now he learned that one of those men had already been captured and was, this very morning, being arraigned for murder in Nassau.

Hawke also had learned that, while the sunrise raid on *Finca de las Palmas* had been a success, there had been casualties. Two of Quick's squad had suffered minor injuries. Ambrose had been hit, but not badly hurt. Most seriously wounded was the man who'd led the raid, Stokely.

As soon as *Kittyhawke* was safely secured, Hawke raced up to *Blackhawke*'s sickbay. Stokely was sitting up in bed, haranguing the doctor, when Hawke walked in. Clearly, Dr. Elke Nilsson was not accustomed to being admonished. A blond, blue-eyed Dane, she had signed on two years earlier, when *Blackhawke* spent one month in Copenhagen harbor on special assignment for the British government.

Alex and Ambrose had successfully broken up a Serbian diamond smuggling ring, flipping witnesses and suspects until they'd climbed the slippery ladder all the way to Milosevic himself. Slobo was a very busy boy. Alex, unfortunately, had gotten a pair of souvenirs of the exploit, courtesy of a Serb gunman.

Dr. Nilsson had come aboard to treat Alex, successfully extracting two bullets embedded in his right buttock, and she'd been hired on the spot. The fact that the new ship's doctor bore a startling resemblance to her twin sister, the reigning Miss Denmark, had no bearing on Hawke's decision. He vetted her qualifications very carefully after hiring her.

Fortunately, she'd not yet learned enough colloquial

English to understand the torrent of undeleted expletives that Stoke was hurling in her direction. The term "booty," for instance, had not yet entered her lexicon.

"Stoke," Hawke said, "what's the problem?" For a man who'd taken a bullet the day before, Stokely looked to be in remarkably fine fettle.

"Problem?" Stoke said. "I'll tell you what the goddamn problem is. Got her little booty parked on that chair right over there! The hell kind of doctor is she, anyway? Goddamn—"

Alex pulled up a chair by Stoke's bed and sat down.

"Calm down, Stoke," he said. "What's wrong?"

"Well, hell, first she tells me how lucky I am the bullet didn't hit nothing important. Nothing important? Hell, everything *I got* is important! Flesh, bones, arteries, all that shit. Not important, my ass."

"Stoke, she's just doing her job," Alex said, smiling at Dr. Nilsson. She had her arms folded across her chest and had gone quite red in the face. At the moment, she was puffing at a charming little banglet of blond hair that kept falling across her face.

"Yeah, okay, then she tells me it ain't nothing to worry about. 'Course it ain't, for her ass! Ain't *her* goddamn chest got shot, it's mine! She got a helluva lot more chest to worry about than I do, don't she? She—"

"Dr. Nilsson," Alex said, interrupting Stokely, "I'm sure he didn't mean . . . uh . . . perhaps you could leave us alone for—" He didn't finish because the Danish doctor flung Stokely's chart at the wall and stormed out of the room.

"Great," Alex said. "See what you've done? Now I'm going to have to go find some way to apologize for you."

"How you doin', boss?" Stoke said, a wide grin on his face. "You heard all what happened? Five of the best, my brother!"

"I heard all about it from Ross," Alex said, slapping Stoke's palm smartly "Unbelievable, Stoke."

"Listen up, my man!" Stoke said. "We kicked us some serious ass yesterday. Serious ass."

"I can never thank you enough, Stoke. I mean I—"

"Hell, ain't me you should be thanking, boss. It's your little buddy Ambrose. That man gets all the credit for this here collar. He been working that case for thirty years, you know. Never told you, did he?"

"I'm sorry, what did you say?" Alex asked.

"Been working on the case for thirty years. Ambrose."

"Good Lord," Hawke said, feeling all the breath go out of him. "I had no idea that Ambrose . . . none. I can't imagine that he would . . ."

It was the first time Stoke had ever seen Alex Hawke speechless.

"Way he works, I guess. Low profile. Him and Ross flew over to Nassau and found some old retired cop who'd kept his file. Had the original police drawings of the three perps. Ambrose took 'em and blew the thing wide open."

"Absolutely amazing," Alex said, still stunned.

"Yeah, pretty good cop after all, ain't he?" Stoke said, swinging his massive legs over the side of the bed. "Now, go sweet-talk your damn doctor and get her to leave my ass alone. I feel great. And I got a lot of shit to do, boss, got to fill out police reports and all that."

"Stoke, lie down a minute and listen to me. I'm thank-ful you're all right. Ever since I was told you were hurt,

I've—Stoke, listen. I'm going to need your help. Now. You're the only one who can help me."

"All right, now you gonna get all serious and stuff. Go 'head then. Tell the old Stoke what on your mind."

"You're not going to believe this, but Vicky is alive."

"What? What the hell you talkin' about?"

"All I know right now is that somehow, incredible as it seems, Vicky is alive. She's a hostage, but she's alive."

"Hostage of who?"

"The new Cuban government. She's being held on an island called *Telaraña,* just off the southwestern coast of Cuba. It's a heavily fortified military base."

"How you know all this, boss?"

"I just listened to this cassette," Alex said, handing the cassette and a Sony Walkman to Stokely. "It was delivered along with Vicky's locket to the Swiss embassy in Havana. You should listen to it, too. She quotes the headline from yesterday's Miami papers. Vicky is alive, believe me."

Stoke donned the earphones and listened for a few moments.

"Holy shit, she really is alive," Stoke said. "That's wonderful. Now what the hell they want Vicky for, boss?"

"The general believes he can coerce me to intercede on his behalf in Washington. Ridiculous, but there you have it. Unbelievably, Vicky is still alive. But not for long unless we can get her out of there, Stoke. Two big problems. One, she made it plain that any rescue attempt would result in her death along with all the hostages."

"Just like them goddamn Colombians. I dealt with 'em up in the Medellín mountains. Always say they goin' shoot the hostages first. And generally do. But we snatched a few live ones, boss."

"How long does it take to put a hostage rescue plan like that in operation, Stoke?"

"Shit, boss, all depends," Stoke said. "At a military installation? Five days, minimum. You got to recon the place down to the inch. Know where your hostage is located. Know where the windows are, what kind, how thick the doors and walls are, all that entry and egress kinda shit. You got to intercept all the communication going in and out, so you know who's who, where they are, and what the hell is what."

"Stoke," Alex said, looking at his watch, "I said there were two problems. Here's problem two, and it's a big one. At some point, in less than twenty hours from now, the Americans are going to launch fighter squadrons from the *John F. Kennedy*. Fighters and cruise missiles from the Atlantic Fleet are going to bomb that rebel compound, and anything else they fancy, into oblivion."

"Jesus Christ. Twenty hours?"

"Maybe less. Now, I know your old Navy unit used to be pretty good at this kind of thing. SEAL Team Six, I mean."

"Good? Shit. They the best-trained, deadliest, most capable group of warriors in America's history. Hop and pop, stuff and snuff. Snatch and grab."

"Stoke, if ever I needed anybody like that, it's now. How in hell are we going to get Vicky out of there? Could the team you and Quick put together yesterday possibly—"

"No way. Not something like this. No way."

"So, who? Who in God's name can help us?"

"Well, bossman, that's a real good question. Real good. I ain't sayin' it can't be done, all I'm sayin' is—"

Stoke clasped his hands behind his head and lay back against his pillow, staring at the ceiling. Alex could almost hear the wheels spinning. A minute later, he sat bolt upright in bed, a big grin on his face.

"Thunder and Lightnin'!" he said.

"What's that?"

"The sons of beaches, that's who. Navy SEALs. They were my two Team Six platoon leaders, now semiretired," Stoke said. "Mr. Thunder and Mr. Lightning. That's what we called them two headbangers. Call one Thunder 'cause he good at blowing things up. Call the other Lightnin' because you dead and he's gone before you know what hit you. Man is one cold-blooded assassin. If anybody on this planet can get Vicky out of there alive, they the ones."

"Where are they?" Alex asked, leaning forward, hope showing in his eyes for the first time since he'd heard Vicky's voice on the tape.

"Martinique," Stoke said. "They run their operations out of a base camp on the cape by St. Marin. Where the St. Lucia Channel meets the Atlantic."

"Operations?" Hawke asked eagerly. "What kind of operations?"

"Well, secret shit, you know? Black ops. They all mercenaries now. Soldiers of fortune. Go anywhere in the world, blowin' shit up for people who don't want their name in the papers. Got their own patched-up old C-130. Flyin' in, snatchin' and grabbin', killing terrorists. All that good stuff."

"Hostage rescue?" Hawke asked.

"Best freelance hostage rescue team in the world. Bar none."

"How many of them?"

"Their team size varies all the time. That business, folks tend to come and go. Like a SEAL platoon, two squads, seven guys each. They got a platoon standing by, generally. Last time I talked to them, they had about fifteen or so commandos down there. Constant training."

"All ex-SEALs?"

"Nope. Got a couple of Viet Montagnards. Three or four frogs, ex–Foreign Legion desert warfare types, couple of real badass Gurkhas from Nepal, and the rest former SEALs, some seriously bad dudes, boss."

"Can you set something up, Stoke? Now?"

"Depends on if we catch 'em at home, boss. They on business trips mostly. Frequent fliers, frequent drinkers, frequent headbangers."

"Stoke, they're our only hope."

"Soon as that little Danish pastry doctor lets my ass out of this sickbay, I'll get on it."

"You're out and on it, Stoke," Hawke said. "Head up to the bridge and try to raise these guys on the sat phone. We can fly down there as soon as *Kittyhawke*'s been refueled."

"Thunder and Lightnin', boss, that's what I'm talkin' about!" Stoke said, throwing back the covers, and literally leaping out of bed. "Boom! Crash! Bang!"

Alex found Ambrose on deck just outside the man's personal cabin. He was standing at the portside rail, watching the gulls dive, and puffing thoughtfully on his pipe. He was wearing a monogrammed navy silk bathrobe with red piping and mismatched red and blue leather slippers.

His hair was standing straight up as if he'd just climbed out of bed, which in fact he had.

Hawke crept silently across the teak decks and joined his friend at the varnished mahogany rail.

He put his hand on the man's shoulder, which made him jump almost a foot in the air. "Hullo, old thing," Hawke said.

"Good Lord! Alex!" Ambrose exclaimed.

"Don't tell me you didn't hear me land a little while ago?"

"Well, I, er, just woke up and—" He pulled two wads of yellow beeswax from his ears. "I, er, use these at night. My own snoring, you see, is so dreadfully loud that it wakes me up."

"Aha," Alex said. "I just came from seeing Stoke down in sickbay. I can't tell you how I feel about what you and Stokely did. It's just too—"

"You're not upset?"

"Good God, no! Ambrose, listen to me. There are simply no words in my mind to describe what's in my heart. To say that I am deeply and profoundly grateful is so woefully inadequate, I can't even say it."

"Since we never discussed the matter, I mean, well, frankly I always felt a little guilty about—"

"There is no vocabulary, Ambrose, that can convey enough to thank you for what you've done."

"Don't be ridiculous. I'm a police officer, Alex. Just doing my duty. The truth is you solved the case yourself, whether you realize it or not."

"Don't be ridiculous! It was all your hard work that—"

"The photograph you spotted, Alex. The old Polaroid. It was the critical piece of inductive information that made all the other pieces of the puzzle fit."

"I couldn't see it. You did."

"You saw it, Alex. Your mind just wasn't ready for it yet."

"Yes. I've had some kind of a—breakthrough. I've never felt better. Hard to describe the feeling. Clarity, perhaps."

Alex put his hands on both of Ambrose's shoulders and squeezed. Congreve saw tears threatening, but Alex blinked them back and smiled.

"Ambrose, time is short and I've some incredible news to tell you. But first, how are you? Ross said you were hit?"

"Oh, good Lord, I'm fine. Just a wee bruise over my heart is all. Ouch, yes, right there. I'd be dead, certainly, had not Stokely made me wear his perfectly hideous vest. Most unattractive."

Hawke laughed, and said, "Ambrose, Vicky is alive."

"What!" Ambrose exploded. "You can't mean it! I mean to say, how on earth—"

"Don't ask me how, I don't know. Nor have I time to speculate. All I know is that she's alive and being held hostage by the Cubans. By General Manso de Herreras."

"The brother of Admiral Carlos de Herreras, the man I arrested."

"Exactly," Alex said. Taking his friend by the arm, Hawke said, "Come for a quick stroll around the decks, and I'll tell you my immediate plans. God willing, I'm off again within the hour."

Alex recounted the whole thing: his meeting aboard the *JFK*, his conversation with the secretary of state, Vicky's cassette, and his most recent chat with Stokely. They reached the stern, and both settled into the comfortable banquette.

"Thunder and Lightning?" Ambrose said, relighting his pipe. "I certainly like the sound of that."

"Let's hope they live up to their celestial billing, old boy."

"Yes," Ambrose said. "We should drink a toast." Picking up the nearest phone, he said, "Congreve here, sorry to trouble you. I'd like two very spicy Bloody Marys, please? Fine. That will be all, thank you."

"I'd love to join you," Alex said, "but Stokely and I are taking off for Martinique as soon as *Kittyhawke*'s tanks are topped off and we've loaded all of Stoke's SEAL equipment."

"I'm very glad for you, Alex," Ambrose said. "You've made a great leap forward, you know, coming to grips with the past. And, of course, it's splendid news about Vicky. If anyone can save her, you two can."

"We'll get her out," Hawke said, his jaw set. "I'm going to make a copy of the treasure map in case I need a bargaining chip for *Señor* de Herreras."

"I must say, Alex, I've never in my life seen you happier."

"I admit I've never felt quite this way before. I always imagined I was a fairly happy-go-lucky sort of fellow. But now—look, here comes Sniper!"

The steward had arrived with Ambrose's cocktail order, and the parrot was perched on the man's shoulder. Upon seeing Alex, the big bird immediately flew to its owner's outstretched forearm.

"Good fellow. Look at you, Sniper, you've grown fat. What have they been feeding you?"

"I saw him eat an entire tin of Beluga last evening," Ambrose said.

"Well, he deserves it. Don't you, Sniper? Speaking of which, I think you deserve something as well, Constable."

"What on earth are you talking about?"

"You've had enough excitement for one voyage. While Stokely and I are gone, I want you and Sutherland to go somewhere and relax. Perhaps play a little golf. I know how you love it and I feel guilty keeping you cooped up on the boat for so long."

"Don't be ridiculous, Alex," Ambrose said. "I've enjoyed every second of it! Bloody marvelous expedition. One of our best!"

"I insist, old thing. There must be someplace here in these islands with a golf course worthy of your mighty swing and delicate touch around the greens."

"Well, in that case, there is one course that Sutherland and I have been looking into. On the odd chance that we might have a little free time, of course."

"Well, there you have it. Pack up your bags and sticks and go enjoy yourselves. It will do you a world of good. Send me the bill."

"Very generous, Alex, I must say."

"Nonsense. What's the name of the course, by the way? The Lyford Cay Club in Nassau, I imagine."

"No, no. A lovely old course down in the Dominican Republic, actually. Blessed with a rather poetic name. It's called *Dientes de Perro.*"

"Translation?" Alex asked, getting up and stretching his legs.

"I'll send you a postcard."

"Well, keep your head down, old boy. Godspeed."

Ambrose watched his friend saunter away, the parrot bobbing on his shoulder. The tune Hawke was whistling floated back to Ambrose. It had to be thirty years old, but he recognized the lovely melody instantly.

It was the famous theme song from Lady Catherine Hawke's last film, *Southern Belle,* the marvelous story of Abigail Lee, a beautiful woman who is killed defending her Low Country South Carolina plantation against a marauding Union army. Coming back from the dead as a ghost, she bedevils and haunts the rapacious Union general who now occupies her beloved ancestral Barnwell Island home.

In a most surprising way, Ambrose thought, sipping his Bloody Mary, Alex Hawke seemed to be coming back from the dead, too. For the first time since he'd met the boy, long ago on Greybeard Island, he could actually say that Alexander Hawke was on the road to peace.

49

· · · — · ·

Alex banked hard left, and *Kittyhawke* slipped down through vast canyons of sunlit clouds.

"Is that it, Stoke?" he asked.

There was a narrow slash in the undulating green triple-canopy of trees below. A couple of hundred yards wide and about half a mile long, this gash in the jungle was definitely not on the chart of Martinique spread across Hawke's knees.

Stoke cocked his head toward the window and said, "That's it, all right, Bossman. Home of Thunder and Lightning itself. That hangar down there, covered with vines and shit, is where they keep the C-130. Big black mother."

Alex came around and lined up on the end of the jungle runway, lowered his flaps, and got his retractable wheels down. No tower, no air boss scrutinizing his approach and the runway wasn't even bobbing up and down. Easy peas, as they used to say during his Dartmouth days.

Only when a couple of Jeeps emerged from the trees and raced down the runway to an apron at the far end did he see any signs of life. Once there, both Jeeps turned so that they were facing the incoming airplane and turned their headlights on.

"Means it's okay to land," Alex heard Stoke say in his headphones, and he eased the little seaplane in over the treetops and dropped in for a three-point landing.

Ten minutes later, Alex and Stokely were in the back of one of the two Jeeps, bouncing along a dirt road that snaked upwards through the jungle. It was good Stoke had asked for two Jeeps. His SEAL toys filled up most of the second one.

"Wait till you see this joint," Stoke said. "It is something else."

Alex had been enjoying the riot of color everywhere he looked. It was like racing through a tunnel of botanical wizardry. Orchids, bougainvillea, and frangipani. Banyans and banana trees. Red, green, and yellow birds that darted and swooped overhead. Shafts of sunlight picked out waterfalls splashing into small pools and spilling across the road.

He was finding the humid heat of Martinique deliciously lush after the dry, sparse vegetation of the Exumas and Bahamas.

"It's an old fort," Stoke said. "Place was falling down years ago, when the boys first came down here and bought it. But the troops spent all their spare time fixing it up real good. Look up there, see it?"

The Jeep came over a rise, and Alex saw the small fortress sitting atop one of the many green hills that paraded down to the sea. It looked to be late seventeenth or early eighteenth century, most probably English, Hawke thought, judging by the design of the crenellated battlements and guard towers at the four corners.

Colonized by France in 1635, Martinique had remained a French possession, save three brief periods of foreign occupation by Britain. The old fort was incredibly sited and gleaming white in the morning sunlight. Stoke had not overstated the facts, Alex saw as they drew near, the fortress was indeed something else.

"See all them shiny cannons poking out all around the top?" Stoke asked.

"Yes," Hawke said. "Magnificent."

"Well, guess what," Stoke said. "They all work. Only fire 'em on special occasions, birthdays and Bastille Days and shit like that. But you should hear those mofos roar. Man, you talk about thunder and lightning!"

"What do they call the fort, Stoke?"

"Well, it had some fancy French name when they first bought it, but the boys renamed it. It's officially called Fort Whupass now."

Hawke laughed. "Fort Whupass," he said, loving the sound of it.

The fellow driving their Jeep, a Martiniquais, who had forearms like lodgepoles sticking out of his olive-green T-shirt, turned around and smiled at him. *"Oui, c'est ça!*

Bienvenue à Fort Whupass, *mes amis,"* he said in his Creole patois.

"*Merci bien,*" Hawke replied, looking up into the trees. "*Il fait tres beau ici."*

"*Oui, merveilleux.*"

"*Vous êtais ici, maintenant?"*

"*Non, pour la journée seulement.*"

"*Ah, oui, alors—*"

The Jeep finally emerged from the dense jungle, and Hawke could see the sandy road ahead, climbing up to the wall of the fortress. He was astounded to see a large rectangular platform being lowered as the Jeep drew near.

"A drawbridge?" Hawke asked, incredulous.

"Damn right, a drawbridge," Stoke said. "Ain't regulation without one. And a moat, too, full of big-ass alligators. You going to have a fort you got to do it right! Besides, these boys don't want nobody sneaking up on they ass."

"You're kidding, right?"

Stoke looked at him for a beat and then said, "Well, maybe about the alligators. There is a moat, though. Big-ass moat."

"A moat, Stoke? In Martinique?"

"Well, no, ain't really no moat either. But they always talkin' 'bout puttin' one in. Can't ever have enough security when every terrorist organization on earth hates your ass. Boys done moved three times in the last fifteen years."

They were just passing under a tree and Hawke glanced up to see a man in jungle camo perched on a high branch. He was cradling a high-powered rifle with a scope. The sniper saw Hawke staring and waved.

The two Jeeps barreled across the lowered platform,

which Hawke saw actually did cover a deep ravine, and screeched to a halt inside the open stone-paved court-yard. There was conspicuous lack of activity inside the fort, just a few dogs sleeping in the shade of a four-story structure of whitewashed stone.

The hot morning sun and the humidity were enough to make anyone, man or beast, seek shade.

"Where is everybody?" Hawke asked, surprised at the sense of total desolation that pervaded the old fort.

"Sleepin', most likely," Stoke said. "Catching Z's. Boys had a twenty-mile jungle run last night. They all sacked out in the barracks, which is the ground floor. Second floor is the armory. Third floor is communications and computers and shit. Top floor is where we'll find our guys waiting. They call it the poop deck."

"Stoke, you seem to know an awful lot about this place. Why's that?" Hawke asked, following his natural curiosity around the building to take a look.

"Well," Stoke said, right behind him and looking sheepish, "I did do a little freelance work down here from time to time. When I was NYPD, you know, I'd take all my vacation time in Martinique."

"That's how you'd spend your *vacation?*"

"Shit, boss, counterterrorism is the most fun you can have with your clothes on!"

"My God, what in the world is that?" Hawke said as they rounded the back of the white stone building.

There was an amazing structure just inside the wall at the rear of the courtyard. It looked like a giant cube of green glass, which is just what it was. Constructed of thick, clear green glass building blocks, dazzling in the morning sunlight, the building had to be thirty feet high

by thirty feet wide. A perfect square, no windows, no
door that Hawke could see.

"Somethin' else, ain't it, boss? I knew you'd get a kick
out of it!"

"What is it? Looks like an emerald as big as the Ritz."

"I call it the Emerald City. But it's really a museum."

"Museum?"

"The 'spoils of war' museum. Where they store all the
things they pick up around the world after the shooting
dies down. Whatever the enemy leaves on the ground.
You wouldn't believe what's inside that place."

"I'd certainly love to see it. How do you get inside?"

"Through a tunnel from the basement of the main
building. If there's time, they'd be happy to show you."

"Right, Stoke, let's get going."

They entered the main building and climbed a narrow
set of stone steps carved into the wall. Four flights up,
they arrived in a dark corridor that led to a vaulted chamber. Beside a massive wooden door, in a chair leaned back
against the wall, a man wearing a white kepi on his head
sat reading a book. The novel *Citadelle,* by Saint-Exupéry,
Alex noticed. Required reading for all Legionnaires.

But he was wearing an old navy and gold SEAL T-shirt
and khaki shorts, the traditional SEAL daytime uniform.
His head was shaved and he had a black beard that hadn't
been trimmed in years. He had a MAC 10 submachine
gun slung over the back of the chair and a burning
Gauloise hanging from the corner of his mouth. He
looked up, saw Stoke approaching, and a huge grin lit up
his deeply tanned face.

"*Zut alors! Skippair!*" the man exclaimed in a heavy
French accent. "*Incroyable!* I heard you were coming

down!" He rocked his chair forward and leaped up to embrace Stokely. They pounded each other's backs sufficiently hard to fracture a normal man's spine.

"Froggy! Yeah, the Frogman his own self! Shit! I've missed your sorry pencil-dick numbnuts ass," Stoke said, holding him by the shoulders and looking down at him. The man was barely five feet tall and almost that wide. "You still smoking them damn lung darts? What'd I tell you 'bout that?"

"I take it you two know each other," Hawke said, a little impatiently. The clock, after all, was ticking.

"Stokely Jones is ze meanest woman I ever served under, *monsieur,*" Froggy said, sticking out his hand to Hawke. "*Comment ça va, monsieur?* I am ze famous Froggy."

"Alex Hawke, Froggy," Hawke said, shaking his hand. "Pleasure."

"Frogman was in the C.R.A.P. division," Stoke said. "French Foreign Legion. One of the few French units to serve in the Gulf War."

"Crap?" Hawke asked, waiting impatiently for the joke.

"*Oui, monsieur! Commandos de Recherché et d'Action en Profondeur!* Ze best!" Froggy said, puffing out his chest and saluting.

"Splendid," Hawke said, looking at his watch. "I think we're expected."

"*Oui-oui, c'est vrai,*" Froggy said, opening the door. "It's true. Let me tell zem you are arrived." He stuck a silver bosun's whistle in his mouth and piped them aboard as they entered the room.

50

• • • — — • • •

Two men rose from a large wooden table where they'd been sitting. Sunlight streamed into the room through open windows on all sides. To the east, Alex could see the dark blue Atlantic rolling to the horizon. To the south and west, the pale blue of the Caribbean Sea. The room was devoid of furniture save the plain wooden rectangle of the table and twelve simple wooden chairs.

There was a sign on one wall, hand lettered in flowery calligraphy. It was the SEAL creed:

> *The More You Sweat In Training*
> *The Less You Bleed In Combat*

There were maps and navigational charts scattered everywhere. Hawke was gratified to see that it was a map of Cuba they'd been poring over. Clearly, they hadn't been wasting any time since Stoke's phone call little more than two hours earlier.

Stoke went to each man and embraced him in turn. There was little back-pounding now, just emotion. For a second, Hawke thought they were all going to get leaky on him.

"Boss, say hello to Thunder, this good-lookin' Injun on the left, and Lightnin', this ugly-ass Irishman on the right. Boys, give a big warm welcome to Alex Hawke, the guy I've told you so much about."

"Good morning," Hawke said, striding across the sun-lit room, smiling at both of them. "And thanks for agreeing to meet on such short notice. It's deeply appreciated. Flying down, I heard no end of lies about you two."

"Congenital liar, Stokely is," Lightning said, earning himself a look from Stoke. He was a big strapping Irish chap, ruddy-complexioned, and weather-burned, with short red-gold hair that also lightly covered his bulging forearms, and crinkling blue eyes. He had the stub of an unlit cigarette jammed in the left side of his mouth.

"You must be FitzHugh McCoy," Hawke said, giving the man a stiff salute. McCoy, Hawke knew, was a Medal of Honor winner. In the U.S. military, such a man is entitled to a salute from anyone of any rank.

"Welcome aboard, Commander Hawke," the man said in a thick Irish brogue, returning the salute. "FitzHugh McCoy is indeed the name, but call me Fitz. My accomplice here is Chief Charlie Rainwater. If he likes you, he'll let you call him Boomer."

"Pleasure," Hawke said to the copper-skinned man, offering his hand.

The keen-eyed fellow studied Hawke for some time, seeming to decide whether or not to shake his hand. He was tall and bristling with muscle, with blazing black eyes and a long narrow nose sharp as an arrow above somewhat cruel lips. His shoulder-length black hair fell about his shoulders and he was wearing buckskin trousers.

He was, Hawke had learned on the short flight down, a full-blooded Comanche Indian. A true plains warrior, he was also the best underwater demolition man in the long history of UDT and the SEALs.

He and Fitz had earned their reputations in the Mekong Delta of Vietnam as part of SEAL Team Two's riverine operations. They specialized in making life miserable for Mr. Charlie on a daily basis. Thunder, because he always scouted barefoot, saved countless lives in the jungle, finding tripwires no one else could see, hearing VC footsteps no one else could hear, smelling a VC ambush a mile away.

Boomer had earned three bronze stars in Vietnam, and one silver star. Fitz had had the Congressional Medal of Honor pinned on his chest in the White House Rose Garden by President Lyndon Baines Johnson himself.

Thunder finally extended his copper-skinned hand to Hawke.

"Boomer," he said.

"Hawke," Alex said, and shook his hand.

"Good name," Boomer said.

"I inherited it," Hawke said, smiling at the man.

"I hear you earned it, too," Boomer said, and settled back into his chair, putting his bare feet up on the table and crossing his arms across his broad chest.

"Skipper here tells me we have a critical time element," Fitz said, blowing a cloud of smoke into the air. "So maybe we should all get to be arsehole buddies later and get down to business right now."

"Brilliant," Hawke said, taking a chair at the table. "I think we just became asshole buddies, Fitz."

Stokely, pulling out a chair, burst out laughing.

"What's so funny, Skipper?" the lanky Irishman asked Stokely.

"First time in my entire life I have ever, I mean *ever*, heard Alex Hawke say the word *asshole*," Stoke said, still laughing.

"That's because I only call you one after you've left the

room," Alex said, to Stoke's evident chagrin and the obvious amusement of Fitz and Boomer.

"Commander Hawke," Fitz McCoy said, moving over to a large blowup of Cuba on the wall, "let's get started. All I know is based on a troubling conversation with Stokely this morning. Trust me, this outfit can do anything. But I didn't like one thing I heard."

"Fitz, I'll be honest," Alex said. "I wouldn't blame you in the slightest if you just said, 'No, thank you,' and sent us packing. Any sane man would. I mean it."

Stoke coughed into his fist, stifling a snort. Alex was unbelievable. Man just automatically knew exactly where people's buttons were located. Man had just located Fitz's number one button and mashed it hard.

Fitz stared at Alex for a long moment, and Alex saw him come to the decision.

"Okay, it's a hostage snatch," Fitz said, stubbing out his cigarette and jamming another one in his mouth. "How many are we pulling out?"

Hawke pulled an eight-by-ten photograph out of an envelope. "Our primary objective is this woman. An extremely close friend of mine. Her name is Victoria Sweet. This is a picture of her taken just last week. And this is a transcript of a cassette she recorded after her capture, clearly under duress. I have the cassette as well."

"Thanks, we'll listen to it. Meanwhile, how about a quick sitrep? Summarize the situation for us? We are aware, of course, that there's been a military coup d'état in Cuba."

"Cuba's new military regime wants two things. One. Immediate lifting of the U.S. embargo. Two. Immediate withdrawal of all personnel from Guantánamo NAS within eighteen hours and twenty-seven minutes from right now."

"These guys are in no position to make such ridiculous demands!" Fitz said. "What is this, the mouse that roared?"

"This mouse has two substantial assets," Hawke said. "A fully operational Soviet stealth submarine carrying forty warheads. And a biological or nuclear weapon hidden inside the Guantánamo naval base set to detonate at 0600 hours tomorrow."

"Holy shit," Fitz said. "These guys are crazy. After bin Laden, and all of Al Qaeda's and Saddam's subsequent bullshit, America's tolerance for this kind of crap is zero. These Cuban dipshit generals would obviously rather have a parking lot than a country. Where the hell is Castro when you need him?"

"Disappeared, Fitz," Hawke said. "He's either dead or a hostage they didn't get around to yet."

"I'd guess dead."

"Probably right," Hawke said. "At any rate, the Gitmo CO is preparing an order of evacuation. First step, get all the women and children safely aboard the *JFK* and other Navy vessels. Once they're steaming out of Gitmo harbor with half the Atlantic Fleet giving them cover, squadrons and cruise missiles from the Fleet are going to carpet-bomb the place."

"Including the hostage site, I assume," Fitz said.

"Yes. It's called *Telaraña*. The Spider's Web," Hawke said. "Just here, in Golfo de Guacanayabo, is a small island just off the coast of the town of Manzanillo. The military installation there is the Navy's number one target. That's where the rebel leaders are holding the hostages and that's where the Soviet sub is parked. And that's why we've got a time crunch."

"I have to be honest with you lads," Fitz said, looking from Stoke to Hawke. "This mission looks like a real goatfuck. One. Who knows when the Navy F-14s will show up? We'll be just as dead as the Cubanos."

"Good question," Hawke said. "I have no idea."

"Conch wouldn't tell you?" Stoke asked Hawke.

"I'd never put her in the position of having to say no, Stoke."

"Two. We've got an island with an area of at least three square miles, uncharted. With no SIGINT, no TECHINT, I'm not seeing a lot of ways to pull this off. And, there's not even bloody time for basic recon. How about HUMINT?"

"The CIA does have men on the ground, inside the target zone," Hawke said, pleased that Conch had just taught him the meaning of HUMINT. "They created a lot of the material I'm going to show you now. Plus a satellite and a dedicated bird in the air twenty-four hours a day. Predator."

He put a heavy leather satchel on the table and withdrew a thick black three-ring binder. A scarlet X on the cover identified it as top secret.

"Have a look," Hawke said.

Both men eagerly flipped through the pages, their excitement growing.

"Where the hell did this come from, Commander?"

"A U.S. Navy briefing I attended on the *JFK* this morning. I'm sure I'm breaking every rule in the book by showing it to you, but what the hell."

"Fitz," Boomer said, tabbing through the book. "Look. A whole section of thermals."

"You'll find a fairly complete set of construction and elevation plans for most of the buildings," Hawke added. "Courtesy of the CIA construction crew."

"Bloody good!" Fitz said. "And here are satellite photos of the whole installation, some taken as recently as yesterday. We can feed these into the ModelMaker downstairs and have a Styrofoam 3-D mock-up of the entire compound in half an hour."

The look of hope in the Irishman's eyes did not go unnoticed. "You're sounding somewhat encouraged, Mr. McCoy," Hawke said.

"Aye. We've moved beyond the hopeless stage, yes," Fitz said. "We still don't know where your hostage is. The way we operate, we clear the room. Four through the door, instantly separate the bad guys from the good guys and eliminate them. We can hardly go building to building, clearing rooms till we find the right one."

"One second," Boomer said. He'd been studying the thermals. Thermal imaging picked up any source of heat, men, or machinery, and turned it into recognizable shapes and forms.

"Okay," Boomer said. "Watch. We overlay these thermal transparencies on this series of sat photos. Now. See this large rectangular building? About two clicks from the sub pen? Watch this. Every twelve hours, a large vehicle, that's it right there, pulls up outside. Looks like maybe twenty guys climb out, enter the building, and then another twenty guys come outside and climb in the back."

"Looks like a guard change to me," Stoke said. "Where there's guards, there's hostages."

"Definite guard change," Fitz agreed. "Gotta be where the hostages are held."

"Okay. That's a start. Now, these are all barracks," Boomer said, pointing to neat rows of buildings in a compound about half a mile from the hostage site. "Soldiers there will definitely come running when they hear the fire and grenades as we enter the target building. We have a serious need for speed."

"Yeah," Stoke said. "Hop and Pop."

"Fitz's specialty," Boomer said. "Here's the primary radar dome, and look at all these cute little sammy and scud site missile launchers."

"The sub pen looks like it's still under construction," Fitz said. "See all the crap still on the ground? Bulldozers? Steel beams and rods. Tell me about the sub, Commander. Building looks big enough to accommodate three fooking subs."

Hawke did. When he described the Borzoi sub with its delta-wing design, retractable conning tower, and forty missile silos, both men's eyes widened with excitement. The idea that this might be more than just another hostage extraction clearly got their attention.

"Can we take out that sub?" Fitz asked.

"Well, it is destroying private property," Hawke said. "But then again, the world would be a hell of a lot safer place without it. And, since the Atlantic Fleet is at this very moment preparing to neutralize or destroy it, the Americans might just look the other way. Let's take it out."

"Good lad. We'll see what we can do. I'm wondering about this large structure here," Fitz said. "The one nearest the beach. It's clearly much older than anything else.

Looks like a small *finca* that's had a lot of wings added over the years."

"It belongs to General Manso de Herreras," Hawke said. "American intelligence has him as the guy who took Castro down. You can hear his voice on the tape. I've got video footage of him as well."

"How and why did he abduct the hostage?" Fitz asked, looking at the photo of Vicky.

"How, I don't know," Hawke replied. "Why is easy. An attempt to get me to use my influence in Washington. Affect U.S. policy toward his new government. Ridiculous, but true. I'm going to kill him, by the way. When I find him."

"Sorry?" Fitz said.

"Thirty years ago, Manso de Herreras and his two brothers murdered my parents. Stokely captured one of the brothers just yesterday and had the bastard arrested for murder. Head of the Cuban Navy, as it happens."

"That'll tend to piss the other two off," Fitz said.

"So," Boomer said, eyeing Hawke carefully. "It's not just a simple hostage snatch, is it?"

"No, it's not," Hawke said. "Somehow, I'm going to get inside this *finca* here and kill the two remaining brothers. That's my problem, not yours."

The Indian nodded his head. "I understand," he said.

"Which leaves me with one question," Fitz said. "Namely, how do we get two squads in and out of there? Look at this place! We got radar here and here, we got fooking SAM sites under every bush, we got two, maybe three fooking thousand troops in these barracks. I mean—"

"HAHO," Boomer said. "Night time."

"Yeah, just what I was thinkin', Boomer," Stokely said. "HAHO."

Seeing Hawke's puzzled expression, Fitz said, "A jump. High Altitude–High Opening. The plane is flying at thirty thousand feet, fifteen miles from the target. It's night. Nobody hears us, nobody sees us."

"We use flat chutes as parasails," Boomer said. "We use minibottles of oxygen to keep from blacking out. We've got lights on our helmets, compasses and altimeters on our wrists. We do a long, controlled glide into the LZ. Done much jumping, Commander?"

"The logic of jumping out of a perfectly good airplane has always escaped me," Hawke said. "But I did a tour with SBS. Jumping was a big part of our training."

Stoke looked at the two ex-SEALs, grinning. "What'd I tell y'all? Ain't nobody got bigger stones than my man Hawke here, huh? Balls to the wall!"

"SBS? No shit," Boomer said. "Tough outfit."

SBS was the British Special Boat Squadron, whose rigorous training was known throughout the special warfare world as even tougher than the SEALs'. In Boomer's eyes, Hawke had just become an official member of the brotherhood.

"Right, one more thing and then we're done talking," Fitz said. He got up and handed Hawke the transcript of Vicky's message. He'd used a red pencil to circle four words in the second paragraph.

Hawke stared at it, trying to make some sense of the thing.

"I've listened to countless hours of these kinds of tapes," Fitz said. "Depending on the hostage's state of mind, they tend to use words only a loved one would understand. Or send clues that would be helpful in a rescue situation."

"Yes?" Hawke said.

"I'm wondering," Fitz said, lighting another cigarette. "Would Vicky ever use a word like 'uppermost' or 'herein' in her general conversation?"

"Never," Hawke said, looking at the paper. "I think I see where you're going."

He studied the section in question, reading it aloud:

> "—so **herein** you'll find me, alive and well but **uppermost** in my mind is that in whatever time is so **far left** to me is getting my **backside** nestled next to yours again—"

"Herein, uppermost, backside," Hawke said. "She'd never talk like that. Rather cute, however, the backside reference."

"So 'herein' is her location," Fitz said, spreading out the plan of the hostage building they'd identified. " 'Uppermost' has got to be this top floor. Far left side of the building is here, obviously, and this is the very backside or rear of the structure."

He put his finger on the floor plan. "That's her room, gents, right there."

"We got it!" Stoke exclaimed. "Vicky, you something else, gal."

"Right, then," Fitz said. "Why don't you two guys go get some hot java or chow or take a walk? Visit the Fort Whupass Museum gift shop. Boomer and I have some serious bone-crunching brainstorming to do and no time to do it. Be back here in one hour. That suit you lads?"

Stoke could see Alex about to protest and said, "One hour." He pushed back his chair and stood up.

When they were outside the door he turned to Hawke and said, "Sorry, boss. I know you want to be in there. But this here one hour is why Thunder and Lightning get the big bucks. Trust me."

"I've got a good feeling about these guys, Stoke," Hawke said. "Thank you."

"Don't thank me yet, boss."

"Least I can do is buy you a little souvenir from the gift shop," Hawke said, disappearing down the stairway and into the tunnel leading to the Emerald City.

51
•••——••

Rita Gomez was sitting in her kitchen crying when the front door bell rang.

The small pewter urn containing her late husband was sitting on top of the refrigerator where the kids couldn't see it. Gomer's will had stated he wished to be cremated, and the CO's wife, Ginny, had made sure he got his wish. Twelve hours after his death in "No Man's Land."

When Rita had climbed up on the footstool to place it there, she'd seen about two years' worth of dust coating the fridge top. *Dust to dust.* That's what she thought, stepping down from the stool.

On the walk home from the small service at St. Mary's, Amber and Tiffany kept demanding to know what she was carrying. Except for her two noisy daughters, the whole neighborhood seemed eerily quiet.

"What's in there, Mommy, what's in there?" they said over and over, skipping along the sidewalk beside her.

She couldn't bring herself to say, "Daddy."

The service had been small but painfully long. A few members of Gomer's platoon sat in the first few pews just behind Rita and the two little girls. Angel, Rita's hairdresser and best friend, was there. There was an organist. Some desultory flowers on either side of the urn. A few sputtering candles that expired halfway through the service.

Gomer's best friend, Chief Petty Officer Sparky Rollins, made a brave attempt to eulogize Gomer, saying that he had been a man who had "died the way he lived, on the edge, living life to the fullest."

It was about as kind a description of her husband's death as anyone was going to come up with, Rita thought, shifting uncomfortably on the wooden seat. She was fanning herself with a church bulletin. Gomer would have leaned over and whispered that it was hot as Hades in here.

Father Menendez, who'd been counseling Gomer without any obvious success these last few months, gave a lengthy benediction and sermon, none of which Rita could remember. Something about a troubled soul now at peace. Not all warriors die a hero's death, he said, some are lost in a battle for the soul.

Anyway it was over, but somehow she couldn't stop crying. The handsome young sailor was gone. There'd been so much hope in her heart that rainy day inside the little chapel in Miami. He seemed like such a fine young man, standing so straight beside her in his brand-new uniform.

And then when they'd had their kids, she'd felt like all of her dreams were coming true. But something went wrong. It wasn't just the drinking, although that was certainly part of it. It started back when Gomer's mom first got sick in Havana. When he couldn't get any medicine for her, and heard her screams on the phone. Finally watching her die in such pain. That's when it started going seriously downhill. That's when he started to—the front doorbell rang again.

"Sorry," Rita called out, hurrying through the tiny living room. "I'm coming."

She wiped away her tears on her apron and pulled the door open.

It was the commanding officer's wife, Ginny Nettles, standing there with a big casserole dish in her hands.

"I'm so sorry about your husband, Rita," Ginny said. "It's just awful. May I come in?"

"Oh. Of course," Rita said, standing aside for her and then following her inside. She was slightly stunned at having the base commander's wife appear at her door. She had been to the Nettleses' house for a birthday party and to play bridge a few times, of course, and said hello to Ginny at the Exchange or the beauty parlor, but still.

"I made this for you last night," Ginny said, placing the casserole on the kitchen counter. "Shepherd's pie. Now, of course, it looks like you won't be needing it."

"What do you mean?" Rita said, thoroughly confused now.

"You mean you don't know?" Ginny said. "Oh—that's

right. You've been at St. Mary's all morning. Well, it's the most amazing thing. We're all being evacuated."

"What?" Rita said. "I don't understand. We're being—"

Ginny had walked into the living room and was bending over the TV, looking for a button. The kids had been watching *Josie and the Pussycats* before going out to play in the back. Josie was still on.

"Do you mind if I put on CNN?" Ginny asked. "I've been glued to it all morning. We're all over the news."

"No, of course not," Rita said, feeling completely disoriented. She dug the remote out from under a cushion and switched channels to CNN. There was that big blue banner running across the screen that said "Special Report." In Rita's experience that always meant "Especially Bad News." Both women sat down on the worn sofa and saw images of Guantánamo that seemed completely alien.

Men in bright yellow environmental suits were pouring from the rear of C-130s out at Leeward Point field. There were strange vehicles manned by similarly dressed men patrolling the streets, and bomb squad teams who looked like Martians. Somehow, life at Gitmo had turned upside down in the last two hours and Rita Gomez had missed the whole thing.

One of the famous old CNN guys from the Gulf War was standing under a palm tree outside the Gitmo HQ building with a microphone. Rita tried to concentrate on what he was saying, but she kept glancing over her shoulder at Gomer sitting up there on top of the fridge.

"In many cases," the reporter was saying, "bacon was frying on the stove and the Monday wash was on the line when the order came to evacuate dependent women and children. Already, security guards protect empty houses and patrol now-quiet neighborhoods only yesterday filled with children's noisy play."

"What is—what in the world is going on, Ginny?" Rita asked, feeling suddenly frightened.

"Shhh, just listen."

"The plans for the evacuation were announced and effected immediately. The base was divided into areas, and responsibility for notification and transportation to the awaiting ships and aircraft was given to the various commands."

"Why are they wearing those suits?" Rita asked, but Ginny ignored her, intent upon the broadcast.

"The Navy Exchange is still open," the CNN guy continued, "but it stands deserted. A battalion of Marines arrived during the early-morning hours, and their general attitude is one of calm watchfulness. Guantánamo is a changed place this morning. The base golf course is dotted with the temporary tents pitched by Marines who now bivouac on the fairways and greens."

"Oh, my God," Rita said.

"Along with the Marines, bomb squads, scientists, and doctors from the Centers for Disease Control in Atlanta, all in their protective clothing, find no relief from the hot Cuban sun. No one will officially confirm why they're here, but rumors are rampant."

Ginny hit the mute button and turned to Rita. "I shouldn't be telling you this, but you've always seemed one of the few base wives who were nice because of who I was, not because of who my husband was."

"Tell me, Ginny. The girls and I've been over at church

since seven. We've missed the whole thing. Why in the world are we being evacuated?"

"There's some kind of bomb hidden on the base. Joe says it's either a nuclear or a biological weapon. Some kind of new laboratory-created bacteria, they're guessing most likely. The 'poor man's atomic bomb,' he called it. They haven't been able to find it to defuse it or whatever they do. So, we're all clearing out. Women and children, I mean. And civil servants, of course."

"My God," Rita said. "Who would do such a thing?"

"The new Cuban government," Ginny said. "They're nuts, Joe says. Certifiable looney-toons. Listen, I've got to run. We've only got a couple of hours before we have to be at the boarding stations. You're only allowed to pack one suitcase for each family member."

"Okay," Rita said, her mind racing. She glanced back at the top of the fridge. There was a family member up there. Did Gomer still count for a suitcase?

"If you've got a dog, you're supposed to tie him up in the backyard. And leave the keys to the house on the dining table."

"We don't have a dog."

"Right. I'm sorry. This is a terrible time for you," Ginny said. "Listen, you get the kids packed and ready to go. Then drive over to my house and we'll go—"

"We don't have a car. The MPs have it impounded."

"Oh. Yes, that's right. I forgot. Well, listen, Rita, I'll pick you and the girls up here then. If you could be out front with your luggage?"

"Okay," Rita said, looking around at the bravely decorated little rooms she and Gomer and the girls had called home for so long. She couldn't stop herself from noticing just how dry the dried flowers looked. God, how she'd tried to make this house a home.

"Can you be ready in an hour? The streets are a mess. Packed all the way to Wharf Bravo. That's where the *JFK* is berthed."

"Sure. We, uh—whatever you say. I would think your husband would, you know, fly you and Cindy out? Something?"

"That's what he wanted us to do. I said no way. I think the commanding officer's wife's place is shoulder to shoulder with the sailors' families aboard the *Kennedy*."

"We'll be ready, Ginny. Right out front on the sidewalk."

Rita followed Ginny out to her car. The sun was broiling now and she shielded her eyes, waving good-bye as Ginny pulled away from the curb. Just as she was about to turn and go back inside, another car pulled up by the mailbox. One of those gray Navy cars.

Two men, one in civilian clothes and the other in Army fatigues, climbed out of the front, then the back door swung open and one of the yellow-suit guys climbed out.

"Are you Mrs. Gomez?" one of the civilian guys asked.

"Yes, I am."

"We'd like to talk to you for a minute. Is it possible to step inside out of the sun?"

"Of course," Rita said. "Please follow me."

Rita showed them into the living room. The two coat-and-tie guys sat down. One had a large briefcase. The man from Mars guy stayed in the kitchen. Rita saw him reach up to the top of the fridge for Gomer's urn.

"What is he doing?" she said. "That's my husband!"

"I'm very sorry, ma'am," the guy on the couch said. "We're doing a house-to-house search. It's his job. Do you mind if we ask you a few questions?"

"Who are you?" Rita said, remaining on her feet, twisting the folds of her navy blue skirt in her hands.

"I'm Brigadier General Darryl Elliot, and this is Mr. Chynsky," Elliot said. "I'm from JSOC, the Joint Special Operations Command at Fort Bragg. Mr. Chynsky is counterterrorist director for the NSA. That gentleman in the kitchen is Dr. Ken Beer, a chief investigator from the Center for Disease Control and Prevention. He has presidential authority to search your house, ma'am."

"Fine," Rita said. "Let him."

"Dr. Beer, I'd start upstairs and work down," the one named Chynsky said. The guy in the spacesuit nodded at him and headed up the stairway.

"Mrs. Gomez," General Elliot said, "I know this is a tough time for you. I'm sorry. But I have to talk to you regarding some things our investigators have turned up since your late husband's death and cremation. We don't have a lot of time here."

"Whatever I can do to help."

"Thank you. Did your husband exhibit any unusual behavior in the weeks leading up to his death?"

"He was drunk a lot. Nothing unusual about that."

"Any strange new habits? Disappearances?"

"If he wasn't sleeping he was over at the bar at the X pounding Budweisers."

"Any new friends or associates recently?"

"He only had one friend. He wouldn't know what an associate was."

"Friend's name?"

"Sparky. Sparky Rollins."

"Yes. The guard posted on what used to be Tower 22."

"That's him."

"Did you ever overhear any unusual conversations between the two of them?"

"Sparky never came here. Gomer always went over to Sparky's apartment at the BOQ. So they could watch the Playboy Channel, I guess. He slept over there a lot, too."

"Please try to think, Mrs. Gomez. Was there anything, anything at all, that struck you as different or unusual about your husband in the last month or so?"

"Well, Julio Iglesias did start calling here about a month ago. That was fairly unusual."

"I beg your pardon? Julio Iglesias? You mean the singer?"

"Well, he called himself that. But he sure didn't sound like any Julio Iglesias I've seen on TV, believe me."

"What, exactly, did he sound like, Mrs. Gomez?"

"Cuban. Very strong Cuban accent. Tough guy."

"How often would he call?"

"Every now and then. He'd call at all hours. I think there were two of them."

"Two?"

"Two guys both pretending to be that singer. Their voices were different, you know?"

"Mrs. Gomez, this could be very important. Did you ever accidentally overhear or eavesdrop on any of those conversations?"

"No. I wouldn't do that. Besides, he always took the calls in another room."

"Ira," Elliot said to Chynsky, "we need the log on all

incoming and outgoing calls from this number in the last two weeks. Thanks."

Ira got up, went into the kitchen, and got on the phone. Elliot opened his leather bag and pulled out an object in some kind of freezer bag.

"Have you ever seen this object before, Mrs. Gomez?"

It was a metal box, about the size of a brick. Little buttons on it. Banged up. It looked like it had been dropped from a ten-story building.

"Mrs. Gomez?"

"No. I've never seen it before. What is it?"

"Did your husband have any hobbies? Like model airplanes or model boats?"

"I already told you. His hobbies were beer and the Playboy Channel."

"This is a radio control device, Mrs. Gomez. You could use it to fly a remote control airplane. Or you could use it to, say, program a bomb."

"Why are you showing it to me?"

"It was found in the mud, a hundred yards from your husband's body."

An hour later, Rita and her two daughters were standing on the sidewalk, waiting for Mrs. Nettles to pick them up. The girls had on their best dresses. They had four pieces of luggage. Three suitcases plus an old bowling ball bag for Gomer.

The two suits from Washington and the CDC investigator had finally left, but not before the spaceman scared the kids half to death when he went out to the garage. They'd come running into the kitchen screaming their heads off. The yellow suit was right behind them, holding some old newspapers. Cuban newspapers, he said. And some moldy twine.

"*Granma,*" he said. "The Cuban daily, Havana edition. Dated five weeks ago. Heavily folded and imprinted. Looks like something cylindrical was wrapped in it."

"Bag it," Elliot said.

When Elliot started asking her questions about a bunch of old newspapers, that's when she'd told them, hey, old newspapers, big effing deal, pal. B.F.D. She'd had enough. She'd spent all morning at her husband's funeral. Now she only had half an hour to pack up all her family's stuff and head to the *Kennedy*. Enough.

He thanked her for her time and tried to be nice. She guessed he was only doing his job. But if he thought Gomer had anything to do with anything at all that was a Special Report on CNN, he was flat crazy. Gomer wasn't smart enough and certainly not sober enough to pull off anything as big as this big magilla thing seemed to be.

Lost in a jumble of thoughts, she was startled by the sound of a car horn. A big white Chevy Suburban cruised right up to the curb, flags flying from all four windows. The passenger side window slid down, and Cindy Nettles stuck her head right out. She had her blond hair in pigtails, with big red, white, and blue ribbons.

"Hop in, guys! C'mon! Mom says we're gonna be late!" Cindy said.

Ginny Nettles was nice enough to climb out and help her stow their luggage in the back with all the rest. Then Rita and the kids climbed into the backseat, one on either side of her. Ginny got back behind the wheel, and they were off.

The traffic, once they got going, was a nightmare.

MPs and marines wearing gas masks were at every intersection trying to keep the endless converging lines of private vehicles and buses full of evacuees moving. Rita was
grateful that no one was honking or yelling, no one was
trying to cut in front of them. If she had expected panic,
she saw none. These were military families, Navy families, and they acted like it.

There was confusion at various checkpoints over who
was going where. Ginny and Rita were headed for the
Kennedy, berthed at Wharf Bravo, and Ginny knew how
to get there. But there were also evacuation vessels at
Northwest Pier Lima, Northwest Pier Victor, and
Southwest Pier Lima. There were no directional signs,
adding to the disorder and confusion.

At Wharf Bravo, there was a sense of barely controlled chaos on the pier. In the massive shadow of the
famous warship, endless rivers of women, children, and
the elderly were streaming up various gangplanks. Rita
watched them disappearing with agonizing slowness into
the many cavernous mouths in the *Kennedy*'s hull. Twice,
various officers recognized the CO's wife and tried to
move them up in the line. Ginny refused both times, and
it took another hour before they were out of the broiling
sun and inside the *Kennedy*.

Seated behind a long table were six officers checking
the evacuees' identification before admitting them aboard.
At either end of the table were Marines armed with
machine guns. The six officers checked every piece of
identification carefully, Rita noticed, even Ginny Nettles's.

Little Cindy presented herself alongside her mother
and handed the officer a pink plastic wallet. It matched the
pink plastic suitcase she was carrying.

"Okay," the officer said, opening the wallet. "Let's see who you are, young lady."

"Lucinda Nettles," Cindy said. "My daddy is Admiral Nettles. Do you know him?"

"I certainly do," the officer said, smiling. "Thank you, Lucinda. Next in line?"

"I hope it's all right if I brought an extra suitcase," Cindy said. "I had to because of my best friend."

"Sweetheart," Ginny said, bending down. "This nice officer is in a hurry. There are lots of people behind us. Let's move along, darling."

"Want to see him?" Cindy asked the officer, putting her suitcase on the table.

"Maybe later," the officer said. "After we've—"

But Cindy had already popped the latches of her bright pink suitcase. A large white bear that had been crammed inside her extra bag exploded out onto the table.

"What's his name?" the officer asked, with a smile of forced amusement.

"Mr. Teddy," she said, hugging him tightly. "He's my very best friend in the whole wide world!"

"Welcome to the *Kennedy*, Teddy," the officer said with a smile.

Everyone got a big chuckle over that one.

52

All was still inside *Archangel,* the C-130 Hercules turbo-prop transport plane owned and operated by the elite counterterrorist group known in international special warfare circles as Thunder and Lightning.

Archangel had been built by Lockheed in the early fifties and was one of many C-130s still flying in every part of the world.

It was a black, moonless night, and as the big plane lumbered along at thirty thousand feet, she was nearly invisible.

The airplane's entire fuselage and wings were painted matte black. There were no lights winking on her wingtips, none showing at her tail or nose. Even the lights in the cockpit were a muted shade of red, barely visible from the outside.

The route of flight had taken them north out over the islands of Trinidad and Tobago, then *Archangel* veered northwest out over the Caribbean Sea. She'd skirt the southern coasts of the Dominican Republic and Jamaica, then vector due north toward the southwest coast of Cuba.

Most of the guys were sitting along rows of canvas sling chairs that lined the fuselage interior or resting atop greasy pallets on the floor. Everyone was dressed in dark camouflage tigerstripes, wearing nothing reflective, faces blacked out with camo warpaint. Thunder and Lightning would be invisible when they floated down from the heavens toward their objective.

In addition to the two C-130 pilots up front and the jumpmaster, there was a platoon of commandos aboard. The platoon consisted of two seven-man squads. Fitz McCoy would lead Alpha squad. Bravo was under the command of Charlie Rainwater, known to his men as Boomer.

They'd been airborne for over an hour. Hawke was checking and rechecking his weapons and ammo. In a coin toss on the runway, he had been assigned to McCoy's squad, while Stoke would tag along with his old XO, Boomer. Since Hawke was easily the least experienced member of the counterterrorist team, he'd promised Fitz he'd stay right by his side.

In what seemed like no time at all, the green light came on, and the jumpmaster was pointing at Fitz's squad.

Fitz, sitting next to Hawke, took a long drag on his cigarette and said, "Saddle up, Commander. We'll dip on down to twenty thousand feet now, reduce our airspeed, and then we go."

"Five minutes!" the captain said over the intercom.

Hawke nodded. He was thinking about his last jump. He didn't particularly want to think about it, but it kept popping up. He felt the plane dropping and cinched up the straps crossing his chest. In addition to his chute, he was carrying a lot of gear. Still, he was probably the lightest man going out.

He had an MP5, the HK 9mm submachine gun favored by SEALs, and a Sig Sauer 9mm pistol, both fitted with what the Yanks called hush puppies or silencers. He also had stun grenades and Willy-Peters hanging like grape clusters from his web belt. Willy-Peters were white phosphorus grenades, lethal and terrifying to an enemy when used.

"Two minutes!" The huge ramp began to lower and the cavernous interior was suddenly filled with a roaring wind. "Ramp open and locked," the jumpmaster said.

Hawke eyed the jump/caution light. It was glowing crimson. He rechecked his Draeger for the third time. Since they'd be jumping into the sea and swimming ashore, all the men were equipped with Draegers. These German-made oxygen-rebreathing units produced no bubbles and made no sound. That made them ideal for secret insertions like this one. Hawke was feeling especially grateful for his tour with the SBS unit of the Royal Marines. He'd trained with all of this gear before.

Most of it, anyway.

Weight was a big problem in the thin air of high-altitude jumps. Many of these men would be going out the door with a hundred pounds or more strapped to their bodies. Two men were going out, carrying two IBS boats complete with motors. In SEAL lingo, IBS stood for Inflatable Boat, Small. Once they'd exfiltrated, each one was capable of carrying a seven-man squad, plus, in an extraction, a few hostages.

The jump alarm bell signaled one minute to drop.

Hawke used that minute to turn everything over in his mind once more. In the plan, worked out over the course of the afternoon, the two IBS boats would rendezvous with *Nighthawke,* the seventy-foot-long offshore power-boat carried aboard *Blackhawke.* The jet black oceangoing speedboat, two-time winner of the Miami–Nassau race, was capable of speeds in excess of one hundred knots per hour.

Nighthawke's huge cockpit and hold below could easily accommodate twenty people. In the likely event of trouble, Hawke had instructed Tom Quick to mount a fifty-caliber machine gun on the stern deck.

If the IBS boats could make it safely to the designated rendezvous, *Nighthawke* could easily outrun the fastest Cuban pursuit craft. And deliver the two teams safely to the mother ship, *Blackhawke,* which would be cruising innocently twenty miles offshore. That was the plan anyway and—Hawke's musings were interrupted—the jump light! It flashed from crimson to green.

The jumpmaster pointed at Fitz and said, "Good hunting, Fitz. Go!"

Hawke stood and followed his squad to the rear. One by one the five men in front of him strolled down the oily ramp of the C-130 and dove off into the blackness of the nighttime sky. It was Hawke's turn. He hesitated a second and instantly felt Fitz's hand on his shoulder.

"You okay, Commander?" Fitz shouted over the roaring wind.

By way of answering, Hawke stepped off the ramp.

His first sensation was that of the freezing slipstream hitting him like a wall of ice. Then the huge black airplane overhead was gone and he looked down. Nothing below but pitch black nothing. He checked the altimeter on his wrist. Four miles up. He pulled his ripcord.

He felt the chute slide out of his backpack and separate.

Instantly, he was yanked violently upwards in his harness. Then, just as he prepared to settle in and enjoy the ride, he veered sharply left and began to descend in a ferocious, out-of-control spiral. Looking skyward, he saw that one of the cells in his canopy had collapsed.

"Bloody hell!" he shouted in the darkness. This was not a good start. He yanked on the guidelines, desperately trying to fill the canopy with air. It didn't happen. What happened is that the crazy corkscrewing continued. Then two more cells collapsed and the chute fluttering above him folded neatly in half. He was at nineteen thousand feet and plummeting in free-fall. His body felt suddenly very cold, and he realized he'd broken into a sweat.

All right, Hawke thought, he'd practiced this before. This was, in SBS parlance stolen from the SEALs, SNAFU. Situation Normal All Fucked Up. But it was not yet FUBAR, which translated to Fucked Up Beyond All Repair. He had a backup.

Hawke did a cutaway, jettisoned the useless chute, and let himself relax into free-fall again. He was now just under fifteen thousand feet, flying on cruise control. He spent the next ten seconds that way, then he yanked the ripcord on his second chute.

The flat chute opened beautifully.

He began a controlled descent of lazy spirals in the blackness. It reminded him of why he'd enjoyed some of his jump training at SBS. Checking his compass and altimeter, he determined that he was descending through ten thousand feet, about five miles from splashdown in the two-hundred-square-yard patch of ocean designated LZ Liberty. Boomer's Bravo squad was going into LZ Nautilus a quarter of a mile away.

Alpha squad's primary mission was to locate the hostage. Bravo was going to create an explosive "diversion" of sorts when the time came for both squads to link up and go in for the snatch and grab.

Five minutes later, Alex could make out the black humped outline of the island called *Telaraña* and the southwest coast of Cuba beyond it. He saw phosphorescent white rollers gently breaking along the island's beaches. He estimated he had about a fifteen-minute glide remaining, so he just hung in his harness and enjoyed the view.

He was so relaxed he was startled to hear canopies fluttering all around him and the sound of men splashing down just under him. He pulled the cord that inflated his BCD vest, a buoyancy compensator device, then initiated a series of S turns to eat up speed and waited for his boots to get wet. Five seconds later, he flared up and hit the water.

He saw black faces bobbing all around him, white teeth smiling at him. He heard a *whoosh* as the IBS partially inflated. One man would stay offshore with the rubberized inflatable. His main problem would be staying out of the path of the Cuban patrol boat.

"You're a bit late," one of the faces said.

"Sorry, Fitz," Alex said. "Minor equipment problem."

"I noticed. Good recovery," Fitz said. "We got lucky. We just missed landing on the fooking roof of a Cuban patrol boat. He's gone round that point now, but he'll be back."

Fitz did a quick head count. Every man in Alpha had made it to the LZ. It was time to don the Draeger oxygen rebreathers and start swimming. They were a half mile from shore. Hawke could see breakers on the white sand and a dark stand of palm trees Fitz had designated as their next rendezvous point.

Before he pulled the swim mask down over his face he did a full 360.

Finca Telaraña, General Manso de Herreras's massive,

grandiose home, sat on a spit of land jutting into the sea. It was a dark, hulking structure, bathed in the pale blue light of a scattering of stars. Hawke said a silent prayer that two men from his distant past were sleeping somewhere inside. But the *finca* was not their first objective. First they would launch a surprise raid on the building where Vicky was being held.

"Go," Fitz said simply, and all eight men dove under the surface and started kicking for shore.

Little more than half a mile to the west, Boomer and his Bravo team were just entering the narrow shoals of the La Costa river. The flashing red and green navigational lights at either end of the jetties were unseen by the squad, which was swimming at a depth of twelve feet.

This is where the Draeger rebreathers were critical. Not a single bubble revealed the presence of seven powerful swimmers moving up the black channel. There were sure to be a lot more guards where Bravo was going than the empty stretch of beach Alpha was headed for.

Hawke emerged from the surf and saw two of his men sprinting for cover into the stand of palms. There was still no moon, but the ambient light of stars and white sand made him feel all too vulnerable. He flicked his HK to full fire and headed for the trees, knees pumping.

He found Fitz and the team already gathered and sorting out their weapons and gear. Each man was being given a Motorola headset and lip mike. There would be instant and silent communication among all the men in Alpha. Fitz's squad would also monitor Boomer's transmissions and vice versa. That way, the two teams would know each other's every move.

Hawke noticed Fitz was wearing a big smile. He had a cigarette hanging from the left side of his mouth, unlit.

"What is it, Fitz?" he whispered. "You seem altogether too jolly."

"I just had a happy thought on the swim in," Fitz said. "Does anyone know today's date?"

"May first!" one of the squad members said. It sounded like Froggy.

"May Day in Commieland!" another commando said.

"Fooking right it is." Fitz beamed. "Which means our little buddies have been partying all day and all night. It's 0230 hours. I should think most of them would be snug in their little beds by now."

"With all ze Stoli and rich Cubano cigars," Froggy said, "zey might be a little sluggish waking up, *mais non?*"

"A bit like Washington crossing the Delaware on Christmas Eve, surprising the British at Trenton," Hawke said, smiling. "Bloody bastard."

"May Day," Fitz said with a grin. "Christmastime for Commies."

"Bravo, you copy?" Fitz said into his mike.

"Copy," Boomer said.

"Anything?"

"Just came up to take a look. Halfway up the river."

"Tangos?"

"Six or seven, guarding the entrance, don't look like they're expecting company. No problem."

"Twenty minutes to hostage site rendezvous, Boomer. Go."

Tangos, or T's, Hawke knew, was SEAL-speak for terrorists. It's what they labeled all bad guys around the world. He felt his adrenaline surge. It had been a while since he'd found himself in a foreign locale, surrounded by so many men who would like to do him serious harm.

"Froggy," Fitz said, "get your NV gear on and see if they've got pickets out here."

"Aye, aye," Froggy said. Hawke watched the wide little Frenchman strap the night-vision equipment on his head and then slip out of the stand of trees. He darted across the beach, staying low, for about two hundred yards. Then he checked up and ducked behind some large scrub palms and bushes.

"Two tangos in a parked ATV," Froggy said. "Shucking and jiving, *mon ami*."

"Have you got a head shot? A clear plink?"

"Aye on both."

"Make that hush puppy bark softly and grease 'em, Froggy," Fitz said. "We're moving up right behind you."

Hawke barely heard the whump of the two deadly 9mm whispers in the dark.

"Two deceased tangos," he heard Froggy say in his headset.

Then Fitz turned to Hawke. "The Frogman is our medic," he said, "on the off chance anybody gets hurt. He's also the platoon's best shooter, which is saying something, believe me."

Fitz then held up his hand and motioned the squad forward. The *Finca Telaraña* lay ahead, sleeping in the darkness. They would leave it in peace for a while. Alpha's first stop would be the large building at the rear of the compound where Hawke believed they'd find Vicky.

If she was still alive.

53

Hawke was breathing hard.

They'd covered the last thousand yards of thick jungle at a dead run. With all his gear, cradling the HK MP5 submachine gun, it had been an effort. It wasn't that he didn't keep himself in very good shape. The fact was, of the whole team, he alone was unaccustomed to twenty-mile jungle runs every other day.

Alpha squad had encountered a total of six sentries. All six had been dispatched quietly and efficiently. Four by squeezed-off head shots they never saw coming. Two had their throats slit from behind before they could sound a warning. So far, there was no sign of alarm anywhere within the compound.

So far, in other words, so good. Everything was proceeding according to plan. An entirely dangerous state of affairs, as Hawke knew from long experience.

They were all crouched at the base of a towering banyan tree when he pulled up, wheezing a bit. Fitz was studying a crayon drawing he'd made of the compound. A tiny red penlight moved over the surface of the map he'd created based on the sat photo analysis. The men huddled close around him, peering at the drawing.

"We're here," he said. "Fifty feet from the sand road. The target building stands there, in a large clearing five hundred yards in that direction. It appears to be surrounded by an eight-foot chain-link fence topped with concertina wire. The last two days of thermals indicate a pair of perimeter guards walking the fenceline. Cosmo, got your clippers?"

"Aye, sir," said one of the Gurkhas. Perhaps one of the smallest, and easily the toughest, men on the squad.

"Go make us a nice large hole, lad," Fitz said, pointing the penlight at an X marked on the map. "Right, I believe, there." He spit one dead cigarette out of his mouth and stuck another one in the corner of his mouth. He didn't light it.

"Don't smoke 'em if you got 'em," Fitz whispered. "These woods could be crawling with tangos."

The little commando instantly slithered into the underbrush and was gone. Fitz looked at his men. "It should come as no surprise that the fence may have electronic sensors. If it does, we'll all know soon enough. Get ready to blow through the hole if all the fooking bells and whistles go off."

Hawke saw all the men flick their HK MP5 machine guns to full fire.

"Bravo?" Fitz said into his mike.

"Set," Hawke heard Boomer say.

"We're cutting wire. Give us two minutes."

"I've got Cosmo in my NV," Boomer said. "We just waxed two guards and are moving along the fenceline toward him now."

The two squads would rejoin at the predesignated fence opening. Once through, Alpha would go left to the western side of the building, Bravo would go right to the eastern entrance. This would be the hard part, the hundred yards of open ground they'd have to cover once inside the fence.

"You see any other tangos outside or inside the building, Boom?"

"Negative. Building is dark."

"Could be a trap."

"I don't smell one, Fitz."

"Good enough for me," Fitz said quietly. In the Mekong, Boomer could smell VC and NVA traps literally a couple of klicks away.

The men waited in tense silence for the sound of alarms and the harsh glare of floodlights. For Hawke, it was the most agonizing minute of the mission. If they were detected early, the guards would surely kill Vicky before he had any chance of reaching her.

"Okay, we got us a hole here you could drive a half-tonner through, Chief," they all heard Cosmo say in their phones.

"Bravo, go," Fitz said, at the same time raising his hand and motioning Alpha squad forward.

Three minutes later, Hawke and the rest of Alpha emerged from the jungle at the fenceline. He saw Cosmo, Boomer, and his men already there. Boomer smiled at him.

"Fun and games, sir?" Boomer whispered.

"Just like the good old days," Hawke replied.

The three-story rectangular building was dark, just like Boomer had said. There was a dirt road leading around to the rear. Three or four vehicles were parked in the front, two half-ton trucks and a couple of WWII vintage Jeeps.

"Somebody check those vehicles for keys on the way in," Fitz said. "We may just need them. No keys, be ready to hot-wire. Alex?"

"Right here," Hawke said, sliding forward to crouch next to Fitz. Fitz pulled out his drawing of the building.

"If we got her code correctly, top floor, backside left, Vicky's room should be right here. Last door on the right at the top of the stairs. We go four-through-the-door and clear the room. You, Froggy, and Cosmo come in on our heels. Clear?"

"Damn it, Fitz, I'm the only one who knows her on sight. I told you before, I should be in the front four."

Fitz regarded him for a hard second. He saw he was unlikely to change Hawke's mind.

"Christ," he said. "All right, it's your ass. We go in low. Acquire and shoot. No fancy head shots. We're firing heavy loads. A hit anywhere will take the tango down."

"Aye," Hawke said, a grin spreading across his face. He'd known he'd get his way.

Fitz looked at his digital watch. "Twenty seconds," he said. The men all pulled their black balaclava hoods down over their faces.

"We blow the east and west doors simultaneously. Clear the stairways and get to the top floor fast. Smoke grenades, stun grenades, and frags. Good hunting, lads. Let's go hop and pop!"

Fourteen men snaked single file through Cosmo's tear in the fence. A hundred yards to go and the large building was still dark, save a yellow light burning over each entrance. Alpha went left; Bravo went right. Anybody looking out a window would spot them immediately. Alex was in a low sprint right behind Fitz. He was expecting the sound of automatic weapons fire at any second.

It didn't happen.

When they reached the entrance, every man stood

aside as Cosmo placed a small explosive-packed battering ram against the heavy wooden door. No door could withstand its impact.

At the opposite end of the building, Bravo squad was preparing the same dramatic entrance. Everybody strapped his night-vision gear on. It would give them a huge advantage over the tangos inside.

"Blow their goddamn doors off!" Fitz said into his lip mike, and, with a loud bang, the two wooden doors at each end of the building breached inward.

Alpha squad was inside the building instantly, hurling flash-bang and smoke grenades into the dimly lit interior. The distinctive sound of AK-47s, the tangos' automatic weapons, erupted as the opaque white fog of the smoke grenades began filling the room. Stun grenades were popping at the rear of the room. The white fog was rolling his way, but Alex saw a set of stone steps leading up just in time.

"Fitz!" Hawke cried, spraying his HK at four figures advancing toward him. "Stairs on the right! I'm going up." The four tangos who'd been there a second ago had crumpled to the floor under the withering fire of Hawke's 9mm submachine gun.

The firefight was intense now. Hawke knew the hostage guards on the top floor would be dazed but already awake. He took the steps three at a time.

"Top of the stairs, Hawke," he heard Fitz say, and then the muffled *brrrrp* of Fitz's HK submachine gun was exploding inches from his right ear. Lead from the tangos above was whistling by his head.

"Down!" Fitz shouted, and Hawke went prone on the steps, putting the sights of his own HK on a mass of figures at the top of the steps. Fitz propped his gun on Hawke's shoulder and emptied a whole mag, obliterating the rush of tangos down the stairs.

"Behind us!" Fitz shouted as he reloaded. "Coming up the steps!" Concrete and other debris was raining down on them as rounds tore up the wall and the stairs above them.

Hawke's submachine gun had gotten trapped under his body. He reached behind him and grabbed a frag grenade off his web belt, pulled the pin, and let it bounce down the stone steps.

"*Adios, muchachos!*" he shouted. The tangos saw the grenade coming and started to retreat in a jumble back down the steps. By then Hawke had his Sig Sauer 9mm pistol on them and was firing into them. The heavy loads were incredibly effective. Men just crumpled at the bottom of the steps. Then the frag exploded and nobody was moving.

"Let's move!" Fitz said, and he and Hawke scrambled up two more flights of stairs to the top floor, firing heavily at anything that moved. The heavy fire was returned, and huge chunks of concrete and tile exploded from the walls just above Hawke's head. He saw two twinkling yellow muzzle flames in the smoke and emptied his mag in that direction. The firing stopped.

There was smoke up here, too, which was good. It meant Froggy or Cosmo had already made it this far and detonated smoke grenades. At the other end of the hallway, he saw shadowy figures. The loud exchange of automatic weapons fire meant Bravo squad was hard at work. As long as Vicky was alive, he didn't care who found her. He saw Fitz in the haze, motioning him forward.

Mounting the final step, he saw that Fitz was standing in front of a plain door and that Froggy and Cosmo were there, too, crouched on one knee.

There was shouting coming from behind the door. He heard Vicky cry out. He didn't wait for Fitz's command, he just lashed out at the door with all the strength he had in his right leg. The door splintered inward.

Hawke, Fitz, Cosmo, and Froggy were through the door low, firing even as they rolled across the floor to either side of the door. Three men, one woman, Hawke made out, as he dove for the floor.

"It's her!" Hawke yelled, "She's on the bed! Vicky, don't move!"

A gaunt, hollow-eyed man with long greasy hair bent over the bed holding Vicky by the throat with one hand, a gun in the other. Another man, fat and sweating, stood bare-chested at the foot of the bed, desperately trying to fasten his trousers, his plans rudely interrupted. Hawke recognized the two Russians instantly. Rasputin now had the .45 at Vicky's temple, while the fat man, Golgolkin, had pulled his little automatic out of his pocket.

When he heard Alex call Vicky's name, Rasputin turned and aimed his .45 directly at Hawke's head. Alex, in the act of getting to his feet, fired so quickly that he'd pumped half a dozen shots into the skeletal man before he knew he'd squeezed the trigger.

He saw the heavy loads blow Rasputin against the wall, several dark stains beginning to bloom on his chest and abdomen. He was already going white, gone. He collapsed behind the bed as Alex turned his weapon on the fat one, the one named Golgolkin, and emptied it into his naked, sweating torso. He'd taken the two Russians out, just as he'd promised Gloria.

"Vicky, get on the floor!" Alex shouted as Golgolkin crumpled, dead before he hit the floor.

His clip expended, Alex ejected it, pulled a spare from the mag-holder strapped to his forearm, and slammed it into the grip of his Sig.

"Alex! Watch out!" he heard Fitz cry. He whirled as the bathroom door flew open and a tall, skinny boy dressed only in his jockeys opened up with an AK-47. The staccato noise of the weapon lasted but a second. Froggy, still on the floor, his Beretta in a two-handed grip, had put a small neat hole right between the boy's eyes.

Alex climbed to his feet. Three down. He whirled around looking for someone else to shoot.

He saw two other bodies lying at Fitz's feet. Somehow, he'd missed all that. He looked at the bed. Vicky was gone. He ripped the bed away from the wall and saw her, half-hidden by the first Russian Alex had killed. She'd done just as he said and rolled to the floor.

He bent down and pulled her up into his arms. Her hair and face were matted with blood but he soon determined it wasn't her own.

"Alex—" she started, but he cut her off. Her eyes were wide, naked with fear, but there was definitely recognition.

"No time," he said. "We've got to get out of here. Can you walk?"

"No, but I can run," Vicky said with a feeble smile.

As he helped her to her feet, Fitz's voice was in his headphones.

"Hostage is clear," Fitz said. "Alive and well. How about it, Bravo?"

"Clear," he heard Boomer say.

"Anybody down?"

"Nobody but bad guys," Stoke said.

"Yeah, same," Boomer echoed.

"Then let's fooking get out of here," Fitz said.

54

Having cleared two rooms, Stoke, Boomer, and the two Gurkha Bravo guys burst into a third. It had only one guard.

When Stoke kicked the door open, they saw the guard had dropped his AK-47 on the floor and was standing flat against the far wall with his hands in the air, red-eyed and white-faced with fear.

"I think you can handle this one alone, Skipper," Boomer said to Stoke. He and the two commandos moved farther down the hall where the firing was heaviest. Stokely moved into the room, sweeping his HK back and forth until he reached the terrified young guard.

"What the hell wrong with you, boy?" Stoke said, sending the guard's AK-47 rattling across the floor with a kick of his boot. "Big old black man scare you so much you ain't even going to put up a fight?"

"I—I have orders to execute him, *señor,*" the guard said in trembling but perfect English. "If there is any rescue attempt. But I do not want to do it. They say they kill me if I don't do it!"

"Execute who?" Stoke asked, looking around the room.

"Him," the guard said, pointing at the bed.

At first, Stoke thought the bed was empty.

Then he saw some movement under the sheets and saw whoever it was had pulled the sheets up over his head. Stoke walked over and ripped the sheets off. It was just an old guy wearing some ugly-ass pajamas.

"Get out the damn bed, my brother, you free at last," Stoke said, prodding him gently with the muzzle of his HK.

"Fuck you," the old guy said.

"Fuck me? I come and rescue your damn ass and all you got to say—hey, hold the phone, I know you! You goddamn Fidel, ain't you? Hell, you Fidel Castro! Man, you world famous!"

"Go away," the old guy said. "Leave me to die in peace."

"Peace? You call this peace? Hand grenades going off, submachine guns firing all over the place? You deaf or something? Now get out that bed."

"Where is my son?" Fidel said. "They promised he would not be harmed. No one will tell me."

"Where's his son, asshole?" Stoke asked the guard.

"They took him last night. To Havana."

"Alive?" Castro asked, staring at the guard.

"*Sí, Comandante.* He was alive when they put him in the truck. I swear it."

"Hey, *Comandante,* get out the bed and put these damn pants on," Stoke said, throwing him a pair he'd found draped over a chair.

"Why?" Castro said. "I'm not going anywhere."

"Why? Look at you! A badass revolutionary like you wearin' them funky pajamas? Why is 'cause I'm gonna save your sorry ass whether you like it or not, that's why. I leave you lyin' here like this, they just gonna shoot you."

"So?"

"So, you a Communist, ain't you? Man, you on the endangered species list! You right at the top! I ain't goin' to let a bunch of dipshit drug dealers murder an old coot like you in cold blood. I'm a New York City policeman! Now, get your damn pants on and let's get out of here!"

Castro climbed out of bed muttering and started pulling the trousers on.

"You, too, dickhead," he said to the guard.

"Me?"

"Yeah, you. You see anybody else in here?"

"No, *señor*, but—"

"Shut the fuck up, okay? Now both of you listen up. Pablo, you go out first, then the living legend, and then me. Pablo, you stay tight, right in front of the *comandante*, got that? Shield his ass. You don't do it, you try and run, and I'm going to blow your ass off anyway. Okay, Pablo? *Comandante*? Let's go!"

There were three Cuban soldiers just emerging from the haze at the top of the stairwell when they came out of the door. Pablo froze and then Stokely shoved Castro to the floor, told Pablo to hit the deck, and unleashed his MP-5. Before the tangos could register what was happening they had crumpled to the floor, shredded with lead.

"HydraShok loads," he informed Fidel and Pablo. "Some serious shit, ain't they? Come on, *Comandante*, get your ass up. We gettin' out of here!"

The firing at the other end of the building had diminished considerably. Stoke was just stepping over the dead soldiers heaped at the top of the steps when he heard Fitz on the radio tell Boomer they had the hostage and were clearing out of the building.

Stoke didn't see anything moving out front when the three of them stepped outside into the courtyard. Clouds still blanketed the stars, but he could sense it was getting lighter out. The closest vehicle was a beat-up old Jeep he'd checked on the way in. Keys were in the ignition.

"Get in that damn Jeep and drive, Pablo," he told the guard, shoving him toward the driver's side. He held Castro's arm, escorted him around to the Jeep's other side, and helped him get in. Then he handed the old man his 9mm pistol. Castro looked down at the weapon in his lap with an expression of mild surprise.

"Now listen up, *Comandante,* I don't know what's going on down here in this whacked-out fucking country of yours. But I do know there's an eight-foot hole in that fence right over there. About five hundred yards past it is a jungle road looks like it might lead somewhere."

"*Sí!* I know it," the guard said. "It leads to my village of Santa Marta!"

"Good," Stoke said. "Excellent. Pablo, this old fella is looking shaky. You take him on home to your momma and get some hot chicken soup in him, okay? Perk his ass right up. You got that? Now you two get your sorry damn asses out of here before the real shooting war starts!"

He looked at Castro and leaned in close to him.

"I'm goin' to tell you something now, *Comandante,* all right? Just between you and me, know what I'm sayin', my brother? The truth?"

Castro nodded, just sitting there, looking up at him like what the fuck.

"This Communism thing?" Stoke said, looking at him, dead serious.

"Yes?"

"It sucks. Try something else."

The Jeep roared off, and Stoke climbed up into the big half-ton truck parked a few yards away. No keys. He'd have to hot-wire it. Just as he bent to do it, the windshield of the truck exploded, showering him with a thousand fragments. He lifted his head and saw more green fatigues than he could count coming at a run down the road from the barracks area.

Shit.

The wires sparked, and the truck roared to life. He jammed it into reverse and backed up all the way to the doorway Alpha squad had entered. By the time he got there, he saw Hawke and Fitz emerge with Vicky supported between them. She looked okay. Hollow-eyed, but okay. Shit, she was breathing, wasn't she?

"Everybody in the back of the truck!" Stoke shouted, leaping from the vehicle. "We got the whole Cuban Army coming down the road!"

Hawke lowered the tailgate and helped Vicky climb inside, giving her a quick hug. "God only knows how you got here, Vicky," he said. "But I am going to get you out."

"What . . . took you so long . . . Alex?" Vicky whispered, trying to smile.

Fitz's commandos, some of them obviously wounded, started streaming through the door. Fitz did a head count as he helped them up into the back of the truck. He obviously wasn't going anywhere until every one of his men had walked or been carried through that doorway.

"Okay, Stoke," he said. "All accounted for. Hit the beach! Hawke and I will ride on the running boards and give you cover fire. Froggy, you guys grab a few RPGs and cover us out our rear. Go!"

Enemy rounds were sizzling all around them, a few starting to rip into the canvas top of the half-tonner when Stoke took off. Hawke, on the driver's side, and Fitz, on the passenger side, each held on to the big rearview mirrors with one hand and fired their HKs at the rapidly advancing troops with the other. The Frogman and two guys in the back of the truck were hanging out over the tailgate firing rocket-propelled grenades at the first wave of green fatigues coming through the fence.

The RPGs slowed the wave of hostile troops down some but it looked like hundreds of them were coming. It was going to be close, Stoke thought, as he fishtailed the big truck in an effort to get the hell out of there.

He held up his arm to look at his watch. He was surprised to see it soaked with blood. A piece of windshield must have caused a deep gash in his forearm. His bloody watch told him they were forty minutes into the mission. They'd been in the building seventeen minutes. If they were going to reach the inflatables and make the appointed offshore rendezvous with *Nighthawke* before the whole Cuban Navy showed up, he had to get moving.

The banging of gunfire and the *whoosh* of RPGs behind him was now constant. It occurred to him that, except for his momma, just about every single person on earth he cared about was riding in this truck. Whatever it takes, he said to himself.

He told Hawke and Fitz to hold on and mashed the accelerator. The most direct route would take them through the heart of the tango compound, just west of the big *finca* that jutted out into the sea.

That's when he saw the huge Soviet helicopter gunship come up over the trees. Soviet choppers made everybody else's choppers look candyass. Big old black bulbous things with glass bubbles and turrets and shit. Scary-looking. Its rotor wash was kicking up a furious sandstorm.

Still, Stoke saw the bug-eyed monster's twin six-barreled miniguns open up and start winking at him. Then he saw it fire two missiles.

"Christ, Stoke! Dodge those things!" Hawke said, firing his HK at the oncoming chopper. Stoke swerved violently right to avoid the incoming missiles and it was all Hawke and Fitz could do just to hang on.

The two missiles exploded about thirty yards to the left of the truck, causing a massive crater. The concussion alone lifted the truck up onto two wheels. It teetered, then finally banged back down again and Stoke got it moving and swerving right. This was bad. Even Stoke knew nine-millimeter rounds were literally useless against armored Soviet helicopters.

"We can't take this thing out with the HKs!" Hawke said. "We need RPG launchers up here now!" He shouted in Stoke's window as the chopper roared overhead. "Have someone pass them up!"

Stoke started zigzagging in earnest now, hearing the whine of the big chopper's jet turbines as it careened around for another pass.

"No! Belay that order!" Fitz shouted in Stoke's other window. "We'll never get a clean RPG shot hanging out here one-handed! Stoke, can you execute a one-eighty in this thing?"

"Hang a U-ey?" Stoke said, swerving to avoid a looming palm tree. "I think I can manage that!"

"Do it!" Fitz screamed. "And come to a dead stop. I want to give Froggy a shot out the back at this fucking chopper. He's the only one of us with the slightest chance to bring it down!"

"Hold on back there, folks!" Stoke shouted over his shoulder. "We're going to flip this half-ton heap around backasswards!"

Stoke yanked down hard left on the wheel, locking it, and sent the big truck into a hard drift through 180 degrees. When it had completely reversed directions, he yanked up on the emergency brake. The truck skidded to a stop, throwing up a huge spray of sand.

He was amazed to see that during this maneuver, Fitz had somehow climbed through the window of the cab and was now scrambling over the bench seat into the rear of the truck. He was yelling at Froggy and the two other RPG guys to get ready.

The monster chopper had completed carving its turn and was skimming back over the treetops. It was probably surprising to the pilots to find themselves now approaching from the rear. But the ticking of bullets puncturing the hood and fenders wasn't exactly soothing to those inside.

"Froggy, you remember where the sweet spot is on these birds?" Fitz was shouting at the back of the truck. "It's an Mi-38 Heckle!"

"*Mais certainement*, ze Heckle's thorax," Froggy said, getting to his feet. "Right below his gullet." He unhooked the tailgate, let it fall, and stood up on it, spreading his stance and lining up the RPG tube, right down the throat of the big black bird. He shifted his feet for better balance. The tailgate was sticky with the blood of his wounded comrades.

"Oh, shit! Don't let him get too close, Froggy!" Fitz shouted, watching the chopper roar toward them at tree-top level. Soviet choppers were designed to get hammered and not even change course. There was one small vulnerable spot, though, and Froggy had his eye on it.

"Settle . . . settle," Froggy said, the tube on his shoulder, ignoring Fitz and all the lead flying toward him, steady as a rock. He was actually calm at such moments. He knew he was probably going to get shot, and since there wasn't a fucking thing he could do about it, he always focused on whatever weapon was in his hand at the moment.

The RPG had a maximum range of 1,000 feet or so. It was designed solely for land warfare. Firing one upwards was enormously dangerous, even suicidal as a few Sammies had learned in Somalia, shooting at U.S. choppers. Froggy, who had been there, knew he was forced to bide his time. The miniguns on the bird were spitting lead, kicking up sand all around the back of the truck. Closing—closing—now!

WHOOOOSH!

The grenade shot out toward the ugly black helicopter, leaving a sparkling white trail of smoke behind it. The chopper tried desperately to pull up but it was too late.

There was a small explosion first, just aft of the nose under its chin bubble where its controls were. The chopper veered sharply left. It went into a rapidly accelerating spin. Fitz and Froggy watched, counting the seconds, praying the hit was on target.

There was an enormous flashbang of light and sound as the helicopter became a huge fireball skidding along the tops of the trees. It tilted violently left, its main rotors snapped and went flying, and then there was no trace of it other than the thick black smoke and licks of fire rising from the jungle.

A cheer erupted in the back of the truck, and then they all held on as Stoke jammed the truck into first gear and hauled ass the hell out of there, headed for the beach.

"Let's go surfin' now, everybody's learnin' how . . ." Stoke sang at the top of his lungs. He could see glimpses of the sea now through the palms. There was still sporadic fire coming from all sides, but Hawke and Fitz and the boys in the back of the bus seemed to be doing a good job of suppressing it.

Stoke was driving with one hand now, firing his .45 out the windshield and the driver's side window. He didn't have any targets but he liked the general idea of fire coming from all sides of the truck.

Suddenly the truck rocked left. Something had slammed into the vehicle hard on the right. He waited for an explosion—nothing. He looked at the right side door. An unexploded Russian RPG had poked its ugly-ass nose right through his goddamn steel door and stopped! The things were two feet long and there was at least a foot inside sitting there pointed at him!

Shit. He was more surprised than afraid. You talk about lucky. Can't get no more lucky than a dud RPG coupla feet from your ass. Can't hang around here too much longer, less luck be running out.

"Stoke!" he heard Hawke say in his headphones.

"Talk to me, brother."

"The big house coming up on your left, *el finca grande*. You and I are hopping off there. Make for the trees and drop us off!"

Stoke leaned out the window and shouted at Hawke, who was still firing his HK at anything that moved.

"Fuck you talking about, boss?"

"Pull inside that stand of trees, Stoke," Hawke said, leaning in the window, grinning his ass off. "You and I have some unfinished business. It might take a while. Fitz and Boomer will get Vicky to the IBS and then out to *Nighthawke*. Then send an IBS back for us. If we're not at the rendezvous in half an hour, tell him to go without us."

Stoke slammed on the brakes and skidded to a stop inside a grove thick with palms.

"I knew you'd understand," Hawke said, smiling.

Hawke then leapt to the ground and ran around to the rear of the truck. He quickly climbed up inside, found Vicky, and whispered something into her ear. She reached up and wrapped both arms around him and he kissed the top of her head and turned away.

"She all right?" Fitz said, climbing down off the tailgate with Hawke.

"She will be," Hawke said. "I'm sure you fellows will make sure of that." He looked up at the commandos jammed into the back of the truck and saluted them.

"Well done," Hawke said, looking each man in the eye. "Remarkable job. Thank you, each one of you, for what you did." There was silence inside the truck, and Hawke had turned away, when one of the men coughed.

"We know where you and Stokely are going, sir,"

Cosmo said. "A couple of us would like to come with you."

"Make it all of us, *mon ami!*" Hawke heard Froggy say.

"Thanks, Froggy," Hawke said, "but we might have a better chance if it's just the two of us. Besides, I need all of you brave gents to protect the lovely lady. Ready, Stoke?"

"Let's move out, boss," Stoke said, and he and Hawke disappeared into the darkness.

There was still sporadic shooting behind them. The fire, though sparse, was getting closer. Hawke heard Fitz shout something obscene as he climbed behind the wheel and the old truck shot forward, spraying sand from the rear wheels, headed for the beach.

Hawke wasn't overly worried. If anyone could get Vicky safely aboard the inflatable and out to the designated rendezvous with *Nighthawke,* it was FitzHugh McCoy, Charlie Rainwater, and the incredible band of warriors inside that truck.

55

Five minutes later, Alex and Stoke were a hundred yards from the main *finca,* hunkered down, well hidden in the scrub palm at the fringe of the jungle.

The place was immense.

Wings extended in all directions, mostly three stories high, some with towers and turrets at least six or seven stories. Towers and parapets and hundreds of yellow lights, oblongs and hexagons, a wonder of golden windows. All was pale stucco, and the many rooftops and chimneys were finished with bright blue ceramic tiles.

Both men scanned the width and breadth of the *finca* compound with their night-vision goggles. There was an eight-foot stone wall, topped with concertina wire, surrounding the entire compound. The main portion of the house lay some three hundred yards inside the wall. Just opposite them was a massive iron gate flanked by two guardhouses with dim blue lights burning inside.

For the most part, the house was surprisingly quiet. Considering that all hell had broken loose in the last half hour, there was remarkably little activity.

One wing, built on a rocky promontory extending out into the sea, was ablaze with light. Stokely and Hawke immediately deduced it was the general's living quarters. They could see a few silhouetted figures moving past the windows. On the very top floor, beyond what appeared to be a bedroom, a large open terrace was built overlooking the sea.

"Good Lord," Hawke said under his breath. "You see that?"

"Yeah," Stoke whispered. "A damn Bengal tiger just cruised by. Look up in the tree to the right of the entrance. Hard to see him, but there's a boa constrictor napping on the lowest branch."

"Are you ready to go rock this boat?"

"I was born ready," Stoke said, slamming a fresh mag into the rubber grip of his Beretta.

"Then let's saddle up," Hawke said, in a perfect mimicry of Fitz's gung-ho cry.

They had previously decided there was only one way

they could both gain access to the *finca* and stay alive in the process.

So they dropped to their bellies and crawled like snakes across two hundred yards of open sand, dotted with clumps of devilish sandspurs. When they reached the guardhouse on the right side, they simply stood up and smiled at the guard.

"Buenas noches, señor," Hawke said. *"Habla inglés?* I am Alexander Hawke. This is my colleague Detective Stokely Jones. We would like a word with General de Herreras."

So saying, Hawke and Stoke stepped back and dropped their submachine guns and sidearms to the ground. Then they each placed their hands on top of their heads. Hawke began whistling an old tune, one Stoke thought he recognized as the theme from *Bridge on the River Kwai*. He instantly joined in, producing a lively if unlovely harmony.

The stupefied guard instantly emerged from the guardhouse, training his weapon on them. He shouted something in Spanish, and the other guard came running.

The second guard spoke English.

"What de fuck you think, amigo? You kill many of my brothers. Now, we take you to the general? No, we shoot you fucking bastards!"

He squeezed off a burst, the rounds sizzling about three feet over their heads.

While the other guard trained his submachine gun on Stoke, the English-speaking one walked right up to Alex, pulled a jungle knife from a scabbard on his hip, and sliced open the blouse of Alex's tigerstripes. Then he stuck the point of the blade under his chin. He'd hooked the thin gold chain around Alex's neck.

The St. George's Alex had worn since childhood

caught the light. The guard ripped the chain and the gold medallion fell to the ground. The man bent down to retrieve it, dangled it in front of Alex's eyes.

"*Vaya con Dios, señor,*" the guard said, twisting the knife blade so that it pierced the taut skin.

"Shoot these gringo bastards," he said, stepping back outside the field of fire. "The white man first."

The other guard raised his gun and racked his slide but saw that Stokely walked directly between the muzzle of the AK-47 and Alex. The huge black man had a small white handkerchief in his raised right hand.

"Yo! Hold up! Flag of truce, son," Stoke said. "You can shoot us, I know, but I ain't recommending it. You think we just walk up, throw down guns 'cause we stupid? No. We got important information your commander wants to get his hands on. This here is Alex Hawke. He famous. Man who been fuckin' with you. General Manso hears you got him held prisoner, hell, he like to pin a medal on both yo' asses!"

The two guards looked at each other.

"Fuck your flag of truce," the guard said. "We have orders to shoot intruders on sight." He fired a quick burst at Stokely's feet, the rounds kicking up sand all around him.

Stoke ignored it, gave them his biggest smile. "Aw, see, you ain't thinkin' clearly. Trigger happy, is all. You just nervous. Get your finger off that trigger a second, 'less you do something stupid. Cheat y'all selves out of a battlefield promotion. Maybe you boys ought to ring the general's ass up and tell him you got Alex Hawke hisself down here? He tells you to shoot us, well, hell, we shit out of luck, that's all. Pull your trigger, Pedro."

The guard looked at Stoke's eyes. He didn't like it, but like all men in his position he was extremely risk averse. He told his colleague to keep his gun on them and ducked back inside the guardhouse.

A minute later, he was back outside.

"*Vamonos,*" he said. "General de Herreras has agreed to see you."

"See?" Stoke said to the guard. "Just what I told your ass. You shoot us, you in the deep severe, baby. Now, you a national hero!"

"I'll take my medal back now," Hawke said to the guard, but all it got him was a jab to the ribs with the butt of a gun.

Hands still on their heads, Hawke and Stokely were marched through the heavy wrought iron gates and inside the compound. They mounted a wide set of marble steps leading to a pair of massive metal doors.

The doors were from some ancient fortification, heavily decorated with shields and lances. A blinking video monitor picked them up, and the doors swung inward instantly. There was a huge entry hall, with candles guttering in heavy fixtures mounted on the walls. Hawke could see a wide stone staircase curving upwards into the darkness.

Six formidable guards, all in black uniforms with red berets, stood in a semicircle facing them. Hawke was astounded to see that the entire group of guards appeared to be Chinese. Then he remembered hearing Conch say that Raul Castro had long been making overtures toward Beijing. Clearly, they'd passed the overture stage.

Conch would be interested to learn there were highly

trained Chinese troops in Cuba. If he lived to tell her about it.

All six guards had Chicom pistols on their hips and lethal-looking Chinese Tsao-6 submachine guns aimed at the bellies of the two prisoners.

Someone then stepped forward from the shadows and, ignoring Stoke, scrutinized Hawke. The man had the dress uniform coat of a highly decorated Cuban general thrown over his silk pajamas. It was barely large enough to cover his enormous paunch.

He poked his silver-plated .357 magnum into Hawke's stomach until Alex winced, then stepped back and smiled.

"This must be Alexander Hawke himself!" the pajama-clad general said in heavily accented English. "Welcome to el Finca Telaraña!" There was the sour smell of rum and tobacco on the man's breath. His eyes were red-veined and watery. He was more than a little drunk, Hawke thought. May Day festivities, no doubt.

"Good evening, General. I don't believe we've been introduced," Hawke said, maintaining the casual smile on his face.

"Why, I am General Juan de Herreras. You've not heard of me? I am in charge of the whole Cuban Army!"

"A responsibility that no doubt weighs heavily on your shoulders, General," Hawke said, eyeing the man carefully, seeing a very old picture in his mind.

It was not the skinny one. Or the very fat one who had the machete at his mother's throat. No, Congreve had already arrested that monster.

No, this was the other one, he recognized the eyes now, the one who held his mother and—it was all Hawke could do not to lunge at the man and rip out his heart. He knew he had to marshal all this anger, compress it, guard his arsenal of hatred jealously. He was going to need all of it if he were to do what he'd come here to do successfully.

"Ah, of course," Hawke managed to say. "Now I remember. I believe I made your acquaintance many years ago."

"Really, *señor?*" de Herreras said. "I don't think so. I would remember. In any event, my brother Manso is waiting for you in his study. Since you and your friend here have caused us so much distress in recent days, I warn you that he is not in the best of moods."

"Pity," Hawke said. "Perhaps I have something that will cheer him up."

"Excellent! Please follow me," the general said, and he strode beyond the curving staircase into the deeper shadows of the great hall. Stoke and Hawke felt the presence of the six guards behind them.

Hawke and Stoke had not seen the second stairway. This one curved down into murky blackness. The sound of the heavy-booted Chinese guards reverberated in the stillness. They had disturbed the sleep of two silky Russian wolfhounds guarding the top of the steps.

It was odd, Hawke thought, how removed this bizarre fortress seemed to be from all the gunfire and bloodshed that had taken place within the huge compound. Perhaps these generals did not dirty their hands with mere soldier's duty.

When they finally reached the bottom of the steps, there was a long red-carpeted corridor leading in both directions. Alex figured they must be a good forty feet underground. The general beckoned, turned right, and walked past several mahogany paneled doors until he stopped abruptly, and knocked on one of them.

It slid open with a hiss, and an elderly Oriental fellow wearing black silk pajamas and white gloves ushered them all inside a massive elevator. He had a wispy little white goatee that looked like milkweed.

"To my brother's study," General de Herreras said to the attendant who bowed, then pushed a button.

The elevator came to a gentle stop and the door slid open. The attendant bowed deeply as they all stepped out of his car. Hawke, expecting some grand room, was surprised as they emerged instead into a dark, smallish foyer with a single table along one wall. A gilt-framed painting, lit by an overhead light, dominated the room. Alex bent over to take a look.

An early Picasso in shades of blue.

"This way, gentlemen," General Juan de Herreras said, pressing his palm against a panel cut in the mahogany. There was a click and a door swung outward revealing a set of steep stone steps leading up. It was suddenly cool and damp inside and the air smelled of, what, chlorine? Alex touched the stone wall. It was wet and mossy. At the top of the steps, two flaming candles hung in iron fix- tures on either side of a narrow wooden door.

"After you," the general said, and Alex and Stoke started climbing.

At the top, they stood aside as the general pushed a number of buttons on a keypad mounted by the door. A green light flashed and the door swung open.

Hawke and Stoke were both struck dumb by what they saw.

The room they entered was circular. The walls and

great domed ceiling were made entirely of glass. They revealed what was perhaps the most spectacular underwater view Hawke had ever seen. Huge underwater lights, all hidden, illuminated the scene beyond the glass. Tropical fish of every size and color swam by. Exotic vegetation swayed from the sandy floor.

Above their heads, a great white shark, some twenty feet in length, swam idly by, above the glass dome, followed by a school of barracuda.

"Man living at the bottom of an aquarium," Stoke whispered. "Look up there."

Higher above them, at least thirty feet above the glass ceiling, huge stalactites hung down and schools of brilliant fish darted through them. Stalagmites, too, rose from the bottom of the grotto, forming intricate cities of pink and white coral.

The glass room seemed to have been constructed on the sandy floor of some deep natural grotto, most likely fed by the river flowing out to the sea. At this river's mouth, Hawke thought, the submarine pen where the Borzoi lay.

The tensile strength of the glass had to be enormous, because Alex could discern no seams, no visible means of support. And yet a massive bronze chandelier hung from a fixture at its very center. It provided the only light in the room other than the external underwater illumination. The fixture consisted of finely wrought rings of hammered brass and bronze, getting smaller toward the top.

The largest ring, the lowest, held at least fifty blazing candles, while the top ring held ten or so. It had to be suspended on some kind of hydraulic or electrically powered wire, Hawke thought, capable of being raised and lowered, otherwise, how could you manage to keep all these bloody candles lit? The effect was certainly dramatic, he had to admit.

"Some weird-smelling shit in here, boss," Stoke said under his breath.

The air was filled with a stupefying sweetish stink, the smell of burning poppy seeds, Hawke realized. He'd walked into an underwater opium den.

"Well, well, well. Alex Hawke himself," came a sugary voice from the center of the room. Directly beneath the chandelier was a massive oval desk. The owner of that velvet voice was unseen, seated at the desk but hidden by the back of a tall leather chair facing away from the new arrivals. "We finally meet," the voice said, floating upwards on a cloud of pale opium smoke.

"A dream come true," Hawke said.

"Let me get a look at this famous Hawke," the voice said, and a tall, slender man rose serenely from the chair. He was naked from the waist up, his well-muscled back toward them. A long black ponytail reached halfway to his waist.

Hawke sucked down a quick gulp of air as he regarded the man.

There was a spider tattooed on the man's shoulder. Black with a red spot on its belly.

Spiders were bad. Alex had been terrified of them ever since he'd awoken one night to find one crawling across his face. On his cheek. By his mouth. Had he not awoken, it would have crawled inside—

Hawke managed to let the shock of seeing and hearing this man wash over him without a trace of it registering on his face. By the time the man had pulled a dressing gown from the chair and turned to face him, Hawke had regained the same faintly amused smile he'd been wearing since entering the *finca*.

As Manso walked around the massive carved oval desk, Hawke eyed him evenly. The candlelight flickered darkly in those dead black eyes set in a face of decidedly feminine beauty. The long hair, still jet black, tied at the back. Too beautiful for a man. Too much raw brutality for a woman.

He was slipping his muscle-corded arms inside a long flowing robe of red Chinese silk trimmed at the neck and cuffs with black pearls.

"The night I first saw you," Hawke said, "I thought you were a woman."

"Really?" Manso said. "How very interesting. When was this?"

"It was a very long time ago," Alex said. "I was just a boy."

"We were both boys long ago, weren't we, *Señor* Hawke?" Manso smiled at the thought. "Something to drink? Or smoke? Our Chinese friends supply us with lovely opium."

"No, thank you," Hawke said.

"How about your friend? Who is he, by the way?"

"I can speak for myself. My name is Stokely Jones, United States Navy, retired. NYPD, retired. And I ain't thirsty either," Stoke said, dropping his hands from his head for the first time. When Hawke saw the Cubans had no reaction to this, he did the same.

"Shall we relax? Perhaps over there nearer the glass?" Manso said, and he indicated a grouping of mandarin opium beds arranged along one section of the glass wall.

He stretched out languorously on the largest of the beds, strewn with silk pillows of gold and black and red. He stretched, flexing the fingers of both hands.

There was something very odd and studied about the general's movements, Alex thought. He moved like a fine athlete or dancer, with exaggerated elegance and drama, as if this were his stage and all that happened here was a performance. One whose significance only Manso understood.

Indeed, he and his brother seemed supremely indifferent to the explosive events that had so recently occurred within their own compound.

"Tequila, *señor?*" General Juan de Herreras said, taking a swig before offering the opened bottle.

"Later, perhaps," Alex said.

Alex suddenly understood the lack of activity in the big *finca*. The two de Herreras brothers had clearly just been woken up. One, Juanito, from an alcohol- and drug-induced sleep, the other, Manso, from some blissful dream here in this soundproofed room.

General Juan de Herreras, weaving slightly as he moved, waved his tequila bottle in the general direction of his brother Manso, indicating that they should all join him on the sofas. Alex and Stokely exchanged the briefest of looks, each of them right on the edge, waiting.

Something about the edge. Having worked together for so long, they both knew exactly where it was. All the time.

Alex sat on the corner of the sofa opposite Manso. Stoke remained on his feet, head darting back and forth, his eyes constantly monitoring the six Chinese whose weapons were unwaveringly trained on him.

"A lovely view, is it not, Mr. Hawke?" Manso said. "I modeled this room on a far more modest construction created by my mentor, *el doctor*. He's the one who taught me to enjoy killing a man like you. You know of Escobar?"

"Enough to know that I wish I'd been the one to put a bullet in his head. Interesting room. But don't threaten me. You know what they say about people who live in glass houses?" Alex said.

"A man with an arsenal of boulders, doesn't worry about a man with mere rocks," the general said, allowing himself a small giggle.

"This guy could go toe-to-toe with Jay Leno," Stoke said, remaining on his feet. Hawke could see that Stokely's patience was wearing thin. He wanted this done so they could confirm Vicky's safety, Hawke imagined. He was having similar thoughts himself.

"Watch this," the general suddenly said.

Reaching back beneath the pillows, Manso withdrew a gleaming sword. At first, Hawke thought it was a broadsword. Then he saw that, of course, it was a machete, polished to a lustrous silver, with precious stones embedded in the ebony handle.

Manso rapped the blade smartly three times on the glass above his head. A moment passed, and then three mermaids floated down through the crystal green layers of water and appeared at the window. There they hovered, naked, save for jeweled tiaras, and their long hair floated about their lovely faces as if blown by a light wind.

"Exquisite, aren't they?"

"Quite," Hawke answered. "Indigenous? Or paid by the hour?"

"You know, Commander, I'm beginning to take an intense dislike to you, even though you have done me an enormous service."

"Service?"

"Yes. You locked up my troublesome brother Carlitos, and so saved me the trouble of killing him myself. Now, tell me why you came here to my island before I kill you."

"I came here to get someone you took away from me. I succeeded."

"According to Major Diaz, you killed at least seventy of my men and wounded many more. Your timing was good. Many hostages were to be executed at first light. Including your whore."

Hawke smiled, letting nothing show.

"Without giving me a chance to meet your demands? Apparently you haven't read many books on business etiquette, have you, General?"

"Ha! This is a good one! Now tell me, Hawke. You are a businessman. Wealthy, powerful, with many, many powerful connections. I am a man with a country to feed, arm, restore to power. Why can't we be civilized and work together to rebuild a once proud nation?"

"Work together? Don't be ridiculous. Victoria Sweet is not the only person you took from me, General," Hawke said, laughing at the man's insipid notion.

"I'm sorry, but I don't follow you, Mr. Hawke."

"Then let me be perfectly clear, General de Herreras. Thirty years ago, you and your two brothers boarded an unarmed British yacht moored in a small cove near Staniel Cay in the Exumas. She was named the *Seahawke*. Do you remember that?"

"*Seahawke?*"

"Yes. That was her name. There were people aboard. A husband and his young wife."

"I've no idea what you're talking about, *señor.*"

"You murdered them. And you laughed while you did it. You and your brothers."

"Ah, he's right, my brother!" Juanito said. "I remember this night! I think we were—"

"Shut up, you idiot! This man is insane. Coming into my house making wild accusations. I won't stand for it. Guards!"

The guards advanced, racking the slides on their machine guns.

"You were looking for something that night, Manso. Do you remember?" Alex stood and walked over to the glass wall, staring out, his hands clasped behind his back.

"I think you're mad. *Loco,* that's all."

"I was there, General," Alex said, whirling around, his eyes blazing. "They were my parents! I was seven years old! I saw it all, what you did to them, you filthy bloody murdering bastard!"

"What are you saying?"

"I was hidden. My father hid me in a small locker. His name was Commander Alexander Hawke. He died saving my life!"

"What is this? I don't need to listen to this!"

"Yes, you do, General, because at the end of the story comes the map. His name was Alex. Her name was Catherine. He called her Kitty. She was a great actress. They loved each other very much. They only had one child. A small boy who had just turned seven. I was in the very room where you and your brothers tortured and murdered them. I saw everything you did. Everything."

"It was long ago," the general said. "Maybe it happened, maybe not. What does it matter? Things are mixed up in your mind."

"You have no idea how perfectly clear things are in my mind. Now. Send your guards out of the room, General," Alex said. He was struggling to get his rage under control, taking huge deep breaths, and he became very quiet.

"You are joking, *si?*" the general finally said.

"No. We have private business to discuss."

"Business? Whatever business?"

"The map, General. The one you murdered my parents for. You see, you killed the wrong members of what once was the Hawke family. My parents didn't have the map that night. I did. I still do."

"The map! You have the map?"

"I do."

"I don't believe you for a second."

Alex bent and ripped open the Velcro seal of a deep pocket on the right thigh of his tigerstripes. He withdrew a small blue envelope and held it aloft.

"Here. This map was drawn nearly three hundred years ago at Newgate Prison in London. The author penned it just before his appointment with the hangman at Executioner's Dock in 1705."

"Open it. Pull it, the map, out. Hold it up. Show me."

Alex did. Since it was a copy, it was far less fragile than the original. The general bent forward, peering at the document in complete amazement. It certainly looked to be authentic.

"This is not a trick?" Manso asked.

"You believe I would come here and chance my life on a trick?"

Alex pulled a lighter from his fatigues, flicked it lit, and held the flame near to one corner of the document. "Now or never, General. Send the guards out of the room."

"Juanito!" the general said, sitting straight up on the bed. "Send the guards away. Now! Tell them to wait outside. This is a private matter."

The man did as he was told, herding the guards outside, shaking his head and muttering. His brother Manso was crazy, but what could he do?

When the guards had retreated from the room, Alex returned the envelope to his pocket and resealed the Velcro fastener. Then he gave Stoke a look and started pacing around the vast oval desk.

"In an odd way," he began, speaking as he moved about, "the rightful owners of this treasure would seem to be your family, General, not mine."

"Of course! Why do you think I have spent years in search of the de Herreras treasure!"

"They won't find it, I'm afraid," Hawke said. "Scribbled at the bottom of the map is a letter from a notorious pirate. Blackhawke. Heard of him?"

"Of course! One of the most brilliant and ruthless pirates in the Caribbean! He's the one who stole my family fortune!"

"We all have a skeleton in the closet. He is mine. I am his direct descendant. His map has been in my family for generations. Just before his capture and execution in

1705, Blackhawke realized his final and greatest triumph. He took the largest single prize ever captured."

"Tell me!" Manso shouted, his eyes glittering.

"Blackhawke engaged a Spanish galleon under command of Admiral Manso de Herreras somewhere off Hispaniola."

"Yes!" the general shouted. "My noble ancestor! He sailed for England with his billions in stolen silver and gold. To deposit his fortune in the Bank of England. But he never arrived."

"Yes, General. Your history is good. According to Blackhawke's letter, de Herreras never reached England because Blackhawke intercepted him and sent him to the bottom. But first, he relieved his burden of all that gold and silver."

"And then?"

"And then he buried it, of course. Fairly standard practice in those days."

"So! It's true! You see, Juanito, all these years, I was right! This Hawke family has a map of our treasure's location! We will find it!" Manso was flushed with excitement. "We will share! Surely there is more than enough to—"

"No," Alex said, turning to face him. "I have a far better idea."

"What could be better than—"

"The map is yours. I want you to have this blood-soaked map, Manso de Herreras. You and you alone."

"You do?"

"I do indeed," Hawke said. "But there is one very important condition."

"I am waiting, *señor.*"

"Tonight, we're going to put an end to the nightmare
you started thirty years ago, General de Herreras."

"I don't understand you."

"Simple, really. If you want the map, you're going to
have to kill me for it."

56
• • • — — • • •

"Kill you for it?"

The general was sliding catlike off the pillowed bed, a
hideous grin pulling his lips back, distorting his face.

"Kill you for it? If that's what you wish, it can be easily
accomplished, *Señor* Hawke."

He lifted his silver-bladed machete, turned it this way
and that to catch the candlelight. Suddenly, it was spinning high into the air above his head where it paused,
then made two or three flashing revolutions and started
to descend. Manso was dancing beneath it, watching it.

He grabbed it by the handle, right out of the air, and
spun toward Hawke, murderous intent flashing in his
eyes.

Out of the corner of his eye, Hawke saw Stoke start to
move to intercept the general.

"No!" Hawke shouted. "Stay out of this, Stoke. This is
unfinished business. Entirely between the two of us."

"But, boss, you ain't got nothing to—"

"An unarmed man with vengeance in his heart is the
most dangerous of enemies," Alex said.

Juan de Herreras, wide-eyed at these amazing events,

brandished his .357, motioning for Stoke to back off and take a seat, which he reluctantly did. Hawke gave Stoke a look that said don't worry about this, but Stoke was hardly reassured.

Manso suddenly lunged toward Hawke and leveled a vicious swipe at his neck. Hawke barely saw it coming but at the last second ducked his head and spun away, unharmed. But the blade had whispered across his chest.

Much too close, Alex thought. Was he really slowing down that much?

"Come now. You'll have to do a lot better than that, General," Hawke said, circling around the man, feinting this way and that, the slightly amused smile still on his face.

Enraged, as much by Hawke's attitude as anything else, the ponytailed general danced toward him again, swinging the blade ferociously as he came. Alex waited for the blade's final arc, swung at his midsection, then turned and arched his spine away just as the tip of the blade hissed by his belly. He'd stepped aside at the last second and the general, who had put all of his weight into this thrust, pitched forward off balance.

"Not quite so simple as cutting cane, is it, *machetero?*" Hawke said, leaping to the top of the general's oval desk. "Cane doesn't move!"

Watching the general circle the desk, Alex had the unpleasant realization that his heavy camo fatigues and boots were making it tough to move about. He'd just have to manage it somehow. Find his old rhythms.

He could easily kill this man with his bare hands, but something inside him, his pirate blood, was insisting on the sword. He'd seen another machete propped up against a Chinese screen beside one of the opium beds. He'd just have to find a way to get to it.

"You English pig." Manso sneered. "I will cut your legs off at the knees and stuff them down your throat!"

He took a vicious swipe at knee level but Alex leapt up, tucking his legs beneath him, and nothing was sliced but air.

"You see what I mean, Stoke?" Alex cried, dancing atop the desk. "This Cubano is very brave when it comes to killing women and unarmed men. Our brave spider Araña is so obviously what they say he is, a *chiquita!*"

"Yes! *Señorita* Chiquita Banana herself!" Stokely joined in, keeping one eye on the one-sided duel and one eye on the drunken admiral with the pistol aimed at his heart.

Hawke looked down at the man circling in for the kill.

"So. Look at yourself, Manso!" Hawke laughed. "What do you see, *chica?* I see a little banana general from a little banana republic! Most men would be ashamed to attack an unarmed man. Most men would—"

"Would what, *señor?*" Manso screamed.

"Would think killing an unarmed man an act of cowardice."

"He wants a weapon?" Manso roared. "Is that his fucking problem? Then give him a fucking weapon! Juanito, there is a machete behind the Chinese screen. Give it to the Englishman and we'll see what he is made of!"

Juanito rose and, never taking the gun off Stokely, wobbled over to the nearby screen. He retrieved the machete, hefting it, and looked at his brother.

"Are you sure about this, *mi hermano?*"

"Give him the fucking thing, Juanito! I've had enough

of his shit! I'm going to slit his throat and pull out that flapping goddamn tongue!"

The man shrugged his meaty shoulders and tossed the blade carelessly toward Alex, who snatched the handle nimbly out of midair.

He took a second to run his finger over the machete blade. It would do. He leapt from the desk and spun around to face Manso, adapting the classic fencing stance, his left hand held rigidly behind his back.

"Do you fence at all, General?" he asked, smiling at the man.

"Fence? What is fence?"

"It's what cowboys do to ranches, baby!" Stokely exclaimed, and Alex laughed.

The general charged, bringing his blade down as he came, and Alex did his best to parry the furious blow, the sound of metal on metal ringing out in the room. The machete felt unwieldy and strange in his hand. And it was clear that Manso was called a *machetero* for good reason.

Hawke had a fight on his hands.

With his left hand clenched behind his back, Hawke went on the attack. There was sheer fury in his face now, Stoke had never seen the likes of it, and his thrusts and blows came so rapidly that Manso was retreating, warding off the attack, clearly on the defensive.

"So. You can fight," Manso said.

"You noticed that," Hawke replied, spinning like a dancer with a razor-sharp blade for a prop.

Manso stood his ground and laid on three resounding blows in quick succession. Hawke parried all three, but the tip of Manso's machete somehow caught his cheek, opening a wide gash beneath his eye.

"Ah, English blood," Manso said. "I developed a taste for it at an early age, you will remember." Then he danced backwards and actually licked the blood off the tip of his blade.

"Delicious! I'll cut your heart out and eat it for breakfast!"

"I think not," Hawke said. He was circling the man now, changing directions, looking for his opening, when suddenly Manso charged directly at him, bellowing like a wounded animal, swinging his blade wildly.

Manso was in his element now, a true *machetero* from the cane fields. His silver blade came flashing down, Hawke raised his in defense but the blow never came. The general stopped short, pivoted on one heel, then whirled around, bringing his bloody machete up from below.

There was a ferocious clang and Hawke's blade, brutally ripped from his hand, went flying, clattering across the floor.

The general's face was suffused with murderous glee as he advanced to finish his victim and claim his rightful prize.

Hawke leapt once more to the top of the desk. The general slashed again, and this time Hawke was not so lucky. He tried to jump away, but the blade sliced through his thick camo trousers and he felt a searing pain in his right thigh.

The little blue envelope fluttered to the floor. The general had sliced open not only his leg, but his pocket.

Two things happened at once. The general stooped to pick up the envelope, and Stokely shouted something at Hawke.

Hawke looked in Stoke's direction and saw that the

man had somehow retrieved his machete and it was now spinning through the air directly toward him.

There was hardly time to finesse snatching it by the handle. He just reached out and seized the machete by the blade, slicing his fingers and palm in the doing. The blood made the handle sticky but at least he now had some ghost of a chance against the crazed *machetero*.

"General! Up here!" Hawke cried. The general had the little blue envelope clutched triumphantly in his upraised hand.

The general looked up only to see the massive chandelier, with Hawke dangling from it, come swooping through the air toward him. In Hawke's free hand, the blade was poised.

There came then a sound, an awful sound, of steel on flesh and bone. Of steel *through* flesh and bone.

An enormous howl of pain exploded from deep in the general's throat as he looked in horror at his bloody stump of an arm. On the floor at his feet, fingers twitching, lay his bloody hand still clutching the blue envelope.

There was an explosion then, and Hawke, still hanging by one hand from the chandelier, felt and heard a round from Juanito's .357 whistle past his ear. He turned to see Stokely on his feet, bringing his hand down with tremendous force on the Cuban's extended forearm. There was another crack from the muzzle of the gun and then the crack of Juanito's breaking bones.

Hawke released his grip on the swinging chandelier and dropped to the floor.

He saw that Juanito's gun had gone flying and turned his attention back to the general. He had sunk to his knees, holding his bloody stump against his chest, taking thin, shallow breaths. Deathly pale, head down, the man was clearly in shock.

Alex lifted the thick black ponytail. Then he laid the razor-sharp edge of his heavy blade across the tendons of the man's exposed neck. Then he raised it and—

"Boss, no!" he heard Stoke shouting from somewhere. He'd lost track of time and place. He knew he had some unfinished business here, something to do with the sword in his hand. Oh, yes. He knew what he had to do.

The machete flashed in the wildly swinging candle-light.

Hawke stopped the deadly descent of the blade inches from the general's neck.

And emerged from his waking dream.

"No," he finally whispered, looking down at the man kneeling before him. He bent down then and pressed his lips near his ear. "Listen to me, you disgusting piece of human rubbish. You killed my parents the day after my seventh birthday. For the rest of my life, I'm going to visit you on the anniversary of that date. Watch you rot in your prison hole. That will be my birthday present to myself each year, watching you disappear."

He put his boot against the man's back and shoved him forward. The general came to a rest with his face mere inches away from his own severed hand. His dull eyes stared at the hand, unblinking.

"This belongs to my father," Alex said, and ripped the blue envelope from the dead hand.

The general spoke, a soft guttural moan. Hawke bent to hear his words.

"I didn't hear that," Alex said.

"I had your mother twice, you know," Manso croaked.

"What did you say?" Alex said, bending closer toward him.

"Twice! Yes!" Manso said, in a guttural whisper. "Two times I had your whore of a mother. Once before and once after. And you know what, *amigo?*"

Alex raised the blade, his face contorted with rage.

"She was better the second time. After she was dead."

The blade came down with such fury that it clanged furiously on the marble floor as it severed Manso's head. Alex watched the head skittering across the floor, then looked at the bloody blade in his hand in wonder.

"Guards! Guards!" Juan de Herreras shouted. He charged across the room to where Hawke was kneeling beside his headless brother. In a blind rage, he roared and bellowed and flung himself through the air. Alex saw him coming, tried to roll away and ward him off with the upraised machete, but the man's eyes were full of a dark red mist and he did not see the blade until it was too late.

Juanito screamed, driving himself forward, further impaling himself on Alex's machete. The blade soon had pierced his abdomen, gone completely through the man, its point visibly emerging from his broad back. Alex rolled away from under the dead weight and got to his knees.

"Behind the desk! Now!" Stoke shouted. Alex saw him rolling across the floor toward the desk as the Chinese guards burst through the door. Alex heard the staccato sound of the Tsao-6 machine guns and saw splinters and fragments from the heavy oval desk flying even as he rolled behind it.

"Christ!" Hawke said to Stoke. "I thought there were only six of them! It's the whole bloody Red Army!"

Guards continued to stream into the glass walled structure and direct fire into the general's desk. Huge chunks were flying off now. It would not take long for the thing to disintegrate.

Stoke saw Juanito's .357 was lying some five feet beyond the desk. If he could reach it—a guard saw his arm stretch out for the gun and there was a loud *thwap* as bullets kicked the pistol beyond any possibility of getting his hands on it.

In a matter of seconds the guards would realize that the two men taking cover behind the desk were completely unarmed.

"Got any ideas?" Alex asked Stoke as they huddled under the withering fire.

"Yeah, I guess it's too late to change the beneficiary on my life insurance," Stoke said. "Everything's going to my ex-wife."

"Well, we could always just shake hands and say—"

Suddenly, there was a huge muffled explosion that shook the glass structure and everything in it.

57

· · · — · ·

The marble floor heaved up and felt as if it might buckle. The automatic weapons fire stopped as the guards dove to the floor. It felt like an earthquake but sounded like thousands of pounds of TNT. The giant chandelier swung crazily from the top of the dome, creating bizarre patterns of light within the curved glass walls.

There was an ominous crack from above, and Alex looked up.

Emanating from the fixture that secured the chandelier, a spiderweb of fissures started to spread in every direction across the glass ceiling above them.

Thin sprays of water started erupting everywhere. You could almost hear the tiny creakings of each little fissure zigzagging across the dome.

"What the devil—" Alex said, looking at Stoke.

"Your new friend Boomer," Stoke said. "His diversionary tactic, remember? Get everybody safely off the beach? Boomer must have just blown the satchel charges of C-4 and limpet mines that Bravo attached beneath the submarine's hull. The main shock wave from that explosion should reach upriver to this grotto in about, oh, three seconds—One!"

Hawke and Stokely sprinted around opposite ends of the desk, smashing through the dazed guards just getting to their feet, headed towards the open door. They saw the massive chandelier hurtling to the floor and dodged it by inches.

"Two!" Stoke screamed, as they dove through the door.

A few of the guards were raising their weapons to fire.

"Three!" They were through!

Behind them the unbearable screeching sound of all that glass finally giving way put paid to any notion of the guards bringing down the two men. Alex, in desperation, tried to slam the wooden door shut behind them, but it was too late. A wall of water was already pouring through the doorway, threatening to overwhelm them. They flew down the narrow stone steps, slipping and sliding all the way to the bottom.

The onrushing tide of water now flooded down the stairwell and into the little foyer with the pretty Picasso. There were pillows, documents, all manner of flotsam and jetsam surrounding him. Alex was totally disoriented. How did we get here? Elevator? Right. He noticed that water had already risen above his knees.

"Ain't no time to wait for that little Chinaman," Stoke said. "Look, here's a door!" The door was invisible, save a thin seam that outlined it. Miraculously, Stoke had seen it, and they slammed into it, splintering it open.

Another stairway, seemingly for service staff, led down into darkness.

Again they descended, the flood of water on their heels, and found another door at the bottom. "Ready?" Stoke said, and they put their shoulders to the wood, breaching it.

This was good. The red-carpeted hallway that led to the main stairway. Which way? Left, Alex decided suddenly. "This way!" he shouted, and Stokely followed. "This is it!" Alex cried. "Hurry!"

They were climbing now, up the great curving staircase they'd descended earlier with the late General Juan de Herreras.

"Good thing about water," Stoke said. "Don't climb steps too good."

They gained the main hallway where they'd first met the recently deceased Juanito and his guards. It was wholly deserted. Both men wished they had grabbed weapons from the guards as they'd left the collapsing room. Alex still had his dive knife at least. Stoke had nothing.

They both knew there had to be tangos gathering outside, perhaps hundreds of them.

With extreme caution, they peered around the massive doors of the entrance. The moon was out now, and the whole compound was bathed in its blue-gold glow. A breeze swayed the palms in a lazy dance.

There was no one inside the perimeter wall that they could see. No one in either guardhouse. Beyond, only the dark wall of jungle. They could see the moonlit sea off to their left. Something was burning out there, sending great tendrils of fire and black smoke licking high into the air.

Nighthawke?

Hawke pushed the thought out of his mind as he and Stoke gingerly made their way down the broad stone steps of the entrance. Unarmed, they had no choice now but to simply make a run for the sea and hope to God somebody was out there waiting in an IBS.

They hadn't taken three steps when the wall of jungle beyond erupted with automatic weapons fire. Hundreds of winking muzzles in the blackness. The air was instantly full of lead, ringing off the ironwork of the gates and fence, kicking up sand at their feet. They dropped to the ground and scrambled back up the steps and inside the entrance of the *finca,* slamming the heavy wooden doors behind them.

"Holy shit!" Stoke said. "The whole damn Cuban army must be out there waiting for us!"

They knelt beneath a window, a hail of bullets showering them with broken glass. Alex saw Stoke pull something from inside his flak vest.

"What the hell is that?" Hawke asked.

"SatCom phone," Stoke said, flicking a switch that lit the thing up. "We get lucky, I can raise Fitz or Boomer."

"Get lucky," Hawke said.

"Bravo, you copy?" Stoke said into the handheld device.

"Copy, Stoke. What's going on?"

"Unexpected delay here. What's burning out there at the LZ? Ain't you, is it?"

"No. Another nosy Cuban patrol boat. We've sunk four. All accounted for here, aboard *Nighthawke*. We're in a holding pattern. An IBS is on its way in for your E&E."

"Yeah, well that's the problem. We ain't evading and we certainly ain't evacuating. We pinned down inside the main hacienda."

"No problem. We'll come ashore and pull you out."

"Belay that, you'd never get ashore. The whole fucking jungle's full of *los tangos cubanos, amigo.*"

"Fuck."

"I was thinking that, too."

"Stoke," Hawke said, tapping him on the shoulder. He had risen and was peering out just above the sill of the shattered window. "They're moving up into position for a frontal assault. I've got an idea."

"All our problems are over, Boomer," Stoke said into the SatCom. "Mr. Hawke here has an idea. Stay tuned. Over."

"Standing by, Skipper, over."

"Follow me," Hawke said.

The rounds were zinging overhead with ever increasing intensity as Hawke motioned for Stoke to follow him. They both ran in a low crouch toward the stairway leading up.

"Remember that terrace we saw?" Hawke said, taking the steps two at a time. "The one built out over the sea?"

"Right," Stoke replied. "What about it?"

"It has to be this way."

"So?"

"If we can reach it, we go over the wall. Can't be more than a fifty-foot drop into the sea from up there."

"Well, it ain't rocket surgery, boss, but it's all we got. Let's go!"

There was a problem with the terrace. The Cubans had thought of it first. Stoke and Alex raced across the broad expanse of white marble and peered down over the edge. There were at least twenty soldiers down there on the rocks with automatic weapons, waiting in case anyone should try to leave the island without saying good-bye. At least ten of them had already started climbing up the rocky cliff that would bring them up to the terrace.

Shots rang out, and pieces of stone just beneath them exploded outwards.

Both men ducked behind the four-foot crushed stone wall that ringed the large patio. The moon was so bright on the expanse of white marble that, if they remained standing, they were as good as dead. Hawke held his breath, waiting to see a grenade come flying over the wall.

"Next idea?" Stoke said.

"I'm thinking," Hawke replied.

"Think faster," Stoke said, but Hawke never heard him.

There was an earth-shattering explosion in the rooms just behind them followed by a deafening roar just over their heads. They caught a glimpse of a massive winged shadow that blocked out the sky, something huge screaming over the rooftops.

"Hell was that?"

"That would be an F/A-18 Super Hornet," Hawke said, a smile spreading across his face. "Black Aces Squadron." Never in his life had Hawke been so happy to see an official representative of the United States Navy.

Two more Hornets roared overhead in quick succession and then three more. The building shook to its foundations with the impact of the Hornets' deadly Sidewinder Aim-9 missiles. Explosions lit up the thick jungle beyond the wall, and Alex heard the screams of wounded soldiers.

Stoke had his SatCom out instantly.

"Boomer! What the hell is going on?"

"U.S. Navy to the rescue, Skipper! Seems like Fidel Castro escaped somehow, got to a phone, and opened Cuban airspace to the American Navy! Friendly fire! Hooo-hahh!!"

"Friendly fire? I'd return their friendly fire if I had any damn bullets! Them flyboys are goddamn shooting at my ass!"

"May I borrow that gadget, Stoke?" Hawke asked.

Stoke handed it to him and Hawke said, "Boomer, this is Hawke. Get that fighter squadron commander on the radio. Tell him he's got two friendlies on the ground. Make that the large west terrace of the main house, facing the sea. We'd appreciate more fire suppression in the jungle and on the rocks beneath the terrace. Our only way out is a jump into the sea, over."

"I've already spoken to him, sir," Boomer said. "He's laying down fire suppression right now, trying to keep the tangos inside the house from rushing you, over."

"How about below the terrace?" Hawke asked. "We're going over the side. And we need to go *now!*"

"Uh, the squadron leader has a better idea, sir. If you look out over the wall, you should be able to see it now."

Stoke and Hawke crept up to the wall and peered over it. What they saw brought, if not tears to their eyes, certainly a hell of a lot of joy into their lives.

Waves of Navy jets were blacking out the stars, the bright flame of rockets igniting under their swept-back wings and screaming toward targets; and there, a few hundred feet below the formations, skimming in just over the wavetops, was the most beautiful sight of all.

A mammoth U.S. Navy SeaKing helicopter headed directly for the terrace, twin .50 cals firing out both sides as it flared up for a landing.

Little more than half an hour later, Alex Hawke was aboard *Nighthawke*, sitting at Vicky's side, holding her hand and whispering to her.

He'd dimmed the lights of the stateroom way down after Froggy had left. The medic had given her something to help her sleep. Hawke couldn't stop staring at her tender profile. There was a thin sheen of perspiration on her forehead, and her long eyelashes were fluttering on her cheeks. Her beautiful auburn hair, burnished with gold in the dim light, was twisted in knots of tangled cobwebs but to Alex she had never looked more beautiful.

He and Stokely had watched the destruction of *Telaraña*, their legs hanging out the open hatch of the SeaKing, sitting on either side of the red-hot .50 cal. The machine gun was still chattering loudly just above their heads as the SeaKing swung out across the island and doubled back over what had been the submarine pen. It was now a blackened pile of twisted steel and broken concrete. Two halves of the Soviet Borzoi-class submarine's hull rose from the rubble. Boomer's charges had broken her spine. The U.S. Navy had finished the job.

"Hey? You the guys took that Russian boomer out?" Alex heard the chopper pilot ask in his headphones.

"Yep," Stoke replied. "That would be us."

"Christ on a bicycle," the pilot said. "How the hell'd you do that?"

"We, uh, used explosives," Stoke replied, and there was no further mike chatter.

The SeaKing was flying at fifty feet, and the tang of sea air and the roar of the wind in the open doors made Hawke forget he hadn't slept in over twenty-four hours. His entire body was thrumming like a wire.

Vicky was safe. With a lot of help from some very brave men, he'd made good on his promise to her father.

The Navy chopper was headed west where the sleek black outline of *Nighthawke* was waiting on the horizon. Behind him, on the rapidly disappearing hump of the island, towers of fire and black smoke were rising from one end of *Telaraña* to the other.

There were other fires along the coast, Hawke saw, rebel strongholds under attack from the deadly Black Aces.

Now, in the soft glow of the cabin lights, Alex watched her sleeping.

"Alex?" Vicky struggled to open her eyes. Her lips were parched and bruised and Alex applied a cool washcloth.

"Shhh," Alex said. "Go to sleep, darling. It's all right now."

"But there's something—"

"There's nothing. Just sleep. We'll have you in your own bed soon."

"No, something I need to tell—important. Please?"

She was straining to rise from the pillow, gripping Alex's arm fiercely. "You've got to know this, Alex. Please," she whispered in a dry, hoarse voice.

"What is it, darling? What could be so important?"

"The guards. Every day. Didn't know I was listening, see? But I did. I did, Alex."

"It doesn't matter now, darling. It's over."

"No! It does matter. I heard . . . I heard . . . something."

"What did you hear, Vicky?" Alex whispered, leaning down so that he could put his ear near her lips.

"They—they were laughing," she said, nearly strangling on the words. "They were laughing about a bomb they had—kill Americans."

"Bomb?" Alex said, his attention now riveted to Vicky's trembling lips.

It had to be Guantánamo. The biological weapon Conch had told him about sitting in *Kittyhawke*'s cockpit on the *JFK* flight deck. Hadn't they found that thing yet? Since the F-14s had attacked he assumed . . . no, that only meant the women and children had been evacuated from the base. The bomb could still be on the base and— Christ, how long did they have before the thing went off?

"A bomb, Alex," Vicky whispered. "They said it was hidden where the Americans would never find—find out. Until too late."

Alex looked at his watch. It was 0520 in the morning. If he remembered correctly, that meant they had about forty minutes until the thing detonated.

"Where, darling, where they did put the bomb?" Alex

could feel his heart trying desperately to get out of his chest.

"A bear," Vicky said in her small, strangled voice.

"Bear?" Alex was sure he'd misunderstood.

"A teddy bear. Not a real bear. That's why . . . why they were all laughing," Vicky managed. Alex lifted her head and gave her a small sip of water.

"Thank you," she said. "They thought it was so funny. The bomb inside the teddy bear. Gave it to . . . to one of the officers' kids," Vicky said, trying to get her eyes open. "Someone hid the bomb inside a little girl's bear. Someone named Gopher, or Gomer, maybe. An American sailor . . . but a Cuban, too. He's the one who hid the bomb inside the bear."

58
· · · — — · ·

"Joe Nettles," squawked the harsh voice on the *Nighthawke*'s radio. "And this better be the most important fucking call you ever made, mister."

"Alexander Hawke here, Admiral. No time to explain who I am. Just ask Admiral Howell or Secretary de los Reyes, but first, just listen."

"Mister, I got a bomb going off here in 'bout half an hour. Talk."

"I have just rescued a hostage from the Cubans. She has important information regarding that bomb."

"Go ahead, son, spit it out for chrissakes!"

"According to Cuban guards she overheard during captivity, you have an extremely lethal biological weapon hidden inside a toy bear."

"What?"

"An American sailor, name sounds like Gopher or Gomer, inserted the weapon inside a teddy bear and gave it to an officer's child as a gift."

A split second of silence was followed by an explosion from the speaker.

"Holy Mother of God!" Nettles screamed. "That stupid asshole who blew himself up! Gomez! Christ! He gave my daughter a big white teddy bear for her birthday! My own goddamn daughter!"

"Sir, I hope this is helpful. I know you—"

"Son, I appreciate the call. My wife, Ginny, and our little baby, Lucinda, and her bear are aboard the *John F. Kennedy* right now, and I hope you'll excuse me but—"

"Certainly, sir," Alex said, but the connection had been broken.

Aboard the *Kennedy,* the secure phone that linked CIN-CATFLT, the commander in chief of the Atlantic Fleet, Admiral George Blaine Howell, to the commanding officer, Guantánamo Naval Air Station, rang on the bridge one second later.

Howell, who was on the *JFK*'s bridge monitoring the takeoffs and landing of nine separate squadrons flying sorties over Cuba, picked it up, knowing who it was.

"Find it yet, Joe?" Howell said.

"Do you know somebody named Alex Hawke?"

"Hell yes, I know him. British billionaire. Ex–Royal Navy. Works for us a lot. Tracked down the boomer the Cubans bought, and definitely on the good-guy side."

"In that case, I've got some bad news, George. The bio-weapon is no longer here at Gitmo. It's aboard Big John."

"What did you say?"

"Hawke has a rescued hostage aboard his vessel who says the bomb's inside a teddy bear given to an officer's child by somebody named Gomez."

"Gomez? Sounds familiar—wasn't he that guy in your minefield couple of days ago?"

"Yeah, same guy. Three weeks ago, the same dickhead gave my daughter Cindy a big white bear for her fourth birthday. It's gotta be the one, George!"

"Jesus Christ, Joe!"

"Yeah. Cindy takes that goddamn bear everywhere. She's got it with her now. That bear is somewhere aboard your flagship, partner."

"How much time have we got, Joe?"

"According to the official Cuban deadline, you've got twenty-nine minutes and sixteen seconds. George, god-dammit, go find my little girl."

"God almighty. Okay, I'm on it."

Admiral Howell hung up and turned to the *JFK*'s CO, Captain Thomas Mooney. "Sound general quarters, Captain. We've got a Level Five biological threat some-where onboard this ship. Came aboard with the evacuees at Gitmo. I've got CDC memos stating that it's probably a highly lethal new bacteria strain, weapons grade, with a delivery system capable of wiping out everyone at Gitmo."

"Yes, sir."

"That bomb is somewhere on this ship. It is hidden inside a toy bear belonging to Gitmo CO Joe Nettles's daughter. I want that goddamn thing found and neutralized. We have less than half an hour."

Within five minutes, Captain Mooney's most trusted aide, Lieutenant Arie L. Kopelman, was sent directly to the converted wardroom where, among others, the Gitmo commander's wife and daughter were housed. He went to C deck, found their room, and opened the door. The sound of snoring filled the room. Everyone was still fast asleep. He looked at his watch. Twenty-two minutes.

Shouldn't be a problem.

He entered the darkened cabin, a wardroom where some twenty-five to thirty women and children were currently berthed and, since he had no description of who he was looking for, simply rapped his fist on the bulkhead.

"Mrs. Nettles?" Kopelman said. "Mrs. Joseph Nettles? Would you and your daughter please step out into the companionway? Sorry to disturb you."

"They're not here," a woman's sleepy voice said. "They were moved yesterday. We were too crowded."

"Where were they moved?" Kopelman asked, trying not to let the rising panic in his voice show.

"I think one deck down. Wardroom D-7?"

"Thank you," Kopelman said, and sprinted for the closest stairwell. He took the steps three at a time and burst into the long companionway of D deck. D-7 would be to the left, toward the bow, he thought. Had to be.

It was. He swung open a door marked D-7 and rapped his knuckles hard on the bulkhead.

"I'm looking for Mrs. Joseph Nettles and her daughter," he said loudly. "Are they in this room?"

"Oh," he heard a woman's voice say. "Yes, we are."

He saw her now, a silhouette sitting up against the far bulkhead. He heard her say, "What on earth do you want?"

"Would you please step out into the companionway? Both of you? It's very important."

Kopelman watched the sweeping second hand on his watch. Less than nineteen minutes now, until the ka-boom or whatever it was. In just over a minute, Mrs. Nettles and her four-year-old daughter were standing in front of him, blinking and rubbing sleep from their eyes. Both were wearing nightgowns and robes. It had taken seconds of precious time to find and put on robes.

"I'm Lieutenant Kopelman. This is your daughter Cindy?"

"Yes. How can we help you, Lieutenant?" Ginny Nettles said, wrapping her robe tightly around her.

"I'm looking, actually, for Cindy's bear," Kopelman said, not caring how foolish he sounded. "I'll explain later. But if you don't mind, ma'am, could you please just step back inside, pick the bear up very carefully, and bring it out here to me?"

"Her *teddy bear*? Is this a joke?"

"No joke, Mrs. Nettles. Believe me."

"Well, I would if I could but I can't. Her bear's not in there, Lieutenant," Ginny Nettles said, giving the young officer a look both quizzical and ominous. "Sorry."

"Not in there?"

"That's what I said."

"This is extremely important, Mrs. Nettles. Where, uh, exactly is the bear as we speak?"

"Excuse me, Lieutenant . . . Kopelman, is it?"

"Yes, ma'am."

"What time is it, Lieutenant?"

"Oh-five-forty-five, ma'am. Fifteen minutes before six A.M., ma'am."

"You know, it's funny. I've been a Navy wife for over thirty years. And I have never, ever encountered anything remotely as ridiculous as this. And that, by God, Lieutenant, is truly saying something!"

"Ma'am, I totally appreciate that. But it is desperately important that I retrieve that bear. Do you understand? I said 'desperately.' I can't say any more."

"What's wrong, Lieutenant?" Mrs. Nettles said, her mood turning from annoyance to concern to fear in less than a second.

"We, I mean Admiral Howell needs that bear now," Kopelman said, looking into her eyes. "That bear is . . . contaminated. Do you understand what I'm saying, Mrs. Nettles? Right *now!*"

"Sweetheart, why don't you tell the nice man where your bear went?" Mrs. Nettles said, bending down to look in her daughter's face.

"Oh!" Cindy said, as if suddenly remembering, "Teddy went up in an air-o-plane!"

"An airplane?" Kopelman asked, his nerves now twanging from the back of his neck down along each arm, all the way to his fingers. He looked at his watch for the third time in as many minutes.

Thirteen minutes.

"That's right, Lieutenant, what my daughter says is true. We ran into Cindy's Uncle Chuck, my husband's younger brother, who is a wing leader of the Black Aces."

"Are you saying that Captain Nettles has the bear,

ma'am?" Kopelman asked. Perfect little beads of nervous perspiration had popped out all around his hairline.

"Yes, I think so," Ginny Nettles said, wringing her hands together, worried about where this was going.

"He took the bear on his mission?"

"Yes, he said his squadron was going on a raid some-where last night and that his niece's bear might bring the Black Aces good luck."

Mrs. Nettles was about to say something else, but the young lieutenant had already sprinted halfway down the companionway and into a stairwell.

"Sir!" Kopelman said, bursting onto the bridge deck.

"What have you got, Lieutenant?" Admiral Howell said, studying his face. "Tell me it's good news, son. We've got about ten minutes till all hell breaks loose."

"I spoke with Mrs. Nettles and her daughter. The bear is with Captain Charles Nettles, sir. He took it along on his mission."

"He's got the fucking bear in his cockpit?"

"I believe he does, yes, sir."

"Are you dead certain about this, son?"

"Aye, aye, sir, as certain as I can be."

Howell punched a button on the bridge console.

"This is Admiral Howell speaking. Where the fuck is Captain Charles Nettles?"

"Captain Nettles is on final, sir, about ten seconds from touchdown," the airboss said.

"Christ! Wave him off, goddammit, wave him off!"

Howell walked outside onto the port bridge-wing and looked astern. He could see all the Black Aces were home, save one. Captain Nettles's F/A-18-E Super Hornet was just off Big John's stern, flared up, seconds from landing.

The yellow shirts were out there, the FSO trying to wave off the fighter. It was too late.

"Lieutenant," Howell said, his voice dead calm. "Would you just go on down to Captain Nettles's cabin and just make sure he didn't leave that goddamn bear there? Is that a good idea?"

"Aye, aye, sir!" Kopelman said, and left the bridge-wing at a dead run.

"He's got his tailhook down, goddammit!" Howell screamed into the mike on the outside console.

"It's jammed, Admiral," the airboss said over the speaker.

"Drop the fucking wire! Have him go to full power! Now!"

"Zulu Bravo Leader go to full power! Bolter! Bolter!" they heard the airboss shout.

There was a howl of turbine whine as the F/A-18's twin turbofan engines instantly spooled up, both afterburners spouting licks of red-orange and yellow flame as she roared past the bridge, accelerating.

"Go . . . go . . . go!" the airboss said as the big fighter rolled and finally lifted off the end of the deck. It immediately dropped, dipped perilously close to the wavetops, then started a climb out.

"Somebody want to tell me what the fuckin' tarnation is going on around here?" said Captain Nettles over the speaker.

"This is Admiral Howell, Captain. How you doin', Chuck?"

"Ah, roger that, pardon my French, Admiral."

"Captain, at the risk of sounding like a complete goddamn moron, let me ask you a question."

"Shoot, sir."

"Do you happen to have a white teddy bear in that air-craft, son?"

"Uh . . . well, as a matter of fact, I do, Admiral."

"You have no idea how happy that makes me, Captain."

"I'm sorry, Admiral, I'm afraid I don't—"

Lieutenant Kopelman appeared at that moment, com-pletely winded, and said, "No bear in his quarters, sir. I turned it upside down!"

"How much time we got left, Lieutenant?" the admi-ral asked, raising his binoculars to his eyes and tracking the jet fighter.

Kopelman looked at his watch. "A minute, thirty-two seconds, sir!"

"Good, good," Howell said, then, into the mike, "Chuck, you're going to need to deep-six that bear, son. Like, right now."

"Sorry, sir?"

"The bear has a weapon in it, son, and it's going to explode in about a minute. Maybe less. Okay? So just take her easy, level off, and reduce your airspeed immediately, you copy that?"

"Copy" was the terse one-word answer.

"Okay, you're looking good, Zulu Bravo. I have you in visual contact. Now, I want you to jettison your canopy."

"Roger that."

The canopy blew off instantly, exposing the pilot and his radar intercept officer seated immediately aft of him to a hundred-knot-plus blast of air. Chuck Nettles felt a shuddering bump and the plane instantly started to yaw left and right.

"I think the canopy clipped the starboard rudder, sir!"

"Yes, it did, Chuck, I saw that. Took out a good-sized chunk. Big old piece. But you've got a more immediate problem. Can you reach that bear?"

"Yes, sir."

"You've got exactly ten seconds to get that bear out of your plane, son."

Admiral Howell waited, tracking his binocs right with the streaking fighter, holding his breath as if that would keep his heart in place. A smile broke across his face.

A small white object flew out of the cockpit, hit the jetstream, and was blasted backwards and down.

He stayed with the bear all the way, saw it hit the water. For a few endless moments, he thought the goddamn thing might float, but a smile broke across his face as he saw the bear slip beneath the waves.

So much for your goddamn airborne spores, *amigos*.

The density of the ocean had instantly neutered the Cubans' weapon.

There was a squawk over the speaker.

"Uh, I'm having a little trouble keeping this bird flying straight," Nettles said over the speaker. "Busted rudder and all. Anybody got any bright ideas?"

"I've had all the good ideas I'm going to have this morning, Chuck. You just saved a lot of lives. I want to thank you for that. I'm going to turn you over to the air-boss now. You just bring that big sucker on home, son. Bring her down safely. There'll be a box of Cuban Montecristos with your name on it waiting in my ward-room."

"Copy that," Captain Nettles said, trying desperately not to let the effect of the blown canopy, destroyed rudder, and the fact that he'd just flown an entire mission with a bomb between his knees show in his voice.

"Bravo Zulu, you are a quarter mile out," the airboss said. "Turn right to 060 degrees."

"I can't do that, she's not responding to rudder."

"Well, you're going to have to land that bird with ailerons and elevators, Bravo Zulu, just like you did out at Coronado in flying school."

"I can't remember back that far, sir."

"Bravo Zulu, you play a little golf, don't you?"

"Affirmative."

"Slice or hook?"

"Slice a little."

"Know how you aim a teensy bit left to correct for that slice?"

"Affirmative."

"You got a little slice in your current stance. I want you to shift your aim left, copy?"

"Left."

"Easy, easy. Not that much, boy. A teensy. You want to draw it in down the left side of the fairway."

"How's that?"

"Call the ball, Bravo Zulu."

"I have the ball, sir."

"Come on home, then, Bravo Zulu. Come on home to Papa John."

59

•••————•••

The third-story sitting room of the old house in Belgrave Square was lit only by a roaring fire. Pelting rain beat against the room's tall, broad windows. The upper branches of the plane and elm trees outside, dancing violently in the howling wind, clawed and scratched at the glass.

It was a cold, sleeting rain, but the roaring fire Pelham had laid in the great hearth warmed the room and kept the chill of late evening at bay.

Savage filaments of lightning briefly illuminated the whole room, where two people sat side by side on an immense sofa before a crackling blaze. The lightning was followed immediately by an earth-splitting thunderclap powerful enough, it seemed, to shake a good portion of London to its ancient foundations. In the silence that followed, the woman rested her head on the man's shoulder and spoke in a quiet, sleepy voice.

"My daddy used to say that all the great romances are made in heaven. But so are thunder and lightning."

Alex Hawke laughed softly, and brushed back a wing of auburn hair, bronzed by the firelight, from her pale forehead. Her eyes were closed, and her long dark lashes lay upon her cheeks, fluttering only when either of them spoke.

"Amazing chap, your father," Hawke whispered. "Everything he says seems to have quotation marks at either end."

"A lot of them are unprintable," Vicky said, yawning deeply, and pressing closer. "He has a few enormously politically incorrect opinions and he's an ornery old cuss when you cross him."

"What did he have to say when you rang him up this afternoon?"

"Not much. Sounded very shaky. It's going to take him a while to get over all those roller-coaster emotions. I promised I'd come right away to look after him. I'm so sorry. I know you were counting on me to—"

"Shh. I understand. You sound tired, Doc."

"I am, a little. We must have walked the width and breadth of every park in London. It was lovely. My dream of a foggy day in London Town."

"We missed one. Regent's Park," Alex said, stroking her hair. "I wanted to show you Queen Mary's rose garden. Why are we whispering?"

"I don't know. You started it. When one person starts, the other just does it automatically. Funny. Do you want some more tea?"

"What I'd love is a small brandy. Curious. I haven't seen Pelham lurking about in the last hour or two."

"I saw him sitting in the pantry just after dinner. Sniper was perched on his shoulder, chattering away, while Pelham was doing needlepoint. Very fancy if you ask me, Lord Fauntleroy. What is it?"

"I'm embarrassed to tell you. It's to be a birthday present. For me, in fact. A waistcoat with the family crest. I've tried to convince him to quit before he goes blind, but he feigns deafness whenever I do."

At that very moment, there was the creak of an

ancient door, and the omniscient Pelham Grenville entered the room bearing a large silver tray, which he placed upon the ottoman before the fire.

"Begging your pardon, m'lord. That last flash and clap made me think a splash of brandy might be welcomed."

"The man is a mind reader, I tell you," Hawke said, reaching for the heavy crystal decanter. "Thank you kindly, young Pelham."

Hawke noticed that, in addition to the decanter and small thistle-shaped crystal glasses, there was a most peculiar box on the tray. It was triangular and made of yellowed ivory, with a hawk carved of onyx embedded in the center of the lid.

"I've never seen that box before, Pelham," Alex said. "Quite beautiful."

"Yes," Pelham said. "It was a gift to your great-grand-father from David Lloyd-George himself. Something to do with a political triad long lost to the mists of history."

"Too small for cigars," Alex observed.

"Indeed," Pelham said. "Do you mind if I sit a moment?"

"You may sit as long as you wish, of course. Here, let me pour you a brandy," Alex said, and he did so.

Pelham pulled up a leather winged-back chair and sat down with a small sigh. He sipped at his brandy, then picked up the box and turned it over in his hands. He focused his clear blue eyes on Hawke.

"Your lordship, I've been in service for nigh on seventy years. And for the last thirty years, I've been waiting for this exact moment," the old fellow finally said. Then he downed the brandy in one swallow and held out his glass to Hawke for a refill. This done, he sat back against the cushion and looked about the room. The firelight was licking every corner of the huge space, even reaching up into the ceiling moldings high above them.

"I don't really know quite where to begin, your lordship," he said at last.

"I find the beginning is usually appropriate," Hawke said with a gentle laugh. But Pelham was not amused.

" 'Tis a serious matter I've come to discuss, m'lord."

"Sorry," Alex said, and getting to his feet, he began pacing back and forth before the fire, hands clasped behind his back. Something fairly momentous was afoot.

"Your grandfather left this box for you in my trust. He was very clear about its disposition. I was to give it to you as soon as I felt that you were in a sufficiently proper state of mind to receive it."

"I see," Alex said, nervously glancing over at him. "A proper state of mind, you say. All very mysterious, old thing."

"Yes. But he had his reasons, as you'll soon see."

"And you've obviously concluded I'm in this so-called proper state now?"

"Indeed, I have, m'lord," Pelham said, a smile passing across his face. "It's been a fairly rough go for you. Especially since your dear grandfather passed on. We all miss him. But I think he would agree that you have traveled long and lonely through a deep dark wood and have just now emerged into a most sunny place."

"If you mean by all that, that after a bit of hard sledding I have come to feel as happy as any man has a right to be, then you're correct. I have. Wouldn't you agree, Victoria?"

She was about to say "Happy as a clam," thought better of it, and said, "Never happier."

"See? And, as you well know, Victoria is something of a psychiatrist. So, assuming the matter of my current blissful state is settled, hand over the goods, young Pelham! Let's take a look!" He held out his hand.

Pelham extended the box, and Hawke took it.

"Like a mystery novel," Hawke said, running the tips of his fingers over the lid and smiling at them both. "Isn't it?"

He placed the strange white box upon the mantelpiece, beneath the mammoth painting of the Battle of Trafalgar. Looking at the box from different angles, Hawke continued his pacing. "Only usually a good mystery writer will stick these intriguing objects right up front to hook the reader."

"For heaven's sakes, open it, Alex," Vicky said. "I can't wait to see!"

"So, in other words," Hawke said, looking carefully at Pelham, "Grandfather wanted me to have this box when I had come to grips with—what shall we call it—the past?"

"Precisely, m'lord," Pelham said, eyes shining.

"Well, then, in that case I think this historic event deserves a toast! Pelham, would you pour us each a wee dram of that fine brandy?"

Hawke received his brandy and stood, glass in one hand, the other up on the mantelpiece. He swirled the amber liquid in the snifter and then lifted it in the direction of Vicky and Pelham.

"A toast," Alex Hawke said, "if you don't mind."

When they, too, raised their glasses, he said, "I would like to drink to the memory of my dear mother and father," Hawke began, his eyes brimming.

Vicky thought his voice would break, but he continued. "These are memories that have only recently come back to me. But as they do come flooding back, they are filled with a joy and happiness I never knew existed. My father was a splendid fellow, handsome and brave beyond measure."

"Oh, Alex!" Vicky cried, and there were tears in her eyes.

"My mother—my mother was equally endowed with strength, kindness, and beauty. And she possessed all three in abundance. In the seven short years we had together, she managed to instill in the boy whatever few qualities or virtues the man might have."

A sob escaped Vicky's trembling lips.

Alex put the glass to his lips and drank deeply.

"To my mother and father," Alex said, and flung his empty glass into the fire, shattering it against the blackened bricks.

"Hear! Hear!" Pelham shouted, rising to his feet. He raised his glass to Hawke, eyes glistening, downed the brandy in one swallow, then threw his glass into the fireplace. Seconds later, Vicky's glass followed his into the fire as well.

"And now at last the mysterious box!" Hawke said, drawing the back of his hand across his eyes. "Let's see what's inside it, shall we?"

He took the box from the mantel, looked at it for a long moment, and then slowly lifted the lid.

"Why, it's a key!" he said, and lifted out a large brass key by the black satin ribbon attached to it. "Where there's a key, there's a lock."

"Yes," Pelham said. "There is. If you'll both follow me?"

Vicky and Alex followed him out into the great hall and then began ascending the broad curving staircase, a spiral that formed the center of the entire house. There was a skylight at the very top of the great mansion and flashes of lightning pierced down into the gloom. Pelham, a Scot, never lit any more lights in the house than were absolutely necessary.

"Where are we going, old thing?" Hawke asked, as they passed the fourth-floor landing and continued upwards.

"To my rooms, your lordship," Pelham said simply.

"Your rooms? What on earth is—"

A violent crack of lightning struck just then, quite nearby, and Vicky cried out, grabbed Alex's arm, and held on. The few staircase lights that were lit flickered twice and then went out. The whole house was plunged into darkness.

"Not to worry, miss," Pelham said. "I always carry a small electric torch on my person for just such occasions."

He flicked the flashlight on and they continued their procession, mounting to the sixth floor of the house.

"Just along here," Pelham said, "at the end of the hall."

"I don't believe I've ever been to your rooms, Pelham," Hawke said.

"Ah, but you have done, m'lord," he said, opening the door to his quarters. "Many's the time we'd return from an evening out on the tiles and you'd insist on having 'one and done' by my fireside before bed. I'd throw a blanket over you on the sofa and try to ignore the horrific snoring."

"Try the lights," Vicky said. "They just came back on down the hall."

Pelham flicked a switch, and two sconces on either side of his small coal-burning hearth came on. It was a simple room, yet rich with books and paintings.

"Let me guess," Hawke said, dangling the key from its ribbon. "There's an ancient chest up here, full of priceless gold and silver heirlooms."

Pelham, meanwhile, had opened a farther door and motioned them to enter.

"What's this?" Hawke said.

"My clothes closet, your lordship."

"Your closet?"

"Indeed, sir. At the very rear, you shall find another door, hidden behind all my old jackets and frocks. It's been locked for thirty years. The key will open it."

"I'd no idea you were such a clothes-hound," Hawke said from inside the closet. "All these linen blazers and— what? Here it is! A hidden door!"

Alex turned the key and pushed the door open. A cold musty wind brushed his cheeks as he and Vicky entered the dark room, brushing cobwebs aside.

"Oh, my God," Alex said.

Casting the beam of the flashlight about the room, Alex saw that it was filled to the rafters with all the fur-nishings, toys, and objects of the first seven years of his life.

Atop a dusty leather chest, he spied a red rubber ball.

"I used to toss this ball into the sea," he told Vicky in hushed tones. "My dog Scoundrel would plunge in and fetch it. And look here!

"This was my pram, isn't it wonderful? Father

designed it to look like a fishing dory on wheels. And here, the picture that hung above my bed. And all my armies of soldiers, and—"

"Alex, come here," Vicky said.

"What is it?"

"A painting," she said. "One of the loveliest paintings I've ever seen."

Later that evening, with Pelham's help, Alex managed to take down *The Battle of Trafalgar*, which had hung for a century or so above the fireplace. Then, mounting the tall stepladder once more, he hung the painting Vicky had uncovered in Pelham's hidden room.

"Is it straight?" Alex asked from atop the ladder.

"Perfectly straight, darling," Vicky said. "Come down and see!"

Alex returned to the sofa without looking back and sat beside Vicky. Then he raised his eyes to the painting.

His father and mother soon after their wedding day.

Mother was seated, wearing the beautiful white lace dress she'd made famous in *The White Rose*. Father stood at her side in his splendid uniform, his hand on her bare shoulder. A scarlet sash across his chest bore all of his many decorations, and he wore Marshal Ney's famous sword at his waist.

He and Vicky sat silently, side by side, staring up at the faces of the happy couple. Alex put his arm around her shoulders and pulled her closer.

He kissed her warm lips, unashamed of the tears of joy and relief that finally, after all these years, he allowed to course down his cheeks.

★ ★ ★

Pelham found the two of them sleeping on the sofa wrapped in each other's arms. He placed the fur coverlet over them, stifled a yawn, and walked out into the hall. It was half past one and he was anxious for his warm bed.

He'd no sooner mounted the first step than he heard the sound of the bell downstairs. The front door! At this hour? Madness.

He descended to the ground floor, muttering to himself about what kind of fool would be out on a night like this, especially at this hour. The bell rang once more.

He swung the wide door open.

There was a man standing there in the pouring rain. He wore a long black cloak, buttoned closely about him. His face was hidden by a large black umbrella.

"Yes?" Pelham said, not bothering to be polite.

"Is this the home of Lord Alexander Hawke?" the man asked.

"Lord Hawke has retired for the evening. Who shall I say is calling?"

"Just give him this," the man said, and handed Pelham a small gold medallion. The old butler looked at it in the light of the carriage lamp mounted beside the door. It was a medal of some sort, a St. George's medallion. He turned it over. On the reverse were Alex's initials and the date of his seventh birthday.

"What do you mean by this? What is—"

"Just give it to him," the man said. As he turned to go, Pelham caught the barest glimpse of his face. He was astounded by what he saw.

The man's eyes had no color. No color at all.

60

"I sure am glad you were able to make it down here, Mr. Hawke," the senator said. "Mighty glad."

"Thank you for inviting me," Hawke said, taking another sip of the delicious whiskey. It was more like some locally grown nectar than any whiskey he'd ever tasted. It was Maker's Mark, the senator's favorite, and he'd brought along a bottle as a house gift.

"Little early to be drinking fine bourbon where you come from, I suppose," the senator said.

"Oh, I'm sure the sun is over the yardarm in some formerly far-flung outpost of the British Empire, sir."

They were seated in a pair of old rockers out on the verandah, gazing down the long allée of pecan trees in full bloom that led all the way to the levee. There were three or four sleepy bird dogs puddled on the steps. The late-afternoon air was cool and heavily scented with the arrival of spring.

Looking over the sprig of mint in his glass, Hawke was thinking he'd never seen a more beautiful place. The sun was a thin band of bright orange and scarlet, lying just along the top of the levee. Everywhere he looked, riots of color had broken out. Redbud trees grew just beyond the faded white railing, and beyond them were azaleas bursting with clouds of coral and pink blossoms. The enormous old rhododendron bushes that rose up to the second and third floors of the house were heavy with crimson blooms.

There was the hoot of a boat, somewhere out on the river.

"You know, my dear wife didn't care much for whiskey, Mr. Hawke," the senator said, with a tinkle of ice cubes and looking over at Hawke with a smile.

"I think a lot of women don't, Senator."

"I agree," the senator said, "but Sarah, well, she had *convictions* about it. None of 'em very favorable, I might add, sir."

"Well," Hawke said, rocking back in his chair, "I've got convictions about those little tiny watercress sandwiches some ladies seem to favor."

"Now, that's damn well said."

They were silent for a few moments, savoring the whiskey and the companionship of the dusky hour, and then the senator again turned toward Alex with a happy grin on his face.

"You know, I used to say that trying to sneak a second whiskey past my Sarah was like trying to sneak dawn past a rooster!"

Alex laughed and raised his glass, clinking it against the senator's.

"That's quite good," Alex said. "Another quotation."

"Son . . . you ever seen a bona fide Parker Sweet Sixteen?"

He picked up a double-barreled shotgun that had been leaning against one of the massive fluted columns beside his rocking chair.

"No, sir, I don't believe I—"

"Finest upland bird gun a man could ever . . ." The senator stopped, overcome by emotion. "Good God almighty,

Mr. Hawke, I don't want to talk about any damn guns. What I been trying to say to you, what I been meaning to do since the minute I laid eyes on you, is to thank you, sir, from the bottom of my heart, from the very bottom of my heart, for what you did."

Alex saw there were tears welling in the old man's eyes.

"Well, I—"

"No, no, I don't want to hear any of your self-deprecating nonsense. No. You found my little girl and you brought her home, just like you said you would, only—"

The senator had to stop and pull his handkerchief from the breast pocket of his old hunting jacket. He rubbed it roughly across his face and stuffed it back inside the pocket.

"Only she's sitting out there right now in the top of that old oak tree of hers writing her new book instead of . . . instead of buried beneath—" The old man bent down and scratched one of his dogs behind the ears. He couldn't continue.

"What's her new book about?" Alex asked, trying to help the old fellow through the moment.

"Pirates, I think," he replied, not looking up.

"Does she still not know I'm here?" Alex asked after a few moments had passed.

" 'Course she don't know!" the senator exclaimed. "She hasn't got the foggiest notion I called you either. But, well, she's been down here with me for over a month now. Not a lot to do around here and I could see on her face she was pinin' away for you. Plain as day."

"Did she talk about what happened, Senator?" Hawke asked.

"Well, she told me a little. I didn't push her. She was funny. Said it was like some ride at Disney World, 'Pirates of the Caribbean with Live Ammunition,' she said. But she was pretty shaky when I picked her up at the airport down in N'Orleans. I still don't know how those damn Cubans abducted her in the first place."

"I'm still trying to put it all together, sir. She'd gone to a club the night before our picnic. She told me she spoke to a Russian at the bar that night. She'd suffered a mild concussion, you know, and she doesn't really remember, but she may have unwittingly told him our plans for the next day. I don't know. At any rate, the Cuban submarine I was tracking was in those waters at the time. And the Cubans at that point were trying to use Vicky to get to me. Suddenly, there was an opportunity for a kidnapping."

"I still don't understand how they managed to get hold of her," the senator said. "Out in the water."

"My guess is that they did know our plans that day. They hid in the trees on the small island just across the cut from the one I'd chosen for the picnic. They probably had us under optical surveillance, waiting for an opportunity. And when Vicky went swimming alone, they had it."

"But you would have seen them, right, Mr. Hawke?"

"Normally, yes, but she was taken from below. Vicky was grabbed by the ankles and pulled underwater by two Cuban thugs wearing scuba gear. Apparently they called themselves Julio and Iglesias. They're the ones she overheard bragging about the bomb being hidden in the teddy bear. Anyway, they dragged her ashore, hid her in the pines, and they were all picked up by the Cubans' submarine later that night."

"Did they hurt her, Mr. Hawke? Tell me the truth. Did those people harm my little girl?"

"No, sir, they did not. She was smart and brave and used her wits to stay alive. But I would say we arrived pretty much in the nick of time."

The senator just nodded his head and took a sip of his drink. In the silver ice bucket at his elbow, there was a lovely sound as ice melted and shifted.

"Needless to say, I'm forever in your debt, sir," he said finally, turning away.

The crickets had come alive now, and great billowing flocks of blackbirds filled the flaming skies above the oaks and elms and pecan trees.

"Times like this, I sometimes think of Tom and Huck and Jim out there on the river, Mr. Hawke. Poling their raft along the bank, looking for somewhere to tuck in safe for the night."

"Yes," Hawke agreed, for the first time realizing that this really was it. The real McCoy, his mother had called it. The mighty, the muddy, the one and only.

M-i-s-s-i-s-s-i-p-p-i.

"My mother was an American," Hawke said, gazing out at the river. "She grew up on the Mississippi, Senator. Somewhere south of here. Near New Orleans. I've never been here before. But I'd like to stay a few days. Maybe Vicky and I could wander down the River Road, try to find her old place. Then, maybe, spend the afternoon in New Orleans."

"I'm sure Vicky would love that, sir."

"*Laissez les bon temps roulez,*" Hawke said.

"You speak French, Mr. Hawke?"

"Let the good times roll. It was my mother's favorite expression. She was teaching me French. Creole patois, I guess. And then—"

"I know all about it, son."

"Mr. Senator?" A screen door swung open and an ancient fellow in a beautiful green felt jacket with brass buttons stepped onto the verandah.

"Say hello to Horace Spain, Mr. Hawke. He's been running the joint for the last seventy or eighty years."

"Pleasure to make your acquaintance, Mr. Hawke," the old fellow said, stepping out through the pools of yellow light spilling from the windows. "I believe we spoke on the telephone late one evenin'. That shore was a sad time in this old place, suh."

"Yes, I'm sure it was," Hawke said, shaking his hand. "A very sad time."

"Mr. Senator? What time we fixin' to have supper this evenin'? Miss Vicky run off without saying nothing to nobody, and Cook, she fit to be tied what with us havin' company coming in all the way from England and all."

"You getting hungry?" the senator asked Alex. "I hope you like honey-fried chicken, black-eyed peas, dirty rice, and hush puppies."

"Senator, I'm so hungry right now I could eat a watercress sandwich."

"Now that's hungry, sir, that's mighty hungry."

The senator picked up his silver-headed cane and rose slowly to his feet. He stood for a moment or two, gazing out beyond the long row of trees to the river. There was a big oak tree atop the levee, with three huge branches starkly silhouetted against the evening sky.

It was, Hawke knew, the Trinity Oak. The place where Vicky felt closest to God.

"Well, hell, son," he said. "What do you say we mosey on down to the river and fetch that little gal home to supper? What do you say about that?"

EPILOGUE

· · · — · ·

"You're teed up too high."

"Sorry?"

"Your ball is teed up too high. That's why you've been popping them up in the air like Ping-Pong balls," Ambrose Congreve said.

"Ah, that's it, then. Thank you."

"Not at all."

"Nothing more?"

"Not a thing."

"You're quite finished with your tutorial?" Sutherland asked.

"Quite."

"Good," Sutherland said, and swung his seven iron. The ball rose cleanly and majestically from the tee, soared over the treacherous patch of ocean and bunkers that guarded the green, and landed softly about three feet shy of the pin. An easy birdie.

"Hmm," Congreve said. He coughed, saying something that might or might not have been "Jolly good."

"Always take the cookies when they're passed," Sutherland said, stepping aside. "A lucky shot."

Congreve strolled up to the tee box and stood gazing at the tiny patch of green some hundred and sixty yards away. A late-afternoon fog had rolled in from the ocean, making an already difficult hole even more challenging.

To his right was the dense thicket of a palm grove and sea-grape. On his left, waves broke upon the shoreline of jagged coral that gave the world-famous golf course its name. *Dientes de Perro.*

The Teeth of the Dog.

"Oh. Did I tell you I received a postcard from Stokely this morning?" Congreve asked Sutherland, bending to tee up his ball. Having witnessed his opponent's brilliant shot, he now seemed in no hurry to take his own.

"I don't believe you did. Where was it from?"

"He's vacationing in Martinique. Most amusing thing. It seems he's been decorated."

"Decorated? By whom?"

"Fidel Castro, of all people."

"No."

"It's true. He received a mysterious package in the post last week."

"Yes?" Sutherland asked, trying not to sound impatient. They were fast losing light with still a few good holes to play.

"It seems he got a very grand medal of some sort. The Cuban equivalent of the *Legion d'Honneur.*"

"Ironic, wouldn't you say?"

"Most extraordinary."

"Chief, I believe it's your shot," Sutherland said, when he could stand it no longer.

"One doesn't rush a delicate par three, Sutherland."

Congreve hitched up his woolen plus fours, which, Sutherland imagined, must be brutally hot in this heat, and addressed his ball.

He then swung the club—and watched in horror as his ball hooked sharply to his left, careened off the jagged coral, and disappeared over the top of the rocks.

"Rotten luck," Sutherland said. "Hit another."

"Oh, I think I can find that one," Congreve said. "Dead low tide. I might just have a shot off the beach."

Sutherland watched his colleague disappear down through a small opening in the coral that led to the sea. There was barely room enough for someone of Congreve's girth to slip through. Sutherland looked at his watch. At the rate they were playing, and with this fog and storm front moving in, it was unlikely they'd finish this farewell match.

It was their last day here at La Romana, on the north coast of the Dominican Republic.

The golf, Sutherland had to admit, had been brilliant. The course was exquisite, the weather had been superb. Even Congreve's eccentricities on the golf course had been more amusing than distracting.

The treasure hunt, however, had been more than disappointing. Using a copy of Blackhawke's map, they'd located the *Boca de Chavon* River the very first day and their hopes had been sky high. Caves much like the ones described in Blackhawke's own hand abounded along the treacherous coast.

Following the old pirate's instructions to the letter, and using a hired motorboat, they'd combed this part of the coastline ten times over and come up empty. Since many of the cave mouths were constantly underwater, even at low tide, Sutherland had the task of getting Congreve comfortable with snorkeling. After a couple of dives, he seemed to actually enjoy it. The two men had explored some of the more promising caves many times over, only to come up empty-handed.

Each evening after dinner Congreve would take his leave, while Sutherland remained in the company of the ladies in the bar at Casa de Campo. Using oil lanterns, spades, and pickaxes, Ambrose, who, unlike Sutherland, seemed to have limitless patience and energy, would dig all night. And still the man had been on the first tee at eight sharp every single morning.

Sutherland had to admire Congreve's bulldog tenacity. The man had entered countless caverns and crevasses, and spent many hours in the tireless, frustrating, and physically demanding search. He was never without a folding entrenching tool that fit in his pocket. Pipe clenched firmly between his teeth, the man was constantly digging. Sutherland stuck with him. But the words "pipe dreams" had begun to flicker across Sutherland's consciousness more times than he would ever admit to Congreve.

He looked again at his watch. The man had been gone a good ten minutes. Five minutes was the maximum one was allowed to search for a lost ball. Congreve, however, would rather do anything than take a penalty stroke for a lost ball and tee up a fresh one.

Nothing to do but go fetch him.

Sutherland slipped through the opening in the coral and emerged into a small crescent-shaped grotto, white sand ringing the gently lapping opalescent blue water.

Somehow, they'd missed this tiny cove. It was invisible from the sea.

He immediately saw Congreve's seven iron leaning against the jagged coral beside a small opening in the rock.

At that moment, the sun dipped below the thick purplish band of clouds that lay along the horizon. It sent brilliant shafts of gold streaking across the water and into the crooked mouth of the cave. What had been a dark hole in the rock was now lit up like a tube station.

Sutherland ducked inside and took three or four steps forward. The walls of the cave were tinged a brilliant gold by the sunlight streaming in.

"Hullo," he shouted, cupping his hands round his mouth. "Where have you got to, Chief? If your ball's in here, it's clearly unplayable!"

A voice came back to him from deep inside the cave.

"Sutherland!" he heard the voice say. "Come here! You must have a look at this!"

Ross Sutherland dropped the golf club still in his hand and ran forward to find his friend. He was at the rear of the cave, and Sutherland was astounded to see him kneeling next to his golf ball in a shallow pit. Remarkable. Could his ball have ricocheted off the walls of the little coral cove outside and found its way back here? Was it physically possible? Ross had seen golf balls do stranger things.

But Congreve was paying no attention to his ball. He was digging furiously with his portable entrenching tool. He stopped and looked up at Sutherland, his face beaming in the golden light.

"Here's our first victim, Sutherland," he said. "I'm now looking for the second chap."

"Victim?" Ross asked.

Congreve picked up an oddly shaped whitish object and scraped off some of the wet sand that still clung to it.

"Murder victim, actually. One half of a double homicide. A cold case for some three hundred years. The other half has to be somewhere in the immediate vicinity. Here, take a look."

He tossed the object to Sutherland, who turned it in his hands. It was a human skull.

"Good Lord," Sutherland said as a tiny scorpion crawled out of one gaping eye socket.

"Turn it over. Severe skull fracture, as you will see. Blunt instrument, obviously. A blow to the back of the head. Never saw it coming, poor chap. He and his mate were leaning over with their lanterns, staring at the hundred-odd bags of gold lying at the bottom of the hole, this hole, when the pirate Blackhawke swung his mighty spade."

"Absolutely astonishing, Inspector!" Sutherland exclaimed, and turned to go. "I'm off, then!"

"I say, old boy," Congreve said, "where the devil do you think you're going with my evidence?"

"Back to the hotel to retrieve all of our torches and shovels, of course! I'm also going to put in a call to Alex Hawke. Tell him that after all these years you've finally managed it."

"Managed what?"

Sutherland laughed. "Why, your most cherished dream, Inspector. A hole in one!"

ATRIA BOOKS
PROUDLY PRESENTS

PIRATE

TED BELL

Coming soon from Atria Books
in hardcover

Turn the page for a preview of
Pirate. . . .

Cannes

Hawke emerged under the hotel's porte cochere entrance, pausing for a moment to see if his scalp itched or if his spine tingled. On assignment abroad, one expects to be watched. He saw no quickly averted head, or raised newspaper, however, and so he turned right, descending the gently curving drive that led to the avenue. There was little traffic, and he sprinted across the four lanes and grassy median to the beach promenade. Following the curve of the harbor west along le Croisette, he kept the *Star* in view on his left. From this distance, it looked like normal departure preparations were under way.

Beyond the twinkling lights of the Vieux Port, the glittering coastline lay like a necklace beneath the dark sky. He was, he thought, ready. It promised to be a simple business, to be sure, but it was not in Hawke's nature to pursue any objective with less than the maximum of his ability.

A pair of rope-soled espadrilles had replaced his evening shoes. Here in the south of France, the thin canvas shoes were conveniently stylish and stealthy. Moments before, approaching a brightly lit carousel just outside the Palais du Festival, he had spied an elderly man shivering in the cold. He bequeathed his tie, waistcoat, and dinner jacket to the chap and kept moving.

Walking quickly toward the palm-lined fringes of the marina, he spoke softly into the lipmike of his wireless Motorola.

"Hawke," he said.

"Quick," a distinctly American voice replied in his earpiece. "Good evening, sir." Former army sniper Sergeant Tommy Quick was responsible for security aboard *Blackhawke*.

"Hi, Tommy," Hawke said. "How do we look for this thing?"

"All the telephoto surveil monitors look good, sir. Normal last-minute activity aboard the subject vessel. Ship's radio officer has been monitoring the *Star*'s transmissions and reports business as usual. Idle chitchat. A pair of cargo cranes loading the midships hold now, as you can probably see from where you are. Looks like heavy equipment. She got her final departure clearance from the port authority an hour ago, confirmed a midnight sailing."

"Good."

"Skipper, again, I have to urge you to reconsider some backup. I don't want—"

"It's a civilian vessel, Tommy. Not military. The hostage is being smuggled out to China by a single guard. I'm good."

"With all due respect, sir, I really gotta say—"

Hawke cut him off. "I'm allowing myself just twenty minutes. Time. Mark."

"Yes, sir. Time: coming up on 23:29.57 GMT . . . and . . . mark."

"Mark. Twenty-three thirty GMT. Twenty minutes. Mark."

"Sir, I confirm a fast Zodiac standing off the vessel's portside stern at precisely twenty-three fifty."

"Zodiac mission code?"

"She's mission-coded Chopstick One. Twin Yamaha HPDI 300s. She'll get you out of there in a hurry. I say again, sir, I believe there should be at least minimal backup. If you'd only—"

Hawke cut him off again.

"Tommy, if I can't handle a simple snatch aboard an old rust-bucket like this I really ought to pack it in. Chopstick One, stand by and confirm pickup at eleven-five-oh. Okay? Chop-chop!"

"Aye, aye, sir. There is one thing—"

"Make it snappy. I'm about to do this."

"If you look back up at your hotel, sir, you'll see someone standing out on your terrace with binoculars trained on you. One of my guys has a long telephoto on her now. She's . . . uh . . . not wearing much, sir."

"That will be all, Sergeant," Hawke said.

He snapped his mobile shut and quickened his pace. He had deliberately left the Ikons hanging on the balustrade, left behind like all the few recently acquired and untraceable possessions in his suite. But why the hell would she—he paused and looked back at the Carlton.

With the naked eye, he could just make out Jet's tiny black silhouette standing at the balcony of his suite. There was a glowing orange dot, her cigarette. He smiled and waved. The glow was immediately extinguished. Interesting behavior. Was she sad that he'd left or curious about where he was going? Make a mental note, old boy.

Hawke made his way past the long row of charter boats, all moored stern-to, in the Mediterranean style, and then out along the curvature of an outer breakwater that culminated in a deepwater pier. There was a trickle of passersby, mostly lovers linked arm in arm, out for a stroll now that the weather had changed. Otherwise, the harbor was quiet. The only activity was dead ahead where the *Star of Shanghai* was moored. Lights atop a pair of very tall cranes created an oasis around the ancient steamer. At her stern, the faded red flag of the People's Republic of China hung limply in the light breeze.

All the intel he had from Admiral "Blinker" Godfrey at DNI Gibraltar and his old friend Brick Kelly, the new director at Langley, suggested this nocturnal visit of his would be a complete surprise to the Chinese operatives on board the *Star*. One of them was a Tu-We secret police officer whose dossier Hawke had read twice just to make sure he wasn't seeing things. The man, whose home base was an ancient enclave on the Huang-p'u River, was apparently a human killing machine.

On the plus side, the Chinese skipper aboard the old tramp steamer had no idea the Americans even knew for certain their deep-cover man had gone missing. He'd simply missed a pickup in Morocco, that's all. Happened all the time. Besides, this guy Brock, whoever he was, was a NOC. Such agents, captured in the line of duty, were simply dead men, no questions asked, no answers given. Unless Hawke got him out, his slow death at the hands of the world's most sophisticated torturers was a given.

More importantly, his superiors at Langley would never learn what secrets were imprinted upon his brain. Kelly wanted him alive. Badly.

Hawke stepped over a mooring line running from a hawser on the *Star*'s stern to a bollard on the deepwater pier and brought the scene before him into focus.

A couple of seamen were lounging at the stern rail, smoking cigarettes, watching the fog roll into the harbor. Most of the crew was engaged with the loading going on amidships. There was a single lookout standing at the bow. They'd posted a pair of standard-issue guards at the foot of the gangway. Both were wearing greasy orange slickers with rain hoods. One of them was looking at him now, carefully observing his approach. Unlike most such practitioners of his chosen field, this one looked almost alert. Hawke plastered a drunken smile on his face, dropped his right shoulder, and walked loosely towards the man, concealing the narrow blade along the inside of his right forearm.

"Beggin' yer pardon, Cap'n," Hawke said slurrily to the big fellow, laying his left hand easily on his shoulder. "This wouldn't be the HMS *Victory*, now, would it? Nelson's barky? Seems I've lost me bloody ship."

The guard sneered, showing his unfortunate teeth, and reached inside his slicker for a weapon.

Hawke instantly inserted the long, thin blade precisely five millimeters below the man's sternum and upward into the thoracic cavity on his left side, found the heart, and ruined it. One small gasp . . . his eyes went vacant.

Before the first man was dead, Hawke turned and performed an identical procedure on the second, smaller guard. He caught the newly deceased by the collar of his orange waterproof and let him fall silently to the concrete, the dead man's arms sliding out of the sour-smelling garment as he did so.

In a trice, Hawke shouldered himself into the slicker and raised the hood so that his face was in shadow. As he did, he stifled the wave of self-disgust that usually accompanied such vicious and unexpected violence. He actually hated killing, though it was his duty. He took pride in doing it well. It was scant consolation.

Tendrils of fog snaked into the harbor from the sea and wrapped around the old steamer's stacks as Alex Hawke ascended the slippery gangplank. The *Star*, save the loading activity amidships, was quiet. Having gained the deck, he paused and looked up at the dimly lit bridge. Shadowy figures moved behind the grimy yellow glass of the pilothouse. Two men at least, maybe three. He would start his search for Harry Brock there. He looked at his watch. He was two minutes in, right on schedule.

To his left was a steep corrugated stairwell leading up—more of a ladder than a staircase. He raced up it, and another like it, and arrived on the starboard-side bridge wing. He paused and listened, feeling the faint shudder and thump of the engines beneath his feet. Inside the pilothouse, he could hear muffled voices and laughter. The door was slightly ajar. He shot out his left leg and slammed it inward, stepping inside the hot and stinking bridge with the Walther extended at the end of his right arm. The look of the faces of the two Chinese told him his information from Brick was indeed hard fact. They were hiding something. And surprised.

"Evening, gents," Hawke said, kicking the steel door closed behind him. "Lovely night for it, what?"

"Huh?" said a squat man in grimy coveralls who now moved in front of the fellow in a sheepskin-lined leather jacket who was levering noodles from a box to his hungry mouth. The man advanced toward Hawke, protecting his captain.

"Bad idea," Hawke said. Somehow, the gun was now in his left hand, and a long bloodstained dagger had appeared in his right. The man kept coming and retreated only when Hawke flicked the blade before his eyes. He had little interest in killing these men, at least until he learned the location and condition of their prisoner. Then he would dispatch them without mercy.

"I'm looking for a reluctant passenger of yours, Captain," he said to a man in a leather jacket who wore an ancient captain's cap cocked rakishly over his bushy black brows. "Where might I find him?"

The Chinese captain stopped eating his noodles and, placing the container and chopsticks carefully on a stool, stared at him. Hawke saw something in his eyes and instinctively dove for the floor as rounds from the captain's silenced automatic pistol stitched a pattern in the bulkhead inches above his head. Hawke rolled left and fired the Walther, carefully putting one slug in the captain's thigh and sending him crashing back against the wheel.

There was little time to celebrate. Five fingers that felt like steel bolts sank into the ganglia at the back of his neck. He relaxed, then sucked down a lungful of air at a new sensation: the cold press of steel at his temple. The pressure increased and he dropped his own gun.

"I am in charge of all passengers," an oddly musical voice whispered in his ear, "and you are dead."

"This is all a bit more complicated than I was led to believe," Hawke said, twisting his body carefully and smiling up at the man. The eyes were like a pair of small coals burning twin holes in yellow snow. Then the Tu-We officer racked the slide on his gun.

"Easy, old fellow," Hawke said calmly, getting one foot under him. "Easy does it, right? I'm going to get to my feet now and—" He never finished the sentence.

There was a sudden screech of metal and then a terrific jolt as the ship's entire superstructure shuddered under the violent impact of something slamming against it, just below the pilothouse. Hawke, trying to scramble to his feet, was slammed hard against the bulkhead. The impact was sufficient to send the Tu-We officer and everyone on the bridge flying across the wheelhouse and tumbling to the floor. He heard shouts from the pier below, and then shots rang out—bursts of automatic fire.

Hawke crabbed his way across the chaos of the wheelhouse, managing to recover his Walther from under a sheath of loose documents and navigation charts and broken glass. Then he was up and out onto the bridge wing. Standing at the rail, he saw that one of the two dockside cranes, the one directly abeam, was now coming under intense fire from crewmen standing on the starboard rail. Then he saw why. Some madman was at the controls of the crane. The cab had turned away and now was spinning toward the *Star*'s hull again, the cable taut, and the crazed operator was about to smash the heavily laden pallet against the ship for the second time.

Hawke could see by its trajectory that, this time, the violent impact was targeted at the pilothouse itself. With maybe three seconds to spare, Hawke turned and simply dropped through the stairway opening, hitting the deck hard, and raced aft.

He didn't look back at the violent sound of metal on metal and shattering glass as the crane whipped around and smashed its payload directly into the four angled windows of the *Star*'s bridge. Agonized screams were heard as bodies were smashed in the twisted metal.

He reached the stern rail. On shore, he could hear the keening high-low sirens and see flashing blue lights approaching the harbor from every direction. *Les flics* to the rescue. Everyone aboard the old tub appeared to have run forward to see what was going on. He looked at his watch. The Zodiac rendezvous was in six minutes. In the pitted bulkhead behind him, a rusted door hung open, steps leading down. Brock had to be down there somewhere. Guarded? Absolutely. It seemed he was expected after all.

How the hell had he imagined this was going to be so simple?

He had one thought as he raced down the steep metal steps.

He'd gone soft. Lazy. Cocky.

Hawke raced down the deserted companionway, a grim corridor lit only by a few bare bulbs suspended from loose wires dangling from the overhead. Doors hung open on either side, opening onto small flyspecked cabins with double- or triple-tiered bunks, empty. At the far end, a large door in the bulkhead opened into the galley. He stepped inside. The stink of cabbage and rancid grease was overpowering. He was about to turn and retrace his steps, when his eye caught a thin edge of yellow light between two tall cabinets loaded with rusty canned goods, stocks that appeared to be long past their best-by date.

He ripped at the shelving and dodged heavy falling cans of undoubtedly exquisite Chinese delicacies. The cabinet swung open easily, revealing a tiny broom closet of a room, no bigger than six by four. There was a metal rack upon which lay a man, pale and gaunt, who looked as if he'd not eaten or slept during his days in enemy hands. A tin plate with what appeared to be dried vomit rested on his chest, just below his chin. A foul slop bucket stood under his bed. At the sight of Hawke, he tried to sit up, and the thin scrap of blanket fell away, revealing his legs. They were severely bruised and held fast to the frame with strips of heavy canvas.

The man smiled weakly up at Hawke as he entered.

"What part of China you from, mister?" he said, slurring his words.

"I look Chinese to you?" Alex said, and he had the knife in his hand, cutting the canvas from the frame, starting with the left leg.

"Can't see too well. Where are you from?"

"Place called Greybeard. Little island out in the English Channel."

"English, yeah. Thought so. A limey. I'm Harry Brock. From L.A."

"La-la land. Never been there. Have they been torturing you, Harry Brock?" Hawke asked, inspecting Brock's horribly swollen feet and ankles.

"Nothing Dr. Scholl can't fix," Brock said, laughing weakly. "I don't know. Been on the run. Can't remember much of the last few days."

"Drugs, Mr. Brock. Chlorides. Pentothal. Anything broken? Can you walk?"

"I think so. Any chance at all of us getting out of here?" the man said. The fear that this might not be so was writ large in his dilated blue eyes.

"That's the general idea," Hawke replied, cutting the last of the bonds. "On your feet, Mr. Brock. Let's get off this tub before it sinks."

"Sounds good," the American said, and, with Hawke's help, he swung his legs painfully off the frame and got his feet under him. He swayed and Hawke put one arm around him.

"I won't be much good to you in a fight. I think the bastards have broken my wrists. One of 'em, anyway. Ever hear of an ugly little shit named Hu Xu?"

"Can't say I have. We're going to make straightaway for the stern. As fast as you're able. Over the rail. I've got a man waiting below in a Zodiac. He's expecting us now. Can you make it?"

As he said this last, Hawke heard a now familiar high-pitched voice behind him. He whirled, and his right hand came up in a blinding motion, the Assassin's Fist already on its deadly way. The Tu-We officer appeared to move his head less than an inch to the left and Hawke's blade twanged into the wooden shelving, the knife handle vibrating just beside its intended victim's ear.

"You are knife fighter?" the man said in his disturbingly childlike voice. "Good. I, too."